Praise for Louis Zukofsky's fiction

"[*Little* is] a gnomic and gnomelike amusement, privy to prodigies, a careenager's tale, a fiddler's playful family tale, acrid and affectionate, stuck with proper names like cloves." —Robert Fitzgerald

"*Little*'s plot is intriguing, its details consistently enjoyable. Its puns, puzzles, and word games are genuinely funny. . . ." —William Heyen, *Saturday Review*

"Anyone who has responded to Kafka or Walser or Borges or Donald Barthelme will recognize [in Zukofsky's short stories] a similar breathtaking deftness of narration, and feel something of their remoteness from the interchangeable themes and styles of the large part of current fiction. . . . As in Kafka, the emotional intensity of his vision excludes that comforting realism which fiction feeds us as so much pabulum."—Guy Davenport, *New York Times Book Review*

Collected Fiction

Louis Zukofsky

with a Foreword by Gilbert Sorrentino
and an Afterword by Paul Zukofsky

Dalkey Archive Press

Library of Congress Cataloging-in-Publication Data
Zukofsky, Louis, 1904-1978.
Collected fiction / Louis Zukofsky; with a foreword by Gilbert Sorrentino and an afterword by Paul Zukofsky.
I. Title.
PS3549.U47A15 1990 813'.54—dc20 89-23697
ISBN: 1-56478-156-9

Partially funded by grants from the National Endowment for the Arts, a federal agency, and the Illinois Arts Council, a state agency.

Dalkey Archive Press
Illinois State University
Campus Box 4241
Normal, IL 61790-4241

Printed on permanent/durable acid-free paper and bound in the United States of America.

Contents

Foreword by Gilbert Sorrentino ——— *vii*
A Note on the Texts ——— *x*

Little / for careenagers ——— *1*

It was
- *It was* ——— *179*
- A Keystone Comedy ——— *185*
- Ferdinand ——— *197*
- Thanks to the Dictionary ——— *264*

Afterword by Paul Zukofsky ——— *293*

Foreword

Zukofsky somewhere writes of Thomas Wyatt "thinking a prosody" in the act of composition: this exercise is not to be confused with counting stresses and straining after rhyme. If we may consider prosody to be a theoretical system which informs genres other than verse, it is not too much to say that Zukofsky thinks a prosody into and through these wonderful prose texts, happily here gathered.

It was, the little book originally published by Origin Press in 1961, included *"It was,"* "A Keystone Comedy," "Ferdinand," and "Thanks to the Dictionary." *Little,* Zukofsky's only novel, was published by Grossman in 1970. The time span of composition ranges from 1932 ("Thanks to the Dictionary") to 1969 (completion date of *Little*). Nowhere is the prose less than arresting, even in the intriguingly dated "A Keystone Comedy," which reads amazingly like a presage of Paul Goodman's early fiction. Reading these works in chronological order, one can register, as if on a graph, the subtle changes in the author's writing—from the accretion of elegantly shaped periods, which gingerly and rather distrustfully inscribe a discourse planted uncomfortably in a "picture theory" of language, á *la* the *Tractatus,* to the near-imageless precisions of *Little*'s free signifiers creating their own reality in a kind of linguistic heaven of infinite play. Here is Zukofsky, in "Ferdinand," serenely refusing Apollinaire, by means of deft metonymies, entry into the text:

In modern literature it was the war which moved him and only one poet—a cannonier dangerously wounded so that "a star rayed his forehead"—who wrote concretely for him of a new mind in process of overcoming existing barriers.

And here he is, in *Little,* tuning prosody so carefully that his sentences can quite easily be "mistaken" for a fragment of one of his poems:

Little forgot in modest homage to Little and fiddle that six months had lagged into twice six. As Dala *pithed it* (an expression Little discovered for him): work drives beyond promise, craving and time.

And, from *A*-9,

> So that were the things words they could say: Light
> is Like night is like us when we meet our mentors

Such rigorous and loving attention to language's registrations, its possibilities and nuances, creates these present light-drenched and wily texts, an exemplary shorthand display of careful foregrounding. For example:

Ferdinand still imagined he heard a hidden drift of melody over the landscape: songs gathered there from all nations, like the birds, and bringing up former days despite present casual sounds.

—"Ferdinand"

As is usual with me I would not go on with the rest of the story and come back to the difficult sentence later. With others it may be different—but when I am that far in a work the story must exist in each word or I cannot go on.

—*"It was"*

He saw a frail lady uppermost in mauve gauze, head wobbling at first, cheeks rouged into two small suns that with the frenzied decisiveness of a pinwheel on its stick whirred quickly past three oblivious parishioners . . .

—*Little*

"Never, never, for shame, shame, in church, in church one never applauds—in church," Dala heard James Madison's outraged, tearful voice—feeling every drop, drop of blood of her piety. "Heathens, heathens," she sobbed.

—*Little*

"Not to put you to shame in front of Verch," Little went on, "I adventure to say there's as much variety of timbre—pronounced *tam 'b'r* in music—as there are trees before they become confused in one stupid word like *timber.*"

—*Little*

With the passage of time, the importance of this great and unique artist's work—wherein, he often insisted, one may find all one need know of his life—becomes more evident, so much so that he seems, now, to stand alone among the poets at the later end of the Pound-Williams generation. His fiction is, finally, not the work on which Zukofsky will be judged, but it is, nonetheless, beautifully made, serious, and lovingly *attentive* literature—not a bad thing to have to hand in this sad time of valorized demotics. To give the author the final word, from *Little:*

"The omniscient observer," Dala said continuing for them out of another day, "reads from the first word to the last with great care for the spaces between them so they are unframed by enthusiasts or detractors."

GILBERT SORRENTINO

A Note on the Texts

Little is offset from the first edition published by Grossman Press Publishers in 1970. The four stories comprising *It was* were reset from the 1961 edition published by Origin Press and incorporate corrections made by the author in his wife Celia's copy, graciously made available to the present publisher by Paul Zukofsky. Any remaining irregularities in orthography or punctuation can be assumed to reflect Louis Zukofsky's preferences.

Little is dated 1950-July 28,1969. The story "*It was*" was written in 1941, "A Keystone Comedy" also in 1941, "Ferdinand" in 1940-1942, and "Thanks to the Dictionary" in 1932. The first eight chapters of *Little* appeared in *Kulchur* (Spring 1962) and as a limited edition from Black Sparrow Press in 1967. Some of the stories appeared in *Combustion, Nomad,* and the *Quarterly Review of Literature,* and "*It was*" and "Ferdinand" appeared as *Ferdinand* in a jointly published edition by Jonathan Cape and Grossman Publishers in 1968-1969.

LITTLE

for careenagers

A Note on the Pronunciation of Names

As in Latin: names of two syllables are accented on the first (with a few exceptions, Drícháy, Uńzúng Phárétte); of more than two syllables, on the penult if that is long (Verchádet, Babállo, Sweetsíder); otherwise on the antepenult (Teárilee, Beármeout).

Where coincidence
intends no harm
who will sue the
first stone in
celebrating?

Thanksgiving Day
1967

L. Z.

When Little Baron Snorck was born into universal society (only about six thousand years old) his first cries were music. But it will be a question until the end of his book and after whether he learned to speak words. The logic of doubt later became very clear to his mother.

He has a lovely head (the windfall of a caesarian) Madame Verchadet von Chulnt, his mother, said.

His father, Dala Baballo von Chulnt, immediately saw Baron as a dolphin. The curve made by his nightgown as his chest rose above the sheet of his crib positively soared as over the first chaos of sea.

It was Christmas and something should be said about his family that had come to greet Little Baron.

As Dala Baballo found no time to see family there is no need to describe them individually. They always arranged to meet in town to assure their arrival together and were in a sense one person—that is the Contessa Murda-Wonda, Dala Baballo's sister, who for all her stature depended on the family's attentions. She never had enough of them and would never have had enough had the family been twice its size and many times as compassionate. She suffered. She suffered at births, christenings, confirmations, receptions, weddings, at all happy occasions, remembering things—for no one remembered as well as she. And when she remembered she took on the centrifugal power of a revolving-armed Hindu goddess of the fierce type running her faithful down as an act of love.

Verchadet's family loved more elegantly. They had accepted Western ways. Medicine had made them mild. They exchanged sedatives, vitamins, and antibiotics—in time of great need, aureomycin—and on happy occasions such as this Christmas eve, mild capsules for digestion no more harmful than lozenges.

Verchadet's mother, Tearilee, "believed," and had hazel eyes which disarmed Dala Baballo, indifferent himself to belief, and his sister Contessa Murda-Wonda, not so indifferent, with the tearful piety of their look. Delicately with an expiating lozenge in her mouth Tearilee was trying to convince them, not overtly at the moment, how happy little Snorck would be if brought up in the faith.

"Don't you feel better already, mama," her eldest daughter interrupted. This was Lucy Drishchay all of ninety pounds of model and well-being, continuing her disquisition on the efficacies of the lozenge she had just given her mother. Hiram Drishchay, her husband, noticed politely that "mother" had not swallowed it yet. "But Hiram," cried Lucy, "you don't need to swallow it—it works instantly." Tearilee hurried to assure them—"Bless you, it has opened my eyes."

Mr and Mrs Esfelt, Tearilee's youngest daughter and son-in-law, sighed heavily, judging Verchadet's ash trays as they looked for a cigarette. Not finding one, Esfelt turned to Lucy, "May I have one of those lozenges. We had an early lunch."

Uncontrollable cries came from Little Baron's room. "I wish I could give him some of this candy," mumbled Mrs Esfelt after she had ravished a huge bonbon herself.

But it took Verchadet six months to find out that Little Baron, still toothless, would be quiet only when he was soaking thru a crust of bread as she played him his music box.

c c g g
a a g
f f e e
d d c
right to the window
left to the door
up to the ceiling
down to the floor

Dala Baballo's expressively long arms were tired. Had his spirit the biceps of a baboon and the zeal of a Turk praying to Allah the flesh would still be weak. He could not bounce his son up and down again. He had counted twenty while singing Mozart's jingle to the words already given here, and as if rocked by a boat he set his son down in bed —still pleading "more, more"—amidst his set of rhythm band instruments.

"My ear drums," he said with casual sickishness to Verchadet who had come into the nursery.

"I know," Verchadet sympathized, "but they can't always be tuned to your projected works."

Baballo had been put into his place, that is into his own mind, again. After all he thought: poems come as you live them. Life's long, time fleeting, lovers bleating lovers greeting, endure.

"It's time to go to sleep, Snorckie," said Verchadet.

"No," said Little Baron, ringing his triangle. "Baballo, I wrote a composition. Like Mozart! You think only you're a great artist, you're a jealous pig."

"Yes? How's the piano?"

"No good! I know 41, let me see, 51, no 61 songs," Snorckie added rapidly as he clashed his cymbals. "Dalo, is Mozart dead? What's dead?"

"W-e-ell, never mind."

"What do dead people do?"

"Nothing, they sleep."

"Where?"

"Under flowers."

"Does everybody have to die?"

"Not really."

Little Baron looked serious and tearful. "I don't want to die and I most certainly don't want to sleep. Is Mozart dead?"

"Not really, if you play his music he's alive."

"Then composers don't die?"

"And—poets don't either."

"You mean the man who wrote *right to the window, down to the floor* too?"

"Maybe."

"Why maybe? You know, Dala, we picked a good profession," said Snorck kindly as he dozed off to sleep.

3

The porch of the music school Little Baron went to had slender pilasters ordered from Europe that stood right in the center of the city. The lobby inside was dimly lighted like a theatre when the curtain is about to go up. On its pseudo-Tudor walls hung old instruments, programs advertising concerts of the season as well as seasons gone by, and an illuminated testimonial hung by a golden braid from an hautboy—this in honor of the old director who had once played music. All his friends, and he had many, had signed the testimonial, and since they never died they swarmed continuously. The director himself walked thru them as tho his violin cushion were tucked under his chin.

Verchadet and Little Baron went there twice a week. She was not vain, and no one knew that Little Baron could play "41, 51, no 71 songs and the Star Spangled Banner" —as he told everybody who came to his house and was an excuse for staying up late—on the piano. He had started at three and was constantly swelling his repertoire. Now he was four.

But Mrs Runnymeade whose class Little Baron attended did not know this. She had a bit of a moustache and was as gentle and as accentual and as round as old Vienna. As much as he spoke at home, he never spoke in class—not a syllable!

"What did they do in class?" Verchadet, itching to know, asked him.

"Nothing!"

"You mean nothing?"

"Nothing!"

"Then what did they do after that?"

"Nothing!"

"Nothing?"

"I won't say something when they did nothing!"

"Did anyone sing or play?"

"A boy."

"Can he play?"

"No!"

"What's his name?"

"Stewie."

"Why don't *you* play sometime?"

"Because they don't know how to and I won't tell them!"

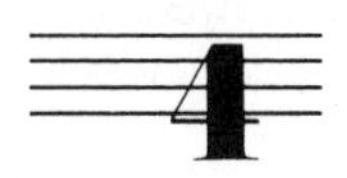

Several weeks later Mrs Runnymeade was confiding to Verchadet.

"And you know, he clutched the little violin and wouldn't let anyone get near it. That's the first time he has participated with the others, tho he still hasn't said a word. And what's more wonderful, he played the piano," said Mrs Runnymeade, pronouncing the last word with such tenderness she smiled all over her moustache. "Mind you, at least a score of songs and the Star Bangled Spanner—of course I mean the Star Spangled Banner—to which we all stood up and sang. I don't know that he approves of our singing because he turned around and scowled," she said with a titter. "And you should see him hold that violin. I must speak to the director because he's much more advanced than the other children and is ready for individual instruction. Won't you come in now because he doesn't seem to want to let go of the little fiddle."

Back turned on the world, on home, on plaudits, on praise, Little Baron, leaning his forehead on the curved portion of a grand piano, choked the fingerboard of a quarter-size violin.

"No!" he shouted as Verchadet came into the room.

"Little Baron," said Verchadet.

"No!"

"Little Baron," said Verchadet. "It's the only one the school has. You may play it here sometime when you can."

"Leopold Mozart wouldn't have said that to Wolfgang Amadeus," he replied bitterly.

"Well you can't play it, can you?" smiled Verchadet.

"I can so," he said tucking the chin rest in place and assuming the stance of the director of the school.

After a few fierce open strings followed

c c g g
a a g
f f e e
d d c

"Why you don't say!" said Mrs Runnymeade.

"Why not," said Little Baron. "What did Nicolo Paganini do when three strings of his violin broke? He played on the fourth. Which was the fourth?" he asked his mother.

Verchadet anticipating what Snorckie's second display of "reading" within a minute or so of the first might bring on was, she thought it over later to herself as always, perhaps too soon embarrassed. Unlike all mothers, for she talked to very few, she had never read *What Mother Should Know For Peter—Aged 4,* nor the rest of the series, *Aged 5, Aged 6,* and *Pre-Youth.*

Shortly before Little Baron was born she was so disconcerted by him she decided on a pediatrician who pooh-poohed the word *psychology*. At that time also she composed an opera that Baballo thought would surely mean an honorary membership in the Club of Music Composers. "I'm not interested," she told him. "When I'm preoccupied I don't think, and I wish everybody were like me." Verchadet, who did not mind learning tempered by politeness, did not at all mind Little Baron's saying to her that he knew three Henry's—Henry Adams, Henry James and Henry Filler—a neighbor's little boy, provided Little Baron had enough manners not to bother the wide world with overheard confidences of Baballo's midnight preoccupations.

Otherwise a nice person, Verchadet was occasionally obstinate to the point of refusing to read—considering she was a mother and that reading all the time in constant reminder of being a mother is the least there is to it.

In short, since her day meant only cleaning a three story house, making the beds, answering the telephone, adjusting the thermostat for the hot water, setting out Baballo's breakfast and aspirin, ironing his shirt collar so "*that* at least" (his words) would be without a crease, again sweeping out the fuzz from the blankets which Little Baron had dragged behind him into the hall while imitating Carmen clicking her castanets, and by this time of day getting home to set out the dinner service—Verchadet was afraid that Little Baron might delay her by telling Mrs. Runnymeade all of The Life and Four Tunes (as Little Baron insisted the title should read) of Nicolo Paganini by—she didn't have time to remember—and illustrated in color. For Little Baron remembered all the words of every book Baballo and she read to him, provided he heard them right the first time. If he didn't, no amount of pointing out his error would convince him that he was wrong. She was not at all surprised a year later when he remembered all of Bach's Third Partita after he had hurried thru it a few times as he said at "brake-no speed." With notes it was different, but with words—"it is just too bad about you, Verchadet, you're wrong, why," he would insist, "I'm are (I am, Verchadet would correct him) I'm are," he would say, "saying it right." And remembering a wisp of comment Baballo on one occasion permitted himself, he would add: "Musicians are noteworthy—eh, mummie?"

In short, Verchadet afraid she might be delayed said, "Little Baron, Mrs Runnymeade isn't interested."

Since Little Baron could be moved by the tones of

voices and hints he put his thumb in his mouth—he always did when innate goodness placated his temper—, laid the unwanted violin on the piano stool, and turning his back on his teacher walked out of the room.

"We'll air you," said Verchadet in her most highhanded manner to Snorckie. He walked on beside her still with his thumb in his mouth.

"Mummy," he said, beginning tentatively to remove it as they came to the park some streets away from the school.

"In the Egyptian wing of the museum. You've seen him before," she said, as she noticed a troop of young men wheeling baby carriages—actively participating in planned parenthood.

"I'm sorry," said Snorckie, finally taking his thumb out of his mouth.

"What good does that do?" she said somewhat relieved.

"That's the surprise," said Snorckie talkative again. "We'll surprise Dalo." (Whenever Little Baron's thought took a crucial turn it played a variation on his father's name, as the reader may have noticed.)

"Verchadet, does the poet-professor, you know whom I mean, Lada Dala, make as much money as Einstein? I know—*because* Baballo told me Einstein is a science-t," here Snorck stressed the last letter, "and knows all about the stars and what's more plays the violin."

Before Dala became a "poet-professor" he had lost his source of income. Snorckie's most unrewarding impression of him was his dropping in for a hurried lunch, burdened with blue exam books from the "institute." But for baronial honor, let it be said that he earned enough to keep the piano in tune.

"Now let's see," said Snorck babbling, "was it the piano tuner or the plasterer whose name was Einstein?"

It was, in fact, the plasterer whose name was Einstein. Listening to Snorckie's repeated playing of a Brahms Hungarian dance on the phonograph and slapping the hanging ceiling under the attic by way of accompaniment he had stopped to say to Verchadet, "Lady, any child who listens to one record for a whole day will be a great virtuoso."

"The plasterer," Verchadet replied to Snorckie.

"Right," said Snorckie glad that peace was restored. "And do you know what he said?"

"That you would be a great virtuoso."

"That's the surprise, because tho a tuner knows his pitches, he doesn't know what's on my mind as much as the plasterer."

"That's why he's only a plasterer," said Verchadet sadly like a musician.

"That has nothing to do with it," said Little Baron, "because our ceiling is almost as high as the sky and you remember when he was working on it he said, when he was a boy he could play the violin like Einstein—*because* his name is Einstein."

Verchadet was slightly baffled.

"And if Dala, Lada, Dalo Baballo knows what's right" —Snorckie sounded righteous—"and what can make more money for him than a mere tuner, because all a tuner makes is a good accompanist, he would buy me a violin. Why don't we buy it now and surprise him?"

"Why not," said Verchadet thinking how she had stepped thru the hanging ceiling and paid for it.

"Verchadet," said Snorck, "and do you know what our secret is? Beginning tonight we must tell Baballo you're my accompanist and that I'm a violinist."

"Balo, it's a Stradivarius," said Snorckie forcing his father's nose close to the *f* hole.

"Antonius Stradivarius Cremonensis
Faciebat Anno 1724 "

With unstudied surprise, his left eyeglass lower than his right Baballo read back what he had seen, including his bibliographical note of the trade mark: "within two freehand concentric circles, a cross over A S." Eyes still unaware that his glasses were not focused, he looked completely credulous at Verchadet as if to ask "at what cost?"

"They all have that," she smiled at him as he still seemed anxious to be gullible.

"They all have that," said Little Baron, "or it wouldn't be a Stradivarius," not realizing that his mother meant it wasn't.

"No, really?" said Baballo to Verchadet feeling the loss of an antique.

"A good buy," he said sadly turning to Snorck, "why the case must be worth—" "Twenty dollars," Verchadet whispered. And as he tapped it he straightened his glasses. He patted Snorckie's shapely head: "Play something!"

"What would you like, Bachmonitor or Johansenbach?"

"Snorckie, you say Rachmaninoff or Johann Sebastian Bach."

"Not really," said Snorckie.

"As you wish," said Baballo, "a violinist ought to know. Anyway, tonight I'll settle for Bach without Johansen and monitor."

Amidst fierce squeaks Baballo thought he recognized "America."

"That's *My Country*," said Little Baron, not completing the title, in a hurry to get on to his next offering.

"You've an ear, son," said Baballo obviously trying to forget his own. "What about some reading before bedtime?"

"The Illicy," Snorck requested. (Sometimes Baballo read *The Odyssey* and sometimes *The Iliad.*)

"*The Odyssey*, Snorckie."

"The Illicy in English translation."

"Yes, but called *The Odyssey*," said Baballo.

"If you want me to understand, you'd better speak in a different anguish," said Snorckie impatiently.

"A different language," Baballo corrected him.

"All right, a different anguish," Snorck nodded.

For some weeks Dala had been able to shorten the reading sessions by enacting a little scene very familiar but fresh to his son who took part in it. Dala donned a sheet which made him Eurycleia. Holding an imaginary torch, he led Snorckie acting Telemachus, Greek as a drawing of Flaxman, but in shirt and pants, to his bedroom.

At the same time Baballo read Homer: *opened the door of the handsome room and sat down on the bed, and stript off his soft shirt which he gave into the wise old woman's hands. She folded it up and smoothed it out . . .*

"Not there," Snorckie inevitably ordered wherever *there* happened to be, and after some delay Baballo concluded: *hung it on a peg beside the bed-frame and left the room pulling the door.*

"Don't forget the bolt," said Little Baron, after Baballo had purposely tripped on the landing, over the sheet which he had dropped to be picked up later.

"It had to be a violin?" he answered his own question, when Verchadet and he could at last enjoy the blessing of speech.

"I have my own fears," she said, forcing a peg of the violin she was trying to tune. "Don't interrupt me."

Sybil Greate taught Snorckie the names of the strings by colors. She herself was always a smiling brown study, arriving late for the lesson, almost too straight, Verchadet could not help thinking. Miss Greate never brought her own too valuable fiddle. She illustrated on Snorckie's quarter-size:

"Little Baron, my fingers are too thick to hold down the right color," she said.—"I'm not used to your fiddle, but you must get used to it.—I'm surprised, Snorckie, why Snorckie, the red is flat.—Good, good, Little Baron, the blue sounds true.—O the green that's as if it had never been," and she would hurry to strain a peg, ending her sentence a minute later, "tuned."—"O but you must play with expression, dolce, sweetly, dolce that's Eyetalian for sweetly, Snorckie, and the white must be heard very, very bright! Little Baron, will you ask your mother to give me that last note on the piano?"

"What color?" Snorckie questioned.

Verchadet accompanied him in a text of exercises called *Scratch A While.*

Miss Greate also taught Snorckie "the notes."

"Every good virtuoso," she told Snorckie who held his mouth open and Verchadet who watched the half-hour go by on the clock as her left eye—the weaker one—acquired crow's-foot, "studies theory. Now this big round empty thing is a full moon. And if you add a stem to it, it's a half-moon."

"No, Miss Greate, my father who's a Greek—or is he a Turk, Vechadet?—calls that *phi.* That line, let me show you," Snorckie said, applying great effort to Miss Greate's pencil, "goes through the center. Or is it *fee?*" he asked exposing the Greek letter to Verchadet. "Full fathom fi'," mumbled Verchadet.

"No," Miss Greate interrupted him gently, firmly taking the pencil out of his hand, "this is music—it's different. And this with a stem attached to a bright black darkened thing is a quarter-moon!"

"Now don't tell me," Snorckie begged avidly, "don't tell me, Miss Greate, I know, this" he said pointing to a blank space of a staff, "is a new moon."

Remember that Verchadet was only a mother that Little Baron had made his accompanist, and she had never read *Pre-Youth.* All this musical moon kind of teaching was very hard on her. After stretching patience over half a term of lessons, she came home one day and asked Baballo, "what do you teach?" She had never asked him this, so that all he said Hamlet-like, or hammock-like as Snorckie would say who had seen the movie, for Baballo was rocked and racked continuously by passion, was: "Ha?!"

"Is all education today moon and sub-moon?" asked Verchadet.

"Moon Mullens, what do you mean?" said Baballo.

"And the spectrum? What about the spectrum?"

"Are you out of your mind, Verchadet?" he quavered.

"Don't quaver," she said, "my right ear is queasy as it is. All I mean is, I shall soon be as moonstruck and as color mad as the dye industry."

It was St. Valentine's Day and Baballo, who was not

unromantic and sometimes not too slow at understanding Verchadet, said: "Don't be that way Verchadet. Isn't Snorckie learning the fiddle?"

"He is, but not his color exercises. Maybe I'm wrong. With me, you hear him every evening don't you, he's up to Bach's Third Partita, but with Miss Greate he doesn't know green from red."

"Tse-tse-tse-tse," said Baballo, looking like the poet-baron behind the Great Wall of China he felt he was at the moment. "Wait a minute, Verchadet," he said, as he hurried upstairs. A minute later he came down. "Verchadet, St. Valentine's Day—your poem!

We may be old-fashioned,
But—we're impassioned.
When a fiddle string's red
Music is dead!
Then up with Johansen
Bach and his ensign
Or we'll be singing with colors
And painting red hollers
A note is a note
And comes from the throat!"

"Stop, Baballo," Verchadet said. "That makes sense. I'm too run-down to make Tuesdays at four any more. Snorckie's getting a man teacher!"

8

In the house of Murda-Wonda all spoke at once.

"No let him *play* first, that's what he came for, didn't he? Let him *play* first, then he'll take off his hat and coat."

The vestibule was filled with relations and neighbors. For the first time in his life *Snorckie* was stymied.

"Does he have a good teacher?" Contessa Murda-Wonda asked as Snorckie still wearing his ear muffs opened his violin case.

"A woman," said Verchadet.

"A woman?" queried the Contessa with a profound look and a tone of grief in her voice.

"A woman," called Count Murda-Wonda from his bed in the next room, "no good!"

The Count, the blueblood of the family, unmentioned till now, did not come along with the others to celebrate Little Baron's first day in the world, for a reason that will become apparent soon enough. Years ago—he carried his years like a debutante—Count Murda-Wonda had left his food and chattels abroad and arrived in the States with his title only. Six feet seven inches tall, wiry but not broad, hired by the day—continually threatened with being fired at any time—he had worked up to the position of reception-ist in frock coat decorated with a white carnation at the ele-gant dress house owned by his nephew, a commoner by birth. Every slack season the nephew unflinchingly approached the Count in an all too familiar attempt to ruffle his composure and asked him to look more dignified so as to avoid offense to absent buyers. Not that the establishment could not have thrived without the commoner—the Count sometimes confided to the shipping clerk, his son, four inches his junior and clearly a less robust replica of himself—because it was an inheritance from the commoner's father who had worked hard and died of heart failure to employ a Count. But Count Murda-Wonda never talked back. Instead he retired to the men's room where he padded his inner soles with lamb's wool carried surreptitiously from the operators' tables, so that he might stand an inch taller in his shoes as he emerged to serve all the more.

His chief task was to insist that his nephew's customers sit. In effect he stood guard over them after they were seated in gilt cane chairs padded with shot velvet which he rushed to them at the door, tho he never appeared rushed but impressively lean from noblesse oblige as he strode toward them thru the reception room. His height convinced them when he insisted: "Sit, it's a treat."

In the twenty years he had worked in the establishment he had himself forgotten the pleasure of sitting. In himself he was the wished-for client of the modern interior decorator to whom the sitting position is unsightly. He never sat in the subways and was at once recognized by conductors, stenographers and messenger boys as an aristocrat.

In forcing his nephew's customers to sit, he was by nature on the side of the gods of health and good breeding. His nobility without forethought caused the commoner nephew—nearly his height and twice his girth—who never cared to do anything but sit, legs wide apart, to puff over twenty feet of reception room from his office to the door where his clients remained fixed till he greeted them.

In the men's room the Count not only grew taller but ate

his lunch, stretched out on a rug which he vacuumed with maternal care for his son who joined him. Count Murda-Wonda ate gingerly because his dental bills were mounting.

After using some dental floss by raising himself on one elbow and staring into the black tile of the side wall, he turned on the other elbow to his son, who looked not at him but up at the coffered ceiling, and invariably said: "Ah, poetry!" He had an extreme fondness for the German language which he had learned as a child, and still felt for as a child:

> Hören sie, sehen sie
> Wissen sie was?
> Kochen sie, picheln sie
> Essen sie das?

And receiving no answer, went on:

> In alten Wald
> In finsteren nacht
> Sitzt einer alter
> Italiener und tracht—

DASH! it was time to get back to his watch.

Leading this hard life all day, it was natural that the Count should immediately take off his frock coat as soon as he came home in the evening. Then his only garb was a deep red pair of pajamas of Canton crepe heavily embroidered with his monogram over the breast pocket—in which he always kept a neatly folded handkerchief of lighter red—and a rampant dragon over the other breast, the end of the dragon's tail writhing somewhere near the Count's solar plexus tied in by a flowing contrasting white sash of satin. He was always lying down, whether eating his meal in stages or receiving neighbors and visitors in a steady stream—smoking constantly and infuriating the Contessa with his gracious request for a sixth glass of tea and another teaspoon please. He slept only four hours a night, sometimes even in these hours making the rounds of the rooms of his large apartment—never sitting down, one reason for it perhaps that the comfortable antiques the Contessa had collected "were too good," as she said, "to be rubbed out." She often forbade her immediate family to sit in them. It tired her "chasing the dust all day from the furniture." She herself always ate standing.

Accordingly, everyone had eased over to the Count's bed where the family usually sat in his house. Verchadet had finally persuaded Snorckie to take off his hat, ear muffs and coat. Between obeying others' wishes and mother's Snorckie's first choice was others' tho his actual choice was mother's. With this interlude weathered, Snorckie stood at the heavily valanced foot of the bed playing the Loure from Bach's Third Partita—especially the chords. Intent on showing everybody that music was serious, Snorckie always picked what seemed to him the most difficult piece in his *studium,* as the Count termed it, stressing the German word in a wordly manner.

"SNORCKIEEE!" roared the Count, who had a good heart and had never yet raised a young violinist to the ceiling, at the same time that Little Baron executed the last chord with a flourish, "Easy does it!" And while guests and royalty roared "Hurrah! Hurrah! Hurrah!" up went Little Baron in shirt sleeves as Baballo, lost somewhere talking to an old gentleman, his father, would never dare bounce him.

"Please the Count and his money's on the table," shouted the Count back on his bed. "ROULETTE! Ha! Ha! Ha!" The contents of a change purse crashed on the teatable beside the bed before Snorckie could see how the purse disappeared. "Ha! Ha! Ha!"

"He's a baby," said the Contessa of her husband to Snorckie, showing embarrassment in the presence of her nephew's talent. "Say! what are you so happy about? You'll break my table, Count!"

"Truck on down, Count!" yelled the usually mute but Westernized young Count to his father, as the Count leaped off the bed to comply while the radio played an Armenian folk tune and the family continued talking all at once.

"My rug! Count!" The Contessa keened with despair at the floor.

"Easy does it," the Count outbraved her as he fell back into bed.

"That's where he learns manners," said the Contessa attempting to smile at Snorckie.

"Never mind, my Contessa; Baron, play more, Fantasia Capriccio!"

"No," said Little Baron hurt to the quick, "do you know what I just played?"

"Who wrote it then Piotr Ilytch Leonovitch Stepanovitch Ivanovitch Dimitricki Zhikovski?"

"Bach," said Snorckie with venom.

"Oh Bach, I know him. He was an old friend of mine. For years—"

"No!" said Snorckie, gulled it seemed, somewhat pale with jealousy. "He's dead."

"Dead!" said the Count. "My old neighbor, dead! Who told you? Ah, oh, my old neighbor Bach!"

"Do you know his first name?" asked Snorckie.

"Snorckie, what does it matter? Dead is dead. Play another piece to remember him by. Snorckie, please!"

"What!" said Snorckie, "don't you know enough—that music is music—Brighteyes—you Zeus Cronion—and peace is P-E-A-C-E?"

"Ch . . ch . . ch . . that's the forbidden kind, Baron, Baballo," yelled the Count, "what kind of language are you teaching him? Brighteyes? Zeus Cronion?" Baballo did not seem to be around.

"What do you MEAN?" said Snorckie.

"Leider, leider, Forbidden to Walk on—Defense de, Verboten!" said the Count abstractly.

"You thermo—" Snorckie began tentatively and then snapped out at him, "you thermotitious mouse!"

"And what do you mean?" asked the Count with a slight pause before happily bursting into a wailing song:

"Ah - ah - mouse
In - my - y - house
How - do - you - slee - e - p
Ah - oh - oh - my - shee - p."

And then decisively: "IN ALTEN WALD!" Snorckie clapped his ear muffs on, chortled tearfully, and walked off.

After some time the music was forgotten. Verchadet heard herself talking louder than the rest of the company dawdling around the still bedded Count as they were beginning to leave.

"Verchadet," said Baballo, "don't leave burning cigarettes in ash trays," as the Count nodded gravely to him by way of farewell. The Contessa stood beside her largest wing chair with a look of vague severity, oblivious to Snorckie and the old gentleman sitting in it now that she would be—of all people—alone again.

"Snorckie, come often," said the old gentleman. "Tell Baballo come. Tell you-mama. Come you-self?" he asked kissing Snorckie as he neared the end of English.

Snorckie understood perfectly: "I come ma-self!"

"Good! good!" said his grandpa. "You smart guy!"

"You smart guy!" laughed Snorckie.

As they neared the door, the Count bowed them out somewhere from the top of his six feet seven. And hardly on the other side, Snorckie asked Baballo: "Why, Dala, if everybody loves grandpa are they always telling him what to do?" The answer seemed simpler to Baballo, when, some months later, after being told that his grandpa had died, Snorckie asked tenderly if he might have a real skull and cross-bones for Hallowe'en.

And Baballo wrote his poem

You are old Dr. Gluillens
Your fiddle is bent
Its father was aery
And played it in Ghent

It sang in Cremona
And bōwed where it went
With its strings tied to Florence
He played it in Ghent

Its mother was rosin
And never forlorn
To the bounds of spiccato
The mellow French horn

The ferment of spruces
That flowed thru its wood!
The firkins for juices
Are now gone for good

Sweet gherkins and spices
Were not untoward
Pizzicato, vibrato
Each note was their ward

A mite of St. John's bread
That fiddle of Ghent
With ninety staccatoes
To one bōw it went

But look! the low elders
The hut which is thatched
The sounds by the wellhead
Are taken detached.

What else was there to do?

Snorckie too had felt "detached" (as in Baballo's poem) for almost two weeks with scarlet fever, no better tho sitting up playing the violin in bed. "Let's play st–" *staying down,* Dala was going to say when the compassionate musical von Chulnt in him hiccuped "–even, son."

Little, who heard with at least a *double* sense when he played, took up any chance hint his own way:

> "when I was sick and lay abed
> with none to tell me what to do

—fertherover—

> in winter I get up at night
> and dress by yellow candle-light
> it is very nice to think"

Inextricably Dala felt himself bound, Little's playmate:

> "Great is the sun and wide he goes
> more thick than rain he showers his rays
> and thru the broken edge of tiles
> grasses hide my hiding place
> and winter comes with pinching toes
> the eternal dawn beyond a doubt"

Verchadet looked in on her ninth climb upstairs, a hand shading crow's-foot of her aching eye from the strong sun in the room, to report Tearilee's third telephone call of sympathy within the half-hour this morning. "Still not resting?"—and left.

The game went on thoughtlessly, largley at Little's urge not to stop fiddling:

Lada: "all grow up as geese and gabies"
Little: "and turn the turtles off their legs
fly as thick as driving rain"
Dala: "and it moves with the moving flame"
Little: "the red fire paints the empty room
and flickers on the backs of books
that crumble in your furnaces"
Dala: "humming fly and daisy tree
in the hedges and the whins"
Little: "water now has turned to stone"
Lada: "when I was down beside the sea
a wooden spade they gave to me
to dig the sandy shore
my holes were empty like a cup
in every hole the sea came up
till it could come no more"
Little: "where shall we adventure
today that we're afloat"
Dala: "a-steering of the boat"
Little: "to where the grown-up river slips
and with bell and voice and drum
cities on the other hum"
Dala: "waves are on the meadow
like the waves there are at sea
the organ with the organ man
is singing in the rain"
Little: "it rains on the umbrellas here
all made of the back-bedroom chairs
with trees on either hand"
Lada: "thousands of leaves on a tree"
Little: "in the sky and the pail by the wall

half full of water and stars
I could not see yourself at all
how great and cool the room"

"Dala, we perfected it."

"Have we?" queried von Chulnt wondering, what.

"Well! If you'd stood still, like a good violinist when he plays in one place and listens to himself and creates, you'd have heard our *you'rephonie*," said Snorckie for *euphony*, "you'd have *heard* what you-and-or-we did with those so-called child's gardens of verses. We were tired of them but still liked them, so we rearranged them—I call that *perfected it*. We've changed not a word: leaving some out you know they sound only more grown-up. Baballo," Little asked very tenderly, knowing very well that Bach had twenty-two children, "how many children" etc "was he patient with them?"

"I should judge he was," answered Dala.

"Dala," Little Baron said, "do you want to hear *something?* It isn't for you to judge. Lada, I like your line, 'To one bōw it went.' *To,* not *on,* that's just right with *ninety* staccatos. Dala—when is Doctor Prunejuice coming? My throat's—bookmatches which got wet—dry again. What's the use of bed?"

"Matchbooks," Dala said softly to correct him.

Doctor Prunejuice, whose real name was Gluillens, had been coming every day without being called to look over Little, for two weeks now faithfully making him his first leisurely visit in the afternoon, after many urgent morning patients. The brisk doctor, years gone from Baltimore, still looked as if he had carried off some of its convict sunlight from the three white steps of stoops lining red brick rows of completely deserted streets. He had himself played the fiddle as a cultured lad, and—psychology's enemy as has been said before the Doctor was—Snorckie's case history was enough to relieve his serious medical diagnosis. For the rest, Dr. Gluillens' pediatrics was simple: prune juice and fresh air. One look at the von Chulnts convinced him his insistence would have to be with them. "The history of medicine in its contention with ignorance was always the story of patient centuries insisting against hiding acid—well, what is life?" But the Doctor liked the almost foreign courtesies of the boy's parents and acted not to notice Verchadet demur as if she was not there—for both she and Balo could endure chill less easily than smoke.

"Fresh air never caused neuralgia or neuritis or a cold." And again he would tell the story of how his half-Welsh granny forgetting him as a baby in his cradle on the back porch overnight (she herself had dozed off after some prune whip and ambrosia by the fire) found him as he woke up before dawn covered with a blanket of snow, but warm as a fresh brewed pot of tea, none the worse. "Or I wouldn't be here," he assured Snorckie.

"Persisting with the fiddle? Good! Wish I were. There's not much you can do with a virus of *this* type anyway—just let it play out." He had been following "the young man's career" out of self-interest from the time of his first examination a month after birth, when he watched the infant follow his finger until the little head turned to make up for the eyes' incapacity to roll on. "There!"—the doggedness of it was the most intelligence he'd ever served at *that* age.

The Doctor stayed on a while after replacing his instruments in his twenty-year-old case. He believed that whatever thoughts he might express as he sat back the few minutes after the all around unconcern on receiving his check most effected his patient's cure. "Why, sir, I see your gift has come."

"Yessir," Snorckie nodded in its direction, "my Brand Mew Fidelity Recorder."

"I finally wrote to the president," Verchadet smiled.

President
Station WAIF

Dear Sir:

You must agree we are both scoundrels—I for allowing my son to appear over your station, you for not keeping your promise to him after three months. But still under five he refuses to take us lightly, noticeably these last two weeks he has been down with scarlet fever. I would rather not say I trust I may hear from you.

Very truly yours,
(Mrs) V. von Chulnt

She did not of course hint to the Doctor at the substance of her letter, which flashed on her mind. The insult of having to write it shamed her less than her feeling that it was her son's lowered resistance, brought on by his video debut, that had caused this illness. How stupid she had been to let him *persist,* as Snorckie worded it, *perfecting* Mozart's minuet from *Don Giovanni* and *Home on the Range* under the hot lights while the director of the half-hour roared "Roll 'em!" Especially after she had learned that Little had been programed with a ventriloquist and a chimpanzee. Why! the chimp had shown more resentment than she had at the commercial intercalating on the same set, some effete youth of thirty or so syncopating his foot on the floor cluttered with cable, as he sponsored his *Tiny Feed* with a lisp she only once made out:

When the goothe
ran loothe
in the kithen
my baby thaid
maybe
we cath him
with gravy.

"Was it worth it?" smiled the Doctor.

"Not to me," Verchadet agreed as if he had addressed her. "Tuning a fiddle with klieg eyes is a bit worse than pulling nipples over baby bottles."

The Doctor laughed. "When your young man is well, I judge in about two weeks, he should be shanghaied to the country. I would not risk another variety of spring bug growing up for the summer epidemics. Well! I didn't sleep deliciously last night listening to our neighbors' young dog locked up in their apartment while they went off.—Bye!"

"Bye!" Little chuckled.

10

They found it thru *The Biweekly Literary Emporium.*

> Vacation in New England
> "Substance and shadow." ANTHOS, five miles south of Sider, four miles north of Sweetsider. Dining in commons live in your separate cottage. Quiet guests.

And pretty soon Dala, Verchadet and Little were walking the one road under mostly elms either the five miles north to Sider, past the Egyptian lotus pond on the estate of Antonio Viertel Achtel, or past the general store, church and graveyard the four miles south to Sweetsider.

The separate cottage backed by a knoll of rock in the trees looked down from across the road on the sunned and shadowed classic architecture of the several-gabled roof of the "commons." The exterior of the cottage of heavy boards hastily put up was still unfinished. Inside, dusty sheet rock, broken in one wall repaired with a grate of wire, safely caged Snorckie's first pet: a field mouse.

"A vole," said Dala.

"Jawohl!" said Snorckie.

Dining—three meals—chilled the obviously unmovable heads of the quiet guests in the long glass-enclosed north porch of the main house or commons.

"George Washington, John Adams, John Alden," Little whispered to Verchadet seated next to him, so hushed that Dala facing them and these three personages, all women, at the large table at the far end, could not hear him. Little Baron had looked long but accurately on entering. Now nibbling at a salad of turnips and beets sprigged with parsley he looked only straight ahead at Dala, and did not dare turn his head to see if his mother was smiling down sideways at him for his good manners. The von Chulnts felt too numerous to break the quiet of a first impression that the three distant, immobile personages shared a doubt of a least stretched smile of welcome. Nearer to Dala before him, dressed sprucely in black at his own small table—not a guest but a Sunday visitor they learned a week later—the composer Viertel Achtel ate with relish, looking out occasionally at the shadows of ducks thru the porch's lead-divided panes. By the time the spoonmeat (dessert) was served Snorckie, looking toward the far opposite end of the porch, saw another small table crowded near the entrance, and whispered again almost inaudibly to his mother: "James Madison." *She* greeted them on their way out, adjusting her glasses chiefly toward Little, "My dear, I *am* glad you're here."

After a nod a few paces onward, "James Madison is the Feather'w'st," whispered Little, who by this time had heard something of the Founding Fathers. A retired army nurse she was in her slight arthritic still tall strict figure the most feathery and indeed Federal of the ladies of Anthos. Few years younger than the other ladies—who hardly greeted her—never resentful in her self-reliance, James Madison unobtrusively became the von Chulnts' self-appointed emissary mitigating the natural xenophobia of the others. Her birthplace Lincoln's Springfield, nurse, a world traveller, she could without trying somehow allay the atavistic gooseflesh of most polyglot fathers or mothers and light any little Abdullah, Rabindranath, Iwa, or Abraham with anticipations of Advent, she was so lovingly curious as to their own heathendoms. Only the turncoat impiety of a Christian heathen disturbed her, but of that—unrighteous as she found it—later.

When John Alden fretted, "Why must that child scratch on his awful instrument every morning," James Madison dared the von Chulnts' rock all alone to find out what Snorckie was really at, tho she had no ear herself. And in a day or so John Alden, appropriating the intelligence from her friend Viertel Achtel as *her* scoop, told James: "Mr Achtel says that the boy's Bach is very accomplished." Lately filling her retired life with books, and books about the lives of their authors, James Madison happily chancing on one of Baballo's endeared it as the only poetry that meant anything to her besides "my" Keats. When Little, who unfortunately ran faster than the ducks, horribly scraped his knees her old second lieutenant's first aid kit brought out such stoicism from him she called him major while treating him on her knees. For Verchadet she reserved her consummate praise, "My dear, you are the purest unsentimental mother I have ever met." Thus in her guileless care for the von Chulnts she innocently attracted to them many friends, who years later would loyally travel *to attend* the violinist's recitals in the city.

Cap of a knee
lock of hair
eyes with their pupils
crown of a head

Bridge of the nose
roof of the mouth
nails of the toes

Crook of elbow
shoulder blades
palm of hand
drum of an ear

Calf of a leg
corn of a toe
corn of an ear

Back home polio raged. In the country Dala walked the one road—in his mind. When the three could not walk, or shower in the midday heat on the rock, the turnips and beets grew too fast for the parsley. The Founding Fathers turned into benign Norns brought more adulators. "If only there were a little distance," Verchadet said abstractly, "it would be less wearing and exciting." That day the vole escaped from its rough cage to share Snorckie's bed.

On a southerly walk thru Sweetsider they came upon Archives Lane, where Baballo stopped to look up at a sign —RUSSELL, THROSTLE & THROTTLE LTD, *Realtors.* "But this is expensive property," said Verchadet who had guessed Dala's thought. "Maybe," Little said, "expensive country." "Baronet colonial," Verchadet smiled. "Look at the cow!" said Little. "We sell warm milk," said the farmer who was there, "to those who want it fresh and unpasteurized."

The Archives with Corinthian columns on the main street, rather highway, its circle with the most famous church steeple in New England after its English counterpart, seen from everywhere, and turning the corner of the lane at the realtors, across from the Archives, two substantial dwellings in baronial good taste opposite the little farm—continuing, country lane past low land and rivulet from larger water four miles off *as the crow flies* they heard say, for an eighth of a mile to the edge of woods: some rods before these tho, a shed for sale with a smaller, closet-like, behind it. They secured the deed for both outright in a transaction the realtors bothered to handle only for the sake of future neighborly courtesy.

Their country home simulated gables, one over each side of the wings of its triptych effect—the doorstep entrance, roofed over, coming out at the most two feet and placed somewhat to the right against the frame of clapboard. Originally this front entrance had been centered. The left wing, as the interior showed, was added after—a bedroom not more than a berth receding less than half the eighteen-foot length of the shed. Fortunately for Little what at once became his room was filled with a rope bed (without mattress) with at its foot a wall table and chair, so that he could bounce from bed and sit on the table by leaping the chair. The living room had no right wing, tho the rain gutter between its two windows on the façade had affected a wing. Wingless the original shed then owned an oversize tinder and coal oven near the back door for warmth, and a Franklin stove for burning refuse for more warmth nearer the front. There were enough windows front, side and back —each with sixteen panes—to make both rooms cheerful with their pre-Revolutionary outlook onto the neighborhood. The story was that a Laplander the one previous resident wintered there, the round well of heavy cemented stones not deep but by reputation sweet perennially drew water when the artesian diggings of the neighbors ran a trickle or froze to nothing. As for fauna and flora, there were all the animals Little might expect in New England, besides a mulberry, without silkworms, and elderberry with tangles of bittersweet. Little said later, the one mistake his parents made was not to live with the shed—content in it and the smaller rear structure hidden by cattails with its private view of three-quarters of an acre mostly in length down the lane; *they just had to plan* tirelessly to make it liveable, while they wished the smaller shed could be made to look illusory.

Six of Baballo's impetuous strides over the planks of the living room to the back door and out, and *there*—as he stood on the cement stoop a few feet to jump down from to ground—was the view he conceived a Turner seascape had perhaps looked to find in a Claude Lorraine landscape.

Verchadet saw, as she said, a lovely landscape. But the consequences of vision turned out the same for both, and for Snorckie a constant actual fiddling unlike the kind he observed in their distraction.

More precisely he overheard as he observed thru the corners of his eyes—"That arrowroot in the rivulet like Viertel Achtel's lotus, Lada, if landscaped could be white."

"I was thinking the same, Verchadet, only I did *not suggest it* to you after yesterday's mishap," he said shyly as if *it* might still be avoided by both.

"I'll do it. Only agree not to help, I can weed around the arrowroot much faster alone. It'll be white and float. No, I haven't a cold. If anything I feel better after yesterday's sprucing up a bit in the cattails. Aren't you happy we're rid of that unsightly fill and rotten log almost breaking them down, and I do know now one can sink in a marsh." She smiled, implying that her new plan for weeding was so much foolishness their similar tastes could not evade.

"No, let me help. But after that we stop." Satisfied, Little executed a picchetato with the words in mind, "not on your life they'll stop."

As their happiness would have it the shed had been electrified for light and telephone. With a few installations its one living room could be divided by a third of a partition into smaller living room with a kitchen and miniature bathroom at the rear, the water from the well electrically pumped running to both. For this renovation they hired help. The mingling professionals at their different tasks could not always it seemed keep them separate, and Little helped by passing Dala's only tools, a saw and clawhammer, heirlooms from his father, among them. Habitually forgetting to bring such tools, if they ever owned them, they often waited their turn. Not to appear embarrassed for their help during these restful interludes the gentle von Chulnts occupied themselves with disposal, carrying the rubbish of the operations along with a late Sunday newspaper a quarter of a mile down their lane to Sweetsider's dump. The realtors had told them it was good for the marsh to be filled there for future building.

By the height of summer, only weeks after Anthos, Verchadet and Dala had transformed their shed and acreage. They had untangled the bittersweet from the elderberry, shut the cover of the gaping seat with its odor of stacked hay in the illusory back shed forever from now on to be opened only for Dala's clawhammer and saw and the new rake and lawnmower safeguarded behind the door with its wooden latch over which the rose brier they trained was allowed to fall casually, sold the Franklin stove and oversize oven and replaced them by an electric heater, boiler, two-plate burner and portable freezer, nailed a trestle table and bench of Baballo's make to the floor at the kitchen window facing the morning sun and woods, curtained the part of the window not hidden by the stall shower of the bathroom on the opposite wall to afford a peek at the mulberry only when standing with one's back to the sliding door that negotiated entrance and exit, regretted they could not bake potato scones as their parents might have done in the oven they had sold, consoled themselves with a harmonium from a hilltown site of an old great battle in the border state reminding Snorckie of its history when Verchadet accompanied his fiddle, assembled Baballo's desk that had arrived as a kit with instructions that frayed him until Verchadet and Little in short order stood it up whole at the two windows of the now impassable but still simulated right wing of the living room, persuaded Little to accept a mattress replacing the odd heap of blankets he had argued were comfort under him, and bought themselves a sofa for two convertible into a bed which opened would protect them from night visitors by making it impossible to open the front door from outside or in. Two small not too reminiscent Windsor chairs, for the harmonium and Lada's desk, were delivered late. The place was now full, tho not over-furnished to their taste. They could sit back anywhere and still see space between things, or look out, or walk the path between front and rear doors to the country around the house. For Snorckie too it was roomy. He could lay his fiddle case on top of the harmonium when he performed formally, or when he practiced with just enough room for his own unimpeded bōwing in his own lane between the windows of the left wing and the side of the rope bed he could keep it on the new azure quilting.

It was during one of these latter choices that he found himself reading his father's notebook—tho Dala could not recall how he had come to leave it despite violinist's prohibitions on Little's bed:

> rabelais $\gtrless$ H. *rab*, master, *le(t)z*, jester; *rab lāvī* (Egy. *lawai*) m. lion; or diminutive possessive, *rebele's?*

"Dala," Little called from his room, "take this back e-midget-ly"—the last word enunciated with command and elegance. "If it has anything to do with music, or what is that diminuendo over crescendo before German B? You can't have them together, even if it's you, in one and the same time." Used to reading most symbols musically he summed up his disgust in a query, "What does it *mean?*"

"Sorry, son," said his father who obeyed immediately—he had been looking for his notebook—"I don't know yet." He might never know, and yet the *yet* sounded almost prophetic of incidents that would follow soon, which could if he mused long enough illuminate his arcana.

James Madison was the first to visit the "restored dream cottage," as her enthusiasm expressed it, *the first* to carry the tidings of its improvements and economies to Sweet-sider, Anthos and Sider. Before leaving her trio of dear friends, she christened their place, as they readily let her, *Riding Hood*—omitting the *Little* that she said would be too obvious, and also the *Red* out of respect to her color of Federalism.

"It's my gummamint, too," said Little, and she kissed him on leaving.

While she was not responsible for all the visitors who followed her to *Riding Hood* many came. None arrived walking, all with the speed of a traffic-saving instinct that impelled them to grind their brakes at *Riding Hood* before they drove past it recklessly into the woods. The owner of Anthos, a lady so huge Little could not name her, paid her respects. *Life gives way and our families,* Baballo had been brooding; and the Esfelts, hunting for a vacation home of their own, somehow came upon their sister's dream cottage with greetings from the Drischays touring Lapland and Tearilee and the Count and Contessa more content at home. The young relations did not stay long after a simple snack of imported canned Dutch ham and several frozen deep dish fruit pies, the best and only comestibles for the happy occasion that the general store of Sweetsider and the two-plate burner of the von Chulnts could bring out.

For the constantly surprised three at *Riding Hood* the visits were a kind of fare more quickly absorbed than understood. Interrupted eating an untasted bite of lunch they at once served the unexpected guest or guests all they had hopefully stored in the portable freezer to last them for a week. One afternoon James Madison brought with her from Sider her wise old friend Gwyn Yare, whose memory of youth was one extended eisteddfod. Together they listened to Little's Veracini, Purcell, Mozart, Honegger and Bach—Verchadet constrained to the harmonium for hours, Baballo lurking now and then at the back door open to his Claude Lorraine. When finally the old sage had recollected all his memories and was ready to go, he smiled affectionately at the young mother and said: "I am sure you know, your son doesn't play, God plays thru him." James Madison then whispered a promise of returning with Viertel Achtel.

The plumber, a pious Mr Arrows, who never laid the tiles of a buried cesspool the shortest distance between two points, defensibly on the mechanical principle that would prevent seepage from the waters of a marsh into a cistern, had coffee with the von Chulnts almost every other day. The tank, or cistern as he called it and had told them, was *septic*. He could find no reason for its acting up so often. But he would observe it—that is exhume it each time it failed its purpose—and with time discover why. His faith that the von Chulnts were carrying not only newsprint but every scrap of paper to the town dump was unshakable. For all that the trouble with their—for want of an elegant word—*plumbing* was heartbreaking. As a precautionary measure, horrified by thoughts of admixture in the pipes that should be running to them the pure waters of the well, they were boiling the water from the kitchen tap. It might happen any time of day or night that Verchadet, or Dala, or Little, or all together hearing a by now familiar noise from the general area of the plumbing under the floor beams would pale. Or aroused from sleep, a smiling Little, showing the space of a recently lost baby tooth, often joined them to see *Riding Hood* bidding as it were to sail away. The rise and fall of water from the bathroom onto the kitchen, living room, and front and rear steps was instantaneous and uncontrollable, allowing them only a murmur of a crescendo in unison of the names of a trilogy of Baballo's recension disembodying the pathos, the terror and ineluctable fate of its happening: "Pia Mia, Le Spectre de la Rose, La Forza del Destino."

They were sad enough to want to go to sleep early after one such tiring session—an evening of bailing water for hours, Mr Arrows not in Sweetsider when Dala telephoned. Snorckie disgusted and tucked in, their sofa converted snug against the front door after mutual warnings *not to flush* until Mr Arrows would come tomorrow to observe again. They had turned off the lights, but the darkness sounded a voice: "Anybody in? A friend of Miss Madison, Reverend Loess." He must have seen the lights go out and did not have to ask his question. But a reverend always had the right to call on his flock unannounced, or as the epic poet wrote, *unforewarned.* The von Chulnts were not quick at excuses: "One moment," Verchadet said impulsively and at once regretted admitting they were home. The bedding hidden on Snorckie's table and his door shut, the bed a sofa again cushioned in its corner for the reverend to sit in, and the hosts in housecoat and robe decently long, they let him in after a minute. "Trouble with the lights? *We have* at home; the utilities, a monopoly, are not responsible I'm afraid as they should be." Dala took the reverend's hat and coat-pocket leather notebook and neatly stored these also on Snorckie's table, quickly shutting his son's door which he had barely opened.

"Everything is so spacious in this little room," Reverend Loess said. Regrettably he could not stay. He had heard so much from Miss Madison about their son's precocious talent. Would he play at Sunday vesper service for the community? That was not an easy request to make to Little and expect immediate compliance, but "of course," Verchadet said as Dala nodded.

Reverend Loess' church was not the historic church of Sweetsider, but the one on the road from Anthos—older, at least a hundred years older, the church *du pays* so to speak, architecturally native in the fine craftsmanship of its interior. "One other favor." He had heard so much about Little's mother's talent. "They would want" to inaugurate the new electric organ—he himself had contributed to its purchase, the antique "pumped one" was so old-fashioned, and the community deserved something new. Would she accompany her son at the vesper service—he was not sure how kind the acoustics would be to her son's he assumed small fiddle, or any fiddle for that matter? He did not recall any instrument other than the organ ever playing in the church.

She would, tho she had never played an electric organ. She assumed it might make it easier for one who never played in public except to accompany her son.

"We have so much to look forward to, thank you, thank you," the Reverend Loess rose, and Dala forgetting the reverend's notebook gave him his hat. Handshakes and the front door closed.

Little was awake, opening his bedroom door just enough to startle his father by thrusting the reverend's notebook thru, "Baballo, why this *simonizing?*" Lada Dala, as he felt, was impelled by his son's swiftness to glance at the opened page that read *Sermon Sing,* and to wonder how Little had read that quickly in the dark, and then as to the meaning of the reverend's title page. But he pried no further. The violinist's door was shut, his lights suddenly on.

Staccatos of an unexpected practice crunched above the voice behind the door. "Verchadet! why did you agree for me? I won't, intend to play in any church. I'd as soon—and won't either—play in a *masque* or a *ginagog* than compete with the Bible."

A wistfulness somehow brought on by his son's slight of *The Book,* from which he had read to Little with no motive in mind other than its sense of story, led Dala—hand on the knob of the only bedroom door in his shed—to say almost inaudibly: "Wait until you are older, son, before you decide." Following in an even softer tone: "*Masque? ginagog?*"

"Yes! you weren't made to listen, but I *heard* James Madison and Gwyn Yare jabbering when they left here last week. 'Poor Mr Achtel—where he probably would like to go—to a *masque* or a *ginagog* rather than *their* church with the little steeple when he comes to Sweetsider on Sundays;

or if he didn't have to, as he must, not to *their* church at all, but just next door to it to buy his newspaper like everybody else, from dear Mr Houston the pharmacist.' " (Baballo and Verchadet, who like everybody else bought their Sunday newspaper at Houston's, had of course heard and met the negro druggist both feared and respected by the customary Sweetsider tolerance accorded to descendants in part of historical Southern families.)

"James Madison said, 'It's a pity, *it's a pity*,' she said, 'Mr Achtel *probably* found our congregation more antisemiotic than *their* church' (evidently the one with *the little* steeple topped by a heavy cross, Baballo guessed, vaguely hurt by Snorckie's interpolation of the letter *o* in the word *antisemiotic*).

"Verchadet, all they'll do is jabber when I play, and the *acootsticks* are bad enough without an electric organ drowning me out. And what do you know about electricity to inaugurate it. You did, *you did* want to remove the stuck plug with a nail file, when I shrieked, *Watch out*, STOP, NO!"

Baballo had his mouth slightly open to speak. But Verchadet, knowing storms pass, merely signed with her left index finger on her lips *say nothing*, turned off the lights of the living room, and the lights of Little's bedroom followed suit in a lightning flash.

Vesper adest. Venus starred an autumn sunset over dense gold leaves, James Madison held her arm in Dala's to be safe over the gravel walk of the churchyard. Several paces forward on the evening's cropped grass Gwyn Yare saw the church doors as the "gates" of the 24th Psalm, and Dala moved to compassion by the wide back span of the old man's uplifted head longed to master more than a little Welsh—thinking: if only he could render its sounds in English that made sense, and repay and delight his friend with loyalty in kind.

Verchadet and Little had been alone in the church some hours early for a last test of acoustics—mostly a rehearsal of passages the church walls seemed not to favor. Snorckie could see that she feared, as he tested a small platform under the pulpit for the creak of his new shoes. She had been playing the new organ by herself for a week, and was reluctantly admitting that its effect was not manual.

Soon they would be performing when she would be unable to hear, as now in the empty church she still could from up the nave to her gallery—where electricity seemed to overcome the effort to resist it and hear herself—to hear if they were together.

Little shouted to her: "Don't worry!"

"I'm worried," sounded the respond.

The church filled quickly. As Dala preceded James Madison in her pew to make her comfortable and sit at her right he felt her elbow wrestle. She stammered a name, something like *Th'Fallens*. "Why is she here," she said under her breath, "she never comes to church." "Th'?" Dala queried. There was one empty seat at his right that distracted him. "Oh—" James Madison struggled to breathe, "th'Jezebel—Baal! I've heard her blaspheme at Anthos. Years ago they say she danced ballet in Paris." Dala uncomfortably suspected that James Madison's voice was heard over their row of seats. Looking up he was abruptly aware of staring into the right aisle.

"O she mustn't, she mustn't," Miss Madison whimpered.

He saw a frail lady uppermost in mauve gauze, head wobbling at first, cheeks rouged into two small suns that with the frenzied decisiveness of a pinwheel on its stick whirred quickly past three oblivious parishioners to the seat beside him. Polite he stood up, she was nearly as tall as he. She spoke sympathetically to be overheard as at a performance, "I hope you don't mind." He could only shake his head from side to side, meaning he didn't as they sat down together. And at that moment like the prelate in a painting of her time called "Temptation" his listless smile might have incurred the wayward thought of a resilience which persists in the calves of an aging danseuse who once wished she were thinner. She spoke freely to him, introducing herself as Dea Falin: "They *all* look dead!" His smile did not change. She must have seen or been drawn to James Madison, coming down the aisle. She hovered on her seat—butterfly over a flower. Contrition held the priest of "Temptation" who now turned his head to his left. Were these tears or fears in Miss Madison's eyes behind the thick lenses? The reflections multiplied into a monster moth humming at a window lighted in the night.

Fortunately a brief prayer, a quick offeratory, then

after the *servitude* (as Little later expressed it) the Reverend Loess thanked the community for their share in the organ and the player in the gallery, and with humility and the charity of a great discovery introduced the soloist.

"Lovely," Dea said, then hissed like a fallen angel: "Snakes and pigs, what do they know of the trials of a child of genius, not able to smell out truths from incense."

"So you're the father?" a gentleman sitting next to Gwyn Yare in the row immediately in front partly turned his head to ask Baballo. The father lowered his long, upcurled eyelashes, long a nuisance tangling in the frames of his glasses, as his reply in church. He looked helplessly towards James Madison, but her rapt face, the good angel's, was prepared to listen without the sensuous ear. Tomorrow she would remember to tell Verchadet, "When he plays something happens to his face that's good."

No one heard the organ inaugurated. As Verchadet confided to Dala after, she dispensed with the diapason with all her strength while the voix céleste was deafening her, and only some inbuilt motherly metronome assured her that she and Little were together. Handel's *Largo* transposed for the violin ascended and was greeted with a jungle of applause.

"Never, never, for shame, shame, in church, in church one never applauds—in church," Dala heard James Madison's outraged, tearful voice—feeling every drop, drop of blood of her piety. "Heathens, heathens," she sobbed. He had not applauded, nor had Viertel Achtel next to Miss Madison tho his suspended hands were ready.

Laughing outright at the *faux pas,* as the nymph might in her wild head in the dance of her youth, "Good for *them,* they're alive," Dea countered the good angel across Lada's neutral body. The applause followed each offering of the violinist. Lada heard neither Verchadet nor Little. The contention was too great. The prelate of "Temptation," the good angel sobbing in his left ear and the fallen angel jeering in his right, by the dormant miracle of his philosophy of history that creates backward as well as forward, had metamorphosed into Janus, but not for long. He found himself thinking: "Loneliness is the same everywhere, no matter whom you love." And that was enough to release the bard so that in his grey matter his little Welsh flowed with the song of Llywarch Hen's son from the *Black Book of Carmarthen:*

> O T'd aerie too hid *his* Strad
> dear is 'nt rue cade weary cad
> m' need awe ah gnaw nim(bl') gad

"Sick transit, home again," Little thought and muttered, back in the city, running upstairs to renew acquaintance with his room. It was the largest in their brownstone, with sunny windows nine feet high, and would be his music studio in the mornings and his study in the afternoons. To their surprise Baballo and Verchadet had easily arranged for Snorckie's schooling at home, under their own tutelage. Perhaps the district school superintendent was impressed that a boy, hurrying towards his sixth birthday, knew the difference between an inflected and an uninflected language, and that Verchadet who would be teaching him Hebrew, Greek, Latin, Italian, French and German had kept equal pace. Perhaps Baballo's rank as professor was warranty for his modest somewhat altered outline of trivium and quadrivium that would take care of his son's delectation for the next four years. One of the few apolitical gentlemen, strangely with some authority in the school system, the superintendent was amenable to Little Baron's polite request for "permission" to sort thru various books and documents on the shelves and desk in the office where his parents to begin with timorous soon discussed their own fitness with ease. Little's several interruptions with questions he immediately answered himself were finally rewarded with the superintendent's consent. "Well," he smiled, "I can hazard one experiment in our great city. Little has been a graduate of the Montessori method for almost three years. I was, I may tell you now, in the audience at the *District Schools Festival* last spring, and your son's *Gavotte* stopped one of the older boys in the middle of at least one profanity. Besides you assure me, Little is registered in an accredited music school. He will not be running wild playing his fiddle."

Gaelic *run, rune* = *beloved* or *mystery*, Dala meditated listlessly as he stepped across the threshold of the superintendent's office.

Whatever the solicitous graces sometimes awkward or unexpected of the world, Verchadet was looking forward to the repose of routine at home. She preferred her chores to the graces. The violinist preferred Venetians to shut out the excessive sunlight in his room. "All musicians work best in the dark." To his simmer of protest she responded that she might, like Baballo, profess to go to work elsewhere. Little compromised with unforeseen virtuoso affection: "No, Verchadet, you need me to wash the rosin off my fingers." She then took some cloth a yard wide, cut it in half down its length, to make drapes for the pilasters of the corner windows so as to trap the sun's glare where it shone in strongest, and Baballo hung them from their dizzy height as soon as he returned from the first day of his new term at the institute. When Little saw them descend gracefully to the floor, "That," he said, "is dignified, enough."

The three hours (limited to) morning practice, not without its ten minute recesses every hour, *synched* with the light of the world on week days. His liking for darkness become a side issue, the violinist for years delighted in the curtainless windows—the object of his own wish as it were —as playing his fiddle he ran to stand to the roulade of *The Upanishads,* that is the uniformed sanitation men emptying the barrels of garbage down the street. Verchadet, as Little readily acknowledged, was first to call them *The Upani-*

shads. She was not sure why, except maybe for their lordly uplift in pursuing the discards and a rattling of the brain that went with their work mixed with a sense of purity.

All three von Chulnts received letters a week or so (weeks passed so fast) after returning from Sweetsider—codas as it were to their summer—Little naturally had run to pick up from the postman. They read these silently together as a trio, tho sometimes one or another lagged as their heads bent over them, and unavoidably breathed into one another's ears.

Snorckie's letter was from his friend Curt Budder, dated June, and it read:

> dear friend You played the violin terrifick.
> You will grow up to be a very famous man.
>
> Your friend,
> Curt Budder
> (Mrs. Doody class 4–1)

It was illustrated with a line drawing in pencil and brown crayon of the performer, head of a mixed breed between child and rabbit in profile, body committed to the *law of Egyptian frontality*, one extended hand alone holding the fingerboard rather like the handle of a shovel whose f-holed scoop formed the belly of the largest imaginable viol, all in plan and supporting the violinist as might a perfectly horizontal strut. Little remembered his June triumph, and the "pledgeum allegiance," and as he thought then he heard "and now good-bye," and how the principal had put her arm on his shoulder and he had placed his on hers. "That was when I wore my King of Music hat," he said modestly, "March, then June, and then Octember. What month is it, Verchadet?"

The letter addressed to Professor Dala von Chulnt read:

> Dear Madam:
>
> Your place in the scientific world is such that membership in The Natural Institute must appeal to you for several reasons . . .

These followed for two pages, including a table of various ranks and respective fees.

James Madison's letter, addressed to Verchadet, read:

> My dears,
>
> I miss you. So does everyone here, as you see from this clipping—I'm keeping on second thought but—from *The Sider Recorder:* "Professor and Mrs. Dale van Chant have gone back to the city where their many winter engagements call, but are expected back at their Sweetsider home next summer. Sider remembers their precocious son Little's concert in Sider church at the vesper service that inaugurated the new electric organ so beautifully played by his talented mother; the applause that followed and the presentation of a red leather scrap book by the Reverend Loess to the virtuoso participant in which he now keeps his press releases. We are sure this one joins them."
>
> I am sorry Gale Bright, who edits the *society notes,* misspelled your name. I phoned to tell her that, and she promises to correct the error the next time. But she did have the good sense to print Little's photo which I took before he went off to church that day. You'll recall it, white shirt open at the collar, rolled up sleeves giving room to his bow arm, as you persuaded him—and as you know it turned out to be warm—and navy corduroys with elastic waist. So sweet. Only I hope he chooses Army instead of Navy when he is ready for it.
>
> One sad bit of news. I just heard that your tool shed was overturned in the Hallowe'en pranks of last night. Not all boys are so considerate of other's possessions as Little is. Don't please let this incident worry you. I am sure the shed can be righted.
>
> Ever yours,
> James

Little noticed Verchadet's and Dala's faces as they read the sentences including the words *Army* and *shed.* "Well, if you want letters and friends," he said righteously, "you better not wince, *camel-ionic*—o you know what I mean!"

They did, and decided right then and there, without telling him, to visit Sweetsider briefly in the spring to sell the dream cottage, tho James Madison could see them then only in the city. Nor could Dala ever explain to her what the sigh of his haiku meant.

Ah-me No

Smell of
stacked hay
overturned shed

Little, who by this time kept a "dairy" to rival his father's notebook, did not answer his classmate's letter. His young years arced to his later, as the poet would say: later, he would never flash sentiment, never answer letters after giving up his diaries for only necessary appointment books. But now he still pressed down and flourished his pen in his "dairy":

> *Anent* (*anant*? asked Verchadet, who said *use your dictionary*) Budder—good man all covered with shnow and icy schlush underfoot last winter, when Boomerang the duck bogged in the lake won't leave the floes nor eat and died. Sad thinking of it. And Wednesday is a holiday.

For once, uncertain that the letter addressed to him was meant for him, Baballo was finally saddened into indifference to life, the pursuit, let alone liberties, and did *not* answer it. But still somewhat free from the priorities of professor's blue books he took advantage of the holiday to write

Four Related Unrelated Notes

> As soon as my title *professor* spread—someone had read my mail—we became the most sought-after people. But I must sublime all ethics into

strict geometry—like the *blessed philosopher* whom I call that, I admit, only to salve my own balm. *Blessed*, he saves me the trouble: "This modification of the mind or admiration of a thing is called, if it happens in the mind alone, wonder (*admiratio*); but if stirred up by an object we fear, it is named consternation (*consternatio*): for wonderment at an evil holds man suspended while regarding it, so that he cannot think of other things to free himself, etc. Ethics III, prop. LII

But when I look into the future, an age of space and rockets when even an innocent fiddler's stance may well have to be astro-nautical and political, i.e. for managerial involvement—cool for profits and intrigues of cultural exchanges between enemy states—then will all art whine, croon, yelp from its invisible floor—

A poet, a lost friend once said, they remembered the past of what had survived, but not the future of what had perished.

How welsh Llywarch Hen's *Lament*?

> Alive 'n' I'll my lamb wed
> neat eyed in debt weed dear head
> a mare wee odd no' butt ah mean head

Verchadet, who almost never wrote letters, intended to answer James Madison's to "my dears," while she waited for Snorckie taking his first lesson of the new term at his music school. She was prevented by conversation, chiefly that of another young violinist's mother she had met the year before, as she noticed shyly that the lady had changed her pendent summer cross for another more harmonious with her fall costume.

13

With every new teacher a violinist starts all over—or from the beginning with *scales*, Verchadet was learning. *Nota bene*, Baballo jotted, *and not until he is on his own does he begin: then*, his pen hurried, *extempore*, as he glanced up at Verchadet, *the note that ends well is blessed.*

The old director of the music school, a continuum of the European conservatory, where Little apparently now also officiated, had heard his American boy draw one note from an open string, at the opening of the new term, and immortalized it with the abiding music sounded off the great foreign names on his own illuminated testimonial hung by gold braid from the antique hautboy. When Little ran down the marble stairs ahead of him, the director oblivious that he spoke to Verchadet (or, as happened rarely, to Baballo) would nod: "You should meet that boy—a genius," he doted. Perhaps the director was mistaking the parents for members of his staff. Miss Sybil Greate was no longer there, having left by default of her one open note she had never exemplified on her own fiddle by not bringing it with her to the lessons.

"Sorry to disturb—Little, Signore Agire Onesto Proba, your new teacher," the director said, as Snorckie was crossing strings in *the* Chaconne, and left as has been said pages back with his mental violin cushion tucked under his chin.

Little pressed his own chin by way of greeting and courtesy, but did not stop crossing strings. The slight, thoughtful-looking Italian had brought his fiddle. Yet without taking it out of its case he already stood in one place crossing strings with empty arms completely absorbed by, as the Swan of Avon termed it, *the ground.* Little's stray glances from his violin bridge obviously endeared him. From now on it was only a matter of who could cross strings faster. They stopped together.

"—da Torino."

"Sì, Turin," said Little whose Italian had somehow advanced.

Signore Proba was the (Scriptural) *type* of Dala's look into the future: the displaced violinist of a late war that left him all the world except his own country to play in, the cultural exchange of concerted enterprise between two erstwhile enemy states. He had come to the States on a temporary visa with *much* hope that the old director's *inflúence* would make it permanent. He spoke, for most purposes, all languages and so spoke none, dreaming his wife might join him some day, *when he had fortune.* If grammar were a test, he was these days forgetting his Italian.

"La mia moglie—weefè—miss—how you say—mi?" he confided to Dala and Verchadet when he met them together. But while the ninety-day visa held, Little, as his aunt the Contessa Murda-Wonda worded it, "was proud of his man teacher." Proba exemplified on his own fiddle, pupil rivalled the sound of the full size, both amplified by duos and a constant run of verbal *espressivo:* "How? Bōw—like how? I'm—*hic opus, hic labor est. Jam post bellum.* Oedipe—you know storia—old member quatuor walk on one (pronounced *wan*) leg. You young, two arms, ten fingers, two legs. Posizione, sta, great virtuoso." (Aside to Verchadet and Baballo: "No, no? you *no* American?" They and Little in unison, "But of course we are, what else?"

Proba: "Maybe, no?" then back to Little—) "Play premier, third exercise Svecik. Bis, more once. Probier. *Moment* (pronounced as in French, probably to mean *momentum.*) Più ah più, *ma*! side of hair—happily!" And the day the visa expired, he was to sail home the next day no polygamist, the conversation took a wistful turn. His eyes shone with a tear or two held back in them saying his good-bye to Little: "Very elegant suit. How much suit? Ever, always *moment* (still as in French) arrivederci," as he bōwed out of the room, still crossing imaginary strings of Bach's *Chaconne* as when he first walked into it.

"Scales all over," Little complained a week later.

His second man teacher was Mr Athens Olympus—by his changeful face a gamin hieratic type or a late Greek deity of Marseilles—youthfully approaching forty-five, reputed soloist constantly on tour with his fiddle. When he had time to sit on his European acclaim he could be friendly in conversation and pert.

He reminisced on St. Petersburg nights, "ah those and the Paris Conservatory's," his "triumphal tour of two years ago with his *crossbow*" (as Snorckie enthralled decided he heard it) and his "great friend" the harpsichordist Rutar Neitsnebur, Bearlean, Warshawa, Prague, Vienna, Buda, Pest ("or as their citizenry feel," he remarked knowledgeably, "vice versa")—and the farewell night on the Acropolis: tho, as she nodded, Verchadet sensed something about him less European than not un-American, not mercenary but subject to checks and balances. She was almost sure she had guessed right when he did not show up for half the lessons the first month, and when he did he had to leave early with apologies and a "rain check for the short hour." She verified her guess that he was not willfully dishonest. Soon after (forsaking scales) he and Little had rehearsed Bach's double violin concerto he enthusiastically promised they would play it together at the next School Anniversary Concert—remarking shyly: "My D.A.R. wife and our five little daughters all of whom play instruments will be there with contingent."

"Pensive man, Athens, after all," Verchadet said to Dala, while Little thumped his back with felicitations on his own good news, "I was wondering why at this point of his career he wanted to teach, I had supposed to perpetuate his method, but it turns out, tho his wife is rich as I suspect, he still can't responsibly fall back on Bach alone for his future."

"I'm glad," said Baballo to Little, only to ask him and Verchadet some moments later, what was it they told him on coming home while he was writing. He left his notebook open on a table for them to read, but Verchadet had expected him to listen and was in no hurry to, and Little, too intent on perfecting his part in the double concerto at once, just glanced and would not even ply him with a question about "such nonsense":

what's the
future of
the future of

Chinese
rabbit hutch
of Demeter

o my girly whirl
not another little girl
any
little boy would
give
equivalent joy

"Honest enough," Baballo said recollectively a day or so later, "and modest too," Verchadet added, "for an Olympian. I've heard Viertel Achtel, who follows reputations, say that Europe's taste prefers Athens' passion to Ztephiah's cold accuracy. I don't, but—." (The great

Ztephiah older than Athens, but from the same East European province, was by now a naturalized American for some twenty years, whereas Athens had just recently filed for his first papers.) "Each genius to his own talents," Verchadet went on, "and if Little ever decides against the violin and for the life of a happy Upanishad let the street-cleaning be honest it's all right with me. I'm not as you know sold to lessons forever." Once Verchadet sheltered the faint shadow of a doubt she held on to it for integrity, unlike Baballo who was always composed to let the sun dissipate the shadow.

The very next lesson, or the one after, Athens remarked casually enough to Verchadet: "I have never taught before, and Little presents a problem. I'm not sure that I have anything to say that would improve his part, for example, in the Double Concerto. I have played it many times and I know of no one who plays it better than Little." Verchadet might have been inclined to agree, but for that very reason Athens' praise of Little's playing impressed her as improbable. Had his D.A.R. wife influenced his opinion? Reasons of propriety? that his prestige might suffer in a joint recital with so young a pupil? Motherly reasons of five little daughters with ten eyes looking into the future of one potential fiddler?

"Already?" Dala said mystified, when Verchadet more or less put her thoughts to him after Snorckie had gone to bed. "Much as I hate psychology," she replied. "Ferther-over, as your Chaucer and Little say, I don't like Athens poking the tip of his bow at Little's navel, European fashion. Little has a way of poking back that risks mayhem." "Ah, Verchadet," Dala sighed mostly to calm her worries, not needing to tell her she roused his: "Maybe all that Athens means by no one plays the concerto better than Little is that what comes naturally to the young is at best later only excavated by life—the bloom of a thought, not the bloom which is never dug up. Or are you a philosopher? You say no, and I hope not," he speculated as she often said to him, "beautifully to no purpose." "I can imagine, as James Madison might, an aide to a brass hat or electioneer toad surveying Little's vita at 21 and asking: 'Sir, you're 21 and have worked 17 years, impossible!' And should Little explain, why yes I've been a violinist 17 years, the response might be, 'boy, you're joking, does it take that long?' But you see," Dala went on generously, "Athens is as they say a patrician among performers and all his regard for Little means is: Youth performs if he has it, age drudges."

Slamming the door one evening on returning from another short lesson, Snorckie confronted an anxious Baballo behind the entrance to his brownstone: "To make a short story long, he's not playing!"

"Who's not?"

"O*whim*pus," Snorckie scoffed, "has to *tour* in Curaçao the night of the School Anniversary Concert," and gave way to a profanity.

"Ah," Baballo said, "I'm glad you know where to use the word, but just add the suffix *ah*. Sit down, calm down. There's the name, son, of a precious wood in the Scriptures, as Verch will tell you, that avoids dullness by ending in *ah* in the singular and *im* in the plural."

"He said he would," Little rankled, "I'm thru, with *him*." He'd have dragged his part swaying anyway and not played in tune, Little added in his mind naming each note of several foghorns in the harbor that happened to sound then.

"And what's after the shortcomings of the *corpus delicti*?" Baballo questioned Verchadet aside.

"For which you have paid," she muttered in anger.

Their impasse promised not to be funny. But contingency is stochastic as those who think it over say, and happenings have a way of coming together. It happened that Verchadet's mother, Tearilee, on one of her rarer and rarer visits—her lonely arrival occasioned by the fact that the rest of the family was that hour shopping for lustreware—quickened to tears by her middle daughter's impasse asked, "What kind of a life could a fiddle lead to in *any* case?" Her mature dissent gave Verchadet an idea. It happened she knew, Olympus had told her that he had spoken of Little's abilities, apropos of his own fortunes as teacher, to his impresario, Warlock Endor, and who but Warlock knew better the future of violinists? Didn't he invest in them? Her telephone call, tho Verchadet put the question of investment only circularly, brought a ready answer: *He* didn't. But, if as Verchadet directly said, all she expected of Mr Endor was his opinion of her son's talent, his secretary answered, Mr Endor would be glad to arrange for an audition. Verchadet felt gratified when the dignified female voice at the other end completed the conversation, saying she believed Mr Endor was aware of her son's name—would he please bring his scrap book—and confirmed an hour mutually acceptable.

The von Chulnts arrived at the impresario's together. A portly, congenial man greeted the "professor" (*had he guessed right? obviously he had*), the mother and "naturally" the violinist. He heard him—Little illustrating the most impassivity as it produced the most accuracy—and complimented him, impresario to artist.

Then lightly: "And who is your favorite violinist, Little?"

"Ztephiah," the answer flashed lightning.

"I thought so," Warlock laughed most of a breath, "the top of my list, but difficult often in his demands. I hope, Little, you will oblige old Warlock more and demand less when he begs for a favor."

"I hope so," Little almost flattered him as seemed appropriate.

"And what are your plans?" Warlock turned to the parents.

"To let Little do as he pleases," Baballo said as Verchadet glanced at him momentarily so only he was aware that she glared.

"Mr Endor's advice, if I'm right," Verchadet summed it up quickly to silence Baballo, "is for Little to plan towards a solo debut."

"Exactly, there is no question of going on," said Warlock, and turning to Baballo, "he should have at least a Strad to play with."

"But the Gretch sounds—" Dala faltered.

Time hung on for Verchadet as Warlock looked thru Little's scrap book of press releases—Little almost leaning on the impresario and, saving himself embarrassment, rapidly turning pages for him.

"Who is his teacher?" Warlock asked Verchadet.

"Mr Athens Olympus," she said.

"Why, yes," he said, "a great artist—who has gone in for teaching. My personal—merely personal—feeling is the *pro* never has the time away from the concert hall to analyse what he does there so he can best teach it to others. But the great teacher is the best soloist in his studio, and can save the precociously gifted the most regrettable subsequent effort." Baballo and Verchadet were both aware of listening, Baballo somehow unsure that he was not lost along the way.

Little's ostensible future impresario went on: "There is Imam Betur who can execute any difficulty of technique to perfection, he can as his pupils say make wood play. I wish he had been there when I played the fiddle, but he wasn't around then. There is an art of bōwing that makes a *natural* aware of what he is doing every moment of playing so that his elbow never regresses to the rear of the player as it were (literally so to the unaware), but always with a forward momentum—the principle is pivotal. I would suggest you at least allow Professor Betur advise you while Mr Olympus is touring. Genius needs watching," he said to Verchadet. "Well—Little! You must play for me again in six months, and the third time will be in Great Hall."

Thru scales to Parnassus, as Little now translated his Latin: the good-byes were as hopeful as Warlock was comforting. Nothing had been invested, so something was gained. For Verchadet there was no choice. Little would not return to Olympus. She must to Betur, he urged.

Little's third teacher—and last, not counting assistants who taught scales and exercises by which their master weeded or finally took over their best pupils—some never reached him so he was rarely prey to boredom—Little's *best* teacher taught as most people eat: biologically speaking, out of need. Known for the highest fees in the industry, he could forgo fees generously for his final aim: that by watching genius be accomplishèd—the grave accent on *accomplished* not exactly his misplaced foreignism but an example of his messianic dedication. Time was no option: he taught from seven in the morning to eight in the evening, every hour a race that never ran short on the pupil, most often running over, if he ever picked a pupil so unromantically modern to test the teacher by stopwatch. So that Betur's day stopped nearer nine than eight in the evening on most teaching days, in some weeks seven.

He taught all ages. Some he had cradled, and from then on to the middle years, so that genius mounted to deeper genius, and when it flinched it could always return to him even if it had hurt him. And when a composer wanted an unregistered note that no violinist had played before on that instrument of all possibilities, Betur in his leisure found it on a string and found a good scholar to play it, tho he himself could not bear to listen to it.

But Little's story is not a chronicle of teachers. The point of it is Little was the pupil all teachers long for—as Verchadet for all her astuteness had still to find out—and Betur the teacher of fortune.

14

In character the von Chulnts arrived at Betur's studio together: Dala Baballo mainly to disprove the academic fiction of *the omniscient observer;* or, as his afterthought skeptically rehearsed on the way, perhaps to throw the first stone at himself as chance propagator of his own fiction. After ringing, Little heard a musical rush behind the door. "Would *be* whippets," he guessed. Mrs Betur opened it.

Two young boxers sat at the threshold and with compassionate eyes on the strangers blocked their entrance. "Sib, Gesib—they're brother and sister both innocent—please step aside first and let these people in. My Georgia father owned a racing stable. May be for that reason they run like colts thru this apartment. They're gentle." Her manner was arch, ladylike and hospitable. The boxers instantaneously rose to the height of Little, the bodice of his mother, and to one third the lean height of Baballo—and stepped aside, that is in front of a waiting room on a line with the entrance. Mrs Betur evidently spoke English, but its registers, suggesting somehow the foreign inflections of world-travelled musicians in a large city, made it uncertain whether her background referred to the Georgia of our South or Gruziya. Verchadet waited a good part of a year before Mrs Betur herself verified that it was precisely Atlanta, "way back," before Sherman.

"Mr Betur will come out presently. His lunch is cooling, but he's had no time," she said drawing back the scarlet tasseled and festooned portieres that served instead of a door to the waiting room. Turning to it, so that the boxers now waited behind in the narrow hall down which they had raced, the von Chulnts could not help noticing a large dining room with beige festoon-blinds half-raised to let the sun in. It shone on a long Florentine lacecovered table set with goodies between appointed crystal stemware and two tall matching carafes sparkling with wine—red and white. "You're welcome to help yourselves whenever you come," Mrs Betur waved unpretentiously toward the display whose sunlit existence had potentially fed the von Chulnts' reserved appetites. Out of habit they declined with triple thanks and grace—and noticed further that the near end of the dining room, like the entrance on a line with the waiting room, was closed by heavy sliding doors. They sensed Betur's studio behind these, tho only a hurried rustling of sheet music reached them from the other side.

They entered a den where a softly lampshaded night eclipsed day. Crowded by two grand pianos, arranged curve to curve, and a row of club chairs, all three walls mounted a continuous collection of portraits of violin virtuosi and their signatures under glass framed by one-half-inch black borders of wood. To Little, the earliest going back a few centuries, when the idea of violin virtuoso first came to life, appeared to have just signed their autographs thru table-rapping hands. "How wonderful!" he said. "It's a bit chilly," Dala whispered. They walked around in the little space there was, studying them, as Verchadet tried to sit back in one of the club chairs much too big for her, thinking at the same time that it would be hard to get up again. From under the festooned portieres the boxers made their way to her and leaned their heavy heads affectionately against her legs and in the ample space to either side of them in the club chair. She had always felt kindly towards dogs but was shy of them. But they were all distracted then by a few measures of a Bach sonata played in the studio. "Out of tune," it was Little's turn to whisper. They heard the sliding doors open and a student's confident voice, "What Bach shall I bring the next time, Professor Betur?" —and the master's quieting voice: "What Bach? Any Bach."

If his reply sounded indifference, sound disappeared when he appeared. Bōwing, the slightest stoop, he seemed not to bōw. He held back the scarlet portieres for them by way of greeting, silent: taller than Baballo, younger than they expected, raven curled hair which the Western reader thinking of Romeo might attribute to Laila's Majnun. His dark eyes perhaps hinted at a smile forbidden to his lips.

An intimate downward glance at the boxers—no audible signal—was needed to make them get up and walk back with great dignity down the hall they had come from to unseen spaces in the apartment. Led politely by Betur thru the sunlit dining room the von Chulnts crossed the track of the opened sliding doors into a much larger room lit by standing lamps in broad day, then the sliding doors were shut. The studio's dazzling artificial night ended in rounded bays and a by now familiar shade of scarlet curtains—drawn. They bulged with a wind from the open windows behind them. Verchadet and Baballo were chilled at once.

They were reminded of daylight only by some motes trapped in a sunbeam across the white plastered ceiling bordered with carved rosettes. Looking down from these as it were—with an impression of being raised on his toes beyond the immediate clutter of furniture—Betur said: "Too much smoke, now too much *drepts*." The elder von Chulnts remained standing tacitly grateful when he walked over to shut one or two of the unseen windows responsible (as they understood him) for the *drafts*. He returned to his previous stance near drawers of music files, stacks of loose music, an executive's flat-topped desk heaped with papers, elegant writing gear and not so elegant stubs of pencils and variegated crayons, several cartons of cigarettes of different brands, and so on, all hiding the gloss of mahogany underneath but removed in some kind of personal order from a large sheet of graph paper apparently his schedule. The other furnishings of the room were too evident but obviously necessary: a concert grand with its partly unrolled rubber and brown canvas cover, weighted with more stacks of music, several violins and or in their cases; a tall bookcase with heavy tomes, placed directly in front of the fireplace and hiding its antique marble mantelpiece; a vast plum velvet sofa with several commensurate armchairs of a matching softness. "Please," he said indicating these.

The von Chulnts sat down. Betur stood. "Mr Endor called me, and has explained. I un'stand you wish my advice. In the situation it would be difficult," he said.

Verchadet assumed that "the situation" meant Athens, and quickly summed up Little's case as against Athens' own statement of his impasse as teacher. She emphasized that for Little it meant there would be no returning.

"I know Mr Olympus," Betur said, "we were fellows at the Conservatory. I'm sure it was on'y a misun'standing easily mended." He looked towards Little, who showing his best behavior looked back and said nothing.

The foreign professor's mixture of excellent English, solecisms and speech impediment puzzled Verchadet as much as his reluctance. Obviously what he did not wish to hear he did not hear. Nevertheless she was certain he had heard her and even respected her as contender—"after his kind" as the Scriptures say. What with a prospect of scales depressing her by this time she was ready to advance her Little. Dala gratuitously interjected for her: "Mr Warlock, as you know, believes that your method is indispensable to our son's debut, but as impresario he assures us of our son's talent. Tho we're his parents, we don't expect your assurance that you will make an artist of him, if by the age of twelve he doesn't show that he is enough of one to go on alone—without a teacher. Until then if you will teach him technique that is all we ask." Dala's wisdom or idiocy as a really omniscient observer might see it—especially his use of Endor's first name and the words "by the age of twelve" —left no more change on Betur's face than the sunbeam on a rosette overhead, which everyone in the room for an instant seemed to eye. Betur gazed above Baballo and turned to Verchadet: "You see, I don't prepare anyone for a debut. I just teach, and in recent years my *shedule* has been too full to accept boy*s*" (the last word ending in a soft *s*). "Still if you wish I'll hear him." Unexpectedly he addressed Little: "Play me."

"Bach?" Little asked firmly.

"For me that's not important. De Bériot?"

Betur had called for an old war horse concerto that young violinists must learn if they expect to become virtuosi. Little had mastered it and, tho *he'd* have preferred to play Bach, proceeded leisurely after an indifferent look to open his fiddle case, unswathe his half-size from its satin sack, remove his bow from its clamps, eye its straightness and tighten it, by which time Baballo tense over having to hear *that piece* he could not bear to hear again could have sworn that Betur's lowered gaze at the procedure betrayed impatience. It might be saying: young man, to save time my students do all that best on the street, or before entering my studio. How could the strange Betur divine that Snorckie's unhurried preparation was his way of letting the De Bériot flow thru him?

"Does the *modder* wish to accompany," the teacher asked. "No," she answered. Not wasting words Betur transformed into apocalyptic accompanist gave Little his *A*, made sure of the boy's tuning and they were off—if not abreast, not in tandem.

Betur stormed the piano with the orchestral part and

flooded it with wrong notes, on purpose as Little suspected, to throw him off pitch. Obviously Betur could wake up in the middle of the night to play any part of this score to fulfill any peer's test of his mastery of it. In the violin part Little kindled his own fireworks, wherever Betur leaped or skipped furiously turning, almost tearing pages—not playing them straight thru much as Little hoped he would, all the glides, slides, heralded coloratura of a century gone before Little was born: obdurately always in pitch. For once Dala, insensitive to Betur's wrong notes, appreciated the musical structure of the piece despite himself. During a cadenza Betur rose from the keyboard and danced as he stood in place, eyes, arms, hands, quickened breath, once catching himself singing, icon of Byzantine saint and Kurdish awe—the historic observer in Dala hopelessly looking for metaphor—what—before vandals covered the mosaics of Santa Sophia, brilliants long before the vulgar glutton's *come hither, shishke bab.* Never, never vulgar.

"*Ver' talented poy,*" Betur said to the parents, "but it would be difficult with my present *shedule.* If you are sure as to Mr Olympus—there is no *horry,* he is *gut*—maybe I can arrange with Dr Presha my assistant, *moch* better, *moch* more patient than I with *yong* people, and I could hear your son *wance* a *manth.*" Verchadet, who knew honest art—whatever the artist might be when she saw his "merchandise," a word for which she would thank Betur in the future—"would rather *arrange* now, to save time," she said. So it was agreed.

Dala, who paid his bills immediately and would rather diffuse into a dew than suffer the touch of money between himself and those he respected, had moved shyly with wallet in hand to Betur. "Please, no—not for advice—there is no reason this time," Betur said. Dala's eyes still offered—yet as it is sometimes generous to accept he accepted. But he was quite aware of the extravagance of his tastes—such as giving of himself to his bluebook students, or paying ten dollars (having misread the price tag as one dollar) for a six-inch square of Irish linen handkerchief for Verchadet who knew more about finance than he, or buying Snorckie a unicorn for his birthday—and honor gave him courage to venture *sotto voce:* "May I ask what is your fee?" "It would be half the usual, but I shall *probeably* be able to arrange a scholarship at *wan* or th'other of the institutions I teach in," Betur said simply.

Thru all this session Betur had spoken only the words *play me* to Little. Obviously part of his method was to demonstrate, not to talk. But he now turned to Little and asked, "What is your name?" "Little Baron." Betur smiled down and they shook hands. "He is to play only scales until I see him. To hold one note for a long time is the hardest," he said to Verchadet, who took this information to heart while looking at Little. He nodded. After the door closed on thank you's, he still seemed content.

In the subway its din in her ears prophesied a shadowy evening of rattling off musical scales. Dala, on his own time before another evening class completed his long day, transliterated, on his wallet's memo pad, from *Gorhoffedd* of Hywel ab Owain Gwynedd:

is the dent roc towered

15

Teeth help to keep the tongue quiet was Welshman Gwynedd's literal meaning.

Dr Vasily Presha's troubled small white teeth, misleading a foreign man with an ailing heart, did not stop him from speaking too much. Researchist in the French style of violin bōwing, whose method he had fed to Betur's more instinctive use of it, Presha often remarked how much better Imam had fared since their young days as equals. "*Nu, zat's natural,*" he memorialized in concluding a story or lesson. "*My fāter wass Proshian,*" he told Verchadet, "but I'm *Roshian.* Betur and myself *ferst studded in Roshia.* Nu, zat's natural."

How *natural* anyone with a sense for status, after having been at Imam's, could see on coming to Vasily's. Little entered Presha's studio crossing his one threshold into the squeezed long end of *one* room, as he judged at once from a lid of ceiling which extended beyond yet weighed over this area. In itself it formed a narrow proscenium between a row of leaded windows and a purple divider of thick folds of curtain hung from heavy brass rods along its entire length. Three highbacked overstuffed armless armorial chairs were backed against the windows. An iron violin stand, a marble and ormolu table completed the properties. Not until summer, in another setting after a winter of discontent, would Little solve the mystery behind the curtain. It was Mrs Presha's domain and (*as if Shakespeare had anything to do with it,* as Little would then tell Lada) her *printless* flight while her husband taught. "Dear *Blume,* Mr Presha pronounces it as in Heine, is a beautiful woman," Mrs Betur would soon tell Verchadet. "She still studies singing, her lifelong ambition's to act Carmen, and she very well does her by twining a rose in her hair or flinging it." On his part, Vasily's preamble to Little's very first lesson with him also hinted at flaws that prolong friendships: "Ada Betur give up violin when she married Imam." Not that Verchadet was curious to hear about it—she dreaded gossip.

The lesson proceeded. "Imam wass ver' imprest, ver' angshoes to have—" (Little's name?) "f'r pupil. Wass afred you no come, he loose, like on stock market, he said, can happens. He toll me," he turned to Verchadet, "won'r'ful ta-lent, stronk character. I say him, Imam, all-wace you say *wait, they come.* You cam. Nu, zat's natural.

"Ass far me," he turned back to Little, "I titch then he take you. Far me iss all-wace from the beg-inning. Bot dis ferst time, play me!" After Presha's disclosure of Betur's anxiety, *play me* echoed Imam to Little.

"*The Devil's Trill?*" he asked.

"What-you-want," Dr Presha said, picking up his own heavy fiddle as for an emergency. He had opened his collar on giving Little free choice. A small golden cross hung from his broad white neck as he tuned softly now and then while Little played, deadpan but checking on him as well. "Humidt af-fects," Presha sweated, obviously annoyed and breathing with effort. "Out! out!" he'd say vehemently from time to time, elbowing, forearm forward.

As I'm doing all along, Little thought, where does he think my arm is—prepared to hear him say, "Nu, zat's natural," as he finished the piece to his own satisfaction. He was not prepared for insult.

"Not moch ima-jinn-ation," Presha said. "I don't hear what Imam—. Needs mat-urity. Bot f'me pieces not interesting."

"You're no jinn *eyether*," Little looked away silently, wondering about Presha's short pronunciation of *ie* in *pieces* and Dala's confidential advice on such matters.

"Far me it's the bōwing wrong. Not so moch trouble with finger-rink. See, ev-ery stroke, ferst leetle, den more, mo-re, more-moch presha." He stressed the increase of pressure with bōwed-out knees and fiddle sagging to the floor. "Iss hard. Nu, zat's natural. We have sayink in Roshia: feedink de peegs t'honor de livink."

Had Baballo been there the saying would have reminded him of his sister, Murda-Wonda—her pitiless capacity for suffering, only *she* was not male.

"What do you think," Little asked Verchadet, once out of earshot of Presha.

"What do you?" she asked *him*.

"If it leads to Betur maybe?"

After an Institute *function* Dala was walking home with an equally questionable variant of Gwynedd:

is that eye hant rack toward—

16

"Rather life is longwinded, art is winded," Dala reverted, compassionate over Little but hoping for his sympathy. Now six, Little, sitting, looked up—with as much established maturity as most humans ever need have—and said: "Ah peeg-poet h-it saze in my hoss-Roshian science't's book-a in quesh-wan-able Een-glish, *We live in an ocean of air with our feet on the ground.* It's almost boring," he confided, "no, not the scales, the feesh"—he rose to enact the authority sagging to the floor—"*Preh-eh-eh-sha!*—Dala."

But the month came round. After three lessons with Presha, the family were all together again at Betur's. Little played the G-flat major scale—and perhaps the C-sharp minor—Verchadet wasn't listening when Betur leaped suddenly and said: "I take him." Except for promising "a piece in *a-nodder manth*" he said nothing else. So till then it was back to Presha.

Finding another occasion, "we don't seem to sit together or talk much these days," Dala said sitting down next to Little. "Read me a *Sonnet,* Dala," Little said, his head heavy on Dala's shoulder. "Don't bother to *fetch*—I feel so Een-glish—your *Complete Plays and Poems.* My little vest-pocket leather one of the *Sonnets* is right here next to *Babar* and *Leopold Mozart.*" "Which?" Baballo asked, stretching his free hand to pick up last year's Christmas volumette of

Shakespeare's *unannotated Sonnets,* inscribed *from Little to Lada.* "77," Little said.

"Good," he said when Dala had finished, his head nestled heavier on Dala's clavicle. "Won't your head ache that way, son?" Dala asked with no intent to stir him. "No, it's just right. What were *you* reading, Dala, before *77?*" "O—*My Institute News.*" "The new issue—is it funny? Read a bit of it, Dala?"

His father leaned back ever so slightly in the little spindle-back rocker, so as not to show himself bucking the transfixions in his collarbone, and after half a breath read:

> A trough of the enrollment wave was reached in 1949, and it is this class which has just graduated. This fall there are already twenty-five paid deposits. Dr Kite whose studies of natural products especially nucleic acids, with the ultracentrifuge, are internationally known. The present Institute represents a continuation and expansion of the Shellac Bureau, supported by Importers Associates, which has carried out practical tests of the solubility of various types of shellacs, its adhesion to certain base metals, and other properties. Investigations by Winger, Hotch, and Yodbull and new applications of natural rubber ingraft copolymers. Dr. Conrad Cubinis, who now spends three-fourths of his day in his bathtub, appeared briefly at yesterday's meeting, admitting he was somewhat fagged from deep salt studies.

"And is that why he had a dream, as he told you, of a hurricane warning in Chinatown, his *lowers* blown off, turning to face a faceless Chinee, shrieked and fell off the bed?" asked Snorckie. "Maybe," said Baballo.

"Are there any student letters?" Little asked.

"One—and it's signed *I. Count Jr.*—which reminds me of your young cousin—years since I've seen him, I should. It reads:

I am happy to be in the Institute, but still not resigned to your Humanities program. Why should I be, considering my world. Prior to being a Vet I didn't go to college partly because I was sure I'd be drafted. Maybe I thought it'll build me up physically—if it does, there'll be some good in it. I've learned since like almost everybody else who read a book overseas that your Humanities list is the same as the Army's, part of the setup of a world that will ultimately come out of a test tube and be so refined and 'beautiful' it'll just die."

"Will they be tested first?" Little asked—and then, "it's always touching when a good man uses the word *beautiful*. How moving he can be." Not sure that Little meant what he said seriously, Dala nodded affirmatively.

"And how are President Gluck Coma, Dean Kittenhoare, and Chairman Rumples?" Little asked.

"About the same," Dala said, "they have all, from Coma down, asked me to take on another assignment."

"Have there been any rumors—" "of a raise? no. It wouldn't do to assault them. It's harder to be unkind. Why should one be ungenerous, tho I suppose they also think of themselves and find quiet easier, as I do," Dala said, noticing that Little glanced with impatience.

Outside the house a neighborly radio abruptly blared a commercial, *o what a beautiful morning, o what a beautiful day*. "Must be Henry Filler taking out the garbage, he carries his portable everywhere these days," Little said of his yearsmate, who—the blare stopped—was done with the chores of this evening.

"I was thinking, Dala, of our situations and *77* and *time's thievish progress*," Little said, "only scales and no music for days yet, and with so much time on my hands I've (quote) *enriched* my diary with some writing." Something had changed and Dala felt sad: Little *had* said *diary*.

"(quote) *To take a new acquaintance of thy mind*. If

(quote) *thou wilt look,* Dala—under *Leopold* there—and hand me my old *dairy*—thank you. It's a what do you call it, mostly a mummy play—a mummer's play?—a mummy play. And if you will read it so to speak (quote) *from thy brain,* I can judge better of its (quote) *blacks,* not *blanks* as my poor text misprints. Never mind my spelling and handwriting, just edit these—unvoiced—as you read aloud." Dala read as instructed.

FRIENDS—GLOCKENSPIEL, RUMPLES & FATHER XMAS

(*Pump and circummarch, enter omnes*)

FATHER XMAS. Glockenspiel, Rumples—and Father Christmas.

(*Exit Xmas. Glocke and Rumples salute with candystripe canes.*)

RUMPLES. Pshu—we build house.

GLOCKE. Pshu—(*admires while* RUMPLES *exits and enters with galleon can of paint and giant jar of putty.*) What color? (*opens gallon*) Good. Now we hose! Go buy me steel wool—but what color, Rumples? Red—yellow hay blue—

RUMPLES. Shu' (*walks off*)

GLOCKE (*yelling after him*). No, bring me black! (RUMPLES *returns with black*) I'm sorry I meant to say brown. Go bring that back!

(*Scaena. A store, Glocke on doorstep*)

RUMPLES. Oh he really meant brown!

GLOCKE. What'n hell, Rumples!

RUMPLES. Gr-r-

GLOCKE. I can't help you. Go to *this* store, it sears. Not this store, *this* store.

RUMPLES. What color? Oi wus idus!

(*exeunt omnes*)

Epilogus

FATHER XMAS (with KITTENHOARE)

my days at the zoo
are to few
I wonder what
this means to you

the seals shivers
make my quivers
all an'mules from lion to monkey
are in the zoo
except the donkey

we're of the zoo
to hear the lion roar
sincerely your
new universal vacuum corps

(*pump and circummarch,*
exeunt omnes)

"*Explicit?*" Dala asked—in his mind helping a late Latinist with his coat—"tho there seems to be more here under *Mozart*—an epilogue to an epilogue?" he hesitated.

"Oh no!" Little looked down at an old page he had forgotten was out of place. "Juniorviler," he said for *juvenilia*, "don't you remember, I wrote that almost two years ago." They read together silently:

> Who doesn't like Mozart's *Lullaby* and Papageno and *A Minuet*, and *Ah vous dirai-je maman* and *The Sonatina*, or does not remember Leopold carrying the baby Wolfgang downstairs and the Prince asking about him? When Mozart was five Leopold taught him the violin. He wrote arithmetick, or numbers, all over the wall because there was no paper in that day. One evening when his father and two old cronies—their names alas long forgotten—were playing trios Wolfgang asked to join them for quartets. "You may play but very softly," his father said, "so nobody hears you." But Leopold's love was not abated. He couldn't

believe his eyes, because little Mozart played every
single note.

"That was about the time you spoke to the collie, who barked only at night, and complained, almost whined, *he doesn't answer me.*"

"Pshu," Little said, and closed the diary, "you put too much expression into it. Dala," he raised his voice as one *might* say compulsively, "you're more of a child than I am—do an imitation after all these years?" "Which one," his father answered aware now that his collarbone had fallen asleep, and gladly rising from the rocker, "J.D.Sr. with his dime and golden throat, or Wozzeck *zeig mir deine Zunge,* or Papa Leopold?"

"Ach lieber Papà, gewiss heute es Leopold sein müsst," Little pleaded to encourage Dala's equally fantastic German.

At once, half his height, bent under an imaginary periwig, Papa Mozart beseeched him: "Fliessender Sohn, Wol-l-f-gang! wo hast du meine sperlingseule geige verfluchtet, mit den bogen, mit den gehobenen bogen, nicht dein spielzug achtel, meine geige mit'n stolzen bogen, ach zauberhaft, ach magisch, hochherzigkeit, entweder entweichend entwendend 'ch habe gesucht in die gewölbte Decke, in die Wände und sinke den Flur an—und so forsch wahnsinnig—"

One morning as Baballo sat writing, still unrushed before his one noon hour of teaching of that day, Little thru with his own stint of scales and ancient history was moved to teach *him.* Looking down over his father's shoulder, he read and said: "I agree, 'Aside from amazing things writers do with genius, I don't believe they have said the first sensible thing about the melodic and other meanings of words in their relations.' But all this about—'in music seven notes may be sharped and flatted, or it's another scale of five or twelve or higher multiple of tones in relation, but words are not multiples of tones (or are they?) and presumably endlessly related'—is nonsense: partick'r'ly from somebody who admits he can't count higher than three, and never in equal time." "I agree," Baballo said, "that's what I'm getting to."

Little offered *himself*, "May I ever teach you the fiddle, Dala, tho you always pick up the bow with your left hand? You could start with the piano, an instrument which I don't especially respect, its keys are always there to lap one up. Come Dala, sit down at the piano." That much Dala did, snorted, baffled like someone who is tickled, then balked: "It's no use, Snorckie, I wouldn't even attempt it, I have two left hands," and looked up with reverence. "Ah, you need *teem-merity* of musical attack," Little considered, "ancient history tells me you're no Memnon. When the sun struck, *he* harped back: action and reaction. Physics: if a stone plays possum to trip me I go back and kick it"—as Dala agreed he had seen Little do. "A string breaks, I restring. A fiddle needs playing *in* before it plays. It fights its bouts before it sings." Again Dala agreed and added, "the word is *temerity,* Little."

Verchadet, who had just stepped in from looking at the crab apple blossoms, overheard Dala's scrupulous diction, and not anxious to engage discussion said, "you're two of a kind," and walked out.

"Not to put you to shame in front of Verch," Little went on, "I adventure to say there's as much variety of timbre—pronounced *tam'b'r* in music—as there are trees before they become confused in one stupid word like *timber.* Lada Dala should know, *The man that hath no music in himself, Let no such man be trusted. Better can teach wood. Zo:* I've written a short treatise for students such as Presha. Obviously it is not meant for me. What I like about writing is the mystery of how it turns out. It (quote 77) *shall profit thee,* before I come back for your first lesson."

Little left to join Verchadet in the garden, and Dala stayed on alone to read:

THE YOUNG VIOLINIST

for Curt Budder

(INSERT) figure 1. violin with arrows to parts
figure 2. bow showing tip, hair, frog

Scales

Number	Sharps ♯	Flats ♭
1	G	F
2	D	B♭
3	A	E♭
4	E	A♭
5	B	D♭
6	F♯	G♭
7	C♯	C♭

Scales are important to those who know music. Look up at the table to scale number 1. Which is it, first or second? (answer.)

The eighth note of the scale is always the octave. (Number 1) G is the eighth from G. The reason why the eighth is always like the one is: the eighth to the one is an octave and one to eight is an octave. So you can see what is meant by an octave.

Now try it on the C major scale, or if you don't have it ask your mother, if she's a musician, to buy it. (Scale books are very expensive, you never know how much they charge.) When you have the C major scale, ask yourself which is the eighth C and the first C.

satis quod sufficit

Practice

The young violinist keeps his violin in a case. His mother prepares the room for practice. When he is ready he tunes, or she must try to turn the pegs. (figure 1)

An hour or two at one time of very hard practice is *in effect all the time*—as the great Ztephiah, whose teacher was Dlopoel Reua, cautions. In any case, don't just run thru everything because you are consciously mad, but proceed slowly. (No rewards—except: if the practice is good and the weather sunny the violinist's mother *may* urge him to fix the swing in the yard as inducement to more practice.)

Any bow (figure 2) can be heavy enough, especially a heavy bow. The popular entertainer's way of holding the bow at the tip and weighing it down with the frog does not show a sensitive player, nor does nervous stroking of the hair as a proof of its being rosined. Both of these actions are probably caused by early training that encourages constant yelling and screaming. (As a child this writer attended a school where a missing piece of picture puzzle led to such fighting and screaming to find it his health was nearly impaired. He went home, with no love for picture puzzles, to listen to his fiddle, and never returned to that school.)

Music to Play

Scales, exercises, concertos, sonatas, etc—is the ancient orderly course of study. But depending on competence or musicality—and most often in practice this holds oppositely for student and teacher—if competent, scales and exercises; if musical, mostly *etc*, which includes concertos and sonatas. Especially musical teachers and students will of course confer with other treatises or between themselves.

Little never again mentioned his treatise, which Baballo stored with his own papers. Either too modest to presume on musicality or whatever it was in himself that involved him in it generally, habit had convinced him he was not the kind who sits down to confer with a piano.

Betur who might have suspected Little was capable of a treatise never read it, but must have felt it coming. It was late spring when he made good his promise to have Little enrolled, at some saving to Baballo, in *wan* of the institutions where, in the opinion of less silent musical colleagues, Betur's prestige as distinguished teacher transfigured his competence. "Apart from my lessons and Dr Presha's," Betur explained with enigmatic judgment to Little, "the *on'y odder* obligation of the course of study is that the administration needs theory, but *wan* hour on *Sat'day* won't take away too *moch* time."

Verchadet and Dala were present at Little's matriculation—waiting behind a closed door during his placement test for the theory course. To Baballo, as much as he could overhear, it consisted largely of marching in step and metronomic rappings. When the elderly, severe yet sympathetic lady who taught theory stepped out for a moment during the short written examination and stopped to ask them what they wanted, Baballo could not help saying gallantly, "I am afraid one of your minors who is having his difficulties." She responded with a silent hauteur of a veteran teacher, so that let down he felt, as in a recurrent dream of his childhood, he had spoken in class out of turn. The examination qualified Little for Theory IV. As there was no such class in the undergraduate school, he would be registered in Theory III, "for the duration beginning in the fall," he told Verchadet.

But the musical year had not ended she learned at Betur's last lesson before the awaited summer. "A violinist accomplishes most in summer, along with vacation," Betur advised her as they were saying good-bye. Lessons would be free if Little could attend his summer school at Garden. "*Op* state," he added—"Little is too *yong* to board at school where parents are not allowed, but *ludging* involves compensation, perhaps the family could instead rent a place for vacation in Pamphilia not far away. It would be good for everybody."

18

Dala was thinking about Sumer when Little told him and Verchadet he supposed they *should go*. They went.

"Welcome to the human race—the bon mot is Mr Betur's greeting. You *are* Mr and Mrs von Chulnt and Little?" The blond lady, in her thirties and her paler blond replica about eleven, tall for her age but pretty out of a fairy book Little and Verchadet thought, were reassured by his violin case before the attired and travelled had quite stepped down from the train. After ten hours of spur track along the river and lakes north of it Baballo breathed mountain air, looking straight up at a span of blue—prolonging day. But he interrupted himself soon enough to say to the lady: "Yes, how very kind of you, we were thinking of taking a taxi."

"I am Lambeth Potiphar—my daughter, Unzung Pharette. And it's our third summer at Garden. Unzung's father Dr Potiphar teaches surgery in Constantinople—Istanbul—but we're native. I was thinking—our youngsters are so fortunate having Mr Betur for their teacher. He happened to mention you were not coming up in a car, and as Pharette has a neuritic finger from practicing vibrato we've taken his advice to do some shopping here in Piraeus and meet your train. May we give you a lift into Pamphilia? The town does not have any taxi service, tho a seasonal arrangement can be made with private owners of sedans. But the five mile drive there with you should be so much more delightful for us." "Do we go past Garden?" Little asked. "No, Garden is five miles further north from the house you will stay in in Pamphilia—ours is across the bridge from yours," Unzung Pharette replied. "Rentals are scarce in Pamphilia. Mr Betur has sixty students and most families rent a year ahead," Mrs Potiphar said. "A few years from now, when our youngsters are of an age to stay at the dormitory in Garden, perhaps we old folk can stay home. We were almost too late to keep our place this year. I had intended to spend the summer in Turkey, but Unzung could not bear to think of leaving Mr Betur for so long a spell." The von Chulnts crouched too obviously for courtesy in getting into the accommodating car. Little took over the conversation which diverted to preventives and cures for Unzung's injury. She stared kindly and listened to him as to a much older authority. So understanding for her age, girls mature faster, Verchadet considered, warding off a yawn. She was shocked when Mrs Betur told her a week later that Unzung Pharette had tacitly celebrated "sixteen plus" some time ago.

"A castle!" Little looked with wonder across the highway from their new address where Mrs Potiphar's sedan had stopped to let them out. His elders looked also: behind a long town block of rock wall, hedge, a private bridge arched over a natural moat created by a fast running stream, ended in high ground, lawn, meadow; led to ascending woods, a mountain—in the foreground a castle. "The family estate of Lieutenant Governor Castle—he died last year. Yes, you have a pretty view—." Mrs Potiphar admired it. "We must go home presently, to a half-hour of healthy détaché—as Mr Betur urged—without vibrato, Pharette? We'll let you good people settle in, and meet you refreshed no doubt at the post office tomorrow, just below the Castle estate down the highway in our direction. There's only one incoming mail, at noon—'bye." "Bye." Mrs Potiphar effected part of her U-turn for home in the driveway along the side porch of the house still unopened by Baballo's new key. Little effected—*"that, there—open!"*

Meanwhile Verchadet looked around at the single choice writing several letters had offered her. Evening recalled shades of Riding Hood. She lit the bare electric bulb of the front porch. The house of three stories, too high for its width fairly rambled upward with porches and verandas —those at the rear and shaded side evidently storage space for the landlord's old bedsprings and broken furniture. They decided at once to use only the ground floor, unless Dala himself wished to clean up one of the upper verandas as a retreat for thought. (He did in time.) As always, Little's room was readied first, so they could fuss with their rooms alone while he slept "sensibly," he said, "like anybody sane." They went on cleaning and ordering long after midnight, startled by glares from cars making their U-turns over cinders of their driveway—confusing the flashes at first with summer lightning. Finally before drinking a sixth coffee, which they intended to enjoy sitting down, they dismounted seventeen highly colored reproductions of martyrdom in heavy gold frames and stored them in the pantry—beyond use to them—Dala carefully noting from which walls they came so he could hang them again when their vacation was up.

"Pamphilia among rocks and falls," Little greeted them out of his guide book, with the light, birds and his open violin case. With Betur in mind he said, "I see you have *accomplishèd* old curtains after working all night." Verchadet sipped her coffee, wondering, as the sun shone in, if the flimsy lawn curtains exposed the distasteful living room to the highway. Her worry could not have been justified sooner. They heard a gentle rapping, and the shadow of a head pressed against the outside of front porch window. All three went to the door together.

"Good morning. Today will be lovely. I hope I am not very early. I shall be your fortunate neighbor in the house next to yours—I hardly leave my porch. Mrs Potiphar told me I will hear a violin again. I thought about it all night—the happiness for me—and fortified myself to thank your dear little son. You must be very good to study with Mr Betur. It was wonderful in the years before Mr Betur moved his school to Garden—violins sounding all over Pamphilia. I'm afraid most people here didn't think so. They'd rather drive their cars to hear the music in Garden on Saturday night. But I'm too old for the concerts, more content to listen here—as I was a half-hour ago. I must not disturb you and go now. Do when you have time say hello—I'm nearly always on the porch." The small country lady with hunched back and thick coils of white braided hair turned slowly to follow her cane home. She had not given her name. "She seems *content*—quote, unquote—to forget it," said Little, "let's just call her Mrs Weatherbureau."

She proved loyal to the surname: beginning indeed later that morning, recalling by their titles the pieces Little had practiced and forecasting exactly what weather the afternoon would bring: it happened for their part they had encouragingly nodded to her porch a half-flight of stairs above ground. Thanks to her the von Chulnts were made conscious of weather all summer. Except for rainy days when she listened indoors they missed no forecast. Snorckie warned against inviting themselves to her house. He could not forget her first and only actual intrusion on their privacy. An old lady's happiness and weather reports were not his reasons for practice. "She should try playing a fiddle herself and see if it's bliss—or do some other work," he insisted.

What baffled Little was that *work* in Pamphilia meant everyone minded somebody else's work. Greeting the von Chulnts anywhere, without having met them before, seemed to be a great part of this work. "Their main *bitzness*, including the druggist's," Little whispered to be overheard, "is that I am a violinist." He asked Verchadet if she thought Betur was to blame for this "adwanz spying." She reserved her opinion, while in her mind Betur's bon mot about the human race implied a contest or just running, that at some time she must be as wary as he was. Dala was always so impersonally puzzled Little did not bother to ask *his* opinion. "The best he could do," Little said, "is to appear naked at the porch window or the door and drive them off when they peer or knock. But No-oh! He can never refuse a fool the *hoarsepitality*" (a good pun as he heard it) "of his living room especially when his *leetle* boy is playing Mozart and for some nosey reason a fool wants to hear it!"

To blame or not for Snorckie's annoyance, in Pamphilia Imam Betur whether worshipped or feared "was legend." Sponsorial (or vicarious) rather than not the human race gathered at the post office, and when the von Chulnts arrived hopefully to pick up their one letter from Tearilee or Murda-Wonda they were cornered by throwbacks to Babel. "With only one intention," Snorckie insisted, "to find out our Betur connections, as if we don't know they gossip." Their talk always involved in Imam "pounced" at Little, as he had to face it, from three types of "ambush": that of the infants Betur still weaned or almost had weaned into perpetual youth, some weary in their thirties with their parents and pianists while Betur worked mostly with his mouth shut; Betur's public at the Saturday night concerts, folk who had not "studied" the violin, but "loved" and were dedicated to support it with charity and sentiment—like the help at Garden whose ancestors had left them heirloom fiddles or equivalent fortunes, and in contrast to these somewhat extinguished, musical doctors, dentists, artists and writers reputedly "great"—summering at a near Indian reservation—but only one songstress, Mrs Presha; last and *foremost,* as Little had heard, two rival impresarios (one of them Endor) who vaguely "visited," and more openly their "patrician" virtuosi who *had made it*. The rumors were they had been brought up or sent by the impresarios so Betur could finger for them some lately commissioned concerto. Their flying from Battersea to Helsinki had left them no time or taste to finger it on their own.

Ceaseless tales of Imam: Little recorded the personal annoyances in his *dairy*.

Three Ambushes or The Envious Variations
(spelling by an omniscient observer)

Ambush I
Lambeth with her blossom Unzung: "Goo'd morning, and how are you this mourning? *We're* so overjoyed. Pharette has just come back from her first lesson. The school's not officially open. This was a make-up lesson we had come up for, a week early, postponed you know by the accident to her forefinger." (I'm sure she said yesterday they were almost too late to rent their place this year.) "Well—to heal the wounds Mr Betur has told her to *practice me good* Wieniawski's *Ecole Moderne*. That's advanced for exercises, isn't it, Little?" (To wound my heels—lurking to find out how advanced I'm.) "Oh! do meet the Rilty's and son Panza—violinist and best tackle on high school team." (Catty: to line me up against him. He's not Betur's pupil, Presha's best.)

Mrs Rilty: "Next year Panza will study mental music too." Broad education! "Maybe you can tell me," opening vile *Mixed Melodies* to a bit of Bach partita, "is this fingering for a boy or girl?" (Harmless? Also asked if my fiddle's dark or bright. To price it and me: thinks the best "violinists" are Stradivari or Guarneri. Itching for Panza to study with Betur.)

Mr Schwerscheide, old-school violin teacher: "I'd never let my Lona" (daughter, very nearsighted, not young) "study with that—*that* stableman Betur." She studies with Serp, Betur's rival, whose one great prodigy *was* Nihunem. She's his last pupil, besides his son, this summer in studio near Indian reservation.

Mr Noë and son Solo at private adjoining P.O. boxes: "Have you arranged for your lesson with Betur, Solo?" "*No!* I'm not taking lessons this summer." "No?" "*I told you* I'm going to relax playing in my orgon box. How do you expect me to have a sweet tone when Svengali snaps his fingers like B-B guns over me, *forcing* me to keep time without rubato? Fact is the fiend's grown gentle since he filliped his index finger into the middle of Josh Slider's forehead for a wrong note and he fainted. No lessons'll teach him a lesson." "So *with whom* will you study?" (abruptly to me) "I bet *you* think Mr Betur's a great teacher." (I smile politely.)

Mr Ambrose Flutit, Garden's chaperon pianist: "Mr Betur is *exhausted*, what with the two boxers chasing the porcupines and their having to stop at every comfort station coming up. And the two grand pianos still to be tuned not off the trailer—o my! Our first lesson may be delayed, Little." (Not too convincing. There's enough litchr'chew'r *for the violin alone.*)

Mrs Bearmeout, daughters Marj and May, 14 and 17: "We've just received a wonderful letter from Eichel Practice about his triumph in Antigua." (Eichel, 17 like May, Mrs B. probably thinking of a match with Betur's greatest prodigy to-date. All the fools here blabbing he outdoes Ztephiah. Due back in Garden soon. I'll hear.) "I keep urging the girls, they don't listen to me, 13 hours practice a day did it." (31 hours wouldn't bear her up or out.)

Dr and Mrs Cyclops and son Tremor: they model his "own musicality" after Eichel's practice. "We all have our own style, don't we, Little?" (A grudging greeting?)

Ambush II

Druggist tries to sell us the family heirloom. "Been in the attic 40 years and goes back at least 40 years futher." The violin looks like a Blutwurst.

Hushlushes, two gray sisters, have worshipped Eichel "since he first took up the prenatal position"—my mother's spry *hapax legomenon*—but really that's all they talk about.

Miss Nasaltwang stays at Anthos style of hotel, tho much quieter, grave-like, where Chamber of Commerce allows no violin practice. She's driven around in a black Cadillac by her chauffeur Diorcle. Very cordial. Has offered to take us to Garden Saturday Night Concerts "whenever" her "favorite little violinist Eichel plays." Chief interest's ethnic dances, but hopes I'm as good as Eichel so she'll have *two* young violinists in Garden. Back in the city she attends—for her much older friend's sake, Miss Nishgut—the Sinfoni concerts and goes to hear the old virtuosi in Great Hall. Both convinced the old are fading before Eichel.

Mme Kupeh, the wife of Pamphilia's one doctor. He came here with a fatal illness years ago, but since there are too many patients refuses to show it. Has no time for Garden, so Mme Kupeh gives a big concert party every summer in *her* garden where Betur and Serp, *both* her friends, can appear together with their students. This year it's a benefit for Schwerscheide's Lona. The invitation reads, *Invited to hear great artistry*. All Garden's *registered,* as Betur calls his pupils, *must* go, if only to say later, "her pitch is so erratic, she hears less than she sees." Mme Kupeh, "gracious and active grandmother," also studies pots and paintings at Pamphilia's art school, *The Northern Propylaeum.* A tremendous shed, full of earthenware pots, bottles, portraits, and pepper-and-salt paintings of clipper ships on the St. Lawrence. The director Feminore Coupran, honorary member at the Royale Academy, has just accomplished, Mme Kupeh tells us, a remarkable likeness of Betur done all in various blues, and would like to paint me. All I have to do is to pose! When Dala and Verchadet said nothing, as I did, Mme Kupeh looked surprised and said, "Why, Eichel leaped at the honor."

"Unbelievably," to quote Mrs Presha. At last we have met her. She *is* Carmen. *Very gay:* "After wondering all spring behind the curtain what you looked like and how your fiddle bore up so nicely under Presha—but everybody in Pamphilia meets at the post office. Here there is nothing to do but practice and babble. I prefer my solfège or nothing —and the movies in the evening. I must show you where it is the first time. It's good for breathing, away from it all—one must have a vacation."

Mrs Ototot, elephant lady with chest arthritis—from trying on children's dresses and underwear: companion of the two ancient Mrs Hemdlach sisters, who own the only other castle in Pamphilia's outskirts. Exulting in highest praises of Betur she tells us as executrix (I wonder) of her old friends' charities that she is responsible "among other things, for the scholarships to Garden" and my free lessons. Betur will notify me soon, she surprises me, about my musicale at Hemdlach Castle. First I hear of it. Is it possible he trusts her between one belch ("pardon me") and another? She wants to be kissed hello and good-bye. Faugh! So far I've escaped by picking up my fiddle case.

Thru all this madness, sardonic (?) snardic Ira Taignit ("a great writer" I've heard from Mrs Rilty and Panza) smiles wordless from the darkest corner of the post office at the people coming and leaving. Mrs Potiphar says he has smiled that way for three years at the Saturday Concerts in Garden, disdainfully, not speaking to anybody, and not so much as a handshake for Betur.

Ambush III
No one's seen him tho everybody whispers Warlock's secretly visiting Garden.

En passant Caasi Nrets, Ztephiah's "most mature" rival for bookings (which Ztephiah refuses—to play tennis instead—he's so fed up) has nodded to us. Hear Betur has teased Nrets: "In *shut* the public is promiscu*os*. Come a midget and hoo-hah! Genius's alone, suffers mismanagement. You know what au*tt*ority is. Ztephiah plays with au*tt*ority. And you I un'stand—from your publitzity—*witt auttority!*" Nrets whose broad public smile winces a bit when he overhears someone talking of Eichel is a short man. Dala, coming out of the post office and almost stepping on Nrets' heels, recalls some Institute joke about some notable, so short he sued the civic authorities for laying a buckled pavement too near his *annus mirabilis*. It's all right for Dala to pun badly, he's so tall.

tuner wresting resting wrĕst pins oreful
oarful

Guy Esor Octa Leber, black curly hair and only famous bass viol player in the world has psych'n' liced and formed the chamber music groups at Garden for this year: they include all the non-virtuosi who need encouragement.

I've met so many people, heard so many names, I wonder if I've really heard them or am making them up, reading backward as in a mirror—mirror fugue.

Eichel not hear yet.

19

The von Chulnts would not ask anyone to spare them the encumbrances of a Cadillac and its cabby owner who drove them to the weekly half-hour lessons in Garden and back. Nor did the meddlers watching the time of Little's departure and return offer their cars, as Mrs Potiphar had offered hers (Dala would not forget) once in Piraeus. On these self-supported drives the father sat next to the cabby, Verchadet and Little less responsive to summer drafts and chatter in the back seat where Little possessed his violin case. Perhaps it was during the second trip going the cabby said, "Curious —Mrs Potiphar—the name *Potiphar*, my Bible concordance says it means *belonging to the sun or gift of the risen one*. Professor von Chulnt, I've been meaning to ask, would you know if the unleavened bread, after the slaves went out of Egypt, was kneaded." Attentive and thwarted Dala shook his head the least bit from side to side—ignorant—and looked silently to the road ahead.

It approached them bumpy thru mountain, rock slides at its sides, passed under a ski coast, a deer hurtling, a scurrying porcupine, and widened flatly thru woods. "These woods have been felled many times," the cabby said, "but enough's still virgin." "How do you know it is virgin?" Little leaned subdued over his case to ask his father. "I guess—like the close columns of trees where there's no underbrush, no grass, no flowers, no ground cover." "I see." A freestanding wrought iron gate appeared, and in curlicue of the grille work GARDEN. "I'll wait for you on this side of the gate, you can walk round it," the cabby said.

Betur was a gardener *by nature,* as the expression prevails. "I (must) *moss,*" he once said to a colleague whose solicitude for Betur's health on an enforced day off over a bourbon had provoked him to a subtle fingering for the colleague, "*torch'r* (torture) the children I nurse—*moch too stronk the drink—wat iss?*" "He putters like a gardener it seems for an unbearable time and then something happens," the colleague would say. " 'Sopsurd (it's absurd)" Betur was given to say, "sometimes happens." The von Chulnt triad first saw Betur in Garden standing on the largest rock of his considerable circle of rock garden—a content profile of care—just to the other side of the freestanding gate. He must have heard the motor of the Cadillac, yet as tho it were better to go as Betur by ear, his eyes perhaps hinting impatience with some small flower slow to come up on the rocks, he did not turn. When he did he saw them, smiled and moved forward but stopped, holding his long hands away from himself only to cross them over his forearms, cradling them soiled with earth as an excuse. The triad waved at a distance: they were not the ones to press toward him. He waved back and hurried off to the two story sprawling house in the classical style of over a century ago, which they knew must be the dormitory and summer studio.

"He was not wearing his black *smokeative* jacket with the sashes," Little said. "His velveteen smock, Little," Verchadet laughed almost inaudibly, not too pleased by Betur's greeting, "perhaps he likes to be rustic in the country." Even Dala had an afterthought: "Well, it is not exactly the *fêtes galantes,* or is it?"

They were early for this first lesson and looked around they felt perhaps longer than Betur's reserved welcome prompted. But what they had taken to be the front of the house was the back. The front was a new tessellated terrace whose granite balustrade crenelated a precipice above checkered green upland and red barns. They were surprised, looking down judging a drop of one thousand feet, that this was the entrance to Garden as well as one end of its wooded plateau.

As they turned to face the woods again Mrs Betur coming out of a long shed under these at the side of the main house hurried to greet them. Ada—Presha had called her, and Dala remembered the Biblical name meant *ornament* —her Georgia self.

"It's the *salle à manger* I've just come from, preparing their big meal—they're all big. I was tempted to shriek *hold on* when I saw you, but Garden Cliff is the least of Garden's dangers. No one has yet jumped off. Aside from overeating, it's the woods that bring most of our worries. Our faithful boxers, Sib and Gesib worry the porcupine quills. But you wouldn't believe that our most serious talent gets lost in these woods. And it's always the best mannered young man and nicest young lady together, as happened last night. I had seen them shortly after dinner talking to a visitor behind the gate. Except for appointments and the Saturday concerts *no visitors are countenanced*—Mr Betur's rule. Cars may not park inside the gate and crowd the grounds, we must keep them clear in case of fire. Well our gifted blockheads were lost circling in the woods for the night, without matches, or too scared of fire to send up flares—and mistaking our flashlights for heaven knows what. I'm responsible for the girls' curfew, and Mr Betur for the boys'. He almost had my head off. He feels so keenly for their proprieties. I could be Delilah in these mad upsets and snip his locks. But his silence becomes more punishment than I can stand when I need his advice—and I'm not allowed to proceed without it. When all lessons were postponed late this morning our lost ones turned up. They'll get the silent treatment from him for weeks. He's sick over it.

"Poor man he's sleepless in Garden—on night rounds to cabins and studios of older students—making sure all is safe. I keep telling him he should allow them *some play* in the newly built swimming pool, but afraid of accidents he insists on using it as a reservoir. As if there is not enough celery tonic, soda pop and fruit juice punch to round off the sixty gallons of milk quenching the daily hundred pounds of beef, lamb and chicken I cook in troughs whose scouring I surpervise! I run it all spic and span like a paddock in Georgia.

"You *would* think knowing how sensitive Mr Betur is, constantly urging them to sing on their instruments and drawing pure tone out of them, they'd spare him such pranks as carrying off their friends' bathroom equipment into the woods—the embarrassment of checking every night, when he can barely get himself to stutter the word in French, 'you have your *cabinet?*' I know you speak French, Little, and it is funny." (He did find it so, with propriety.) "Of course *you're* fortunate to have your own place this crowded summer. There's enough work too to do for the younger ones upstairs here, turning their beds inside out and their laundry, and seeing they write home occasionally. I have just retyped a letter for Mr Betur to a parent. I had typed *request*—but '*no,*' he says, '*I said ask.*' Wasn't he on the rock garden a moment ago? Most likely he has hurried back and is waiting anxiously for your lesson. Let me show you in."

Ada's summer talk overflowed, while Imam's remained in his mouth, except for some squibs impelled by disciplines of curriculum. Scales, exercises, pieces—his traditional rigor never wavered from his competence. Yet he was not the fool to spite his own public face and overrate a friend's or a pupil's endurance. Compassion for Presha in Pamphilia (where he needed him, he was welcome unobtrusively on Garden's Saturday Nights) evoked some musical relief, at least that summer, for his old friend's subordinate fretting over scales and exercises, and at the same time soothed Little's avidity for sightreading the repertoire that Betur sadly knew only maturity can "project" (a word the von Chulnts disliked). Without blinking at Snorckie's tacit flash of gratitude (they were two of a kind, again Verchadet saw) he would, after a surprise review of a scale or an exercise, flaunt Mozart's G major or the Mendelssohn on the music rack and say: "You like to read, READ me." While Little did Betur pencilled the fingering on the music, following the boy's most comfortable reading expeditiously. "Moch better," Betur'd say, and as Little was playing it for the first time he'd wonder why the comparative. He decided that Betur had no use for *best* and that *good* was his niggard superlative.

As Little played the boxers, who wore bells in the country so they could be heard if lost, appeared outside the uncurtained lateral French doors of the studio and listened with tilted heads. In the freedom of outdoors Betur's shooing glances could not move them away. Little noted they did not appear when other violinists played and was pleased. He sensed that Betur too was pleased, murmuring once, "Stupid, (hurts) *huts* you—from porcupines?" Little heard him express equal sympathy years later over a neuritic finger: "Oi I know it goes to the head!"

He could finger a movement of a new piece in a leisurely last fifteen minutes of a half-hour lesson, then signal its end, handing over the music with a flurry of comment: "Here, give Dr Presha, practice me good, I have my spy system." Little collected Betur's advice to others, passed on to him: "Next time don't stand like *vet* (wet) chicken.—Stand like melt'd butter—no!—Must play? no I say, work like dog(k)." He invariably refingered most of his first fingering, especially if the pupil in his practice followed him servilely, and if he had not Betur would substitute some finer difficulty, some mathematical subtlety of fingering that played even more expeditiously. Such changes were most likely after a time of letting a piece lie fallow, when the pupil least expected it, after Betur's saying "Put aside —I don't want" had seemed final. So it happened with the Mozart that summer.

Betur told Little, "The Ladies Hemdlach would appreciate if you play Mozart at Castle." Little did, but Betur did not go. Nor did Presha who might have hinted—in French —at a claim *f'r inter-prétation.* It turned out that Guy Esor Octa who was there, *spy system* Little deduced, exulted in praising thruout Pamphilia "that little one's" masterly handling of a slight slip of memory caused by the sudden distraction of sighting Mme Ototot's elephantine landscape. "Who wouldn't wander," Esor laughed.

As for the Mendelssohn there was one phrase Little bōwed after hearing Ztephiah. "Wrong(k) again!" Betur insisted, "I marked before. Mendelssohn don't want this Ztephiah bōwing, editor don't want, I don't want. How many times you want I write it, I write it *for you.* What color?" Little who admired Betur's pastel collection had one of his own. Betur had impulsively hinted at Little's markings all over his music. Unmoved but disciplined Little handed the master the faintest of yellows. The Mendelssohn was put aside.

Whether Betur's fallow concertos intended some secret *torch'r* for a future garden did not worry Little. He read. There was one piece that Betur reviewed in every lesson that summer, if only for a moment refingering his previous refingerings, paradoxically to spur Little to "R'member practice me good." When Little gently responded, "Don't worry," Betur severely retorted, "*I* say *worry.*" The uncalled-for rebuke caused Little to infer that the piece was meant for his imminent Garden debut. Rumors in Pamphilia somewhat confirmed his guess. What piece more suitable than the soarings of Onangni's *Praeludium and Alle-*

gro, serious hoax of Ztirf Relsierk's own melting strings, which he had modestly attributed to the archival Onangni when audiences were all *Parsifal* and still innocent of Baroque, at least twenty-five years before Ztephiah had touched a string—so *he* would have a literature to play: Garden's musical expectants had older loyalties.

They listened to Little play Onangni behind the curtained interior French doors of Betur's summer studio, *after* Guy Esor told them of Betur's trustful prophecy for his youngest prodigy: "Comes sometime Relsierk and Ztephiah in one and knows more than they music." The most rabid cornered Little in the post office: "When are you scheduled for a public Saturday Night, Little? You will play for us won't you? We're dying to hear you." With Betur for mentor, he did not answer them. "Let them—" he would say to Verchadet and Dala and laugh when they shuddered a little disapproving his vehemence. Truthfully, the three rather expected a Garden debut. Or why had Betur without forewarning allowed Little to play the *Praeludium and Allegro* when, unexpected, Oniz Narf dropped down on Garden in his private plane. The friendly rotund Ladin virtuoso, well on in his fifties, always travelled with his youthfully vigorous mother and sometimes with his young obviously aging wife. This time they were all together. He pinched his own jowl (as Ztephiah, whose enemies said he spurned a chin rest, could never do) and then Little's cheek in praise. The mother blessed Verchadet apart: "My dear, it's *you* who will need all the strength." The wife steeled herself to a shy *au revoir*. Betur himself warmed to a muttered *very gut* as he closed the door behind the von Chulnts to celebrate with his friends.

The last three of Garden's Saturday Nights were still to be scheduled. The order of surprises turned out as the public in Pamphilia expected: Tremor would precede the greater Eichel, but the soloist of the Farewell Concert remained unannounced. Little's ambushes persisted: *they* knew *who*. The embarrassed von Chulnts replied honestly they did not know. Their ears rang with chatter. Tremor Cyclops was practicing more hours than Eichel—nowhere to be seen. Who could afford not to emulate Eichel, whose very name was Practice. No genius out of sight but gained. Did Betur believe that Little practiced only four hours a day? The von Chulnts were minimizing. Mrs Bearmeout was "distraught." She had almost been run over by Eichel in a white sports car, an elegant Triumph. He begged her not to tell his mother, frantic over his disappearances before his recital. Poor Mrs Practice the huge accompanist in tears, the thanks for her devotion.

Miss Nasaltwang true to her promise drove the von Chulnts to both solo concerts. Of Tremor's, Little had but to see the stance, the two prodigious round sweeps of the bow arm preparing as it were to wrestle with an antagonist, then the clamped hesitancy before placing the first note to know something would be lacking. He played as anyone trained by Betur played—at least visibly competent, rarely off pitch, and (if sadly it happens the heart or the head cannot keep the same pace) overwhelmed most of the audience.

Little was soon more absorbed by the circumstances. They sat on folding chairs at the rear of the grand ballroom rearranged for the concert. He knew Betur was listening at the far end of his studio, its door now open to the central stairway and entrance hall behind them. With its packed audience the ballroom was altogether too electrified, crowded for the *general* on their folding chairs and excessively comfortable for the elect sunk in sofas flanking two fireplaces that yawned to each other across the room divided by a red carpeted aisle. Drawing attention to themselves by their bells the boxers acted as ushers might, running up and down the carpet, or all the way back to Betur it would seem for instructions, infallibly skidding on several gay colored scatter rugs in the entrance hall on the return errand. The walls were mostly open leaded windows, so that

Dala struggled with the drafts all evening. Turning his neck in longing towards one sheltered corner he suddenly flinched self-conscious under the meaningless gaze of the smiling Ira Taignit. Tho Little did not expect attention from Betur during the intermission, he could not help noticing the ceremoniousness with which the teacher he thought of as reserved kissed the hands of the Hemdlach sisters, the cheek of Mme Ototot; the courtesy of conversation extended to Mr and Mrs Cyclops seemed far in excess of the casual nod to his parents. The ceremoniousness at Eichel's concert was even more extravagant—Betur a gallant European kissing Mrs Practice regaled in diamonds.

As Dala's most devious reflection might put it, the enthusiasm of the audience was as affectively as it was infectiously unanimous, no omniscient observer who had not become nescient. Eichel had whipped thru several styles of two hundred years of violin literature in forty minutes, allowing his admirers to breathe only their gasping praises. To Little, despite the impressive facility, all of it had sounded as tho it went nowhere, except for one Paganini caprice. Its unstalled brilliance, the leaps of the most sensitive racehorse, had been endangered by too much cherishing, too much currying. The same horse plodded thru the encore, a fluff of songs "my mother taught me" preceded by his softly spoken homage. "It's no compliment, Verch," Little whispered. "To me it wouldn't be." Only her lips spoke. The boy tried to wink one eye at her, but inevitably both eyes winked, and he looked down to avoid a chuckle. In the shuffle of everybody rising "I doubt—" she started to say to Dala, and stepping into the night on the way to Miss Nasaltwang's sedan—Miss N was still chatting with Eichel—"I am sure Betur has cancelled Little's Garden debut for this summer." "What did you say?" Little who was walking adventurously ahead called back. "Nothing," Baballo said, "just that the headlights of these cars cast shadows, it's hard to see what is level." "Follow me," Little called back again, "or you'll be lost in Ada's woods."

Verchadet's firm doubt proved right. When the triad arrived at the entrance hall for the summer's final lesson they stopped to read an announcement of the Farewell Concert: a septet with Ambrose Flutit as pianist. They showed no concern sitting in their usual chairs as Little tuned. Again Betur asked for the *Praeludium and Allegro*. With no show of anger, Little played it at a speed that they sensed almost caused Betur to gasp. In the last wisp of bravura the bow masterfully poised above the strings flew out of his fingers across the room. The three laughed spontaneously. "Don't laugh, no laughs at concert," Betur reproved them, while cosmopolites they detected he smiled like a bedbug who seems pleased.

20

Summer's end was celebrated in Garden with an annual Farewell Masquerade Ball. On Betur's part it was a lingering *fête galante*—a courtesy to those of Garden's patrons who, after the Farewell Concert, did not flee Pamphilia at once to their autumn ways. To Little's second sight it was perhaps a way of saying in behalf of ambushes and musical followers, *Lest we forget.* Not that the ambushes needed a reminder. Not to miss a trick they would have stretched awake to the shining dark on Garden's grounds until the first frost, when the studio and dining hall were shut down and boarded for the winter. But it was the *manth* (month) he wanted loneliness for his rock garden, or Ada tacitly following advice, or a mute over a bourbon. "*E-noff* (enough) studen*t*' (students), they come more than I want in October." The only breaks into his vacation would be a lesson forced on him by his fears over Eichel's lack of interest in an early fall recital, and two free lessons he would give to the marine band boy on furlough. Jon the marine: his violinist's life had been interrupted by a summons to military service. Betur's dedication to the precious violin as instrument of worldly culture—he had no opinions on political illegality or war—was sufficient reason to sacrifice some hours of his vacation. "How's bugle?" "Fine, sir—easy." "Mm . . . for *that* one study *nineteen* years violin . . ."

Distantly, perhaps because he was farsighted, he would then look at Jon's uniform with compassion equal to that for his boxers smarting from porcupine quills.

Miss Nasaltwang in ethnic costume drove the von Chulnts to the Ball. Summer's lease a week to run out, Mrs Wetherbureau's forecast fair, they too longed for "a little vacation," Snorckie for adventure, for some fun that seemed likely after the letdown of no debut had estranged all the curious, none of them working. He was masked as Hammurabi in an old satin dress of Verchadet, so that he moved like a short block of black diorite as he imagined it moving by some mechanism out of his ancient history book. On or about his chest pinned by a tiny safety pin was THE CODE in white on a small oblong card framed under cellophane. "Always ingenious," Miss Nasaltwang spired rising after bending and failing to read it without her glasses. Verchadet and Dala had not thought of costumes for themselves—ready, she said, if they were required at the ballroom doors, to say that the summer in Garden had already disguised them. They went chiefly to be with Little, or as her doubt led her to feel for no other reasonable reason. Maybe the reason will clarify, Dala considered—anticipating one or another quick retort for her to as many offenders.

No one embarrassed their arrival, nor was it greeted. A string ensemble of the literally handicapped—Betur's gift over successive summers of the violin to the cure of muscular dystrophy—was playing fervently: backed, perhaps for resonance, along one wall by stacks of folded chairs that only last week had filled the dance floor. It had been cleared, and of the not more than two dozen who had come to the Ball each one wandered rather sparsely in her (or his) costume, the masks eminently recognizable. They were: Tremor as the great Bach; Panza as Verdi; Lona as La Bohème (*da* Leoncavallo); Marj as Constanze; May as Frau von Bülow; the boy Japanese cellist Nogo as Washington crossing the Delaware; etc—that is, a few strangers.

Eichel was not there, but no one who was saw anything recognizable in Snorckie's dress as he walked among them stiffly—he preferred not to smile in public. Jon the marine came in uniform. First, Jon danced with Marj, while Tremor watched them and imitated their dance with Panza; then May danced with Jon, while Panza watched them and imitated their dance with Tremor; then Constanze danced with Jon, while Frau von Bülow, Tremor and Panza watched; then Jon danced with Frau von Bülow, while Constanze, Panza and Tremor danced together; then Verdi, Bach and Lona *La Bohème da* Leoncavallo, Marj, May and Jon the marine who had not missed a partner for a second, and the strangers who had not danced joined in a square dance, while Miss Nasaltwang, not inclined, danced with little Nogo, "Washington crossing the Delaware."

Betur looked up at them from his hand, Gesib at his feet, rarely speaking between hands of his card game with Esor Octa in a pillowed window seat, and Little wandered over to pat her. His teacher did not notice him at first—distantly conscious that the parents had been sitting, silent as usual, patiently waiting for his youngest prodigy in the adjacent window seat. "Unzung gone back to Turkey," Little overheard his considered speech. After a longish pause, he reminisced: "Rogerg, Rogerg Yksrogi"—the Apollonic bass viol one historian of music called him, Esor's great predecessor at Garden—"no one beat me at cards, only once Rogerg, I let him, and he could play—also poker." He glanced down sideways at Gesib and saw Little. "Enjoying?" he asked. "Why Liszt?" he said inferring the abbé from Little's costume. "What does card—badge—say?" Snorckie looked puzzled: "Not Liszt, THE CODE—of Hammurabi." "Ah-há," Betur said, tho THE CODE, while he played his hand, meant less than Hammurabi to the later line of Assur.

Verchadet and Dala rose to tell Little perhaps he ought

not disturb Mr Betur. "Not 't all," he said having heard them, still looking at his cards, and in afterthought, "this dŏz (does) it"—the round, the game his, he leaned in a mere gesture of moving the stakes—a tray of shelled almonds on an end table—closer to himself. "*Moany* (money) no option, gambling not for students"—and in fact his example to them was always exemplary—"if you have the merchandise, *they* come, customers come, not *fest* (fast) may be, but *they* come." Verchadet heard herself having said it after she said it, "It must be trying tho, Mr Betur, for a fast horse in reserve, waiting for ten slow horses to come in first." The slight nearly avoided wrinkle in his forehead showed her he felt her sally, a delayed droll wording like his. Yet his ears did not seem to hear. He understood but did not honor this lady who might be a compatriot. "Not mŏch refreshment tonight. *Pliz* (please)" he coaxed the von Chulnts, "Cake?"

He had seen Ada and Sib approaching with a mocha layer. "I am so sorry," she said to the von Chulnts. "Once school closes and the lessons stop, Mr Betur and I don't go in for heavy cooking. But there is punch in the dining hall, the dancers alas have consumed the pop. I did make and expected ice cream, only it seems to be warming the refrigerators. Calamity on top of drudgery in the kitchen, you know. Maybe the setting will adjust itself if we give it a chance and talk for a while in that window seat—it looks so lonesome empty. Let us spare the men." The parents returned to their seat with her, Little stayed with the men.

Dala felt obligated to chat, "I haven't seen Dr Presha around. Didn't he come?" "O," said Ada, "Blume takes him right back to the city after the lessons end. Dear Carmen, she has her singing lessons when the summer movie here closes." He had no prepared reply, and felt as tho he himself had come out of a bad movie.

"Have you had a good vacation?" Ada asked Verchadet. "As a matter of fact," Verchadet said, "I find it unpleasant living in other people's houses and our place in Pamphilia is exposed to the street." "I know how it is when one is used to one's own, I hope you hadn't too much to clean up, we've had our skirmishes with Croton bugs, but you must learn to *protect* yourself," Ada stressed proverbially, "tho as you know in Georgia we're usually hospitable. The first summer here is the hardest. To those who must return to Garden year after year the sublets are second homes." "Until now," Verchadet revealed thoughtlessly, "we've travelled to different places every summer." "O but what about Little—when one has a prodigy on hand—" it was all too obvious for Ada to say more. "I should think a vacation," Verchadet's answer followed, "would make him play better." At once modest and sure as to her "merchandise," Verchadet meant her concern was his health—it was enough for a mother that he drove his own genius. Dala's gloom dispelled by her answer upheld her, tho he did not see where it would lead her with Ada. "O but for violinists it doesn't work that way, why even Practice," Ada honored Eichel with his family name, "comes back regularly to Mr Betur for lessons. By the way," she quickened, "the Castle estate is to let next summer. If you're interested I can phone the caretaker, it might help." "Everything is possible," Dala said not knowing what he was saying, but certain that Verchadet's mind was this very moment intent on rock wall and castle across the highway from their present shambles. They had been returning the caretaker's greetings on their daily way back from the post office, had even chatted. The coincidence of Ada referring to him moved Verchadet like all coincidences that in themselves are pleasant. Despite her doubt, if she let Dala explain it to her philosophically (which she would not care to have him do) she *entertained* probability if she let it be possible. She was always better at figures than Dala. "Why, yes," she said to Ada, "thank you if you will speak for us. Half a choice is better than one since it offers two." Ada not sure of their minds said, "Will do."

Sparser in far corners of the ballroom the tired dancers were playing cards. Esor joined one group after another. Betur, apparently content to be left alone with Little, thought back vaguely—"What card—badge—say? ah-yes—THE CUD. I can *shedule* you," he said holding his head, "*wance* (once) a week lessons back in city in October. Dr Presha maybe not necessary for you next year, has too mŏch to do, tell *y'māther* I tell him. Next year in Garden, Wizard—Endor—come hear *you*." He had not mentioned Dala, perhaps an oversight, but Little said nothing, obviously gratified. "Good-bá, practice me good." Little shook hands: "Good-bye." "Wait," Betur said, "maybe soup ice cream ready." But Miss Nasaltwang was anxious to go; they were all "leaving Pamphilia the day after tomorrow, *au revoir*."

"I almost told Miss Nasaltwang," Baballo said. "What vanity," said Verchadet. They stayed up half that night bubbling, so to speak, over their fortune by themselves. "What vanity," Little added, "it's good you didn't." "Are you sure Betur said what you said about Endor?" Verchadet asked to confirm it to herself. "Tell me again," Little said, "how Dala nearly spoiled it with Ada about the castle." "Dr Presha will probably feel hurt," Dala said. "He's not your assistant, but Betur's," Little scored, "*that* takes care of that. When will you stop taking care of the world?" "One concentrated lesson a week will be simpler for me," Verchadet said, but her fair enough reason did not clarify. He went off to write in his notebook—'in two removed window seats by telesthesia—' "Well, Little you'd prefer a castle to this hovel, if—" Verchadet said. "A hostel hovel," Little spelled it out for her on paper. "It's late," Dala yawned, "one more day here, tomorrow the caretaker."

They met him at noon the next day—no last letters, no

one at the post office. "I've watched you across the highway," he said, "and I know you won't bother me and I won't bother you." A deposit, returnable if they changed their minds before next June, would hold it for them. "Do you have the return train tickets?" Little asked Verchadet as he looked over the amount on Dala's check. "The boy knows his business," the caretaker laughed. "Come here, let me show you a bit, I'd show you all of it, only the young folk are coming for their lawn party later this afternoon. Twenty-four rooms!" They were convinced by a glimpse of the grand stairway, but Little by this time was coming out of the nearest room. "A library!" was all he said. "We have to pack for home," said Verchadet, "we can see it all next year." They were out on the terrace again. "A greenhouse?" she asked. "Used to be," said the caretaker, "that's where they throw out their furniture. They'll probably have me empty it for the bonfire tonight."

She stood at the door of the glass structure and saw a few dead plants and roots thrust thru heaps of furniture. "What a lovely little spindle-back hickory chair," she said. "They'll probably burn it," the caretaker said. "Burn it? O no!" "Could be used for violin practice?" Snorckie referred to the greenhouse. "Suit yourself," the caretaker said, and spoke again to Verchadet: "Come to think of it, there are three of those chairs—one for each of you—let me crate and send them to you for Christmas, they'll never miss them." He appeared enriched when she gave him a little more than the freight charges.

Meanwhile Dala and Little had walked on to the woods and mountain behind the house. The pine needles that looked as tho they might kindle under them sank cool and soft underfoot as they entered the edge of woods. They rose tall with the mountain. Dala's nostrils whiffed a few short breaths of pine odors. "We'll climb it next year," he said. "Aye," Little said, "with my coonskin hat?"

Droves of the Castle clan filled the lawn towards evening. The lessees of next summer watched tense from across the highway. About midnight the voices reaching them grew louder. The bonfire roared. When the fieldstone walls darkened safely, the von Chulnts went to bed.

Now Betur was his only teacher Little rebuffed the faults of his own practice to spare Betur the trouble. Eight years old that year in taking pains he would say: "Little Baron Snorck, to yourself." Like most people with their own names that suggest a lot is doing, he expected courtesy everywhere, tho he despised the flattery of showing courtesy to everyone. One fall day Dala in an engrossed walk back and forth behind the closed doors of the largest room in his brownstone—wanting to say good-bye before leaving for the Institute but not wanting to disturb his son—overheard three voices. In the past, his good-bye held back by the same scruple, he had often heard only one voice: Little's to itself. But now, tho he was sure Little was alone, he heard three.

"Signore Paganini, that son of—your Nicolo won't keep time, squeaks when he shifts; his A-string the treble of a tinny Signorina Verona Moronica; the G—a German howler raising haunches into his shoulders." "O Professore Betur, let Césare judge—O Caesar, *pian pianino!*" "That little one failing me? No! how? He has extended me superlative contributions, great favors of dedicated compositions; if you don't approve, Professore, why do you teach him? He must never be cowed into what *you* call strenuous practice."

He was never cowed, requiting Betur with more than his due in competence. Yet his musicality, Little's strictly personal gift to himself, craved to be heard in Great Hall. Betur's promise that "Wizard" (he had meant Warlock) would hear him in Garden next year reminded Little of Warlock's earlier promise: "You must play for me again in six months, and the third time will be in Great Hall." Little forgot in modest homage to Little and fiddle that six months had lagged into twice six. As Dala *pithed it* (an expression Little discovered for him): work drives beyond promise, craving and time. Perhaps Verchadet recalled—and not too surely—the chilling words Betur meant for Dala but addressed to her when they had first called on him: "You see, I don't prepare anyone for a debut. I just teach." As tho Betur now encouraged her to forget that first puff of disavowal and last summer's proof of it in Garden, he startled the von Chulnts by telephoning one evening after lessons: "Miz von Chulnt? A lady *colt* me"—*called* me, Verchadet half realized. "Name, Osmir Nishgood, sorority of Chiromeles"—all spelled out. "Would like musicale entertainment like *Ladies of Yesteryear* she explained me. I recommend Little, she very pleased. Could prepare his own program. I trost him."

Like Betur, Little took *trust* to mean a bond for "merchandise" to be delivered. "It won't do," he badgered Verchadet, "to give them what they've been getting from Tremor and Eichel. I'm sick of Onangni and the Cochon *Quicksand Concerto* with piano score, where you'll be sure to end up two measures behind me—that's for privacy with Betur." "But if he hasn't heard you play the pieces, do you think he'll like *Daring Do*," Verchadet worried, "when he hears about it?" "I don't care, he said he trusts me. Besides he will probably be assigning it to Eichel and Tremor to *practice me good* once I've premiered it," Little said with finality. "No Bach for violin alone, no, no Mozart—they won't listen. What do you think, Verchadet—an untranscribed seventeenth-century English piece or some early American—something for fiddle to sound like a French horn, never heard before?" The Chiromeles, most of them ancient widows and second wives of retired garden farmers and fishermen in the export business at Sheepshead, an inlet of the sea some miles from the von Chulnts' brownstone, must have their cheated tastes revived and spiced for the true violin literature, Little argued. "You mean," Dala interrupted almost unheard, "they're—sort of—country people and seafolk, once high class, bored by a century of concert going so they cannot stir to how near the true classic is to work in progress?" "Yeh—yeh—" Little sidestepped, "they've had enough vespers, leit motives, chorale *gehag te lieber Gott,* cantata *ah soul, o test, how cool the*—in organ versions of Beer Hand Baer after grand voluntaries of Tusk O'Ninny—but if you're hinting at modern kitten music by L. O. Quint and Lapping Furtive, DON'T HINT, please." Dala did not answer. At their age the Sheepshead ladies would probably not hold Little responsible for his father's scholarly eyeglasses, if they saw thru their own bifocals. Good—Little obviously required his own research.

The von Chulnts went to the Library. Little perched on a high oak stool over an oak table in the vaulted catalog room, of an age for all the world like the daguerreotype of The Old Librarian, tho without Franklin's spectacles, filling out slips for books and scores, while Dala with his new uncomfortable rimless glasses carted the index trays to him. Verchadet waited at a table in the communing reading room for the arrivals of Little's choice from the vaults of the vast interior. By the time the three gathered at her table for Little to make his selection the music had piled up higher than her head, and the other nearby readers who slept or pored or merely observed were roused to an educated if unworldly family. "Drayhorse," Little whispered as he caught Dala drowsing, "sorry, don't nod, I'll be thru soon—here's a lullaby for piano—if you'd like to copy it out for me?"

Research became a fair portion of Little's winter work or public disappearances, as he worded it shyly to a colleague, a little girl at the music school who had asked him where he had been some previous Saturdays. For his history the Chiromeles concert went well enough. There were other performing engagements that year: *youth concerts* taking him to provincial watering places, as a wry critic described them, annoyed perhaps by young audiences slaking their thirst around the drinking fountains near the wash rooms when *he* was trying to listen and praise a virtuoso of *their* time. "I don't mind," Little said to this critic, "*de gustibus*—just don't give over half of your review to *them*." For all the praise and friendly crowding over the signing of autographs—Little varied these, sometimes his first name, sometimes his last, sometimes *von*—these engagements never brought him a return engagement. Baffled by this result Verchadet explained to herself that Little's fleeting admirers, even the old Chiromeles strove like her son to be original each year in their selection of entertainment.

Behind Little's public appearances she always sensed Betur's permission. Why he gave it she could not guess, except maybe to strengthen practice with audiences. Uncommitted—"They ask," he'd say, "so if you like, good luck." How could she refuse an impartial wish? Fortunately the engagements occurred on week-ends, when Dala not obliged to his Institute could help carry three small valises, one for each of them—their insides mostly Little's belongings. The fiddle case was *Défense de toucher*, the soloist warned them, for him to carry himself, and at intervals his to unlock to tune the fiddle as they travelled.

The weather's *fair*
the teeth ache

the weather *changes*
the teeth ache

the weather's *the weather*
the teeth ache

Despite himself the verses sluiced thru Dala's head. With clinched fists, "Be quiet both of you," Little muttered, "if you don't keep quiet I promise you'll never again travel with me to my concerts."

They sat on their made beds in a room of a fashionable last century hotel in the nation's capital after reading the morning paper's review which Little had run downstairs to bring up to them. The reviewer of his appearance as soloist the night before with The Symphonia had praised Little and taken away. Rereading they hurt with ire for him. "In the tuttis the flying brilliance of the soloist's half-size was understandably but regrettably obscured"—Dala strained at the duplicity of the words. "Who cares!" Little flared up again, "maybe he's saying *cows brayed*!" "They did," Verchadet said, "I've never been deafened by a worse orchestra—o QUIET, both of you." Little saw his father hesitating towards a leaf of hotel stationery: "Don't dare, don't dare, Dala, write the fool or whoever a protesting letter!" The doorbell rang and to Verchadet who answered it appeared a bouquet of American Beauties, so many with a tag wired into them reading *For Little von Chulnt from The Manager.* "O thank you, how lovely," Verchadet said only to realize the bellboy had gone. "I must ask the maid for a vase for these." The roses went with her as she shut the door.

"Father Peremptore," Dala said looking down into his son's eyes. "I say what I mean," Little flustered, "don't dare write for me—and if ever in fiction, to spare me, condense. What were you doing with that scrap of waste paper?"

"Welshing," Dala said.

"Before or after the review," Little teased.

"Last night," Dala said.

Little stalked over, leaned his waist to read standing, his chin in his palms, elbows on the table:

not o' wame a' that
Pan hymn *Dī* go not
am cry am create
o Nine wreathe 'll laugh & knot
o fruit of fruit thew
o fruit to deck or root
o really a blood hue brae
o flight gie to goad dew
o preed o preed rath
Pan hymn *Dī* go not
o flight down at
o dew veer to nine wet

"Taliesin?" Little asked.

"Well, yes," Dala answered, "for my purpose he'll do. You open your mouth sounding off, but sometimes you close it." With the reviewer in mind he said: "I too have been charged with obscurity, tho it's a case of listeners wanting to know too much about me, more than the words say."

"You know me," Little said matter-of-fact and unrepentant: Verchadet had just come back with a vase.

23

Concrete poetry—a hundred years ago it was marble—Dala mulled over a late magazine, I hope my teeth qualify. He mulled further: to be sure is to be unsure, and to be unsure is to be sure? that one's matter in history or out of it was "work," "a useless work," "a fine work," "Square's works," "ZZZ's works," "Etc's." Has not Verchadet said, 'Who hasn't worked, for the rich to dress in the morning was work.'

Also work the pleasures of their concert trips were chiefly historical. Travelling southerly to Little's concert at a Moravian counterpart of Garden, they visited Dala's old friend R. Z. Draykup who had been confined to a madhouse. As he put it, 'he hath spoke sooth'—and for Dala these archaic words completely expressed the sorrow of his friend's incarceration. In time he would be released, but not cleared of the charge of madness implying a sanity for which he had risked being executed. He would never be pardoned for the compassion which inflamed him into raving speech against "gall, vices and lackeys" somehow involved in medieval echoes most modern folk heard as "Gulf whites and gibbet blacks." For him Little played Bach *for violin alone* with results which the concrete reader may, if he can rove while gazing solidly, read as another chapter. For the time being, during this stop Little confided to Draykup that a concert tour involved being the fodder of audiences. "Ah, but you're a performer," Draykup took exception, "Ewe hev to fader"—and he spelled it out on paper for him, much as Little himself might have.

With the Deep South Symphony Little played Mozart's G major for the youth in the afternoon and the mature in the evening. The lady of Welsh lineage Lledil who introduced both occasions effervesced, "What pretty tunes!" But —apparently stone deaf—she only looked straight at him when he asked after the girl, about his own age, in the lilac dress who had helped serve the afternoon tea. He had *thought*, he said, her black skin with her blue eyes and kinky red hair *unusually* beautiful.

James Madison, who aging had been ailing, wrote about that time pleading for news of Little's musical engagements and themselves, and Dala wrote her about two other appearances:

> I am still terrified when Little stands at the edge of his own three-foot square platform, which the conductors always need to overcome the battery of the orchestra behind the solo part, that he will fly up on an upbow and fall off. In The University Hall, looking away from him all the time, I sat in an acoustically dead spot, and when the concerto ended I hurried frantically to Verchadet to ask what had happened. "He played well, that's all," she said. Later we were taken to a colonial brick mansion furnished entirely with antiques—the conductor's residence, apparently open house to everybody any time of day. The uninvited guests serve themselves out of two stocked refrigerators. They may also handle anything on the property. Little did, running upstairs and down to come up to tell us that in the basement music room (the mansion has three music rooms) was Haydn's own clavichord and a replica of Bach's. Simply there they were: wood keys, boxwood painted green.

We finally got him to go to the train where he found the railroad's vice-president to talk to across the aisle—who said it was a pleasure—while I dozed off with pain in my right eye, not having dared to infringe on the refrigerators, which tho free for anybody to open, as I saw, would after all shut.

Easter, in Neufafen Little received a check of $50 and took us out. He spent $14.32 for fare, coffee, milk and hot cross buns, but not a penny more: Bach himself when it comes to economy. Verchadet risking not too obviously to implant generosity hinted he make it a straight 15, but he wouldn't hear of it. Guess I had better go back to my *Bards* and maybe earn $29.50 in three years—and forget the drafty trains that other passengers find comfortable. Little has now read me the praise in The Neufafen Journal-Currier, gloating over the spelling "Mazas" for Mozart—the point being one of his earliest student étude books is by Mazas. A cold wind's in my overcoat.

Affectionately

24

A tang of next fall, was it, in April? Not Little, but Verchadet and Dala lived their past sometimes into the future: the annual gathering of their families on Little's birthday had been delayed by his public disappearances at the turn of the year. With grandpa gone Little did not want to see family, but he could still be persuaded. "Every year it has been the same bickering—you'd think—" Verchadet began the midnight before their visit, when Dala in perspective broke in: "The loneliness of the artist—the loneliness of a da Vinci, no forbears tho there were forbears—yet we live to a convergence, of it with our kin."

For the third time in three years Little arrived without his fiddle. "*Enough*"—the families had heard his first notes, when something to talk about and hail, as any lazy public might say reflecting pride on itself, *for them* he had "arrived." The ever embedded Count and the complaining Contessa—her antiques more dingy in shining from constant polishing—did not remember to ask after the fiddle, nor did the others—the younger Esfelts and the older Lucy and Hiram. They were more interested in the travels of the von Chulnts, as tho, Verchadet suspected, they—not the von Chulnts—had been deprived of confidence in their worldly attainments. Not that Verchadet wanted to disenchant them of what they thought glamorous. *Their* disillusion would give *her* no comfort. Little stood off. Dala swallowed his obligatory burden, feeling less obliged to their envy—tho he could not believe it—in silence. But Verchadet showed her pleasure in the verbal flight of the Count who—when Tearilee with a shiver of her slight shoulders and a pious wish in her hazel eyes said, "Cold today—where's spring?" —whispered in his bedding, "Behind." Verchadet let his one word speak for her too, what good would it do to tell them: Little has played in many cold places; invariably with a cold that hung on tho he had to play warm; over the air without a proscenium before phantoms; for a microphone affording no greater fidelity than a hi-fi; with a string workshop so he could encourage the sloths and in innocence help a famous old lady cellist who coached them keep a job; had, during a year of Mozart celebrations, reenacted (three times) the legend of little Mozart (with ruches trimming gold crewelworked aquamarine velveteen) replacing the first violinist the first time Leopold let his son play with a grown-up quartet, so that an actual first violinist forty years old would begrudge Little the indignity for life; and furthered the Triennial Festival of Recent Composers, only to be chagrined by the dean of critics who, extolling Little for his performance of the work dedicated to him, neglected to mention the name of the composer along with the others who made up the program, all lumped as a "pride" (mere lions) "from whom Little had stolen the show." And if these affronts were due to Betur's attentions where was the glamor?

Saying good-bye at the door the young Count grown more portly not knowing what to say spoke as older cousin: "Keep your chin up." Looking up at six foot-three Little replied, "A fiddler doesn't need a butler for that." And when grandma Tearilee said to him, "You look *so art*"—an expression which held for her all the aspiration for the extraordinary she naturally felt but which somehow could never be close to her—Little said, "Thank you."

Still spring vacation the day after, Dala went with Little for his lesson with Betur while Verchadet tended the hyacinth bulbs in her garden. "Here *pater pote*, you may brood the last page while I have my workout," Little said leaving him with his "dairy." Dala read:

> Courtesy whin do'n' dee wére nighed
> courtesy dear handed me I'm all eyed
> courtesy dire a feather, I vied
> high I see been pour eye gimp again guide
> courtesy chock have a' th' pech, hide—
> when glare irk when garret him dare hide
> courtesy sigh'th ai if quiet gored 'n' gnawed
> courtesy within hall pith path or wider gained
>   is the deigned rock towered

Happy with the brood of words he still looked at Dala heard himself thinking, "May soon." "Lucky I was reminded," he said aloud, leaving his check for the caretaker of the Castle in Pamphilia in the diary and closing it. "Might be *Gorhoffedd*," Dala said returning the diary to Little who had brisked up with a scowl and closed fiddle case. "What's this," he asked. "Check," Dala said, "remind me to mail it." Little shut both eyes several times in winking them.

A gait an unhurried eat gear hastened—

translated the lessee of the Castle walked grateful to be alive in June to a different vacation in Pamphilia, last year's out of mind. Sunlight shed a pearl's luster on him from the twenty-four long windows of his leasehold, the length of a city block to the kitchen. He was up earlier than Little, to rake the embers of the wood fire in the cast iron oven he had assured the night before and to make breakfast where the three would be warmed by risen sun and kindled log. Beyond hearing him Verchadet and Little slept on under six counterpanes, each in an oak paneled bedroom with its door to the library: Little clasping *The Mabinogion* he had pried from the tallest (lowest) shelf of the Lieutenant Governor's unused collection. The violinist's bow hand strained to its fretted place at the end of *Manawyddan the Son of Llyr,* third of the four-branch tale of the Mabinogi. But Dala for their waking toasted white dough to a coppery tinge on aluminum foil, wrapped the crisp rolls in it, and when they were diapered placed them with the intent of his absent mind into the still spotlessly clean antique tole pail reserved for newspapers for the fire. Until now pine bark had served. Abruptly untranslated by his error he discarded the foil and removed the rolls to the oak dining table where a slab of board incised with the word BREAD awaited them: the board's underside similarly encouraged BUTTER. So as the three ate Dala sheepishly had a tale to tell on himself, not unlike the knight Kynon to his own discredit in the "The Lady of the Fountain," the ninth tale of the Mabinogi Little would read this morning. Not uproariously—they laughed.

"Let well alone enough," Little inverted and Verchadet decided against Dala's and her own craving for the rare thing sometimes lost in an attic. After one cobwebby inspection by all three together they agreed for their sensible needs to sublet the upper stories of the Castle to mystery. Betur had definitely scheduled Little's performance of *Praeludium and Allegro* for the Farewell Concert in August, and Little's precise musical runs anticipating Warlock listening deterred Dala from climbing stairs to some blurred confusion like—'Is it Warlock or Wizard cum Endor—well, let August tell.' It was pleasant to listen, a solitary on the terrace, and the distracting birds were welcome. So, Dala had no doubt, Mrs Weatherbureau across the highway also listened to Little practicing in the greenhouse. Let us enjoy the grounds, the terrace and the main floor, the three agreed, and of its eleven rooms leave three with their silver, stoneware and crystal untouched except for an occasional brightening with feather-duster or dry-mop on the way to the kitchen. Country dust is not dirt. And let us not use the outdoor grate to cook on. Mrs Otototot was overheard whispering to them in the post office: "my—where have you kept yourselves, your rent must be enormous." Few visitors crossed their private bridge. Lambeth Potiphar, in confidence "by herself," on a brief excursion from Turkey came to call Unzung long distance and found the von Chulnts' telephone disconnected. Esor Leber saying he was "driven by family"—Verchadet and Dala had not heard or seen the station wagon—invited himself to the greenhouse for practice before Little could "warm" them with a surprised *n-no!* Some hours' rumbles of runs and intervals on the bass viol justified Little's claim to the greenhouse. His parents glared not exactly at each other while he smiled at them chasing himself from one room to another, out to the terrace and in again. Verchadet's migraine commiserated with her geraniums behind the glass walls accustomed to gentler vibrations. Dala immersed himself in *Timon of Athens,* moved as always by it, between recurrences of queasiness. Their release arrived when, expecting to be coaxed to come again, Esor thanked them profusely. Intending a friendly good-bye thru his pallor, Dala said "what for" and suddenly faint but still smiling went on, "I reread it over your bass," pointing to the spine of *Timon.* Esor, quick to analyse others, left abruptly, looking as tho he could never brook a neurotic competitor. "I should've—" Dala gasped, as Verchadet and Little seated him in an armchair to his discomfort, and then resolved more firmly, "had he stayed a minute longer I'd have invited him to lunch." Little was more explicit: "I am hungry too, that's what's the matter with you." On the whole the status or situs of the Castle precluded visitors. Budgeted but not conscious of budgeting they never regretted renting the Castle.

There was romance that summer for Verchadet when her yellow dry-mop swept from her floor brilliant petals and blown anthers fallen from bouquets she renewed daily, and for Little and Dala there was adventure. When they sought it they incurred differences of weather without its being forecast: when they sauntered in hot sun, or raced in cold brake, then bathed under the bridge, feet and legs timid on sharp rock in the trout brook called The Breath—the first dip literally carried the breath away. In the late afternoon, the sun still high Little renamed it The Midges, so pestiferous were "these things" flying in the face of the sun. They were not certain when a cloud over the woods shadowing their meadow might as at will shut out the sun from the Castle. What Pamphilians called *high fog* was not rare. But last year's promise to themselves to climb the mountain they carried out on a day when the blue of the sky was the sun's alone. Perspired (against Verchadet's wishes if she were there) on the warm comforter of pine needles at the edge of woods—their red sagging fired Little and Dala into them: the woods chilled them, they climbed.

"And what a climb," Little reported to Verchadet, "a miracle we've come back with eyes! We couldn't find the path up—so it was over rocks and thru bramble, with the trees to hold onto. What we mistook for a path was usually smooth rock which slid us into other tangles. Branches we held back for each other to crawl under, Indian file, snapped back vice versa." "I don't suppose you had time to say face to face you were sorry," Verchadet said, slightly queasy over their recklessness—"or congratulate each other on not tearing your trousers?" Little chortled, but did not interrupt his story for her: "Craziest thing, there *was a path* a few yards around from the rock where we started—the path we came back on. Climbing we must have skirted it all the time, while looking for a clearing ahead or blue sky above that turned out to be blue spruce until we crawled out at the top into a meadow." At his mentioning blue spruce, "*Those* I'm sorry to have missed." Verchadet said. "Dala might from the start have hung his glasses on a twig—the twigs always angled for them, like the branch for Absalom." A casual look and smile expressed Dala's thanks for his son's use of The Old Testament once read to him. "Coming down took very little time," Dala added by way of apology for the worry their longish absence had brought her, "only I was more winded." "Did you find a horse," Verchadet said to recall to him the one occasion he rode one and "experienced his ribs in his heart." "Are you all right now?" she asked quietly.

They had not told her what they said and saw when they crawled out on the meadow at the top: perhaps because they knew that she had their very same talk on her mind gathering her bouquets for the Castle that summer, and flowers curtailed her speaking of lesser lives not so pretty or candid or magnificent; or perhaps because Little who confided in both his parents preferred not to place his secrets all at once in one basket so to speak and staggered them, often to V, less often to D, but quite sure he'd find them in the long run in one basket in any case—why deprive himself of the pleasure of showing up either one caught red-handed as having blabbed to the other? The top of the mountain received Little and Dala gasping near Indian Reservation they had visited with Verchadet a year ago by car at less hazard. It led them to where the musical doctors, dentists, artists and writers lived—Little's last summer's ambushes. On the road circling the meadow was Serp's place still boarded. "Serp, Lona's teacher—you remember, Dala—Betur's rival who once taught Nihunem, tho Lona is his last pupil." "Poor Lona, we wish her well," Dala said out of personal wistfulness. "Like Manawyddan, whose story you read last night, tho we try hard someone is always pushing us out of a livelihood, or could it be *we* are a bit envious." "No," Little said, "it's just that we strike them so sure and don't bother them for false sympathy like they do us that makes them hate us. So like the thievish boors or bad craftsmen whom Manawyddan's competence infuriated they'd kill us. And I'd just as soon kill them first." "Not so," Dala said, "we will not *slay* them—take it in the new or in the old sense—as Manawyddan said, *if need be do our work elsewhere.*" "Then let's get back to Castle and Verchadet fast," said Little, and they did. And tho he had forgotten to bring his coonskin hat from the city—or secretly felt too old to bring it—he bounded down as if he wore it, protected from falling boughs and all dastardly reservations.

The fiddle of sprucewood was fortunate. Hoarfrost on yellow petal in mid-August dawn, followed by cold and clear, token of more frost the night of Little's debut at Garden, protected the bouts from humidity. There is always the risk of the bouts' minutest splitting, "when the fiddle moss go to th' o'pital"—there was no hospital for fiddles in Garden—Betur was used to stammer before enunciating, "then it plays *too* open, *too* resounding." But with his music in mind, tuning occasionally was all the worry Little spared himself the long day before the concert. He was to play last, after an evening of Flutit and Esor. "It's the waiting that's dullest," Verchadet whispered. Dala could not hear her or the bass under the blunt thud of Flutit's piano. They stood in Betur's studio, all the interior doors of the ground floor of the main house open, looking beyond the entrance hall into the concert room. When the crowd separated them by an arm's length Dala saw her as in a gap between them thru a mist of Welsh sorcery. The playing stopped: he heard fainthearted applause, and while it thinned, hurried worried Betur—was turning, examining Little's fiddle, belly, bouts, back, furlings, tailpiece, pegs—retreated to a corner. From there Little was to walk down the length of carpet, the boxers having anticipated him jangling their bells on their collars, to his two-and-a-half-foot cube of platform. Dala glimpsed Little in possession of his fiddle, but waited till he was well out of the corner before edging to replace him in it. And there, standing or in their seats, were the peers straining to look at the fiddle, all the eyes the von Chulnts had avoided that summer alone in their castle: Panza Rilty, Schwerscheide, Lona, Solo, Noë, Slider, Bearmeouts, Cyclops, Tremor, Hushlushes, Nishgut, Nasaltwang, Mme Practice, Otototot, Hemdlachs, Taignit, Presha, Blume, Eichel—the many who sipped Ada's punch after music in Garden.

Little was playing—shod in one place, unswayed outstripping flights of fingering all true pitched to the bow arm—Dala saw its sinuous excellence, but heard nothing. His heart hurt, his lungs forbidden a gasp. He felt breath on his nape, and turned partly to face a furious puffing from Betur's cigarette. In the little space there was he extended his left palm forward, somewhat above his knee, with the most thoughtful gesture of inviting Betur to squeeze in front of him where politeness felt Little's teacher should stand. But Betur lighting a chain cigarette and shaking his head from side to side held Dala where he was, for an instant with the pressure of a hand on his shoulder, as tho to hide behind him, with a thankful look at Dala for shielding him. Far-sighted, intently listening, Betur obviously wanted no one behind him in his corner.

If Dala had turned deaf by a freak of mind (or *lusus naturae* as some still say) while his son was playing, the applause he now heard was deafening. "Could you hear him?" he pleaded to Betur, "Esor's bass, too, sounded very faint." The reproach which faced him was more than he had hoped for: a contorted handsome face whimpering, averting the tears, "He was won'r'ful!" And Betur stalked off recomposed thru the crowd to shield the pupil of his eyes from the visitors "countenanced" by Garden's rule only on Saturdays. His hawk vision had seen one dentist collector of fiddles speaking to Little, very likely minimizing the tone of his instrument, which was only a half-size; perhaps putting vain thoughts in the boy's mind, telling him the Guarneri, the Stradivari never bothered to make them.

"You bet you were won'r'ful and *he* knows it"—meaning Betur: Verchadet flared at her men, impatiently turning the key to the Castle, "But where was Warlock!" Her question had occurred to them quietly. "What's the matter?" Balo swallowed. "What's the matter?" Little said. "In the hoo-hah of it, all those false best wishes," she almost wept —she had been approached by Mrs Bearmeout, who had it "in confidence": Warlock had been in Garden that day, but only to look at Tremor's purchase of a Stradivarius and to talk over with Betur the young Cyclops' debut under the impresario's management at Great Hall in the fall of next year. " 'And now Eichel was worried'—as if I cared!"

"Chatterminestra," Little said not looking up from *Agamemnon* to Verchadet, "am I to suffer another version of this *tradegy?*" He was ten, and trying to read a not too happy translation of the Greek. "And what has Mahmud," Verchadet pronounced it Ma Mud, referring to herself as much as to Betur, "*done* to deserve your faith?" "I put no faith in him and don't mistrust him *yet,*" Little said. She recalled Tearilee's name for Dala (an aside) when she first met him—*The Turk,* elicited by Dala's gentle insistence on some trifle he'd rather avoid as *he* saw it. Uncompromised future compromiser of battles Dala did not look up from obstinately, silently sounding Aneirin:

> Gear a grief's ascent be ant geat night
> girt eye gilled o wade we eye hay night
> agh y' be at anger is good dour angry man
> agh yet heel descend weal a dash sand
> nev 'r eye teem here neat at coursin'

"When has my advice been wrong," Verchadet persisted, "all I said was what Mihcaoj who played Bach for violin alone said before me—the prodigy grows up and the child remains. You're too good a player to beat the second-raters to Great Hall. Last year you were quick to see thru the business, older you swallow its insults. Why?" "Because in business insults are not false, they're evident,"

Little parried. "O you're *so* witty beside the point," she said out of patience, "if I were variously gifted, like you, I'd know I've had enough lessons, and do something else now to support my fiddle later, if that's what you must do. *And* I'd tell Betur to keep his scholarship *and* Theory III for his other children until the year they qualify for Theory I. By that time Betur might show more interest—in you." "I'm not so sure you don't want your child to remain and a prodigy to grow up," Little said, "besides my scholarship doesn't cost us anything, and education should never be expensive." "There you hurt us both," Dala said, "that's hardly *our* consideration. The obligations that go with accepting a scholarship can turn out to be costly for the unowned artist—and money, sometimes the little that's there, money—" "So?" Little queried, expecting more logic. "Cannot—to us," Dala said.

Wintering in the brownstone, Verchadet—as Little turned a cliché—"to give me the doubt of her benefit"—declined to take the subway with him to lessons and theory. Dala asked to go with him: Little had once nearly lost a shoe, when the vise of a train's shutting doors closed on the family together but slipped his shoe off him for a kind lady on the platform to return it at the next stop. So it was on one of these self-effacing journeys (when Little would have preferred Dala to stay home) it happened while Little was packing his fiddle out of earshot and patting the boxers: Betur, aware Verchadet had not been accompanying Little to the lessons and perhaps fearing she was not at the piano during his practice at home, commended Little to Dala, "He plays very well, you know—please remember me to Mrs von Chulnt." Dala thanked him and, since Betur had confided that much as it were, added: "Little told us the summer before last that you said Mr Warlock would hear him at his debut in Garden this past summer, and we've wondered what prevented him." Betur, first as tho he hadn't heard, said after a longish pause: "Little must have misun'stood, I am sure it was a misunderstanding. I cannot tell Mr Endor what to do, I can *if he asks* sometime only speak as teacher of pupil, I am an honest man." A more negative conviction followed abstractly: "I am not sure early appearance in Great Hall helps anybody, it is better to study and hold on to merchandise for later."

Dala kept no secret from Little or Verchadet, and Little conveyed the "soap-stance of Betur's position," as hissing it he told her at once on coming home. "How did you guess he did not speak sooth, you—" he dramatized after Dala's old friend R. Z. Draykup—"you always guess right." Relenting to his show of ebullience she said, "You get one more chance, I take it you want Ma Mud to go to the mountain" —meaning Endor as Little (Baron) was quick to gather. "That makes sense," said Dala. "As *ho oikeús* of this house," she said to him, feeling the Greek word appropriate, "*you* can phone Warlock's secretary."

"Miss Shield, Mr Endor's secretary," her voice remembered Dala and offered to "connect" him with the impresario, "if he's in." "Why, yes, I've wondered what happened to Little—you say you went to Betur?" Warlock questioned affably. Dala for once listened and heard him say, "Yes, I shall be glad to hear how he's grown. Come directly this time to my little hall with the flat ceiling. Its acoustics are not so good if one sits in the middle of it. But that's where I've auditioned the best of them—all my concert artists. I shall have time for several accompanied pieces and one unaccompanied." The von Chulnts paid Flutit for some hours of rehearsals, assuring Little "more than less" of the pianist's compliance, and the four greeted Endor together.

Warlock had two undeclared reasons for sitting in the middle of his little hall: 1) if Little's half-size could be heard there, it would be heard anywhere in Great Hall, where the acoustics, contrary to the fears of the unaccomplished, actually aided accomplished virtuosity, 2) the impresario wished to be affected by the "projection" (as is said in the trade) of the performance rather than the close impassivity of the performer, which had impressed him sufficiently the first time he heard Little play. On his part Little, aware that the music would carry best to the dead spot under the flat ceiling if he enforced Flutit's compliance to accuracy, took extreme care not to project his fingerboard toward Warlock. So while the music moved impeccably for his ear, Endor put off by Little's wrapped up stance and profile found himself looking mostly at one hip and the slightest convex below it of the player—feeling it an insult absolutely intended. The audition over, "My—you've matured, very fine," he said—"why didn't you face me?"

Little felt let down inside him, but his face showed nothing to conciliate Endor. "You'll need a better fiddle, this half-size may not carry safely in Great Hall," the impresario said. "Relsierk said," Dala half queried, "that except for the ease a fine fiddle offers the virtuoso, audiences can't tell the rare instrument apart from the inexpensive." "Ah, yes, he's said it," Warlock replied knowledgeably, "but has publicized his three Guarneri." No one explicitly mentioned a debut in Great Hall. "Well, keep up with Betur," Warlock said, "and come back again, speak to my secretary on your way out to arrange it."

"Mr Endor will be away most of the spring and fall," Miss Shield explained, "you may meanwhile arrange for a city recital with our affiliate Metro Management, if you are disposed to cover the necessary box office receipts in advance." "But Mr Endor will cover those for Tremor Cyclops next fall," Verchadet came out with it, "and isn't Little just as worthy?" "Mr Endor doesn't cover anybody," Miss Shield said, "even Ztephiah Achsai must assure Mr Endor that the attendance will pay for Great Hall. And young Mr Cyclops, who's older by the way than Little, has proved immensely popular in Curaçao."

"Since you cannot escape inviting Betur to Great Hall, Little, you should tell him about our signed contract with Metro Management," Verchadet argued against obstinacy several months later. "He promised and says he didn't," Little gritted his teeth. "I'm in no hurry to invite him, it's not even May and my concert is in Octember, and I'm not going to Garden for him to *prepare me* (quote) with *his* stale program—if *I* feel like it *I'll* concede later to one transposed concerto for Flutit's flushing piano, or compliment them both with Postlude and Fury of Einem Pferd Schmitzik for encore and that's that. My program is my affair. You be polite if you want to, don't nag me. Did you dream I'm going to Garden again to be lied to—never! Our garden's right here—the backyard—while Dala mopes in that vile Institute this summer, to keep up with the bank's equity in the old brownstone." (Actually he was quoting Verchadet.) He hesitated: "How inconsiderate of both of us can you be?" His question pitted one against the other, and he was sorry before he finished it as he sensed his punishment—her silence. He might now not get a word out of her for days. He gazed at her even more at a loss as she looked off and he remembered "as a matter of fact" (her one bit of verbiage) she had recently at her own insistence again taken over the chore of going with him to Betur's lessons, of listening to them in that den of a waiting room, where "dear Imam," she hoped, would not be likely to step in to greet her, he had been ill and was too busy teaching two makeup lessons for every one he had missed.

"You quarrel and don't think of my bursitis," Dala also dreading her silence began tentatively. "I was able to move my left arm before you started bickering." "Nevermind, don't strain it and don't tell her about it," Little said. "How many times, Little, have I asked you, since you're less likely to hurt her with silence to—" "Now *you know* I want both of you to keep still," she ordered. "Neither of you makes sense," Dala said, and then from a long distance, "when you fall out—I might as well be in the Institute where they don't know half the things I drive myself to think in my trust of them. It's all mad. We're sensible, sensible, and suddenly there is no sense." He spoke gently, without any literal intention it seemed, to his words. Annoyed as both were with him, they could not help feeling the something of a classic frenzy that probably frightened people as often he made sense. "We've been practical for once," he said, "let's not spoil it. This concert should be as it happens, with no regrets that it might have been arranged —with other's luck—by Warlock. I rather trust Miss Shield and believe the art of bōwing is evidently for those who pay management, even Ztephiah pays before he plays," he looked at them vaguely. "If you find it so noble," Little taunted him, "you play my concert and wait until you're forty odd to mature for Great Hall. By the way when's your birthday, Lada?" "You're so sure Betur lied," Dala said sadly, "and we don't really know he did, do we? may never know. Or whether he can recommend or can't, or what his influence, or if he has any, or if after some Oriental system he looks on would be sons in size place and favors the oldest first tho he likes them all." "He's downright upwrong, if he likes us all," Little said. "But it does seem common sense even if we can't prove it," Dala said, "that a reputable teacher like Betur would not run Endor's business to be exposed in a conflict of interests?" "If you're so generous and aseptical, Sir Horse, you verify, here's the telephone, you tell him about your contract with Metro Management, I'm only Betur's baby," Little said. Verchadet's face lightened with the slightest smile. Dala was strangely aware that Little had been perusing the dictionary. It was of course the star shower of Little's puns and affection that bursitis could not twinge that fired Dala to the telephone—and his fate. He explained.

"I say iss no gut," he heard, "why you want?" Was this the suave Betur, or by some quirk his assistant Vasily Presha, Dala apprehended psychically. "We don't—or we do only because Little wants this recital," Dala said. "No! impossible, Little und'stand, you don't. Little is my friend —*you* want, I say cancel," Dala heard with Verchadet and Little straining to listen to either side of him. "I hope he will always be your friend, that's what a good teacher earns as I know it after a pupil goes on on his own," Dala said as to a friend. The voice in the receiver sounded exactly what it meant to say: "You're not my friend, Little is, you follow your teaching, I know what I know. I expect you will cancel the contract." Dala, disgusted with having said too much, blurted: "You make no sense, I can't cancel what I've signed to." "Then I won't teach," Betur said loud enough for Little and Verchadet to hear. "Don't teach," she spoke right into the mouthpiece now out of Dala's reach, and, as she hung up slowly, the receiver rattled, "b . . but Miz von Chulnt we must talk."

29

"And what will you play?" Verchadet asked. "Friends again," affectionately offering to rap her head with a restraining downward flapping of his vibrato hand, "My own program for the innocent progress of Betur, tho the reviewers may say he prepared me," Little said. "Perilex," he flashed, cabalistical, "danger—Dala—Phaethon Weaver's *5 Pieces—5 Stars—5 notes ascending the lantern crowning the cupola,* tho our pseudo friends will not like it sha'n't I be original?"—as Dala half heard over Hywel and Aneirin and wondered what Little meant, but did not dare being asked, "Where have you been living?" His son's choice predated by some years the octogenarian composer I. Gloss Dazzling's acknowledgment of his debt to the genius of Phaethon, who were he alive would always be one year younger than Dazzling.

The telephone rang. "I've a hunch it's the mountain again calling on Mahmud," Verchadet said, "I'll take it upstairs." Betur had called back almost at once after *their disconnect,* as he abbreviated perhaps after talking with Ada, to concede to Little's recital, if the contract date could be delayed *only one manth.* He would speak to Warlock about it to save the Professor embarrassment. ("Good, that leaves me out of it," Dala then noted, tho she had taken care to tell Betur she would pass on the message and that incidentally since Mr von Chulnt would have to be elsewhere the coming summer the family would not be coming to Garden. "Not necessary," Betur said. "I have confidence Little practice me because he wants. There will be time for rehearsal and dress rehearsal if we have until November. He's fast, as you know, and it's better always to play freshly.") "Tell him," Little called after her as she climbed, "that this isn't like his old joke of his school friend who didn't want to play his exam, pleading a *colt* that would spoil the varnish of the fiddle—tell him I'm not competing with who'ver he wants to play in Octember, I'll only be more original a month later!" "You tell him," Verchadet said, "I shall only list your program so he will feel he arranged it." Little's eyes teared perhaps for an instant grateful for her support. "Squall," Dala said with tact, looking at him thru his bifocals.

30

Verchadet and Little worked in the garden on the upper level of their city back yard. Dala wrote in the shadow of the privet, his eggshell (he called it) protected, under his Borsalino, from neuralgia the sun's direct rays always caused at a small table on the uneven pavement of the damp terrace below. She clipped a blossoming spray of privet hanging over the neighbor's wire fence, but kept it arching for shade and for them. "Much too much sun for the morning glories," Little said. Their large leaves had become a weed as he untangled a small brier from them to train it on the rock back wall. "Mostly thorns," he said. Then, overseer, he walked toward the hydrangea. "Hope springs coternal," he officiated, some eight feet above Dala, blending his Latin and Greek—*eternal* and *cothurnal.* "It's a far growth from the stump it was in Admir's sandbox when her governess, no less, wondered why it didn't grow. Cockeyed little cherub she could look mature with her blue-rimmed eyeglasses, painting the radiators with vegetable colors at three—you remember the mess we moved in on, when we exchanged apartments. She forgot to say good-bye to me and I missed her left to myself in our brownstone when she moved to the country: inconsiderate of her after all the lunches she invited me to and the rhymes we made up together to the weathervane of the retired fireboat in the dock where the old firemen held out." "That's what I call remembering," Dala heard Verchadet say, "you weren't much older, are you sure you're not repeating what I told you." "Obviously you can't remember for me more than Betur could," Little said, "Let me talk with this philosopher," and abruptly ran down the steps to the terrace to distract Dala with a slight snort: "Philosopher, your company."

Little with both hands on the top slat of the chair pushed most of his weight on him. "Ah, Manawyddan, son of Llyr," Dala said, "still a trace of your summer cold? I'm inclined to say this is finished, would you read it to me, please?" he asked removing his glasses. "*Parens., Hywel ab Owain Gwynedd*—

> panic air eke it pan arc y'pate frying
> a league grew three fate
> a' quietly argued
> a gat land a granary gruelled"

"Does it make sense?" Dala said shyly. "Maybe—the noises, but they won't translate back into Welsh. You always seem to be wanting to say something else—like Mrs Bearemout's letter we received yesterday, about all the excitement in Garden because I'm preparing my recital myself, Betur perhaps put her up to—" "Then it does," Dala said. Little then read the last line in Dala's notebook: "*Parens., Aneirin*

> lour mom ai dagger are y' ham rant

You may have noticed," Little said, "it's some time I've dropped my middle name Baron from my autograph, it takes too long signing."

Little's cold went with the summer, and Dala's head avoided neuralgia from the hot sun. Three months without his complaints the other two were grateful. Soon like a music box taken down from an upper shelf the musical year ground its round again—October—Verchadet bringing in bouquets of crisp globes of hydrangeas for a winter's display.

in sanie

semper

mon chair Dala

I am Dee-lighted that you-ah *coq de combat* has spurred a recital in Megalosaur, and foresee in ten years a series of such (recitals) as his range browdens. From what I hear'd here of his J. Batch it should bring him glory, if less e-mid-jet bliss to his progenitor. BUT all need NOT be LOSS e'en while you "hold" the unstringed purse. A sentiment of old daze of bein' regisseur calls me a-gayne. I can get no reprieve to come myself, and know yew feel as I do that for every Luna tick within these walls there are millions tick out there. IF you can get some of 'em to ATTEND. I mean —if you can PAPER Great Hall. 'N'if yew see no objection I shall be glad to contack my list here of such as still whirl in the world. Better not send me tickets, nor (xcep very few) direct, as they WILL lose or forget them. Let me exact promises and send you list of those *pledged* to honor rite to a seat picked up the night of the concert—*at the box office*. Overheard Self-announcements would add mystery of distinction to Little's audience. Cannot hurt if Baroness Yolda occupies a box (she needs) and / or two with her circle, or if Princess

Lwan Tan officiates in tiara in another with Unique
& other chawmed males.

Fair once use yer horse topknot and doan shy.

Yrs
RZ Draykup

Durable fire singing an old tune filled Dala's mind: the sane mad RZ *from itself never turning*, heartened and heartening in *that* madhouse cold. "Sith the practice of the world is to be impractical," as R once summed it up talking, Dala wrote at once to thank him for bothering—pretending to look off (with glazed eyes) when Little said, "*He* is a friend." "Tho how else but PAPER," Dala's afterthought followed. "Charge a friend for what I have paid?" "Feign *free* with the throng."

Over a plan of Great Hall's orchestra, loges, dress circle, first and second balconies, and four tiers of boxes—the claws as it were of ascending horseshoes, in the reversing order of a climbing heart's unprivileged status Verchadet and Dala PAPERED. And grieved: if with absolute equity they could give everyone the best seat. The first Law would not let them. Yet they tried. 2,999 seats, Ztephiah and Neitsnebur alone were known to fill them by advance sales months before their concerts. Of the late overflow allowed in on *their* concert nights the fire laws permitted as many standees as ticket speculators contriving with ushers could crowd away from the exits; also several rows of spectators, weaker for their money, pitted on folding chairs on the stage where they became part of the distraction of the properly seated audience—especially when the aloof diminutive Ztephiah and no taller but lively Neitsnebur stepped out for curtain calls, the violinist from behind his accompanist's keyboard, the unseen harpsichordist from behind his, and when they remembered bŏwed to the folding chairs, swallow tails arched over the footlights instead of unobtrusively away from these for the greater plaudits. But in the case of so young an artist's debut Metro Management finally told the von Chulnts there were no such problems. A maximum of 299 tickets left at the box office two weeks before the concert would be more than enough to meet the demand for cash sales they might hope for. Of course that left 2,700 tickets to do as they wished with.

"There must be ten easier ways," Verchadet said summarizing for Dala the trials, comforts and errors of 800 telephone calls pursued further by correspondence enclosing tickets expected to cross their lives again—Little's sustaining audience in Great Hall—as follows:

> *Orchestra.* Rows A-B: critics (pro-Metro), last minute purchasers (sustaining?) box office (also scattered seats for them thruout Hall). Rows C-N: Dala's colleagues, faculty, wives, their friends, batches for Dr Conrad Cubinis' Shellac Bureau Importers Associates, Chairman Rumples' Apogamicfungi Society, Dean Kittenhoare's Civic Club. Rows O-Z: family, city and select country friends, neighbors.
>
> *8 Loges.* 4 tickets max. each: (2 center) Yolda, Tiara (recognizable distinguished authors now dispersed thru Rows C-N Orchestra, following Draykup's latest advice); (3 Right) Imam & Ada, two violin virtuosi in separate loge (Betur's request), Warlock & Associates; (3 Left) President & Mrs Gluck Coma with 2 Distinguished Trustees, President & Dean (Betur's Institute), Little's theory teacher by herself.
>
> *Dress Circle.* Sweetsider and Garden contingents, Presha, Blume &; Metro office staff, night help etc.
>
> *First Balcony.* Students, families, Dala's and Betur's Institutes.
>
> *Second Balcony.* Students other music schools (nominal fee passes, unreserved seats valid concert night).

Boxes. Orchestra Level. (L) Dr Gluillens; (R) Misses John Alden, James Madison, Messrs Viertel Achtel, Gwyn Yare. *Dress Circle Level.* (L) Dea Falin; (R) Misses Nasaltwang, Nishgut. *First Balcony Level.* (L) Curt Budder family; (R) Jon the marine's party. *Second Balcony (L & R)*. For children who like to climb & hang over?

Estimated total 2,693, leaving two Orchestra tickets, Row E on outside aisle near the stage entrance—for Little's scrap book and for our own use during the concert in case he doesn't want us backstage during encores; the other five for emergency should Esfelts, Hiram, or the young Count forget Tearilee's or Murda-Wonda's tickets (five each to remind them) as an excuse for seeking us backstage before the concert.

[As happened.] "Why do you anticipate?" Little fretted, "I'd rather they'd listen than whisper comfortably when I play. No one will thank you for the best seat when their eyes chance on the next one. When you pay to PAPER the Hall it isn't easy for the complimented NOT to envy the music. I could do as well with one-third *that* audience." Dala sensed something sensible in Little's gripe, but tired said listlessly: "I found it hardest to remember that the odd seats in the orchestra 101, 103, 105 etc are on one side of the center aisle, and 102, 104, 106 on the other. I hope I did not send ordinal numbers to those I want to sit together." In one instance at least he was lucky, tho no omniscient observer was the wiser for it: thinking of 100 and 101 consecutively he sent 102 and 104 to his friends the poets Narodnev and Hecsteud who would be surprised and delighted to meet again after twenty years living around the corner from each other. Had he placed them in ordinal numbered seats each would have faced a malign disguise who would at once recognize him as Narodnev or Hecsteud.

32

"Going on twelve," Little said after puffing on twelve candles celebrating his eleventh birthday. "Everyone has so much to do about my Great Hall debut," he teased Verchadet—"nervous?" "Purchases," she said. He needed the largest size *boy's* formal shoes—the widest for standing thru his concert in comfort. "Not easy to come by, they might have to be ordered, along with a tuxedo?" she questioned. "I guess so," he replied not the least prest, "Nihunem's days of velveteen shorts and bare knees are gone, let Betur's *registered* or Serp's nobles wear what they will, I won't be there for ruches." She remembered how he had once sent his toy Navy blue, American red and white leather dog with Admir instead of himself to school. "Well, you had better go with Dala on one of his free days soon and at least see what you can find ready made," she said without seeming to urge him.

In the five weeks before the evening of Little's first recital in Great Hall, the trio found time to buy his concert wardrobe. Verchadet, whom Little persuaded to come along, again suffered the beginning of a tale Dala's honesty would in time relive to his own discredit. He had led them straight to a legendary turn of the century department store and genteel shoes. Bemused by his success, eyes lowered toward the floor but following the tied shoe box under

Little's arm, he nearly missed seeing the satin trim on two stylish legs of midnight blue cloth: the color almost indistinguishable from black that never browns or grays. "Sir, where are the tuxedos?" he asked without looking up. When Little and Verchadet tittered Dala raised his head to catch himself addressing a mannequin. "Laud nose: knows," Little scored. "Doesn't a nose lead," Dala said, "now if only they have your size." What blessed idiot spoke of *mental music?* The mulled note sounded: *Eskimo fashion a man and a little boy once rubbed noses*—'Nose-ick.' The store *had* the size requiring *no* alteration. Dala was content having shopped as he had planned. Had he tho? His taste wavered once his purchases were made. Did quotations pursuing themselves in his head foreshow good? "No doubt they rose. .Valentine. .wood-birds. .can no longer live by thinking"—the quotations decided. "Don't forget my tuxedo," Little said, "some day you and I will write an opera and you may need a tuxedo." "I won't forget your tuxedo and don't you forget the opera," Dala smiled, for no reason vaguely visualizing the Great Wall of China he hadn't in some years. "By the by," Little said, "while they were packing the tuxedo I read an item about Ztephiah Achsai making his debut and *for years* his career on an indifferent, what did they call it, *biscuit tortoni* or something, even *now* not worth more than two grand—how much is it, Verch?" Little was of course hoping for a contingency.

In the five weeks before the evening of Little's debut in Great Hall, Betur suffered the fears which his pupil's summer's absence from Garden obliged him to dispel as *the stretch.* The first words Betur said to Little on their reunion were, "Half-size won't carry." He ran from his studio and returned shortly to display the unwrapped three-quarter violin in its battered case. With a tenderness reserved for a newborn infant, "I borrowed for *you,*" he said. It might have been his. "You see with like boy's treble stretch change." "I know," Little said as the wise might after having simply observed. But with the three-quarter under his hands and fingers shifts and intervals soon leaped accurately. "Not too moch the first time," Imam cautioned, "might hurt 'self stretching." "Don't worry," Little said. "I say *worry*," Betur recalled a previous summer, then added slowly, "See, if you strain would hurt concert. Enough today."

The sliding doors opened an inch to Ada whispering, "Mme Ototot has just stopped by." "Must?" he said. "I am afraid so," she said and told him what Verchadet had despite herself overheard behind the drawn portieres of the waiting room. The sobs and tears of Mme Ototot could not dampen the news that the older Hemdlach sister had passed away after willing her grand piano to Garden. Her last breath had *ordered* it be delivered at once. "Now?" he asked. "A strange bequest," Ada said, "but where shall I store it meanwhile with our three pianos here?" "In the studio," he said in fidelity to the deceased, "until I can arrange with the long distance movers." Verchadet again overheard the voice which could not whisper, brighter from the end of the hall: "Imam, how's my boy doing?" Thinking of Little but speaking to Ada Betur said, "He has a head not just to hold a fiddle up." Little was too absorbed packing the three-quarter size into his own case to hear. "*Un moment*," Betur waved backward to Mme Ototot while Little caught up with him at the portiere he held back to greet Verchadet, their dispute of last spring conveniently forgotten. "Miz von Chulnt," he asked earnestly after suggesting three free lessons a week during the remaining weeks before the recital, "please see he does not overdo." "I don't control Little. But *you* must not overdo, Mr Betur. Two lessons would be more than a great kindness," she said uncompromised. "Then two," he agreed as tho she had, "beginning next week. Would happen I moss go to Garden out of season," he added to his pupil's bewilderment. In

Little's mind his fingers had been on *the stretch* effecting the higher positions—why this a—*non squitter* (he punned to himself on his Latin) to Garden?

Compassing *the stretch* was as painless as growing up in tuxedo trousers on every upbow the evening of his debut in Great Hall. Lucy Drischay, her listening limited to watching their rhythmical lift, told Verchadet that they were two inches short—mentioning it only with the future of *her* nephew in mind. And so many hellos out of the hollows of Great Hall, generous and envious saying the playing was beautiful, asked why didn't he smile. The leading newspaper critic in his lead column echoed: "A child with *nary a* smile, but a program that might give older virtuosity pause —in short, stretch of his fingers on the button and a bow arm of threatening genius to match."

Two dress rehearsals with Betur standing in front of every acoustically critical seat in empty Great Hall had calmed his fears that "an important pianissimo" might not be heard the night of Little's recital. "It will be heard more properly," he assured Little, "with full audience as soundboard." It was during this second rehearsal that Verchadet, by chance turning her head, saw Warlock slink in and out at the rear of the dark orchestra. She soon forgot him, settled comfortably with Dala among the vacant rows of seats —both callous to Imam's remote consultations with the soloist and his accompanist onstage. For the parents the two rehearsals replaced the debut with the added delight of a repeat performance. For guarding the wings from friends on the night of the concert they would be listening backstage, handing out and taking back the music so the players could proceed smoothly between bŏws. Verchadet and Dala both took it for granted the debut would excel the rehearsals. But Dala huddled with fever on the night of the recital could not convince her or Little that it was *not* the recital which distressed him.

From Little's first note on she was happy there was no

one to talk to, singing—a faint hum in her throat—the violin part Little had left with her—Dala on his folding chair hushing her under his breath as he tried to listen shivering in his overcoat. Her humming did not stop, and he could not sit. He rose to a temperature of 103 and walked to the coulisse to steady himself with a glimpse of Little's bow arm, but she motioned him back to his folding chair—not for long. He rose again to peer thru a chink in the backdrop, for all his aches a stagehand overseeing all's well. But unable to see anything of Little, his eyes focused on someone he had known and could not name in a seat he had 'papered.' She let him be, knowing he would sit down and be up again, while she gave Flutit the piano score of the concerto Betur had picked for the showpiece before intermission. She appeared almost too happy to Dala when Little's razzle-dazzle tidily eased Flutit over an accompanist's blunder. And in the second half of the program, as Dala deplored biblically in his fever, her felicities seemed to outweigh the years before Jubilee: gay, gay with the Bach solo partita, with the Weaver Imam had refused to teach leaving complete responsibility for it to Little, with the Mozart Allegro for balance. Betur was the first, after tipping a cordon of ushers, to congratulate Little in the green room. Verchadet, who had hurried ahead to avoid the immediate deluge of cranks and autograph seekers, foreboded from Betur's crisp judgment how the reviewer would read next morning: "Good, but smile sometime gives audience confidence. *Bot* good. Glad you played on'y two encores, not like who was—coming out to ask, 'you want anodder?' Don't get tired now you know what 's all about. Moss go—getting late—we speak at lesson."

"Remember my old neighbor Bach? Ah Snorckie what a concert!" For an instant Little hesitated over the sound of his childish name he had not for some time been called by. "Ah yes!" Little greeted, "Count Murda-Wonda?"—who had left his bed "to make it . . . such impeccable, unsentimental Mozart . . . Who was that gentleman? I heard what he said about smiling, and I see no reason why you should have to the pigs I sat next to!" The Countess, young Count and the others stood by abashed, so that Little made the mistake of not recognizing them. "Lucy" Esfelt (of course Little had the name wrong) said, "The Sabbath—almost any day of the week now—prevented grandma Tearilee from coming, but you know she *really can't* bear the strain of watching you play."

Aging friends from Sweetsider, Garden, where—shook Little's hand and left. A wizened, obviously musical lady in figured lilac organdy, at last approached Dala whose fever had subsided into the demands on his courtesy. "Dea Falin," she said, "Sweetsider Church. You are so kind to have thought of me. Your son was even more wonderful today. Please congratulate him and yourselves—no, I must not impose." The electrician was dimming the lights, and telling everybody to leave. "I will," Dala swallowed, insisting on leading her carefully from the green room and downstairs to the exit. "I looked for old Warlock in his usual loge," she said vaguely, "in all his evil years he has refused to meet me. He wasn't there tonight, only his disaffected associate I would never speak to. Thank you, I live nearby." By this time Little and Verchadet catching up behind them had heard what she had said about Warlock. They nodded to her as Dala held the door for her, and again before they turned the street corner for the subway home.

When leaning over one another they read the review the next morning Little paled somewhat and said nothing. Dala, who read the last sentence (the reader has read before) first, flared to the sting of the adjective "threatening" before "genius." As he read backwards he was even more infuriated by the reviewer's guileful attentions to Flutit and Betur as Little's teachers. The ring of the telephone interrupted the cheerless von Chulnts and Little went to answer it. Verchadet and Dala were so still most of the impulse coming from the receiver reached them. "Little? Betur. The reviewer," he said, "know nothing. When 's good they say *bad*, and when 's bad they use word like *'strawdinary* or *unb'lievable.* Pay no attention—we speak at lesson." "Thanks," Little hung up without turning to his parents who had more or less overheard. "I guess your friend had nothing to say about "mangement," Verchadet said brooding on Dea and Warlock. "No calls from impresarios—only a lesson on Monday 8 A.M." "I'm not listening," Little said, hurrying up three steps at a time to his room. Dala felt *nothing* inconsolably inside him. "It's easy for Imam to say 'they come, *mangement* come,' " she said—"I'm tired, I'd rather not remember." "Don't," Dala said. "Well, if he wants to he can be insulted again," Verchadet said meaning Little.

He reappeared for lunch two hours later. "Medusa Flutit," he started out, expecting his pun involving upper and lower case would make them happy, "*would* make the same mistake at the recital that Betur called him down for at the second rehearsal. 'Jellyfish,' " he glossed when neither smiled. "I forgot to tell you," he persisted, "because giving up my *dairy*" (here both eyes winked) "is no aid to the memory: the other day Jellyfish complained of a backache from sitting down so long and having to repeat his run three times to get it right. Betur said: 'Pliz, listen, don't wash! It won't matter if you play the recital half sitting down, half standing up. *Bot* keep time reg'lar. Strongk! like washwoman in Bretagne river! Where—how—you going—Luxembourg, Istanbul, Vienna, Warshawa, Bucharest, Reykjavik, Curaçao?' "

"Fugue or phugh, almost spring term, and I'm tired of abiding immortal Theory III on *Sat'days*," Little yawned slightly to Verchadet in January after his Great Hall debut by then safely historical. "I told Betur this morning—" For two months he had been riding the subway by himself to continued violin lessons on Mondays. "I told him," he finished his yawn, "that I have my high school diploma and I am ready for college." "And did you ask him why the advanced student should be retarded," Verchadet said. "Shut—" Little said too briskly, "but excuse me, Betur is not my enemy!" "Nor your friend," she said as tho unconcerned. "If you'll listen—" Little began again: "First, he missed his chance to sing at the opera, he has a *colt*—but he's not sorry about that; worse he has to save himself for 'worse engagement' tomorrow when the Musical Institute of Neufafen 'extinguishes' him with an honorary doctorate, 'I need a doctor's like waste time,' he sighed," Little laughed looking toward Verchadet. She looked the other way. " 'But why violinist need college to take time from practice,' " Little quoted Betur, " 'we renew your Institute scholarship and maybe arrange special Theory IV on Fridays when you would be the *only* pupil. I know Administration consider you too yong for Institute Upper School, bot *why* you need *humonities* course? I' sure you learned already.' " "Constant and neutral, along with of course free lessons," Verchadet said, looking noble with her least smile. "I see I can't get advice from you," Little chided.

He could always interrupt Dala in the little room opposite the largest in the brownstone. Dala disliked spreading thru space, preferred things small and compact, a small table for desk, a narrow shelf of books over it: so that when he was not writing it was a blank table, never a display of creativity or a sign such as exhorted him in a colleague's study, THINK. But this time when Little breezed in Dala was ghosting—for a banker—between ever heavier chores for his Institute at his permanently stalled salary. An oversolicitous friend, who had ghosted the banker's previous books—of a political campaign nature against government that assumes too much—had tendered Dala this extra income. And when his friend assured Dala and the banker face to face that Dala would do better by the banker's latest than 'I myself have time to do,' Dala and the banker both appeared gratified by their bit of luck. Dala, as he told Little, had been unreserved with the banker, *told him* that while von C might not agree with B's ideas—obviously a banker could not satisfy everybody—that B must tell von C, whenever in doubt, what B wanted to say—that as a writer von C must be sure he is the banker's true statement and ghost. As it turned out (the book's faithful eloquence delighted the banker so, he could never find a publisher for it) Dala's great difficulty was as Verchadet said, some ideas are just not clear: and she stood often over his editing to see that a word from the point of view of hourly pay did not bankrupt him for an age. So when Little breezed in Dala's small table *was* cluttered, tho in seeming orderly fashion, to his distaste, with the banker's original elegant typescript, three pages of handwritten editing in sequence, a neat pile of ninety-nine blue examination books to be corrected for his Institute classes, and last year's Institute Catalog he had been assigned to revise "minimally" for this year. Little always had the right to pick up anything from Dala's small table, tho Dala had no right to displace anything on Little's large desk in his room, and Little picked up the Catalog.

"What is this *Strength of Materials* course," he asked Dala, "like *Materials of Music,* Theory III?" "I guess so, but for engineers, not music students," Dala answered not looking up. "What was the question?" he asked some minutes later, "O I remember, why do you ask?" "Would *Strength of Materials* be more *viable* than *Materials of Music,* Theory IV—I know music takes in its physics, and physics does not go out of its way for music, or will it? But if as Manawyddan said, if need be sometime we have to do our work elsewhere—" Little stopped talking, looked at Dala's face, then away a distance as tho he were travelling the railroad with his fiddle. "What can I say," Dala said, "knowing little of either, merely human enough to believe that both physics and music are humane." "Probably neither is humane," Little said. "Does your Engineering Institute grant scholarships for the same sham humane reason as mine, which flatters a minor into thinking it costs nothing to be a violin major forever?" "I suppose physics might be as easy for somebody as music, I didn't know you were thinking of changing—" here Dala stopped, then added: "Would you want me to ask my President about a scholarship for you? The Institute has some fringe benefit offering free tuition to sons of professors with tenure and little means. When he called me in to discuss the new curriculum the other day he greeted me by your first name, assuming it's mine. He was enthusiastic about your debut, which he attended you know—said he *envies* you, still dreams of conducting an orchestra, having himself majored in *sound.*" "This convinces me, thank you, *no,*" Little said, "I'd just as soon follow mad Draykup's advice, *but you're a performer, Ewe hev to fader.*" "That's *just* it," Dala echoed slightly, "who is it's responsible, who is accountable—it happens *ewe hev to.*" Here Dala lingered. "Don't be too sure about that," Little said, "you may notice I have just made my choice." "But—" but taken up by Little's new slant of thought, Dala shied at *But,* looking at Little and feeling in deed very responsible. "How can you stand it—teaching there?" Little said riled, not in the least thinking why Dala looked very responsible. "Oh—it seems all right when I'm actually there, and I vary what I must say from term to term by speaking extempore—I hope—so it doesn't mostly seem to come out of my own ears. And to new students it's new, and a few old ones say it's all they've learned. Not that what I say isn't good talk—you know I'm not proud of talking—the kind of talk maybe that gets other more serious they'd say, or shall I say less fortunate professors a Chair! But it isn't silence—well, not business either." Dala looked worried: "I hope my banker is not disappointed; that I have not falsified one word he meant to say, but if one edits can one—" "Dala," Little said to distract him from that topic, "I was trying to find it the other day, was it Parahelsus who said, 'I don't shun the music of yesterday, I look backwards new to old, not old to new.' " "No, not quite that, but very near what you just said—'You run off, I am new.' "

"For want of a Warlock, whatever your frets over Betur's intrigue with Wizard or vice versa, expect *man'ger* and find none, or as *heppens* expect none and find one." Little said on another day to Dala—apropos of nothing, as neither Dala nor Verchadet had openly rankled for some time. After nearly six years of Betur it was the teacher noticeably grown old who always seemed to run off while Little with apparent loyalty pursued him, unexpectedly from time to time with a new "chance" score of dots, dashes and carets that bypassed note, line and intensity to the discretion of the performer. About which, Betur would say, "*This* I moss leave to you, we have still Beethoven concerto to do. As for former—whether in Tabriz where I wass born, or Hamadan where I stud'ed, or Mrs Betur maybe tell you in *Jawjaw*—

would be difficult to play when's hot becus summer flies change composer's score." Betur said this with a straight face turned sadly to Gesib. The aged boxer no longer stirred to see Little off at the door. "She old lady now," Imam condoled. Her brother Sib whom both father and sister missed had suffered a brain hemorrhage, was no more.

With no summers in Pamphilia and Garden, or lessons to sit thru in the waiting room stretching the time for Verchadet and Dala, soon it was eight years since Little came to Betur and played the De Bériot for him. " 'Wonderfully,' " as Guy Esor Octa, whom the von Chulnts ran into once, in his embarrassment in meeting them again, recalled Betur saying, " 'Perhaps as I shall never hear it again.' " Reminded again Verchadet was not salved on top of her recent grievance against the Administration of Betur's Institute, tho it had finally conceded to Little's matriculation in the Upper School after his solitary year of Theory IV—largely spent teaching his composer-tutor how to write for the violin. To her annoyance it was Betur who convinced the Administration to "make exception in this unusual case," after she had *submitted* (academic transcript along with annual renewal of scholarship application) and hinted how else do you expect to keep him. "But I think," Little confided to Verchadet towards the end of that year, "Betur looks forward with dread to marching with his youngest pupil in purple in June—'stupid ceremony,' he said today, and what he fears most is that I might complete my master's degree in one year. He inhaled so much smoke when I told him the Administration will let me do it, he sneezed and saluted me in German, 'Gesundheit!' He treads carefully even with his older students these days and seems resigned when he can find them a job at thirty. It isn't that he wants to teach them, but knows he has so much to teach them. Ada actually had to pin him down in his sheets and blankets when he had pneumonia yet pleaded with her to help him out of bed—he simply *had to* prepare Unzung Pharette for her recital." "She's back, then, from Istanbul?" Verchadet asked absently. "Where else would she be back from," Little answered, impatient with her, in his mind aware of Unzung's age, at least eleven years older than he—"twenty-five, if a day. She's in my Greek literature in translation class," he said, "and in her Islamic frenzy the other day asked me, 'Who is Jesus,' meaning Aegisthus. They're all that brilliant. I never answer, just mumble to myself, *Kunst der Fuge*." "Betur doesn't give up," Verchadet scoffed. "Really, Betur's wonderful," Little differed, "true he can't demonstrate in pitch anymore, but when he plays out of tune, '*sory that wass wrongk*,' he says, as if the wrong note had been wrung from him. A little paunchy, but when he dresses up in white tie still Imam, tho he hates public occasions and is for the most part tied in by the sash of his smoking jacket." Observing Verchadet Little wasn't quite sure whether she was the least bit jealous or sad.

Meanwhile the brownstone was aging for want of repairs. The three were lucky to be out for a walk together one spring day when a large chunk of ceiling plaster rosette molding above Little's bed unexpectedly came down. Overriding his objections Dala and Verchadet *badgered* him, as he protested, into putting up with Dala's small room while they risked the larger. The next day Verchadet's left eye throbbed and reddened. "What causes it?" Dala worried. "O nothing much, the plaster dust maybe." But the following day recalling the pain a sty gave her as a little girl she took one look at the eye in the mirror and fainted—"like a classical Chinese actor in transfixed anguish, a bird settling spirally," Dala said later. He was on hand shaving, and cried out for Little as he helped her fall without hurt. He chafed her hands on the wood floor and whimpered, but Little ran and filled a glass with cold water, which he dashed into her face. "What is all this water for?" she moaned coming to, and feeling chilled she rebuffed him, "what—are you crazy?"

"Tse-tse-tse-tse," Dala chirped, for the third time in his life *having seen* (he said) *behind the Great Wall of China*, "we've had enough brownstone." Then managerially: "its basement and three stories are going up for sale, and we move to a brand new apartment where you can have less furniture all on one level. And since we won't be mortgagees sharing in equity with magnates of high finance, it's a long time we've had a vacation, we'll travel on their down payment to *us*. O di mi, on second thought," Dala spoke shyly to himself, "interest cannot be avoided on real estate transfers, but we will make the new owners happy by accepting the legal least."

When Little told Betur that the von C's had moved and were going abroad, he wished him well and impressed him "not to forget the *same* to your parents: also especially tell them it would be good you give another concert in Great Hall in February of next year. The last I think was good for you, bot if you don't come back audience forget."

Miraculously Dala's lawyer sold the brownstone faster than they expected. Verchadet, before sailing, neatly arranged their four room apartment for their return. She gave the pussy willow stems and other plants to Miss Madison who had come from the country to see them off. And before closing the door for the summer on all their possessions she secured a towel rack over the kitchen sink by *gluing* the screws into the wall lath, that is after forbidding Dala's and Little's assistance, otherwise they wouldn't have made the gangplank in time. They sailed on a small ship, an overhauled freighter—the decks crowded with students conferring, studying, lectured to, so the von Chulnts had to step over their heads or laps to get to bow or stern—seasick 9 days out of 10 in their own private cabin—to Europe.

34

"What's that he's sweeping the garden with?" Little asked. "That's a besom," Dala said. Thanks to the fine graces of Gwyn Yare, James Madison's friend, tho it would never have occurred to the von Chulnts to ask him, they had been invited to an ancient type of Betur's Garden in Cornwall. The girls and boys of Cornwall School, whose old gardener tidied a green almost blue grass, played consorts of viols. In kind Little gratified them and their master with a solo concert of bōwings and fingerings never short of Betur's method. Cornish, the children marveled and courteously served their guests three recipes of potatoes and two of tomatoes every meal of the day. The von Chulnts ate and in return praised the great stones of the medieval refectory. They stayed a week, then started their travels.

"In Rome you don't have to as the Romans and nowhere else eyether," Little said, "it sickens me when you flatter foreigners who won't speak their own language." In Oxford, a bookseller bemused by Little's fiddle case brought out a facsimile of Bach's manuscript of the partitas for him. He glanced and looked off, purchased *a tract on the oriels* instead. They then sent, *air mail*, identical souvenir postcards to their families, two to each, addressing the one of Baliol to the young, and the interior of Baliol to Murda-Wonda and Tearilee—all bearing the same greeting: *Here we are—well! Hope you are. Love.* This taken care of, they boarded the train for London without conscience, riding privately in a second class compartment. "I say," Little sounded British taunting Dala, "this arrangement disposes of your theories of *clahsses.*" "But if the national railroad were busy enough to fill the two seats occupied by your fiddle case—" Dala queried, implying in his tone—*would you feel so uppish.* Little ignored him, and now wrote on the back of his postcard of Brasenose (which Verchadet always instilling courtesy had distantly suggested he might mail from London to Betur): *Worked well in Cornwall. On to London. Kindest regards.*

In London it happened (without thinking of Great Hall ahead) they bought Little an expensive Tourte bow (*never mind the Bach one,* Little said to Dala absorbed in it, *that's vanity*) and (as they still felt the affluence of their vacation) a not at all expensive fiddle with an original belly prized for its maker—its eighteenth-century back forever broken to splinters since matched by a less esteemed early nineteenth-century violin maker, a wine merchant. "Try it," Verchadet urged, liking the yellow in its amber narrow waist. "Pretty comfortable," Little agreed as he chinned it, "but has to be played in." "Let's buy it, Little," Dala said, "since it happens this way."

They took the Channel boat and shuttle train to Paris, where on the first kiosk they saw they tried to read an old rainworn poster the print of which they could not agree about—each reading differently:

(Little)	Athé	QUATUOR
(Dala)	Ah-The	QUATUOR
(Verchadet)	ah the	QUATUOR

All agreed as to QUATUOR.

Whether in Bath or Florence, Verchadet would not condescend to the continental tour. Her test of great art was that she should not be dragged to it. It would justify itself drawing her glance, as she looked while she walked at a distance. One glimpse into the interior of a landmark was enough to keep her out. Also not sightseers Dala and Little were still afraid they might if they hurried on miss something. She waited too often impatiently for them as appearing longer for their shyness they came out from a landmark, fortifying themselves to praise a chased tendril on a tomb or the rib of a vault. Little would then *forestall the situation* "Well, Mrs Shriek—" enticing her sometimes to smile at Dala and say, "Well, Mr Weak—"

Nearly three months of travelling. After crisscrossing the Alps from Italy to Switzerland, again somehow in Italy in Switzerland and on to France, they would be recognized warmly by other travellers they *must have* met before overnight at some stop quite nameless now, tho the others knew them at once: the lean gentleman, the slight well-dressed but not showy lady, their growing son with a fiddle case, whom they greeted by his first name while the compact family longed for home. They had privately been sensing it all thru their journey in their dread of seasickness on the ship that awaited them. Again inevitably they faced the chaos of sea. Very sick indeed, the three bumbled in their cabins past the point of no return impeding and pursuing their memories at once West and East.

After the pavement of their city home stopped rolling under them, Verchadet remembered for Dala one midnight the eight wonders that had made their European vacation worthwhile:

> the besom and gaiters of the old gardener in Cornwall
>
> the porter who—having placed their luggage on the train to be delayed for two hours at Victoria Station stood by them until Dala failing to persuade him to seek elsewhere and aching for the man's loss of livelihood, having only a crown and six shillings in English money to give him asked,

"is that all right?"—shook all their hands and said, "lovely"

the French customs inspector first unduly detaining them for his tip until they understood the custom, then rushing and hurtling their luggage over ten rails, to lift each of them safely off the ground, luggage after, on to their train that had begun to pull out

from the train window near Nantes an ancient woman powerfully washing her laundry on the river stones in high tide

a publishing house still firm since the last war over the edge of a bomb crater seen at the end of a long English day

a rainstorm in Keswick on just getting off the bus from Grasmere

The North Sea come upon a bleak streak in Edinburgh—Portobello (?)—Firth of Forth—

Little's black feet, on returning to their hotel after walking several days out of the rain the whole length of the arcade called the rue de Rivoli

He had not shined his shoes once in Europe. Verchadet did not urge, resigned, he might think of doing it himself. As to *life* she felt useful people should not harass misuses. "Why are your feet so black at the end of a day?" she finally asked one evening as merely a type of question. "I don't know. I've been bathing." "Is the dye coming off your socks?" He was in the shower and did not hear her as she felt the socks thru the holes and no leather. He had worn out his concert shoes.

35

Snow was a foot high when they came out of the subway at Great Hall. Fortunately for the trousers of his first swallowtail accenting his return Little wore boots over his new concert shoes. *One cannot chase a need,* Verchadet thought herself saying. She might at this instant be thinking instead of Dala—these words not voluntarily her thought. But how extricate her legs in their boots sunk in two holes in the snow: Little way ahead hurdling pure heaps in the flaky downfall, Dala floundering behind him, not too sprightly while assuming her sense of things would lead her into the holes he sank for her in the heaps. He returned to help her trudge, making new tracks for himself.

At the stage door Little obtusely saw Betur stooping out of a taxi—in the icy flurry emptying a coat pocket of its bulge of coins to the sheltered cabby. Little did not feel like talking, but Betur caught up with him, squeezing thru to the other side of the door as it shut. "Frank," the unassuming teacher said to the guard in the drafts, "see no one disturb Mr von Chulnt till after encores, and please tell Brown to keep the crowd from the Green Room so I can hurry upstairs 'head of ev'body and go early." In asking these favors his good manners seemed to hide the exposed stance of the guard, as turning his head somewhat aside Betur thrust his customary excessive tip into the man's coat handkerchief pocket. Little's glance observed his teacher's, then his back, heavier these last few years, aching perhaps girdled under the styled tuxedo. He had heard him call him mister. Imam was—and well *was,* after eight years, *Imam,* Laila's Majnun—"Romeo" to Frank and stagehands and ushers. He was their intimate who had brought so many prodigies they could listen to for free, judge—and whose futures they weighed as said "in the balance": *young von Chulnt is great or Betur would not let him come back in two years.* In the Green Room Betur took the fiddle—anachronous belly and back—from Little's hands to examine it again and then leave him on his own. "Not bad, you know, for mongrel—and just as well: belly nicer than back." He took a last look out of habit at the bouts. If their seams had opened he could do nothing, and if he could—"it's always safest to play the fiddle one worked on." He looked around: "Careful you don't touch all this velvet furniture—they never dust here. What you might say integration make fingers slip. Good luck, see later."

Verchadet and Dala sat in about the middle of the orchestra. This time they meant to watch and enjoy Little play. Waiting for the hall to fill they looked up into the cupola, the golden glows of the lantern above it making its white paint marble. Below—the orchestra was almost empty. They did not wish to make themselves conspicuous by craning their necks to count heads in the climbing horseshoes. Draykup released from the madhouse and parted from them by the seas was too far to recommend again, "PAPER!" This time Little insisted, "Papering is not a fair test of an audience." His parents' thoughts ranged singly parallel. Should they have papered? Whether by papering and newspaper publicity artists find their valid audiences sooner than later? "I don't suppose many 'll appear at the other concerts tonight either," Verchadet said. She had skimmed advertisements, in Little's recital program, of several concerts elsewhere in the city that evening. "Regrets?"

"No, except why did we pick February, it's so cold," she answered him. "Still some days to wait for Valentine to give a beggar a cloak," he said indifferently himself as he touched her hand. She predicted silently their families would stay home: wasn't it true, *their* homes were their deepest wish. Not to blame them: simpler. A few rovers straggled in from the storm. Someone behind joshed about the snow stealing his stalled car. It was nearly nine o'clock when the stage lights arced and Little followed by Flutit walked out and bŏwed, both taking in how few were there. Presumably they had friends dignified only by papering. They had known these friends as not stingy with self-gratifications called "gracious." Little nodded to Flutit with a look that might say *don't coax your wares,* and played. *Not tomorrow* flitted past Verchadet's ears. *For the snow—a mysterious compliment to nature, like,* and Dala omitted the "like" in his mind—*the snow.* "Are you listening?" Verchadet urged. Dala pretending his eyelashes had misted his lenses wiped them—"Yes."

During intermission most of the small scattering of audience remained seated, advised it would be brief. The few who rose worried, two's or three's, how they would get home. Dala had got up to stretch. He saw an old man smiling, to him perhaps, shadowed by the columns supporting the loges. He was reminded of his father. Who was he? *In this storm?* he wanted to ask, but his personal remembrance, if he did, might wrong the momentary closeness he felt for a stranger. The impulse to speak passed both when someone venturesome for a glimpse of the sidewalk fronting Great Hall was hurled back by slamming doors and covered in white coils of blizzard, so that Dala without his far eyeglasses could not make out whether it was man or woman.

Soon the long concert and encores were over, Little the happiest for it—it had gone well. The night guard rushed to the stage to ask everyone to use the side exits on leaving, as the front doors were now shut. Few followed Betur to the Green Room—autograph buffs who did not lag. Betur's *good night* at the door after a hushed *good* to Little perhaps beggared intimacy when he also addressed Verchadet and Dala, "unfortunate the storm—there should've been more to hear him." Past Great Hall's alley they came out on stalled cars at all angles. Exactly when had motors refused to rev, brakes to screech, horns to stop blowing, and churned into—Dala gaped at what had been an avenue—a conclave of rear ends to bumpers, hoods to door handles, windshield wipers poised, all transmuted of the snow's hooded societies. Bent into the updraft of the subway the von Chulnts, the three together now, felt the highest tread of the entrance stairs thru snow above their boots.

The lower steps felt more certain as they tamped the snow down them. As happens in blizzards on the platform a pleasant if sparse party (they might have met these four people before somewhere?) informed them with smiles (that recognized them?) they had just missed a train. The few trains not stalled in the air were running only underground between this station and "theirs," the next in about an hour. They waited two and reached their stop at two in the morning, when after saying good night the party left them. Quietly the confetti of snow hurled down on a beaten way of friendship *Shake-spere* reminded Dala as they trudged: what responsible neighbors—asleep now (?) had cleared this path one foot wide and one foot deep for them between walls of snow taller than Verchadet? "This is great!" Little said, the gloved palm of an affectionate hand hovering above her head, as tho fearful of his son's impetus Dala cringed for her. Little's hand stopped with patting the snow of her wool hat. "This goodly frame the earth" Dala's trudging metered out for him, *the gracioso of it*—his mind flew before him as usual—*came with the effort.* It took another half hour. "A congregation of vapours," they opened their apartment house door with their own key—the night doorman nowhere around—and brushed off in the foyer.

Coats hung up and boots aligned in the bathroom, they changed into dry stockings while Dala recalled the summer evening of the hurricane when he returned from work with his shoes in his hands. "You wouldn't remember, Little"—who said (he was a year old then) "I do." To appease hunger, Verchadet faster than everybody asked Little—"and, tell me, do you want coffee?" "I have never tasted of it yet," he said. "Warm milk, then?" "Why ask? I recall tea." From their twelfth story view of the city's harbor indistinguishable from the snow they reported the blizzard to her in the kitchen. Plentiful, even courteous, as Dala now thought of it, the snow whirled its merry-go-round of profusions. "I could watch it all night," Little said. "I'd like a fire behind a fire screen," Verchadet said. "Do you really intend an all night session?" Dala asked yawning thru his nostrils. "Aren't you tired, Little? tho I wonder what the reviewers said, if there'll be any papers today—it is today."

They were gazing listlessly when the intercom startled them. "It's that smart night doorman who's back," Little said. "Mr Curt Budder," the voice announced. "Are you sure?" Dala questioned. "Saw your lights on, has two newspapers for you," and with less aplomb, "I hope I haven't—disturbed—" "No, no," Dala said, "please send him up," now aware of the name of Little's boyhood friend. "Wait, I think he's gone off," the doorman said. "Sorry, I thought he'd keep the papers for you until morning," another voice said not too near the phone, "are you sure it's all right to say hello, I can't stay." "Sure, please do," Dala persuaded him. He showed up at their door more wiry than Little, snow on matted brown hair, eyes out of an afternoon sky brilliant blue—matched against a short sailor's coat, navy corduroys, and ankle height hobnailed o-live shoes, Little punned inwardly. "Felicitations," his friend said, perhaps sounding for him a bit literary. "Come in, come in," Dala repeated. "If only to warm up," Verchadet said. "I trust that's a dry wool shirt under your elegant costume," she spoke moved by gaiety, hopefully not like a mother. "No, I like snow," he said having stopped at the threshold. "They're wet," he added for her care looking down at his shoes, "but boots in this blizzard would be wetter." He had been to the concert, he explained, and not to bother Little in the Green Room decided to walk the two subway stops to the Square and pick up the papers, since there would probably be no deliveries for days. "One review's very good, and the other—well I don't agree," he said quietly. "I expected I'd meet your train at the Square, but just missed it." "Won't you come in tho," Little asked. "No, my family came to your concert with me and must be worried where I am by now." (Were the four they met in the subway *his family*, the three thought as one—too shy to ask, never to be certain.) Little walked him back to the elevator. "We didn't urge anyone to come to this concert," he said, frankly not sorry before the one proof of his test of not papering. "Why should you have," Curt said. "It was fine, that's the difference." "Thank you," Little said, "drop by again," wondering when there'd be time. "Sure would," but he'd be with the merchant marine for a year, ultimately to get to the north woods for a while, he hurried to tell Little holding the elevator door: "I like snow, and I don't suppose this kind of weather's good for warming your fingers—see you!"

No one sifted the gist or gruel—she'd think when newspapers clogged her throat—faster than Verchadet. When Little returned from saying good-bye to Curt he saw that she had read the reviews. For Dala's ascetic back turned to the door, forehead close to window pane, eyes looking but not seeing, meant he did not want them to see his face suffering their dismay—did not want *a* thing—or if his hurt was not that serious after he excoriated it, a reserved personal note like: "the pother over birthpangs of writing, pupa sealing images at the threshold of stupefied larval thoughts—confident moths for the bonfire." "What is?" Little asked. She did not answer giving him the newspapers. "What purfles?" Little asked again, nodding toward Dala. "A friend could have done better," she said, "please, I'd like quiet." "Another seizure of Betur?" Little champed his teeth and read for himself. Of the two newspapers which fed the city's musical taste at large and—as an ample classical critic versed with an opposite slant—'not of an age,' the older less circulated paper whose senior critic's quirk or temerity was to legislate 'for all time' did not affect the violinist's *present* future. Teased by a seepage of unanimous condolement for pure mature musicality entertaining empty halls in the blizzard, Little hurried thru reviews of other concerts before absorbing his own. None of these cordial reviews mentioned competence, but in Little's case neither of his critics so much as referred to a snow. As Little understood it, the review Curt thought "very good" perhaps missed a point in unstinted praise: "excellence thru grace of means . . the program might have taxed his only comparable elder over three times his age." That won't touch anybody one bit, Little thought very maturely, Oldman is hinting at his friend Ztephiah, who if he is curious will care less than his manager Endor.

As for the newspaper with the greater circulation it stung. Perhaps Little expected that its leading critic, who knew good playing from bad, so cavalier with the precise virtuosity of his nonage two years ago—and Little himself knew he had improved—would say, if only to show up less bald than Oldman, that the former child now has a mind of his own, and as for smiling the reviewer once gave him a clean slate for the future. Little could imagine some such remark his slightly stooped violinist's shoulders might shrug off if he had to make amends in the style of the reviewer. He was more than a bit jarred that the lead column was not about his recital. Timely as the weather the critic had written an informal piece: (informed by the grapevine) / At home in the blizzard / while hardy patricians played / to not too warm but an intimate few. / An unknown name—A.Gnith—reviewed Little—inconspicuously near the inside margin of the page. The minor notice, after listing the program, expressed "a question of psychology" in one sentence: "What motivated parents to expose a growing talent yet to be spared an empty hall, of all halls Great Hall whose warm audiences time out of mind comfort the great performers?" "Psych'n lice thyself," Little reverted to his tenderer years. *Psychology*, the one word Verchadet had fought before he was born and that brought cat's bristles to Dala's spine. His shock over, Little again felt for their duo of silence. "A. Gnith—Dala," he whispered tentatively.

Dala turned still not seeing, riddling backward as in a mirror, "a thing," he said, "the dishonesty. He should know us, I could *kill* him."

"*Gentle* Dala," Little said with superior irony as he squared to the height of Manawyddan in *The Mabinogion*. Verchadet forced a smile: "he," meaning Dala, "should go in for vaudeville—the legitimate stage. No, Mr Gnith need not know us, we'll see to it you avoid him, Mabinog von Chulnt." They would too. Who else, after his two asinine assertions of one irate subject, *I* could kill, *he* should know —tse-tse . . no honor to Sextus Empiricus? no ballet for Verchadet and Little? His thought bŏwed in a minuet going right into his act of old Leopold. "Raupenfliege so wie verbum, ohne Wetter, und so hin, und so weiter, Amadeus Allezeit!"

Nerves would not let him clown that night. To feel—want to, yet false? He stood at the window and with a finger melted its crystals recalled as it were to his eyes.

> He had dozed then for an instant—after asking to hear The Fantasia!—to be startled beside himself — yet heard—Verchadet played each note so

evenly no rubato of Neitsnebur rippling at the moon could steal from her

Rocking in Dala's rocker so comfortable, outgrowing his undershirt hitching above his navel—unlike Athens poking his bōw at it Dala thought 'There had been little, and *there is Little*' playing an 'early' tape of his own and saying, 'As to listening to yourself something there not now but something now not there'

The blizzard whirled faster and thicker woods of white leaves.

Dr Gluillens or maybe his banker saying, death and (it) taxes; eleemosynary, distracted sometimes to the arts. Not charity, Dala believed he said—*Infernal revenue*

'I appreciate,' she (James Madison) said carefully with a sibilant *c* instead of her breath of a laugh, 'your telling me. Do you indeed hurt? You always say it as if it doesn't.' To which Verchadet winked with accomplishment and added: 'The illness is human, but there aren't very many people we ought to be disturbed by—being really never sensitive when we're *around* others, that's what he's trying to say.' 'That seems honest enough to me,' James Madison agreed.

Gathering crystals at the sash

Joined in the storm James, Gwyn, Dea—welshing to Welsh Llywarch Hen, Welshing Aneirin:

pye, you bed whom?
bed whom and whom. gone i' me. me ag´ōn.

air panicked   dire our aneirin
new night his score has   not a gododin.

Each now stood at a window—leaving two white and black, —unaffected window: but even as they stood at the other three, instead of black of the unlooked thru two iced deep blue. The blizzard stopped almost instantly after. "Dawn," Little said at his window, "and I'm not sleepy. There's a thin chalk dust out there blowing but not falling." Not very long the dawn reflected brilliantly in their west windows. "Today it will be lovely," Verchadet said, "no prima donna beats nature," and walking away from her window, "breakfast."

There was Dala's little table Little called *tabula rasa* at the window nearer the warmer wall, where his legs out of their way they breakfasted. "No path for the cow" (meaning milk) "today," Verchadet said, "since you stayed up all night, Little, coffee?" "It would be disgracious to refuse gifts," he said. She set it down for him. He took one wry sip. "Needs sugar," he said. "Not coffee," Verchadet said. He took another, and pushed the cup in its saucer a bit away from him, "Hot enough." "The omniscient observer," Dala said continuing for them out of another day, "reads from the first word to the last with great care for the spaces between them so they are unframed by enthusiasts or detractors. I read now—present tense—the moon is made out of magma." Little responded with a pizzicato in the air,

"Ex-plic-it,"

then with the ball of a finger of the same hand vibratoed on the wood of the table (for *good luck* Verchadet and Dala thought together) as on his instrument.

1950—July 28, 1969

It was

It was

IT WAS fine weather in mid-August when I awoke anxious to go on writing the story that in the dark hours did not let me rest.

I had promised my wife not to stay up and strain my eyes, and had failed her. So I was happy to be up before she was, to tell her that I was not tired. The birds had anticipated me with their song: early birds—a dark comedian used to say—catching worms. As I listened before the mesh of window screen which a few hours before in the dark had let through only the hot wave of midsummer, a drop in the temperature brought in a breeze as from some basin filling with torrents of air.

We lived then opposite the park and not far from the zoo. The river that flowed from up the country, and passed the side of our house, fell in a cascade we saw from our windows. This morning the falls came down heavy with the rain of the day before, and brimmed to the top of the stones forming the river banks under the viaduct, which was the crossing in our street. I could hear the roar of the lions hungry for their morning meal.

Thanks to the park commissioner who had recently landscaped the grounds of the zoo, the animals wandered or rested on imitations of their natural terrain, attracting thousands of visitors who before this novelty had lost interest in seeing them in cages. The lions ranged apparently free on earthworks, meant to be African plains, though surrounded by abrupt ditches they could not cross—and our apartment was thus favored by the natural noises of Africa. It was not always we heard them a quarter of a mile away, but this morning the wind carried every roar.

The park across the street, the early sun and the morning shade thrown between tall old trees, tempted me to go downstairs before breakfast. The visitors and picnickers would soon be coming up our street in droves. We did not like to look down on them from our windows when we could not get away on Sunday afternoons. The park was then too crowded for us to walk in. But if we managed to get out of our apartment by eight in the morning we could still have it to ourselves for about two hours before noon. Part of it near us was woods and few people troubled to enter it.

I wanted as I said to write, but not on paper. I hardly ever found the park helpful to writing on paper, even in fall and winter when no one was there, especially if I were writing prose. This time it was the sentence opening the last part of a story I had worked on for months: a sentence as is often worked off paper first. The pace of narrative and interest in character do not readily help the writer's hand to set down a sentence of that order. For though characters must take things in their own stride—somewhere in his story the writer cannot hold back this sentence that judges them. He wants it unobtrusive to his pace and the characters that caused him to write. The difficulty is to judge without seeming to be there, with a finality in the words that will make them casual and part of the story itself, except perhaps to another age.

The sentence kept me up all night. As is usual with me I would not go on with the rest of the story and come back to the difficult sentence later. With others it may be different—but when I am that far in a work the story must exist in each word or I cannot go on. The halt seems likely to be permanent in the worst of the grind—when the words of an insoluble sentence written down, written over, crossed out, add up to indecisions making situations and characters empty. I feel I have not the sense in which, along with the story, I must live—and seem merely to glance at a watch

This story was a story of our time. And a writer's attempts not to fathom his time amount but to sounding his mind in it. I did not want to break up my form by pointing to well-known place names and dates in the forty years that I had lived—events familiar to most of us, to some more than myself. I wanted our time to be the story, but like the thought of a place passed by once and recalled altogether: seen again as through a stereoscope blending views a little way apart into a solid—defying touch. I was saying something that had had a sequence, like the knowledge of taking a breath, and hiding it, because one breathes without pointing to it before and after. Having tortured myself most of the night to get down just that in one sentence of my story, I hoped that the freedom of the green, the sun and the air of the park would make the task easier.

My wife was still asleep. She was used to making breakfast for us. I disliked to deprive her of the seclusion she found in it, since it made her happy and—she would assure me—did not tire her for the rest of the day. This morning I decided to risk her displeasure and make it for her so that we could both go downstairs early enough for me to get back to my story.

By the time I had put up the coffee she was about and taking over the job to herself without a word, doing it faster than I in my hurry. She did not ask me how late I had gone to bed, which pleased me.

Still anxious to get back to my story, I became busy straightening out things about the house. Somehow we could never leave it with the necessary disarrangements of the night unsettled, even if we did not intend to return to it for days. For always when we returned—in this my wife shared my habit—we liked to find it undisturbed so that our attention would not be distracted from whatever occupied us at the time.

I dusted the bookshelves and the desk of unfinished maple, and a small table of the same wood over which hung a large landscape painted by our close friend in another city: he was working on a "Defense" job—had made our walls cheerful when he had the time—and if he were coming to see us that Sunday I would gladly have put off the sentence still on my mind. I watered the plants, then covered the couch with the white cotton print hand-blocked in blue with early American scenes of a naval battle, Indians, date palms, mules and elephants. Why elephants happened to be drawn into scenes on authority depicting the history of St. Augustine, Florida, I have never been able to answer with the knowledge of history I have. Though I was still thinking of my story, I regretted as always that writing too often leaves little time for the pleasure of looking up answers to the unfamiliar. I found myself saying the sentence aloud.

—You were good to me.

A *Keystone Comedy*

FENIX sniffed and rubbed his nostrils with the back of his thumb. Thru a tiny sieve he poured a measured quantity of white powder into a small cardboard box marked 1 oz. There were stacks of these boxes on the kitchen table. The process of filling them had been going on for hours.

His sister used a large sieve to filter sugar from two ten pound sacks which evidently had spoiled the neatness of the kitchen. "Watch out now, Helen, you're spilling a little," Fenix said. "That sugar is worth fifty cents an ounce."

"I'm not spilling it," Helen said. She looked around at her sister-in-law Ann, bent over the sink, with her back towards the family, whose old father, Peter Schreck, dozed where he sat near the steam pipe. Billy, his younger son, had his heels on the middle of the kitchen floor and the front legs of his chair lifted and rocking.

Fenix went on as if he had not heard her. "I don't know what's wrong with your generation. Why do you, such a nice girl, run away from Billy? When I met your sister Ann, Billy, neither of us ran. The only running I did was over to my mother's to tell her that at the age of forty she didn't have to put me to sleep anymore. Ask Ann if she's sorry she met me." He sniffed again and rubbed his nostrils with his thumb.

"I wouldn't breathe too much of that stuff. It isn't sugar," Billy said.

"But it dissolves better," said Charles. "If I knew as much chemistry as you, Billy, I'd find something more soluble than sugar."

"That's not my business," said Billy. "I've told you before that stuff is extracted from a plant."

"You don't have to tell me. Who's the expert? I know it's a plant. I tell you addicts don't care what it is so long as it dissolves."

"This plant happens to grow in China," Billy said.

"If I were a chemist, I'd extract a drug from Chinese celery. Ann," Fenix said, "how would you like a whole garden of the stuff! Wasn't marihuana found in a Brooklyn lot? Gee, it looked pretty!"

She did not answer.

Billy smiled and showed a little impatience. He started to whistle from Mozart's "Eine Kleine Nachtmusik." Soon he looked very indifferent as if his whistle were not for any one around him.

His mind lulled, his brother-in-law's name evoked the bird that went up into flames every five hundred years to appear restored from its ashes.

Now his brother-in-law was silent, Billy considered his face as he moved about—almost sensing in the ravages of its old eczema traces of the bird consuming himself.

The alarm clock began ringing by accident and was shut off. "What is it?" asked Peter Schreck, his eyes half open.

Billy touched him on the shoulder. "Why don't you go to sleep, Papa, instead of roosting all night like the bird in the sole Arabian tree out of Shakespeare?" It was no use speaking to Ann. Like the legendary turtle-dove, also out of Shakespeare, she was probably set on finding her right in the phoenix' sight.

The kitchen of Mr. Charles and Mrs. Ann Fenix seemed policed by its dark window and by the light from the burnished drain-pipe under the sink which Ann had angrily finished scouring. She looked so tired the sink might have been a holy font over which she performed a service to show off the broken-hearted pallor of her face. For a moment Billy felt too sorry for her to sympathize.

"You're smelling the stuff so often," she complained, "you'll soon be taking it like your customers."

"Quiet, please," Fenix said lightly.

"Quiet yourself!" Ann said. "Mrs. Sapphire keeps asking me, Mrs. Fenix what does your husband do with all the sugar he buys from us? If Bobby weren't around I wouldn't know what to say. He told her you're in the restaurant business."

"Pigeon," Fenix said to his wife, "isn't our four year old wonderful! At nineteen he'll be the champion prizefighter and knock out every girl with his eyes! I swear he'll be the Einstein of his day!"

He left his work, tiptoed to the bedroom where Bobby slept, and came back beaming, "You should see my heir! He's just swell!—As for that grocer's lady, Mrs. Sapphire, tell her instead of being so crudely suggestive as to my business to pay more attention to her washed out husband. Do you have to act down to her?"

"I'm not acting! It's impossible to keep a straight face. I can't do it anymore. I won't! even if I have to stay in the house for the next—"

"How many months?" Fenix suggested. "Stop it! Do you think you're a holy personage confining yourself that way? Aw, go to sleep. I'll get there in an hour."

"You needn't bother, Bobby'll be up. It's almost time for his breakfast."

"Well, between meals," said Fenix.

"Please talk less," she said. "Do I have to worry about my father sleeping in a chair to keep a fool like you company? The kid's probably breathing your stuff in his sleep. Tell me, what's to prevent the police from jugging us?"

Charles laughed. "Billy, professor, won't you explain to your sister that dope ain't contagious? After living forty years—I never met such ignorance."

She all but wept forcing herself to keep quiet.

"Dope," said Billy feeling stupid, "ruined China, a great empire."

"So! And what happened? They had a revolution. If I had as much dope as they've had in China! Please, Ann, look at the facts! My brother an elegant clown at the game sells dope pure and does not get into trouble. It takes a fool like me to tell him that you can mix it with eighty percent sugar, and pass it off for pure. His clients like it just the same. They're doped less without knowing it, as under the government cure. We sell sugar for almost as much as dope. And I'm a man among men—in my own business! Suppose the cops do come and ask, 'Whadda ya got?' I say, Sugar! What's wrong with that!"

But are you sure Mitchell is safe on to-night's errand?" asked Ann still trying to persuade her husband that his racket was involving the family.

"The Mayor? Why, of course, he is, pigeon."

Peter Schreck heard his older son's name in his broken sleep and remembered an unfortunate relative after whom this son was named: "I can see him as tho it were now. Poor boy, his feet sticking up, his head down, nine feet deep in the well, and his mother scolding him as if he were still alive. 'I told you not to play in the well!' Mitchell takes after him. A great sense of enterprise, no responsibility, finds pictures in running strictures, bankrupt, too proud to meet his creditors, he makes me his creditor. Well, at seventy I suppose I'm too old to be delivering sugar as a substitute for snapping pictures like Mitchell."

"Father," Ann pleaded.

"It's alright, Ann, we're still alive. Did you finally get Bobby to bed?" said the old man.

"Hours ago, papa."

"Good," he said, "I take after my grandson. Now please wake me when he wakes! Good night, all."

"That's a man to be honored," Charles said after the old man left, "and who honors him? Nobody!"

"You ought to be going, Helen," Ann said. "Your mother'll worry." Helen who had been helping Charles all night out of family loyalty felt free.

"Sure, Helen," said Charles. "You're not afraid to go alone?"

"I'll go with her," Billy said.

Charles bowed like a gallant to his young brother-in-law and said, "Mr. Bach goes to town!"

"Have you heard that, too?" Billy asked.

The Fenixes lived in a neighborhood of the Bronx where a goat was still to be seen sometimes. The apartment house Helen and Billy came out of stood on a hill a half mile from the East River where motor launches some hours later would take their owners from Westchester to offices overlooking New York Bay. The youngsters headed west for the subway which was on an avenue flanked by solid ranges of tenements. Midway, before they crossed the railway trestle at the bottom of the hill, the occasional deep hollows were not sites of new buildings coming up, but kitchen gardens of farmers from abroad growing their own lettuce. Basement doors below the sidewalk led to these sunken plots. Passers-by on the asphalt above could stop and look down, but could not walk there uninvited, unless they cared to risk a drop of twelve feet or more and a chalked warning—"Beware—The Dog."

Now an early riser of a goat lurched from behind a slatboard fence and followed them.

"These people know how to live," said Billy.

The milkman passed, assuring Helen it was dawn. "Yes, I see they have a car."

"I don't mean that," Billy said.

"I know," Helen said, "but they have that too."

"Hm," said Billy. "On the other hand, why do I live with lunatics?"

"The family?" she ventured, "I guess you like it."

"Well, let's not speak of the family," Billy said.

"Of course, I do wish Charles could find some other kind of work," Helen said.

"That's not the worst of it," he said.

"I must admit he talks a lot, too much," she said, "but he likes you, you know. Why don't you interrupt him sometime and talk about music instead of just whistling it?"

"Music?" Billy said.

As the two walked to the subway they did not know they were the subject of mutterings between two men on their knees, peering over the edge of the roof of Fenix's house. The men grumbled to each other as follows:

"Sure those two ain't bulls?"

"Nah! Wind's from the west, gonna be fair."

"You don't say!"

"Sure! Wut in hell would they be walkin' the udder way for?"

"Guess they're scared of ya."

"*You* don't say!"

"Well, I guess they ain't."

These two had rung Charles' door-bell shortly after Helen and Billy had gone out. They had come up thru the vendor's entrance of the big apartment house to avoid meeting anyone coming out of the more respectable entrance. Charles was bolting a piece of coffee cake and listening to an early morning broadcast of setting-up exercises accompanied by the tune of the Highland fling, before going to sleep for the day.

Ann, in bed but not sleepy, heard the bell and appeared at the uncurtained French doors of the bedroom.

"The wife?" asked one of the men looking at her from a corner of his eye.

Fenix waved his thumb backwards. She disappeared from the doors as suddenly as the curtains when she thought they needed washing.

"What's up, boys?" Fenix asked, business-like.

"Ya mean ya don't know!" said the other man.

"How was the delivery?" Fenix asked, apparently not disturbed. He lit a cigarette.

"There wasn't no delivery," said the first man.

"There sure wasn't," said the second.

"What!" Fenix said. "You mean my brother-in-law didn't show up? Why, he was sent out hours ago."

"No use gettin' panicky," said one of the men.

"Nah, not yet!" the other said. "But we just come from your brudder."

"Yes?" Fenix said, waiting.

"He says ya better get rid of what ya got. Send it down the drain-pipe."

"There's over ten-thousand dollars worth." Fenix was hoarse.

"Yeh, but the police may be grillin' your brudder-in-law," the first said.

Suddenly fearful of being questioned himself, Fenix was about to ask if he'd better get rid of his sugar, too, but stopped himself in time. Fenix! he said to himself, these guys don't know you've been feeding your own brother sugar.

"You think you need to stay around?" Fenix asked.

"We got orders to watch from the roof," the first man said.

There they went, as it turned out, to watch Helen and Billy walking in the early morning.

When the bodyguard left the kitchen a cry from Fenix went up for his wife. He called his pigeon, his turtle-bird and his dove. "Ann, hurry!" he cried. "What's my time worth, save me!"

Even before he called, she had started to pick up the one ounce boxes filled with the drug—carefully as the family was used to—and ran to the bathroom again and again to empty them into the toilet as she flushed the water. Fenix laughed harshly, feeling the depth of the washout every time the bowl was flushed. "Ten-thousand dollars worth," he mourned. All his efforts flushed down the drain.

Ann remembered her brother who might be in trouble. She did not dare think of arrest or worse happening to him. This was no time to think. Maybe the police would come—but at least she would be rid of dope once and for all. After this muff, her husband could no longer rival his brother. The latter was the racketeer after all, not Charles. The sugar followed the drug, but in such large quantities that repeated flushings supervised by Charles caused the water to run over. The caked sugar spread over the tile threshold of the bathroom, into the foyer, and on the newly waxed floor of grandfather Schreck's bedroom. He was still sitting in his stockinged feet asleep on the edge of the bed when it reached him.

To the old man who slept mostly sitting up, his wet feet sensed thru his drowse were like his alarm clock's signal, a call to get up and go to his job. "What on earth!" he exclaimed when he realized the water around him. "What is this? What is this!" he cried.

"Father-in-law, please get the mop," pleaded Fenix, "or the police will be drowned in this flood."

"You'd think I was Noah," the old man sighed. "Have they caught up with you?" he asked, his voice betraying tears of compassion. Then confused by the sticky feel of his socks in the palms of his hands, he asked, "What is this, must you get rid of the sugar too?"

"Why not! What's ten dollars worth of sugar, when I've lost ten thousand of the real goods," said Fenix bitterly.

"What's ten dollars!" exclaimed the old man as he fetched the mop. "Have you ever worked for it? Is it a crime to own sugar? I'd have bought it from you if you had asked me. My heavens, even the police would call that honest!"

Whenever his father-in-law disputed the matter of honesty or integrity Fenix knew enough to keep still.

Ann still brooding about Mitchell broke down and wept. "Why worry Charles about his affairs, papa," she said, "when Mitchell hasn't come home." But just then the door-bell rang and Mitchell came in.

"I'm thru" was the first thing he said.

"You are?" asked Fenix, his voice very steady.

"Yes, I'm not doing this again."

"What are you thru with and why won't you be doing what?" Fenix stressed ever so casually.

"I'm going back to snapping pictures," said Mitchell.

"How, now that you've pawned your last camera?" Fenix asked, aware that question would stump him.

"I'll answer all questions after I've started," said Mitchell. He looked at the floor where the white trickles of sugar were flowing in from the living room. "I suspected this would happen sometime," he said.

"But, Mitchell, *what* happened?" Fenix persisted.

"Do you know the cop on the corner beat here?" Mitchell asked.

"Denis, the cop?" asked Fenix.

"I guess that's his name," Mitchell answered, "I usually don't pay attention to such trifles."

"Well?" Fenix said.

"He met me as I was going to the subway with those little boxes of yours. Of course, they were wrapped, but—I don't know—he's probably had an eye on you for some time," Mitchell said.

"Not on you?" Fenix asked.

"That's just it," Mitchell said.

"Wasn't he anxious to talk?" Fenix asked.

"Oh yes! he walked me all the way to the subway, talking all the time. He even took the train downtown with me. You know what he said?"

"I don't know," said Fenix, "I'll tell you after you tell me."

This reply seemed to disturb Mitchell slightly. "Oh, he said his wife just had a new baby and he was going home to celebrate. What a stream of talk! You should have heard him—beats you! Like this:—*A pint of Irish couldn't hurt any man. Sure a man can't honestly say he's sober and not stand up under a drink. Character is what you are. You've got to give it and be ready to take it in my profession. I don't know, he said, but I wouldn't even refuse a taste of snow just to see what it's like sometime. Ah well, but you seem an educated person, he said to me, you probably don't know what snow is mister.*

"*Mr. Mitchell Schreck,* I said to him."

"You didn't tell him my name?" asked Fenix.

"*Mr. Schreck,* he said to me," Mitchell went on in character, "*snow is narcotics. That's what it is. And many's the time when I was in the narcotics squad I nabbed them racketeers and had 'em put out of the way where they won't harm anybody but themselves. Well, they couldn't bribe me with a whiff of that stuff after all.*"

"Did you get off at the same stop?" Fenix asked.

"Well, when he got off at Mott Avenue," said Mitchell, "I had half a mind to."

"Only half?" asked Fenix.

"You see he asked me to join him in some good cheer at home with his wife. They must be nice people. But I thought I had better continue down to the Ferry."

"South Ferry?" Fenix asked.

"Yes."

"What made you do that?"

"I had your package on me."

"By the way, Mitchell, where is my package?"

"I threw it into the water after I walked out into the air."

"Well, that was the right thing to do, Mitchell. I suppose the ten thousand dollars worth that went down the drain here will flow to the same place."

"You're not angry with me, Charles?" Mitchell asked. "Are you?"

"Mitchell! You know I always take it easy. Forget it!"

"Charles!"

"Yes?"

"How would it be if you and I went in for photography—together—I'll do all the specialized work—you'll—"

"Oh well, Mitchell, you know me, I'm just a simple fellow and know nothing about that."

The door-bell rang again. This time it was Billy. He was still whistling "Eine Kleine Nachtmusik." Tho he usually never whistled more than the lively Allegro, the fantastic and intricate Romanza movement now flowed out of him—modern, as if he himself had composed it. His father and sister had just finished mopping the floor.

"Let's have coffee," Fenix said, "we're all here, ain't we!"

The door opened again, a crack. The two who had been on the roof all this time showed their faces. "Alright now!" said one. "See you sometime," said the other. The door shut.

"Company?" Billy asked.

"We had," Fenix answered. "Billy, there's no other dope in the house now but coffee."

Billy made no further inquiry—"I'm going to get married," he announced casually.

No one there needed to ask if the girl was Helen.

"Good luck, son," Peter Schreck said.

"Oh, Billy," his sister said, "I'll go get some rolls."

"That's love!" Fenix said. "You better! A few weeks from now—who knows!"

"Is there any sugar left for the coffee?" Peter Schreck asked clearly not meaning to rub salt into anyone's wounds.

Ann nodded quickly and smiled prudently to Fenix. She looked happy and not at all tired after her mopping, as she closed the door quietly behind her.

"Cha-arles!" the heir of the family called from his crib. Now everybody was up.

Fenix answered the summons.

"Good morning, Bobby!" He sang as he *trucked on down* into the bedroom.

"Good morning to you!" Bobby chanted. "Did you go to the movies last night, Charles?"

"Sure, I went to the movies."

"And what did you see?"

"Pitchoors!"

"And?"

"And they played a game."

"Yeh? What did they play?"

"Bingo!"

"Bingo! Bing O!" Bobby shouted. "Did you win, papa?"

"No, I lost."

"Aw-w."

"But, listen, Bobby. I'll tell you what the man on the platform said. He said: *Ladies and Gentlemen! Now comes the greatest surprise of the evening! Just to show there's always money to be given away at your neighborhood theatre! And remember your theatre—it's your theatre—your theatre is what you make it! Every morning, noon and night, you can see here the best pictures shown anywhere in town. The surprise! The surprise to dazzle your eyes! I OFFER a prize of ten dollars—one crisp ten dollar bill—to any or every man in this audience here to-night who is NOW wearing at one and the same time his belt AND SUSPENDERS! If you are, come right up and get it! This $10 bill is yours!*"

"You won!"

"No, Bobby," Fenix said. "Last night for the first time in three years I was not wearing my belt."

"Aw," Bobby said looking serious.

Ann came into the room. "Good morning, Bobby. Charles, what are you telling him?"

"It's true, isn't it, pigeon?" Fenix said to her.

"I guess it's true, Charles."

"And what do you say, Bobby?" his father asked.

"It's true, pigeon," said Bobby to his mother.

Ferdinand

1

ABOUT 1900 an expensive limousine rolled out of the public square of Portofino and up a mountain road of the Italian Riviera. Wearing a pinafore like a girl, a small boy in front of the family fiacre turned his head back toward the car as it disappeared. Tearfully he made out people at café tables. Before all these his brother, older by almost a fifth of a century, shamed him.

A while ago, breaking loose from his party, he had sat down on the running-board of the limousine from which he was jolted. Monsieur le Millionaire was having dinner at the inn. Ferdinand insisted he would wait for Monsieur and ask: Monsieur, please, please, Monsieur, will you drive me home? It's my birthday and I've never been inside an automobile. My friends don't have to come. The gardener will take them!

His aunt had said that his father, minister of affairs in the nation on the border Ferdinand had never seen, must know Monsieur le Millionaire.

Ferdinand, the gardener whispered, see, our horse is waiting for you. He's just as nice as the limousine. Nicer. He's your friend. Step in, won't you? It'll be hard to see if I have to drive in the dark.

Trying not to sob the boy climbed into the fiacre. His aunt

helped him up and placed his head close to her bosom and his legs on the knees of his uncle sitting next to her. His brother riding backwards faced them.

As they followed the road the automobile had taken, the boy fell asleep. Aroused later by the clog-dance of the horse's hoofs on a slope over the sea, he turned uncomfortably in his aunt's arms and looked at the lamps burning in clefts of the coves. A beam from a lighthouse scanned the mountainous shore on the other side of the bay they were rounding so that the highest rocks appeared like the air. The boy's eyes roamed, and his aunt seemed worried hearing him repeat in a low voice:

Fire — water — water — fire.

It was dark when the party reached home on the piazza across from the monument to Columbus, who was said to have been of their old suburb of Genoa. Feverish, the boy shunned the landmark wonderful to him by day; and as his brother lifted him from his aunt, he turned from the arms taking him. The Italian gardener, who had held the door open for them, moved toward the child and allowed himself to be embraced.

Ferdinand is alright, he said, tomorrow he'll play with my Nina.

Leaving the family, the man appeared diffident, sensing their unexpressed regret that the child had been disciplined before he had a chance to approach the millionaire.

Our boy, his aunt remarked as they sat down to dinner after Ferdinand had been put to sleep, is like Columbus out there beset by a sea of intrigues. If we are always to be flustered, we should not have accepted his charge.

The face of her older nephew showed the obstinacy of his little brother in front of the fiacre earlier in the day. But in keeping with his age he replied tacitly by unfolding his napkin. The family ate in silence, troubled because Ferdinand was ill.

Desolate together, they thought of him as they dined in the large room with the heavily curtained windows set off by bric-a-brac of every period.

Letters from Ferdinand's parents instructing them as to

his care arrived very occasionally. His mother, her husband's secretary, not much more than half his age, wrote them. Puzzling letters, they stressed that Ferdinand's development must not be influenced by his mother and father whom he did not remember. They would especially appreciate it if he did not meet people who might be diverted by consideration of the aged minister's incongruous progeny from befriending him in state matters. Should Ferdinand ever decide for himself to follow a diplomatic career, he could in time be introduced to people of influence.

Fortunately for the minister, his sister was middle-aged, had been married about the time the boy was born in the Italian suburb, and expected no children of her own. Devoted to her husband, equally devoted to her, she divided her time between Ferdinand and studying botany while copying the manuscript of her husband's work on Linnaeus.

Ferdinand's brother, whom his parents had raised, lived with his aunt and uncle because his official position, at the age of twenty-one, in the watering place on the Riviera made it convenient. Besides it was his duty to set an example for Ferdinand.

For the minister was the type whose alertness to personal succession in the service of his state affected his older son even at a distance. The minister's foreign interests were not closed though he was home with his wife, not inclined to revert to the routine of bringing up another son so young he could have no pertinence in their everyday affairs.

Aunt and uncle were rarely disturbed by the child growing up. Still, at times as now at dinner, they felt the years spent with him in a foreign country pass in a certain vacancy. It often seemed to them, helping one another out of family love, that the family did not exist. Or if it did it was the shadow of a menage, and they brooded over it but mostly at dinner. If Ferdinand played as he wished with almost the freedom of an orphan, his guardian's responsibilities decreased, his happiness grew. Only the gardener having a little daughter of his own to love pitied him, for some reason probably peculiar to his station in life. The boy's family felt quite apart from him in their thoughts, except for their obligations.

That evening, as usual, a native servant girl put out the lights of the dinner candelabra but for one candle by which the diners retired separately.

But the next morning, under the sun of the Italian sky, the boy's relations found him none the worse. With Nina, he was trying out a new toy, at the end of the piazza where it joined the beach not more than a hundred yards from the house. Seated at the wheel of a shining cart, whose body resembled the limousine of the day before except that it was not enclosed, he worked the pedals, and every now and then Nina climbed in and out over the side.

An appropriate gift, said his aunt who had come out to watch the boy from a distance and to chat with the gardener working at the grape arbor.—It came last night, too late for us to wake him—from his father. Her first words carried an implicit apology for the incident of the previous day, and having said the last, she could not take them back.

Strange that it should be an auto, the gardener said. It might have been, for example, a hoe such as I give my Nina.

Ferdinand's aunt laughed.—Your wish I see is to make a vineyardist, or a vine-dresser, of our boy.

How can one plan surely? the man questioned. For myself I can wish Nina no better future than such a man with a vineyard up there in the hills.

They took deep breaths of morning air happily rid of the sirocco. The sun warmed them. Standing there, they satisfied their eyes on the littoral: green water, sandbars under sunlight; over the dark green trees of the coves, precipitous hills and mountains with still more varied shades of green and blue distinguishing the natural vegetation from the plants farmers cultivated.

Yes, the gardener smiled, and then all they sensed seemed blotted out by a subdued rustling from the waves noiseless till that instant. They were not really sure they heard anything. Perhaps, as the boy's aunt said afterwards, they could account for their impulse to listen by posing second sight—the accident was so unexpected. Years later she would say to Ferdinand—hardly amused—it was because he was fated to live long.

Neither she nor the gardener could respond at first to the children crying from the water into which they had raced their toy. But as he ran toward the sea, she followed. All at once they saw a wave turn the cart on its side and douse its occupants completely. They ran on in silence, till reaching the edge of the sea, the gardener almost stumbled over his little girl whimpering face down in the sand where the force of the wave had carried her. Ferdinand still standing up, shouting, but wobbly in the water, was offering him—miraculously—an impatient hand. He grasped it and picked both children up out of danger without even wetting his shoes.

It could have been worse, he said to Ferdinand's aunt who unable to speak had caught up with him.

What do you say we go in again, he exclaimed, coddling the children to distract them from their trembling.

No, said Nina.

Let us, said the little boy, and we'll get our wagon again—laughing hilariously.

His aunt shuddered slightly, fearing for a moment he had been seized by convulsions.

Alright, said the gardener, Nina stays here. I take off my shoes and in we go!

You see, there's nothing to be afraid of, Ferdinand, said the gardener as he waded out of the water, his clothes dripping, with the boy happy on one arm and the cart under the other.

Then—as if he had been thinking about it a long time—he said to the boy's aunt, I wonder where his fine temper will drive him some day.

The remark was casual enough, yet prompted by overwrought feelings voiced for the gardener himself an unintended foreboding. Sorry he had spoken, he searched the face of the boy's aunt for a sign of misgiving which he might have brought to it. She looked reassured now the child was safe. Her expression had not changed. Footless, his words affected him only, and in a flash his mind sensed that what he had intended to say was not clear to her.

He had wished to confide what worried him, but, in her employ, could now only point to the cart and say: Perhaps Ferdinand won't need this for some time.

In his confusion, the boy was helpful: No, indeed, gardener, it'll take months to dry out!

There's the empty dog-kennel for it, the boy's aunt smiled.

That was all. That moment he knew he would never have a chance to speak to her personally.

A gardener could only be resigned to see plants grow and depend on the weather. He must let live. Yet he had wished to say it was not a matter of stepping out of one's circle, of emphasizing one's caste, to give advice. He was sure Ferdinand's aunt would agree were it only possible to break the habit of reticence. Should the children have to part sometime, pain could not be avoided. In that respect perhaps he was considering Nina alone, but no, he was sad with the thought of the boy possibly wasting a life on a kind of toy such as had nearly drowned him that day.

Everyone's future was less predictable than the weather, the one thing which strangers knew the effect of in common, although children playing together seemed to call for greater certainty. It was a pity that people did not risk enough to speak out in behalf of one another's happiness and their own.

He tried not to think about it—wishing that Ferdinand were *his* son. Yet that would have made two futures to worry about. The irony of this thought reflected his own face wryly in his mind. He had not spoken, and his fear of inviting disappointment did not allow him to pray patently for realizations. A born peasant, and by upbringing a self-taught pagan, it occurred to him that Ferdinand's aunt might be of those who prayed sometimes. Her circle, so unlike himself trusting from day to day, must, he felt, own to a degree the secret of the world's affairs, since they were solicitous enough to pray for them.

Other Sunday jaunts with the family in the fiacre to Portofino bore him out. Against the reassuring limit of the sky of his native village, his planting or pruning, playing with the children, reading an almanac or a newspaper or a book of the times out of sheer curiosity, there was the chit chat of the cafés—on the square where Ferdinand first saw a limousine—saying that all was not well between his country and Ferdinand's father's. Ferdinand's uncle shrugged his shoulders to such talk, the boy's aunt listened. Her older nephew—after approving of Ferdinand's teacher, a new mysterious addition to the family—was now for the most part in Genoa. It was said that he managed an office of a foreign subsidiary of an automobile manufactory in his homeland.

For a while, the gardener consoled himself, the change would not be too great when Ferdinand wrote him his first letter, using capitals in red and yellow chalk. These told him that their garden was beautiful. The children still played together as though the world carried on without rumor.

One day, however, Ferdinand discarded his pinafore. Another day, one week-end at Portofino, ladies failed to show ruches around their necks and wrists. So many novelties came out of a decade, including fine ankles and pretty shoes, while the pace of everything appeared nearly the same as before—except that something in the air caused the gardener to feel he was working for a foreign dynasty.

Ferdinand was fourteen. A lock of hair, delicate in line, like a tendril chiselled in stone, fell across his forehead, giving him the appearance of some old portrait head of young Caesar. He was manly and friendly and his people were friendly. But Nina went to school and kept house. She saw Ferdinand rarely, though they still saluted each other when they met.

The gardener could have taken his daughter with him and set up for them both in the mountains, and avoided the new friendless changes of a time which perplexed him. But the tradition of working where his father had, held him in the same place, as did the cottage he had shared with his young wife, dead since Nina's birth. He felt that his wife left it to him to keep as it was, that it should be so. Loss had matured him quickly.

Finally, a day came when the war was twenty-four hours off for nations on the border. The gardener's own country was still undecided about fighting—questioning the stakes. Ferdinand's family shuttered their mansion "for the duration." Taking Nina with him as a last tacit hint the gardener drove them all with their baggage to the railroad station in Genoa. For years the boy had wanted to show enough feeling to be able to kiss the cheek of this man whom he loved. He did so now. Then he shook hands with Nina. They looked at each other remembering how her father once saved them both.

Knock on the roof of the dog-kennel for me sometimes, Ferdinand said, it's made of wood you know. And besides our old wagon was lucky.

She laughed, abashed, and promised. He never saw her again.

2

In the capital city of the world Ferdinand was accepted at a lycée. The only childhood companion his age had been a girl and by comparison the boys at school in the new country, to which he owed the same allegiance as his relatives, hardly interested him. Yet left alone of his own choice as a consequence, he took to their city as his birthright. Time after time at nightfall he would be late for dinner, after tarrying along the course of the river dividing the city in two. Each bank had its streets paved and repaved through the years, accountable for the squares, parks, public buildings and monuments—the general effect a cross-section of history invoking the rings of an old tree telling its age. Or as he read in a book somewhere, the architects still built colonnades, affecting the ancient for another era of recorders and travellers. Out of all time, through all lands came this city, like the book telling him as newcomer not to be astonished if in the dark he should encounter on a wall the trace of the Hindu, the Egyptian, the Greek, or still youngish Gothic. And people pursued the War here.

He lived with his aunt and uncle as before—growing to approximate a son of their own as he engaged them in talk of his studies and the tactics and strategy of the campaign. His brother, who had returned to the household, handled chassis for the army—his capacity that of supervisor of the main plant whose foreign office had employed him previously. It puzzled the other members of the family to find an occasional notice in a newspaper still calling the branch of the main plant in the enemy country by the name of the parent firm. Since Ferdinand's brother seemed to use his every waking moment to build up the defense of his country, they did not bother him to explain an incongruity easily dispelled by inferring that the control over the two plants was now different. The shocks came from the battle front—four hundred fifty thousand casualties in one sector—receding, however, when an old domestic worry threatened them anew. Ferdinand's parents resided in the same city, and their son would at last have to meet them.

A day in May, his mother sat reflected in the pier-glass that mirrored also a crystal bowl filled with white iris. She talked in subdued tones to her sister-in-law, hardly a sign of animation marking her still youthful appearance. She expected her son. As he stepped across the threshold he wanted to turn back, but somehow forced himself to stay, feeling his weight bearing on his heels. He relied on the rare occasions his mother had been mentioned in his life instead of on formal introduction. Civil conduct, he imagined, would protect him. His eyes were focused shyly on the mirror, and as she approached him, he saw her in the length of the glass move further away. Then unexpectedly blurred but magnified, the irises appeared to come close to him.

He remembered her kiss, and—

Your father is very busy at the *Bureau.* But we should be seeing you together soon. You must encourage us. We're sorry, our lives are not simple.

Yes, mother.

She had left. He wished he could laugh irresponsibly, insult his pity for her and himself, run to his uncle the botanist in his study and ask him, suggestively, by what process *fleur-de-lis* transpires maternal passion. He could never shamelessly tell the story of his parents' desertion and have anyone believe it. For the first time in his life he felt too young to be friendless. He subdued tears of anger as he noticed his aunt, looking old, weeping quietly in the hall which led to his room.

His lot, the result of habit, stopped him from running away from the childless love of aunt and uncle or to a desire out of the past for possibilities like Nina and the gardener. Practical in risking little, he saw in himself and detested the strait-laced wariness of his brother who without real feeling would never give up the duty of taking care of him. In the same way he took care of his own constraints, emphasizing his emptiness and affecting to be quiet.

A senior classmate attracted by his reserve invited him on drives through the woods of the city. Ferdinand accepted—here was something he could do without family, alone or keeping still by the side of another not much older. The classmate guessed right in assuming that Ferdinand would consider him company and not a friend. Casual companionship was the extent of intimacy the classmate required. If he stopped to drink absinth or took unnecessary fast turns driving, Ferdinand, he was sure, would not speak about it.

The young man sometimes talked about books, wanted to write, preferring however to read instead, and was pleased easily by a manner of style at once flashy and hard. Ferdinand at sixteen also thought about writing but read all too occasionally. What literature he picked up outside the lycée was mused over, set aside—if it had impetus at all—to be weighed or enjoyed when he would be free from study. The more the words of others impressed him with their factual content the more he felt he must wait for his own facts before being tempted into words. Behind the cleverness of a shocking trope denying insight, Ferdinand saw as much waste as in drinking absinth, which made him sickish. Yet taking from his companion what he offered, he did not disapprove of the other's drinking or argue his tastes. In modern literature it was the war which moved him and only one poet—a cannonier dangerously wounded so that "a star rayed his forehead"—who wrote concretely for him of a new mind in process of overcoming existing barriers. The mechanically gifted fellow at the steering gear next to Ferdinand would, were it quoted, probably scoff at the weakness of the verse's subtlety. Ferdinand refrained—persisting in being practical and keeping his thought like his life to himself.

Outwardly he was grateful for the drives, for the woods, for the wind on his arm on the lowered window glass, his sleeve rolled up above his elbow, while the car sped through the wind's resistance and he anticipated the unexpected, for himself.

The classmate offered him the controls and he moved into the seat before them with nervous gratitude. The mistakes he made as learner were few—a tendency to step down too much on the accelerator, but soon he drove safely enough. Cars, even of good make, too readily betrayed then in rattling and vibrations every slight irregulity of the road, but Ferdinand was grateful for the surprise in each jolt.

When his companion tired of the "dinghey," Ferdinand was invited to drive alone.—If you wreck it, old son, said the older, you'll buy me another—maybe better.

Ferdinand said—thanks, and tried not to wreck it.

A year later, on a day of rumors of the war ending—America across the ocean had been fighting on his country's side for some time, shells had systematically burst into his capital city—he was driving along, alone, thinking even the car had become too great a familiar, too much of a hit or miss affair, like aimless words, to pass for action; perhaps if the war lasted a few months longer, he would get to the front. Listening to the motor and resenting the thought of his brother who had allowed a stranger to teach him the inchoate pleasure of its hum, he felt the crunching of a few dried branches under the wheels over a narrow path and some drops of rain on his face. The storm clouds that had gathered blew off swiftly. The sun came out again looking—it was he who thought so—sad. He noticed a dead rabbit partly skinned that had been thrown into a hedge. A squirrel with only one eye scurried past him. He wished he had not met it.

He drove on in his companion's car into the afternoon streets of the city and at last drew up listlessly in front of a group of government buildings. Across the street were other buildings probably for symmetry, or so it occurred to him. Another car stopped in front of one of these—a yellow chassis he recognized, fearing he was too late to drive off without greeting the occupant. Suddenly the asphalt buckled and a crash seemed to follow deafening him. Debris fell. As the dust cleared he realized the noise must have come first.

The yellow car lay in a trough of pavement, a sorry heap of smashed metal and springs. It had been hit by a shell. With the reflex shadow of a smile on his face, he neared the crowd of people who seemed to have nothing to lose gathered about the dead body of his mother. He looked up, the building containing her husband's offices before which she had stopped, and which she had intended to visit, remained standing unimpaired.

At the funeral he saw the remnants of the family for the first time together, walking behind the slow motor-driven hearse. Immediately preceding, stepped his uncle, face behind glasses—as if studying a flower in some field—and his aunt with tear-stained cheeks at her husband's arm. She looked back at Ferdinand moved, as she was, not by the dead in the coffin but by an undesired thought—more painful than mourning—that his mother who alive had made nothing of affection in death could exact what was left of it between nephew and aunt. Not daring to return his aunt's look that searched his own, he stared past her towards his brother.

The funeral rites turned out to be an occasion for the latter to walk in formal black. Tall, somewhat heavy and jaunty, he accompanied an old man whose straightness apparently stimulated the pace of the marchers back of him as his alert tread proceeded closely behind the hearse. A feeling of sickness decided for Ferdinand that the man heading the procession was his father, the minister of affairs. The small back of the chief mourner's head, the side of white hair—he was somewhat too short for his son to catch a glimpse of his entire profile—never for a moment stopped to attract his son's bewildered gaze till the coffin was lowered and the head of the old man bowed. By that time the son was certain his father would not see him that day. And turning from the grave, everybody faced completely about as one person. Neither son nor father saw the other's face.

He took his aunt and uncle home where the thought of the dead seemed to have hurried before, and behind closed eyes lived over the day's events. Apprehensive that his wardship was ending ironically for all of them with his mother's death, he saw her as very much alive handing him over to his father whom he did not wish to meet. He was impressed suddenly by the fact that he could think back at least sixteen years but to no ties, while in the future the few he had known continued to dissolve. And he asked himself what he knew of his father, when had he first heard of him. The picture of a cart, a child's automobile freshly painted as on the birthday when he rode his present into the sea, engaged him and he heard his aunt say, as though that early morning in his life had returned—From your father. He could remember him in no other connection. His thought proceeded, however, to form relations previously not lucid. Why did his father remember the child he was on the Riviera with a toy especially designed as an automobile? His brother who had their father's confidence shared it no doubt as manufacturer of cars. If rumors were true, they sold cars indiscriminately—to enemies of their country as well as their country fighting a battle for the last four years to drive the enemy from its soil. What comfort of goodness was there in an enterprise like his brother's? How could his father reconcile it with a task dedicated to his country?

Their mature inconsistencies were like his own inexperience—his empty studies at the lycée which would graduate him some time, his aimless driving of his classmate's car through the city which after all its intimacies proved foreign to him, at best pleasantly foreign. And this was so because his father and brother probably planned his life for him and also—he felt too tired to move—the world as he knew it. Rousing himself out of his doze, out of a thought of the dead, he added aloud—looking around to see no one, yet ashamed that some one might have overheard him—Because I have no friends.

The words he spoke held the answer to his perplexities. He would make friends. He could go to his father at the *Bureau,* before he was called there and say whatever they planned for him was not for him. Old friends should not be hard to know again. They would close up the gaps between his discontinuous years. All he needed was his father's approval and a car to go in. Both could be given without loss since his father did not know him. A car would be useful where the gardener and Nina were, and his worth as a vineyardist in a year or two would defray the cost.

His hope imagined a future so simple he wept for the second time in his life he could remember. Yet he was not ashamed to weep as after a while his mind mated words to an unusual rhythm. He had given up writing poetry as useless some months ago but now the words came naturally.

On that day
on that day
Ferdinand
world without end
heath and sea and they

hurry
hurry
your worry away

gone father
and mother
and
your brother

The matter-of-fact meaning of the experience recalled in the words shocked him and he tried to forget them. He got up suddenly, walked over to his desk where he sat down again to write his brother a note requesting an appointment at the *Bureau* for the next day.

He had been waiting about a quarter of an hour, but that morning it was to be expected. The streets through which he had elbowed still hummed in his ears the din of celebrating crowds of strangers meeting for the first time, yet embracing resourcefully regardless of sex, with the words "the war's over" on their lips. His father and brother must have been delayed. It would be pleasant to wait. Surely that morning should bring him good luck. He recalled the different types drifting through the arcade below the waiting room in which he sat alone—especially faces of foreign emissaries and colonials, African, Syrian, and Oriental, who after their share in the fight to preserve a free Empire looked around with expectancy of reward in a world to be reapportioned beginning that day. His father and brother would share in that adventure, and for a moment he regretted the callow choice of a livelihood as vineyardist that only yesterday had prompted his present visit.

The sunlight through a closed window fell on his hand and made him think of the limitless range even the smallest choice could contain. A grape lit up in the sun reflected his choice. But roads laid over the world, breaking under the never stopping traffic of cars, were civilization's obvious measure of adventure, and to feel that one moved it all in much the same way as one walked home leisurely. He was shy, however. In the wide world his shyness would not do. He was sorry to have avoided greeting the colonials below. Fellow students fascinated by their costumes that morning had greeted them naturally, though they were not Europeans. Moreover, he had known the "foreigners" for almost five years. They were of the same mortar as the architecture of many another world facade that had befriended him with its singularness in the capital city he had adopted in his walks and his rides. Their features were intimated in poor imitations of their ancient buildings which the war had bombed along with the new fashionable hotels of his world city. Were he suited to a more adventurous calling than that of vineyardist, he would have said at least a few words to these colonials who betokened history and travel to most people.

He looked at his watch. A half hour had passed. The girl behind the door had said he was expected. They would call him. They were closed back of the door opposite. Or were they? No sound came from that room and the impressive number of paces he counted mentally from his bench to their door cowed him. He looked around the spacious room. The door opened tentatively its slight creak making him eager. Voices reached him, his brother's urgent speaking followed by a deliberate voice.

Would you agree, father, the time is ripe for an overseas connection?

Well, I would first make certain that the Americans see

our point of view.

Then his father and brother were not discussing him. He sat back, but his impatience returned when he realized he might have to wait long.

Have you—the elderly voice paused, preoccupied it would seem with different matters—have you thought of an agent?

I suspect that Ferdinand's request to see you today will fit in with our plan.

His brusher did not mention the hour of their appointment. The presumption that he would *fit in* offended him and effected a catch in his throat.

Ferdinand?

He heard his name pronounced with sympathy he would not have expected from his father.

—I didn't know Ferdinand had himself asked to see me.

The voice, evidently sensitive to obligations incurred a long time ago, admitted more than surprise. And the failings conveyed in the tones of surprise made Ferdinand feel strangely obligated in turn, though he did not know the speaker.

I forgot to tell you in all the noise this morning his brother said.—But Ferdinand will be through soon with the lycée. Don't you think he might go on with his studies by starting as under-secretary in the office of our embassy on the other side?

He thought of the other side of the ocean, an image too vague to make sense. At the same his decision to seek out the gardener and Nina was swamped by a feeling that nothing ever went right with him and a tardy, as yet unclear, understanding of his father keeping him waiting.

I don't know what will happen in the next twenty years. Do you think he would like it alone in a foreign country? his father questioned.—I owe him much.

Sincere regret compelled the last words—and, evidently, an enormous debt his father had assumed while living his life, which inevitably had reacted on him; the realization of the forces bearing down on the man's old age made Ferdinand cringe. Perhaps the accident to his wife had shaken him.

Ferdinand had imagined his father as always unaffected—as unquestioning and unquestioned command. Possessed with self-distrust, the son now asked what could his father in his decline owe him, and what foolhardiness had made him call that morning to claim his own emptiness when the whole world was unsettled.

Tell me, Ferdinand must have liked the Riviera? his father went on, as if concealing a hope that his young son might still recapture for him the Europe he had known.—Your aunt tells me he had friends there.

I don't know, I was too busy with our affairs in Genoa to notice. The only one I remember was our Italian gardener I met by accident during my trip several months ago. It would hardly interest you or Ferdinand that he is building a new house for his daughter recently married. They marry young, these simple folk. Our staff in Genoa is full if you were thinking of Ferdinand there, his brother said.

For the moment the knowledge of his loss seemed irreparable, but only for the moment. The next moment nothing mattered. He hated himself only for being there. His brother was stupid, stupid and practical, but so was his hate of him. He wondered if it were really affection that had made him think of going to her. If his loss were imaginary, he could forgive his brother. It was not imaginary, the fact that she was married, and he cared nothing about forgiving him. Yet he knew he was alone to blame for neglecting her. In his disgust with everything he imagined her on the slope of a mountain with her lover, walking in a vineyard or entering their house.

When his brother on the way out finally spoke to him, he did not answer and only later remembered words to the effect that his father would see him shortly.

He looked upon an old face notably sympathetic like a monkey's, and able to provoke—yes, from him in answer to its half-question, half-greeting—Ferdinand? What it said after voicing his name in the manner of an apology, which it seemed to take for granted no human listener would understand, mattered less to Ferdinand.

For he had made up his mind not to confide it to anyone. Parting on good terms with all his family, but never expecting to see them again, he would shun talk about them as vulgar.

As he leaned over the handrail of the vessel taking him abroad, this resolution helped him not to look shocked when the steward—a former student at the lycée working his way across—brought him a wire. His brother informed him that an automobile had been stored in the hold for his use on landing.

3

He got rid of his pride bit by bit and drove his brother's gift.

Six days a week he took his car from the outskirts to official duties at the embassy and back, and regretted that his hours of work were not longer. Sundays he walked.

He had sought a room in the country, rather than one near the embassy, out of a desire at first to look around for himself so as to be able to write. He knew after a while he would never write again. And there was nothing to write home about, literally,—granted that home existed apart from his thought.

He alluded to business inquiries of his brother in a half-yearly letter to his aunt, out of deference to her love which he remembered as treasuring any visible evidence of family that she imagined made her less lonely. His brother almost never heard from him except through intermediaries at the embassy or elsewhere.

Saddened by the knowledge that he could use his head to the purposes required by routine existence, as well as others about him with lesser heads, he did not exaggerate his ability to learn quickly. Instead, he judged that a fair assumption of initiative on his part would be enough to attain the compliments of his superiors. His advance therefore was gradual and did not offend competitors, while his apparent modesty disguised an indifference to things he had never wanted. He often thought if he were seriously interested in his job he would be using up his cells faster, but perhaps not to the good of his health.

To his official world he was pleasant but not the man of affairs it recognized in his father. When the latter died, he even picked the right moment—after all equity was assured to his country and all countries—or so at least Ferdinand's compatriots implied when they offered him condolence. Acknowledging their eulogies as one of his duties, Ferdinand was secretly surprised.

The facts readily available to him and to others at the embassy—when they cared to look at them—indicated that the world was discounting nasty skirmishes in an interim between wars. For the present it was resigned to a necessary twenty years of preparation, or to temporising before it prepared, for a second war that in all probability would again see the breaking, or the breaking up within, of nations. The peoples of the world had not benefited by the last war, which had ended, in some countries, in revolutions ousting the war parties. But the Russians, the first to isolate themselves from the armed camp of Europe, had been attacked even after the peace in Western Europe by the armies of fourteen states including Ferdinand's own. The leaders of these states compromised with the fact of a people's government in Russia only when their own armies threatened that they were weary of war.

He wondered if his father's friends had ever shared the old statesman's confidences, or whether overcome by the pomp of his funeral, pictures of which the newspapers printed in their grief, they beheld the hearse drawn by an idea no less than the guiding solace of Europe. Yet Ferdinand thought he in his own way perhaps echoed the findings of others—the historians of the reaction of force—seeing Western Europe that had subjected continents and peoples fast becoming a continent of subjected peoples profitless to themselves.

His lifetime might not decide the question. And now alone, without family, he did not have to beg. Though he owed his start to family, when he looked around he did not seem less hard or soft than the greater number of people, rich and poor alike, whom decisive factors of history had made equal as to indifference.

His aunt wrote more often—about her husband's botanical studies and her older nephew's wife and children. Ferdinand lost track of the scions she mentioned among the plants and how many new nephews he had.

America, too, was still an unfelt entity about which he did not care to write down a quick opinion that might mislead anybody. So he merely bettered his personal position many times. Expecting no friends as a result of his efforts to answer only when others talked to him, he had none.

He tired easily when he first came over, and his twelve mile drive after work over a new highway's dangerous curves made him doze off on his cot before dinner. Still pulsing with the motion of his car, he transferred it into a repeated dream of a toy cart lunging into a sea he knew as a small boy. A nightmare of shame awoke him as he distinctly remembered being grown up in his dream of his childhood. When he left his room, the landscape of his new world then appeared like the old. He had dinner about eight at a nearby farmhouse run by an aging widow who years ago had come from his own country but still used his mother tongue, making her neat, formal service seem intimate. Saying "good-night" to her recalled his aunt, and when he got into his car again, the steering wheel at his right, instead of at the left as in American cars, invariably brought up a continent he had left behind.

This foreignism of his automobile also affected others, and after a year his apparent unconcern and routine were broken into. The odd position of the steering gear attracted the curious unused to the make of another continent. Men working with Ferdinand asked to try it out for themselves. Girls from the office staff leaned on the wheel with their elbows, after working hours, and remarked that it was cute—a word they used also in speaking of the owner of the car. At first he defied these inquisitive strangers of the new world by racing his motor as a hint of his impatience to drive off. They showed no reaction to his impoliteness, and after a time their gift for talk prevailed over his loneliness. He learned by listening to speak English without an accent, though conscious that his features revealed him as Mediterranean. But these too, like his speech, seemed to change behind an acquired American happy-go-lucky air when he attended parties, and later out of the corners of his eyes watched his rider or riders glancing, uneasily thrilled, at the number sixty shifting steadily towards seventy on his speedometer.

He drank with them, always ordering scotch-and-soda for himself, taking the drink his foreign constitution was least used to as a compliment to them, and triumphing over his allergy.

—O, I was sick yesterday from that stuff—but it was wonderful. So sick, you think you're dying but then you're suddenly better!

He realized after permitting himself confidences of this sort that they confessed his relief at being well again—not a great compliment to his drinking prowess—but talked anyway. At such times reborn free and equal overnight as it were, on a par with his American associates, he did not hesitate to speak to them as friends, and amused them with stories of his encounters with the traffic police.

—Well, this morning I was late for the conclave (you know, the ambassador and the other extraordinaries), and a trolley stopped to let out passengers just ahead of me. I didn't have time to pull up alongside to avoid a crash, so I swung around its left side and like a good citizen barely missed the officer at his traffic station.—Where are you going? he asked.

—I'm going to work.

—Is this your way to go to work?

—Why, what's wrong?

—What's wrong! You're on the wrong side of the street!

—Sorry, sir.

—Sorry! I'll bet you'll be when I'm through with you. Hey! What's this?! What kind of a car is this, anyway? Did you have this steering gear installed on the wrong side especially for you?

—No, it's a foreign car.

—Foreign, hey! Where do you work?

—At the embassy.

—At the embassy? You sure you know which one? Well, let me tell you something. There are no special privileges for riding on the wrong side of the street even for the Siamese ambassador, and as far as I know the only side of the street you can drive on in the direction you want to go now is the right side, in this country, and we don't post that information on a traffic sign, because in a civilized country you don't need a sign for every law!

The wisdom of the story's end pleased Ferdinand's circle, and sometimes, when he was not merely the good boy acting bad out of boredom, gave him food for thought about governments and peoples he was too reserved to discuss with others. Life was amusing—at least sometimes—and the wrong kind of talk might spoil it. The seriousness of possible accident to himself, to his acquaintance, and to his country, far away though it was, run by callous, possibly stupid forces like his brother recently installed on the board of directors of the state bank, as it was called, troubled him—on occasion. But since most of his world answered the question as to which side of the road was the right with the customary answer of foregone habit, it became in the long run too heavy for chance conversation.

His acquaintances were a varied lot. With something of peevishness in his nature, he sought diversion among people constantly, till suddenly he avoided them—behaving like an erratic clock that often works perfectly, then over a long interval refuses to go at all. In those days, voided in the calendar as it were, he would give as excuse the rush of work, but unexpectedly turn up most at ease among fellow nationals and career men who could afford good food served by their own countrymen in dining places known as speakeasies in Prohibition days before the depression. Yet when the effort of returning the serious fondness of an odd few, whom his generous moods did not always allow to pay for their food and drink since he suspected they were often short, did not reduce his pleasure in them, he could refer with pride to his closest friends as three. Then he detested in himself the fits of stinginess, for which he blamed the national character of his country, and was delighted by the companionship of a White Russian emigré passionately convinced of the good in the *workers* revolution. An Englishman, who loved to sail with them in a catboat someone had given him, analyzed international desirabilities for them, as though they depended on English common sense and England's will to rid itself of the thieves in the Merrie Isle. A decent British empire, he believed, could be the best government in the world. When he tired of that line, he diverted them with his opinion that poetry sang and spoke best in Firdusi and his growing conviction that after the Shah Namah it almost never sang and spoke at all: an opinion which Ferdinand and the Russian would probably never verify for themselves by studying Persian since as linguists they were remiss—having got around to American and stopped. One other was in this company: a New Yorker of Jewish parents, younger than all of them; Ferdinand called him "the rabbin." For speaking good Hebrew and Yiddish, as a result of early training, this friend had nevertheless steeped himself in English and American scholarship to a degree emulating the devotion of his parents to their religion about which he never thought. Ferdinand had no use for religion, except in a jest marking a friend as among the faithful, who was as far away from them as he was.

To Ferdinand, when he was happy, they were like one these three—though incongruous together—fortunately not of his diplomatic world. They were those strange results, naturally urbane products of other nations, on a new scene—distinguished from Americans who smoked and did not take off their hats before customs officials wherever he had met them abroad. In himself, he was getting to feel more like an American ruggedly free, affecting to send out roots, never long rooted,—like the Creeping Charlie with the blue, mantis-like face of its flowerest, whose Latin name his uncle the botanist had pronounced for him as a child and which he had forgotten: in reality, a weed to be seen almost the first in the spring, its pointed leaves rambling everywhere in the city parks and the countryside—the face of its flower blue as with cold.

Often feigning to chill even these three friends—because whatever pride he had left was telling him that they had wasted less time than he, had kept their integrity, and were each something—Ferdinand teased them while admiring them rooted in their own heads as they seemed to him. When the Russian reminded him of Crèvecoeur's eighteenth century anticipation as to the revolutions Russia and America might one day bring about, Ferdinand, with a false show of malice, prodded him with the fact that Russia's workers and peasants had made an exile of him. But the Russian passionately defended the necessity for his country's acts against anomalies like himself.

Feeling especially puckish, Ferdinand once confronted the Englishman with a gracious but frankly unsubmissive subject of the Empire, a Hindu touring the states in behalf of his oppressed countrymen. The Englishman listened with great interest, and to Ferdinand's surprise, the talk changed from politics to Firdusi. The Hindu, of course, had read him in Persian. With a lasting smile, the Englishman, not intimidated by Ferdinand's evident disappointment that they had not quarreled, took out a card from his inside coat pocket and shyly handed it to his potential enemy, as though he were calling on him. The brown man read aloud deliberately—at first looking up at the Englishman to receive his approval—then quickly and appreciatively as he continued, in a Cambridge accent:

Program of the New Iranian Government

> In the course of his speech on assuming the throne of Iran, the young King, Minuchihr I, said: "Whosoever in the seven regions of the world strays from the road or turns away from right-dealing, whoever causes the poor to toil, or treats his kin, the people, contemptuously, or swells with excess of riches, or molests unfortunate persons, all such I will treat as unbelievers worse than the Evil One. The respectable people who are not worthy of respect God curses, and so will I."
>
> Firdusi Agency.

Ferdinand turned to the *rabbin* who happened to be there and asked distantly:—Wasn't Columbus who discovered this land also something of a *rabbin?* And Barnacle Bill—he said, nodding his head towards the Englishman,—and our Indian friend probably comes from the lost tribes. You don't know how sorry I feel sometimes not to have been born a Negro or a Jew.

The truth was, even the Creeping Charlie, let alone a Negro or a Jew, was too much itself, too much a flower to stand for comparison with him, when he thought about it deeply. That happened when the life around him and his day-to-day course failed to amuse him.

Aside from the fact that his past was nobody's business, he had no reason to keep secrets. Nevertheless he kept secrets from everyone because his life was not very full of incidents. He had mistresses—part of his secret, though everybody knew who they were. Little happened—he became anxious about them. But for all his anxiety was worth to them, he was not compensated by vacations, legs on a beach, on a rock or in a field, release of exercise, affection of a night or a year, a continuous quarrel of ten years broken by regrets and making up every few months or so. He would be generous, then wish he had been otherwise, and be generous again.

If a car lost worth from disuse in storage, obviously the trick was to keep moving. Almost any street seemed too narrow to drive in or out of. Yet if one did not need to make a complete turn, one drove smoothly everywhere, without thought, and the speed however fast was impressively slow, since it never reflected the uneasiness of one's own body and mind. Only shock could do that, and till now the roads of his new world had, in a physical sense, led him unerringly. He passed splintered glass on the highways, looked down from inside his car on wrecks of others in a ditch, or beyond an embankment in the valley. On vacations, he had seen more states of the Union than most Americans. To one who remembered, as part of his European childhood, a car miraculously climbing an almost precipitous mountain, there seemed to be no mountains in the States. There were plateaus, but these failed to rouse seriously a latent fear that some day would find him in a collision.

This thought occurred to him sometimes, as the thought of drowning might, distantly, to a man swimming with head under water. Only his birthdays registered an impact—at that merely empty reflection akin to longing. I am past thirty, he wrote his aunt, and stopped at expressing a wish that something had not happened or perhaps that something else would. Always closest to her image of him as the child that the sea had once yielded back to her, she then answered, hoping for the best, that he was fated to live long. But her hope merely served to becloud his momentary interest in what else she had to say. He had first become aware that he was any age, with his mother's death, about the time he reached his majority. After that he disliked the knowledge that five years ago or fifteen, or whenever, he had wasted time and was no less vulnerable than at present.

The development of successive car models forced him, when he looked back on them, to dwell on parts of himself he had superseded like the machines. He had long ago become successful enough to trade in his brother's car with which he had sailed to the new world for another with a steering wheel not strangely placed. Sometimes he recalled it was then that passers-by had stopped to marvel at him.

With time he hated the New-years—his reason, he was compelled to change his automobile license plates. But year after year, on the same errand, he had them changed. That incident summed up his worthlessness to himself, as did the several newspapers he glanced through impatiently each day—wishing he could forget the half-fact or one fact he drew from the lot of them. If the poorest, for the most part, sought the newspapers only for the "comics" and were unconcerned about the disputes of nations they populated, why should he taken care of be concerned. He imagined, with as much to live on as he had then and without his job he could be spared from the everyday—statutes hindering both rich and poor, politics and national differences not his concern. Still, he imagined he could be worse off. Living in a sphere of influence, so to speak—not of his choice—made him assailable like the savage. Even his good friends annoyed him. They affirmed his fear that almost any unexpected chain of events would some day affect him personally. He lived in a world in which the true pariah, as distinguished from himself, had begun without knowing it, under the impact of the civilized, to outstrip his bounds. The feeling of unlike centuries expressed in contrasted habits of life, persisting at the same time till now, was colliding with new events levelling all grounds of difference. Not far off, his friends appeared sometimes to adjudge like reformers, there would have to be only one century till the end of doom, whether they wished it or merely waited for it, with the same roads everywhere but for distinctions of climate. He suspected that then also he would be dying of inanition, finding no steady pleasure in any bit of the earth as his own and professing to be glutted thinking whether others could. He recalled, in leisure moments, a round Indian face from Ecuador saying mildly that the Second World War, still to come, would see a few countries of Europe left without their empires. He derided his sinecure, which exposed him to this kind of international weather as he called it, to friends out of jobs and obviously detested his work. But when he spoke of the things he could not do in the world without it, a click in his throat consciously disclosed that he preferred his complete extinction rather than the end of his tenure.

Pretending for years to have forgotten his diplomatic brother, Ferdinand nevertheless felt his force—a desire to be safe whatever happened, a passive acknowledgment of the order or disorder he moved in—more profoundly than any rival impulse in himself. He had heard from his aunt that his brother had gone on a sales trip to Indo-China. It was the day that Manchuria had been invaded by the Japanese. He remembered the date because the Americans had protested the Japanese adventure and had called at his embassy to obtain the support of his countrymen and the English. The Americans failed. He deplored his country's policy, but of course he did not determine it. Later looking for someone to speak to—his shyness as time went on was compelled more and more to hint at itself—he remarked to the Englishman:—It is thirteen years since the peace was fashioned that gave power politics its bone of empire, and me my sinecure.

The Englishman was more aboveboard:—I don't approve of what happened today either—a bad precedent for the British Empire to follow—besides you know, the Japanese necessitous poor,—that's a quaint, old phrase—who will migrate to Manchuria to work won't be better off than at home without jobs. The oriental and the savage, he continued somewhat quizzically, make a mistake to want to advance to a job in our sense. I have no job and am happy enough—most of the time—without it. If you don't like your sinecure and the immoralities it forces on you, why don't you resign?

—Yes, and then? Ferdinand complained.

—Nothing, you're a bloody savage, bloody, beastly savage—the Englishman replied chuckling at his own frankness and nodding his head up and down.—You have savings, or haven't you?—and he suddenly shot his fist forward with pugilistic skill aiming at the pit of Ferdinand's stomach. Ferdinand bent double in anticipation and blushed.

—Say, he protested.

—Gentle, too bloody, beastly gentle, disgustingly so, for a diplomat, the Englishman added as an afterthought. Then, becoming seriously friendly, since Ferdinand was exciting his sympathy—looking at least ten years younger than his age and ingenuous despite his abilities, Ferdinand usually compelled sympathy—the Englishman went on rather gratuitously:

—I suppose looking back on life, anyone's life, it amounts to this—everything that diverges from one's aim is a bloody waste of time, except as respite making you less lonely. I know a man, still working, over eighty, and his aim was a family. The sad thing is he has little respite. I mean the squabbles of his children and his amused observation of their eccentricities, their mature helplessness, offer him little solace, though they make him less lonely. But he still supports them and every other task to him would be a bloody waste of time. He has lots of energy, the old fellow. He might have used some of it to write a novel about his family—wanted to at one time—but he knows it would be mere sentimentality, at least for him, to think of them in terms of literature. So, for respite, he drinks beer with me and sings chanteys like—Ferdinand listened, affecting not to be moved, smiling uncertainly—

> Cape Cod girls they have no combs,
> Heave away, heave away,
> They comb their hair with codfish bones,
> We are bound for Australia!

Chorus:—

Heave away, my bully, bully boys
Heave away, heave away
Heave away and don't you make a noise
We are bound for Australia.

Cape Cod boys they have no sleds,
Heave away, heave away,
They slide downhill on codfish heads,
We are bound for Australia.

Chorus:—

Cape Cod women they can make,
Heave away, heave away,
A briny lot of codfish cakes,
We are bound for Australia!

Chorus:—

—What would you have liked to do? Write?

—To be a vineyardist, Ferdinand answered petulantly, like a child.

His English friend looked away from his face, at a wall, and said nothing.

His English friend, who seemed intentionally to plot his conversation so that quite by accident and afresh it turned up from time to time the odd phrase "the necessitous poor"—a tautology of a seventeenth century English economist which amused him excessively—left about that time on one of his perennial journeys: to prove that the tautology really existed, because—as he also liked to repeat—god took care of his own. Ferdinand did not see him again for a long time. He singled out Ferdinand of all their friends as the one who could conveniently pass on the news, if there were news. The Englishman wrote when he was almost mobbed in a café in Unter den Linden, when the nationalistic revolt of a new party in a torchlight parade over that thoroughfare threatened to undo the armistice of 1918. Again, he was almost mobbed in Rome, when his country instigated sanctions against the latest Caesar hazarding a policy of conquest in Africa. In Majorca, his room was ransacked by Italian and German spies. He could not imagine the reason in his case, but felt certain not many months would go by before they ransacked all Spain.

—I am not sure, he wrote Ferdinand, that the program of the military party here has not its advantages for Spain, but I am certain that the German and Italian nationalists are prepared to turn any military program of any nation against the British Empire in the near future. I think it is folly not to attack the enemy now when he is still weak. The British tars are longing to fight.

Ferdinand had, indeed, wondered why his own country had allowed its former invaders to threaten its borders recently.

—Be sure to ask the Russian, the Englishman added in a postscript, what he thinks Russia's military will do.

Ferdinand asked the Russian, who answered:—Russia will in time, no doubt, have to fight with you, even with your own men of empire, alias the men of good will, but knowing that our English friend's "necessitous poor" will thrive neither among you nor your enemies."

—Russia is far away, yet a nation, said Ferdinand.—It has not been the immediate concern of Western Europe—any more than has China—for the past seventeen years. No one knows what Russia will do. Besides who wants to fight for any nation? Do you?

—Yes, the other answered, for Russia and not for Russia, in so far as the world to come must start *some* place, and hold out there till it comes.

—I can never understand you. Can't your world to come ever start here—here? asked Ferdinand.—Or in China?

—Here, too, the other said, or there will be no world. And

maybe one of these days for me, in China.

You're just making trouble for me, Ferdinand laughed, hinting at the slightly risqué story familiar to both of them—about the husband asking his neighbor whether the man whom he had found with his wife and who threatened to make trouble right then and there if he did not leave quickly enough really could make trouble for him.

That conversation, like all their other talk of the past ten years, had come to an end.

The Englishman wrote from Singapore when Japan launched its attack on China. He was in California, looking for work as an extra in the film industry, when the emissaries of the victors in the last war gathered at Munich to defer fighting their enemies at any cost. With little money he hurried back East to the British consulate, to enlist, since he could not believe that the leaders of his country were blind to its immediate danger. The reserves, he was amazed to learn, were not yet required.

The four friends met again, and their talk followed where it had left off seven years ago. The *rabbin,* as in the past brought down the humor of the others on him when he interrupted, by attempting to quote from a book at hand—while there was still time to thumb books, he remarked sheepishly looking up at them and glad there was company to tease him.

In the back of his mind, the Englishman was skeptical of his consulate's advice. Restless, he departed for England, but not before asking Ferdinand to take a leave from his job and to come along. Afraid to admit that not even his friend could help him break from his impasse, Ferdinand lied about urgent duties. Yet without knowing it, the Englishman, by making his life an excursus, had made his friends feel that they were bogged. Thus it was not altogether the Russian's decision that led him to leave for China about that time. He would be foreign correspondent there for a Russian-American journal, he told Ferdinand on leaving,—if I am bombed I shall be one among four hundred millions, rather than one of three as I am here.

And the *rabbin* went back to New York, night work, and the days with his books, till the day when perhaps war here would overtake him.

Left alone, Ferdinand reached the end of foresight before middle age. He had talked theory, though personally he saw no sense in it, while others were there to spur him. Alone, he had no heart left to guess. He could not see how science which invented words for what it did not know could predict anything. Like his world he could not look forward while looking back to a peace it never had.

Everyone knew the enemy was arming at a rate not experienced before, but no one in command was ready to stop him. They admitted the enemy was too formidable to stop. Then the enemy moved in where he pleased, where the chances of resisting were least. Finally when his intention to force England and Ferdinand's country to fight was as plain as day, their ministers shamed by their own defenseless peoples declared war: ostensibly in the name of honor upholding alliances with small nations, in their sphere of interest that had been attacked and the slaughter of whose peoples they could not prevent. Ferdinand everywhere heard these ministers called traitors. Nevertheless, for one year after that, while the leading powers were massed for attack and did not attack, other people said that it was because his country's secret defenses were strong and the enemy could not fight a concrete wall. But the attack came. Territory that had held out for four years of the last war was yielded in a few weeks. In less than six weeks his capital city fell. Those who dared risk their sinecures already unsafe admitted that the facts were, old survivors—heroes of their country in the last war—had sold out his father's memory and that of others like him who had once marched in triumph.

Perhaps if he were alive, his father would be one of the old, helpless betrayers. He was still uncertain as to the causes that had hurried their turpitude. He was not sure that they had feared their own common soldier might turn on them for having left him without weapons in the face of war. That they feared the enigma of Russia more than a foe whose aim of conquest was only too obvious seemed to him the assumption of the uninformed. Only these could assert that the Russians so-called, made up of one hundred eighty-two different peoples speaking one hundred forty-nine different languages, could all equally share as much freedom as the relatively few and more unified peoples of his small country, where the idea of people revolting for their rights had an older heritage. The leaders of his country could not, he thought, have been so skeptical as to underestimate the effect of their propaganda, that a soviet was not freedom, on their own informed peoples.

There seemed to be only one reason for their common defeat in the natural run of things: mistakes are not always avoided. It was easier to be old and a general or a minister and live—while one half of one's country was occupied by the enemy and the other half just as much enslaved though called unoccupied—than to die. Three thousand miles away from it all,, wasn't he more fortunate than a general? It was a moot point at the embassy whether it represented the occupied or unoccupied areas of his country.

The embassy—a parcel of homeland as before its defeat—obviously could represent nothing if the enemy took over his country's assets. America forestalled that contingency by freezing his country's local assets, though it did not grant diplomatic standing to a free army some thousands of his fellow nationals had mustered in England to continue the fight against the forces that had submitted to the enemy at home.

The law governing nations, in peace times effected ambiguously by a balance of power freeing the seas, had been reduced to the hazards of mined waters. If it had existed in the minds of most people like the names of home waters touching on different countries at once, it was now like the English Channel which might well be called German. The Atlantic ferry had stopped to convey passengers home on schedule. Even if he wanted to go home, like a sly child suspected by everyone, he might be beset on arrival with questions on all hands which he could not answer.

—The English who were our friends and our own sons are bombing us, his uncle might whisper, looking up from a book or a drawing of a flower, not daring to say—Let them bomb us. It is useless to pretend that I have studied or worked in this horror.

Anxiety overpowered Ferdinand's listlessness till his mind heard his uncle speak as though he were present:—Why come back, nephew, when we are on our way to a desert? Men don't see it. They think of this war as a lapse in civilian life. They imagine peace as it was—branches spread wide without any of the old sawed off.

Still more an image of his aunt in danger troubled him till he could not sleep. Roused suddenly, realizing he had been awake for hours, he asked himself questions which she might ask him if she were there and which he had weighed to no purpose almost twenty years. He had not married, and he shied explaining even in his own thought that a girl, whom somehow despite all their quarrels he could never leave, had stopped seeing him.

Knowing something of his personal life, she had grown tired of his indecisions—not to marry, not to go home, not to break off permanently or to start anew. Her absence and the unanswered letters, in his desk, of his closest friends sent him outdoors. In his car he was reminded by some part rattling in its engine that it needed a tune-up like himself, but would not be bothered to fix it. Bits of the Englishman's talk came back to him as he drove: . . . gentle, disgustingly so . . . everything diverging from one's aim is a bloody waste of time . . . The Creeping Charlie, attenuate like the Americans, still much more an existence than he, moved in the landscape to be stared at, after a summer storm,—and bored, he wished that the raindrops on the flower would reflect as tears in his eyes.

He ate much, to forget that he could not sleep. His hours away from the embassy were now spent in bars and restaurants where his countrymen waiting on him and his colleagues held to one line of talk:—They're all no good at home. Let's hope the colonies hold out. At least, our general on England's side is a patriot. The patriots these days are few and far between.

In the early mornings he went regularly to one of these places where from time to time the ambassador joined them. The radio, a source of tension, brought bad and indifferent news, easier to accept at these informal meetings. The embassy staff would be reduced after a curtailment of funds from home. Ferdinand was advised by the ambassador one morning to take a six months leave. Ultimately it might assure him his job. He had no choice, and he comforted his mind with the knowledge that a young colleague who was to take over some of his duties at less pay needed his salary more than he did. Over a fine, grape brandy, that was becoming hard to import from home and to which Ferdinand stood him, the younger man talked more than he should, out of gratitude:—The ambassador doesn't always know on which side he is himself. I don't see that there's any question, except that for some reason this government continues to recognize ours. Do you hear from home or family these days? I got a cable from my folks yesterday. They're just about hanging on—starving.

The insensitive, personal approach of the stranger somehow roused Ferdinand's sympathy. He was touched by the younger man's attempt at familiarity, but casually let the amount of drink they had consumed together be his excuse for turning away without answering. It was alright for people's judgment to be green, if they remained strangers. In his automobile on the way home, still seeing something of his own isolation in the younger man, his eyes suddenly filled with tears. He could not help thinking of the Englishman's phrase: god takes care of his own.

Perhaps god would, Ferdinand deliberated, faced with the last resort of the skeptic looking to the favors of chance.

He had not been in his room for two days and a cablegram

from his aunt and uncle was pinned to his door. They were well, had reached their country's possession in South America thanks to Ferdinand's older brother, still there on an official mission, and were on their way north.

Though the unexpected message drew Ferdinand's memory back to his youth and back again into the blind alley of his present, he was inclined to accept the fact of the old people sailing to see him, after all his fears for them, as a sign of good luck. Trusting to chance now seemed less silly than it would appear otherwise. He was not responsible for the cablegram. He knew that back of it was his brother, and for the first time in his life he found it easy to respect his brother's instinct to persist and take care of his own. Still serving the leaders who had compromised with the invaders of his country, his brother had saved what he could, while the leaders were realizing too late, without daring to admit, the futility of their compromise. Such shrewdness on the part of his brother made at least for some kind of life and affection, and after years of stubborn self-pity for lack of these Ferdinand felt he could well greet his brother should he too come north. It mattered little if a vestige of his past disgust sensed that his brother would remain where he was till his present advantage had been explored for all it was worth. In a world for whose institutions he was not responsible, his family suddenly seeking him out was alone worth saving. After twenty years of working blindly to achieve an enforced vacation, he was faced in his mind with the fairly cheerful contrast of his aunt and uncle taking the necessary means of their support for granted. Old, their integrity appeared so childlike, it would be a pity to reject and not to cherish it—all the more pity since like his brother they had been loyal to him over a long time. They had taken care of him as a child.

Free now of his embassy where his family had sent him as to school, he could look after them with all the wisdom he had acquired—which, summed up, said:—take care of your own. Retired and given to secrecy as usual, he felt that no one at the embassy need know they were coming—at least not till he knew where the old people wished to go or where they wished to stay. He had six months to spend as he wished, and if by the end of that time the pace of events did away with the embassy entirely, chance meanwhile might point to something else as he journeyed.

Small talk of his acquaintance was, Ferdinand was leaving again on one of his mysterious vacations.—Who is she? they asked. And while they flattered him, he appeared very happy, as though the creature they imagined existed. Preparations took a week during which he stored his belongings and invested in a new car. He had been too headlong, he thought, in his resignation to run last year's model with the emergency brake not working. The new motor would have to be driven with care till its parts worked in smoothly. And he would have the comfort of old, yet new riders to consider. For once his procedure, without effort, seemed to him rational, even pleasant. He spared himself good-byes and set out with one handbag.

He passed the shabby outskirts of the nation's capital after mid-night and drove to the port of arrival, the greatest city in the world, still extant, it occurred to him as he took the turns of the highway slowly. He had as much as eight hours time, though he figured on reaching the pier sooner than the ship on which his aunt and uncle were sailing. Part of the world was awake and formed the night landscape; a bomber plant, the flash of a furnace on a hill, a huge glass case with a thousand windows, all lighted, behind which biscuits were manufactured. From time to time he checked an impulse to try out his machine at full speed and drove on slightly less than forty miles an hour. For stretches of the road the leaves lighting up in the trees distracted his eyes from the constant path shown by his headlights. When finally he reached the city at dawn, he was aware that he had passed the most depressing industrial sections of the landscape in the dark.

A sense of having all the time in the world during that night and perhaps for as long as he lived had moderated the anxiety he expected to feel at meeting those he had not seen for so long. He could hardly believe, now that he would do all that he once confided to himself he could never do, there was so little to worry him. His loneliness seemed to move in the distance, offering no explanation as to why he had once brought it on himself, seemed reflected like the numbness of bitter cold when several senses at once begin to feel warm. He drove through a crowded street and, behind a long line of taxis also headed for the pier, recognized objects he had first seen twenty years ago.

There, a vessel of his country's merchant marine—its flag painted on the hull as a reminder that most of the world, if not he, was in the war—was already docked. Yet the vessel was safe—he remembered as a child being dragged out of the sea, safe. He walked towards the gangplank. At the top of its incline an elderly couple were looking around uncertainly. He was not sure at first it was they. He remembered them as well built and somewhat above average height. They were stooped now. But his uncle's glasses, with their thick lenses that stopped one from looking into them while the eyes behind them still peered keenly, were the same. The old people saw him—both at once—and his aunt stepping still briskly and maidenly started towards him. But she had to stop halfway down and hold on. As he came up to help them it seemed it was he who had come home.

—The city is built into the air, his uncle was saying.

Unaware of traffic dangerously close, he had leaned his head out of the car and looked up as they left the pier, then sat back still oblivious and entranced.—It reminds me of the tall buildings and apartment dwellings on the Riviera though those were not so tall.

—Do you remember the six story hotel and the monument to Columbus, Ferdinand? his aunt questioned.

They jarred him in reverting to his childhood unexpectedly, as if no present intervened; yet he felt touched, for they had not mentioned one hardship of their exile and were thinking of him. An unpremeditated sympathy—almost a chill at the thought of having to see them helpless or come to harm, as he recalled his uncle leaning out of the car a moment ago,—held him. To his aunt and uncle he appeared worried as he replied:—The hotel, well, yes, and perhaps he did not recall it at that. But, of course, he remembered the monument distinctly.

The three cruised past neglected six story tenements, where the poor lived, on their way to a restaurant once recommended to Ferdinand by a colleague at the embassy. The proprietor, a fellow countryman, catered to a quiet, dignified set. They dined in the same poor quarter, his aunt noticed.

—Quite a number of fellow nationals preferred this district and lived here back of the main railroad station and center of town, Ferdinand told her.

—I see, it's accessible, she said.—Do you come often to the big city? That's what it's called, isn't it? I suppose there really are no other cities like this anywhere?

—No. This was his first visit in twenty years. But it was his first long vacation. He explained with some diffidence his present status at the embassy, over lunch.

—Ah, but poor boy, his aunt and uncle expressed their regret as with one voice.—You must not worry. It's to be expected. We ourselves have fared much better than we expected. We have told you nothing, and perhaps we should not here.

They looked around, asking silently if the other diners were friends.

—If I tell you that we fled our country because our acquaintance in the government trusted us less than the invader, his uncle whispered, staring beneath the rims of his glasses at the white tablecloth—will you believe me?

—I can very well believe you, Ferdinand agreed slowly.

—The invader is an expression, his aunt urged.—Our most trusted led him. They invited his fire on our own: women, children, boys they expected to fight without arms.

Her head shaking involuntarily seemed to be trying to persuade her nephew completely. Small wrinkles in her lips held back a sob. He saw his uncle's sensitive hand reach out as if to hold hers and console her, but it stopped, pretending to be prompted by his food. Ferdinand leaned back on his chair unconscionably—the gist of their talk was sinking in, his food unwanted.

His aunt attempted a smile.—Why do we disturb you, when we were so happy thinking during the worst of it that you were not there to see us suffer?

Ferdinand could not help reflecting to himself that for anyone who yet wished to write, her words were among the best of her time.

—Do you recall the book I was working on, Ferdinand? his uncle asked, to change the subject.—Well, with all of us safe in this country, I should be able to finish it.

—I am sure, Ferdinand said, feeling like a novice that he had invoked a blessing and not too certain that something valuable beyond them, as they sat there, was being granted.

Notwithstanding the presence of his relations, he felt lonely again. The sensation of relief from anxiety, of the day before, while he was travelling alone, was gone.

—Yes, his uncle continued, I want to finish it. When one is on in years, as I am, the confused haste to finish things regulates a sort of trembling existence. Besides, world wars have a way of spreading, I feel too often as if my hands were letting things fall from them. And yet I know very clearly what I wish to do.

—Still the work on Linnaeus? Ferdinand questioned.

—Yes, but more than that. Rather a work on the order of thought he effected by making order in a world of things growing. Isn't that the way science works?

—Or a poet or anybody? his aunt ventured pleasantly.

Ferdinand listened to her voice quite aside from, yet close to their lives.

His uncle continued: He affected others, caused them to

travel, here for example, where they recorded in English, often spelling it as they spoke it, with an accent, their finds of flowers, birds and game. You see, separated from these others by scarcely a century and a half, I can still be one of them.

Ferdinand smiled spasmodically and looked serious again.

—Like the farmer from our country, his uncle continued, who, when his wife passed away could plant only flowers and left for the East in this service for the King; and later bought land here in Jersey where he cultivated gardens and shipped varieties of new cuttings home; explored the mountains down to the Carolinas; went on to Florida, to the lowlands on the gulf, and at last north to the prairies. Till then, Indian companions had not footed his devious paths. The Court let the birds and plants he sent home die. This did not prevent his son from devoting years to his study of the woods of the North American continent. Such men are not among those that another naturalist who also came here from our country speaks of: "gamblers that although playing for nothing are always grieved by losing." He was a wonderful person this particular naturalist. Here are some things from his diaries I have jotted down. Unquestionably his hazards depressed him.

His uncle read from a small pad kept in a billfold of saddle leather which he had taken out of his coat pocket.

—"No doubt that the frogs that whistled so merrily yesterday are well buried in the mud this morning."

—"The winds on this river are contrary to our wishes as that of an old rich maid to the wishes of a lover of wealth."

—Yet he was a lover of wealth. He did not slight such scenes as an immense flock of bank swallows of which he says that "the falling of their dung resembled a heavy but thinly falling snow"; nor did he fail to observe that someone's lawful wife resided and kept a small store with another gentleman—"their partnership," he says, "rendered agreeable by a natural wish of nature." He underlined lightly, you see, the singularities of the difficult life around him, and in another place he says, "I have never been very fond of battles, and indeed have always wished that the world were more peaceable than it is."

His uncle put back his billfold into his pocket. As he took some time about it, Ferdinand, watching him fidget, thought, he stores his years there. It's the first time he's spoken at length to me.

—Perhaps you may remember my mentioning, a good many years ago, the Commelina Virginica, his uncle smiled at him.

That, Ferdinand realized quickly, was the Latin he had tried for years to remember. They call it here the Creeping Charlie—is that it? he asked his uncle.

—Perhaps. I've also heard it called the Wandering Jew. Both folk names laymen find appropriate, I suppose, to a flower which thrives like a weed. It was named after two brothers and you know, it has three petals, two blue which are seen. But there was also a third brother, and there is a third petal not seen which is white. To me it's like the past affecting us and not here. I have often taken that petal out of its sheath and the flower dies. No, I have never been very fond of battles. But how would it be if one could take that white petal out of its sheath and the flower would live? I imagine it would be like the feeling experienced by those queer people who explore again the terrains of old battlefields and sense anew the action that happened there. Could you stand such a trip with me over the old routes that these predecessors in my book took once?

—I don't know what is left of those routes, Ferdinand suggested.

—Probably a good many or sufficient stretches of them.

—Well, of course, his nephew answered, but don't you want to look around in the city a few days?

—Well, it would be like a besieged fortress for me.

—You see, Ferdinand, his aunt said,—he's been so restless, having his work interrupted. Still we'll be driving in your car, and perhaps you would prefer not to.

—Not at all, he answered, it makes no difference.

They were after all old people. Their incentives were naturally not his. The scene of a party that took place near the embassy occurred to him: a group there amused themselves with an attachment to a phonograph that could play records backwards.

But in his mind he was already planning their trip.

Nothing of consequence happened in the hotel lobby filled with furniture dimly reminiscent of living quarters he had shared with his relations as a child. They remarked on the fact that the desk-clerk had not asked them for their cards of identity. But, of course, they had forgotten these were not required by this country. This, they said, made them feel at once that they were not foreigners. As a result they sat in the lobby for a while and chatted. Finally, in their suite they became sleepy, and retired to their own room.

Not accustomed to going to sleep early, Ferdinand sat around, thinking of tomorrow's itinerary. Looking through his luggage for something to read, he found himself arranging some scattered pages of blank stationery. He had not intended to keep in touch with anyone on this trip. But he suddenly decided it might be amusing to write his close friends, the Englishman, the Russian and the *rabbin*—now that they had left his world and he theirs—and ask them to address him at a small western post office where he expected his journey would take him two months hence.

He mailed the letters in the corridor and entered his room again as quietly as he could. But just then in the street below the horn of a car sounded stridently and continued for a few minutes—evidently something wrong with it—till it made him furious. He became concerned that his aunt and uncle in their part of the suite would probably be wakened by the noise, if they had not been already. And for no other reason than that just then he wanted absolute quiet, he entered their room to make certain. They were sleeping, but since he could not hear them breathe, he bent over their beds to reassure himself.

As his pulse, which had quickened, permitted him to hear their separate breaths, he stood up again, perplexed, not daring to admit to himself the absurd thread of life that had led him to fear the death of the old people in their sleep. The blind wish in which he indulged for some world where his own history would not diminish to the vanishing point made him feel at that moment of less use to the world than ever. The street behind the drawn blinds of their room had quieted down, but only in his own image of a channel bearing the impress of a force that had sounded and wasted growing distant. There was a kind of adequacy in feeling that way, though he knew while they slept no one missed him. He returned to an armchair in his room of the suite and sat there brooding till his mind drowsily seemed to pick up the voice of a chorus in the wings of some platform—the room had become so large summing up his life thus, clearly:—

Ferdinand came from a hamlet in the environs of, he did not remember the name. He never said much about his parents, but once over drinks confided in a few close friends that but for his mother he would never have seen his father on the only two occasions he did. Ferdinand's profile was meridional, but in this country quickly took on the aspect of an American. Other friends could tell other stories. He had a brother with whom he might have quarreled in his youth and had never seen again. He avoided having his friends meet his mistresses wherever he happened to dwell by running downstairs to greet them with the excuse that they could not come up because the house was in disorder. He was evidently selfmade since very young, and through extremely generous at times, hard knocks in the past seemed responsible for many of his violent resentments and unexplained recurrent breaches short of sportsmanship.—

He was yawning excessively when he stepped into bed. For once he slept without having nightmares. And being one of those restless people who cannot recall a time when they ever sleep soundly, he awoke so rested the next morning it seemed he had had no need to sleep at all.

Really, it was May. The weather made their morning coffee a delight. An early riser, Ferdinand had the first day of the journey mapped. Leaving it to him and the motor of his automobile that ran so smoothly they could hardly hear it, his relations found themselves out of the city in a half hour's run. They had taken the ramp overlooking the river famous for the width of its estuary and its palisades and were in its valley of rich estates and heading north where the source rose hours away. On the first lawn they saw, the blossoms were falling. Here were indigenous trees and birds aunt and uncle had previously codified in books.

Ferdinand carried a tune under his breath, at first scarcely conscious that he had struck upon an air for viols, seven centuries old. The words written to it at that time, beginning *Kalendas Mayas,* resounded with the festival of May. The dance of the words, and the dance they followed called *estampeda,* was among the earliest that gave his people a tongue. Only bookish people had remained familiar with its simple measures. His aunt and uncle recalled them from university days and urged him to sing the whole song aloud. He consented because they promised to join him.

To sing well, without attracting attention, and to show them another local tree, he stopped the car under a shagbark. No one was hungry and lunch could wait. So they sang of May, the echoes of the rhyme *aya* beating out at the end of each line the stamp of feet. They continued with a full repertoire, while each song seemed to say: the previous song was of a different time.

The effort was tiring them. They had almost reached their own age when his uncle dropped out of the trio. His aunt hummed a snatch of a mazurka; Ferdinand, perhaps deferring to her young days because she had raised him, the lilt of a Viennese waltz.

—Let us end now with the minuet from *Don Giovanni* said his uncle.

Rather childish, its performance broken by an occasional doubtful laugh, Ferdinand's voice attempted to imitate the twanged strings of a harpsichord. His aunt accompanied him, humming.

—Poor as your performance is, the tune still has insuperable balance his uncle said.—The construction it is hides how much of it is solid earth. We don't know how much until we hear the words acted in the scene for which the sounds were meant. Even then perhaps only children can realize fully how mysterious three masks over three actors' faces can be though all the previous action of the plot tells us whose faces they are. Older people who can still hear the tune itself above the action and the words of the lovers can only become wistful.

A child had stepped upon the running board of the car and was watching them.

Later, in the heat of midday, when the gray-haired botanist delighted his wife and nephew in a new role, eating a brick of ice cream on a stick known as an Eskimo Pie that a boy vendor on a bicycle had sold him, Ferdinand still imagined he heard a hidden drift of melody over the landscape: songs gathered there from all nations, like the birds, and bringing up former days despite present casual sounds. He suspected that most of the old numbers they had sung would have rather an enemy status in several nations now at war and that a language of notes alone was still too frail to cement the finer human passions easily greeted by society when contention is not its tongue.

Before going to bed that night in a farmhouse in which his aunt and uncle were pleased to put up, he whistled to himself again, almost without feeling, *The Miller of the Dee,* with its characteristic English refrains, as if they had become his mottoes:

—I care for nobody, no not I, and nobody cares for me . . .

—Let others labor from year to year, I live but from day to day . . .

And yet, while he whistled, he was convinced at heart that neither the tune nor the verses would serve those who feigned to live in his time. He did not need to tell his relations, and much less himself, that whatever out-of-the-way places they went to could be harassed soon enough by events that at best hang fire. Civilized people, they feared the next morning that the inconsequence of yesterday's casual richness would not be the pattern of today or the next day. The recurrence of breakfast in a farmhouse or on the terrace of a country hotel, driving a few hours in the early morning until Ferdinand became tired, lunch, more driving, supper, an indisposition on everyone's part to stir in the evening before going to sleep or to lie awake, made them restless. Aunt and uncle reverting to lifelong habits without meaning to, appeared detached to their nephew. His unintentional manner in turn impressed them as distant. Thinking of nothing or his position at the embassy a half year from then or what might happen to the world meanwhile, he would stroll off alone, as often as he stopped his car, without considering their feelings. After hearing him say he would return soon for lunch, they waited till they lost all appetite. But they ate with him, if he still wished to eat, when he came back.

One aim controlled them all, to avoid the cities. Fortunately the engineers of the time planned highways which occasionally conformed to the aim of Ferdinand and his relations. The newest road skirted the cities. In the legends of maps handed out free at the gasoline stations owned by the leading oil monopoly, these first class, numbered highways, appearing as lines of primary red and blue, meant they made travelling faster and more pleasant. Yet the harder and the more carefully graded their shoulders were than those of second class roads of gravel or narrow paving, the more clipped was the grass at their sides. Travelling faster, one saw less of the country. Skirting the cities, numerous cars ran over miles of road no less urban. The lush grass growing in the memories of aunt and uncle at the sides of earth roads in the homeland—a rare sight in the foreign land they travelled through became a delight for which they wished constantly.

—But surely, his uncle said, there must be side roads more diverting. That one, to the left.

—That leads right on to a rich man's estate, Ferdinand answered time and time again.

The itinerary he had chosen offered indeed almost no chance to diverge from the main road. But sometimes he lied. Instinctively sparing with his uncle's money, he thought of the wear on the tires of his car going over sharp stones. From the moment his position at the embassy had become uncertain, his worries had transformed his own investments and savings into a negative quantity that his needs could not touch except for dividends and interest. But then, as in the past, the selfish streak rankled and he would be generous again, fitfully. Bumping over a rut, in his caprice, he risked more serious harm to his car than the wear and tear on its tires. Like the highways, the ruts, however, did not lead to the old routes as his relations expected—at least never to the old routes as they had seen them in their minds. The discomfort the old people endured in driving over gutted tracks—midriffs shaken as they caught their breaths—was not repaid by what they found.

At best they came always upon ruins which modern times had let alone; at the worst upon cheap tourist mementoes that flattered the bypaths and sites commemorated. With the obstinacy of age and with the feeling of possession that lovers who have shared many years together decline to give up for the sake of any third person, aunt and uncle continued to hope as before for their book. Ferdinand's uncle reiterated *ad nauseam*—They would find it . . . They would find it . . . harking back to words of Jefferson among his notes: "That there was still one bird, absolutely unknown to science, which he had heard and some hunters knew, that sang divinely from the tops of the highest trees."

They were not aware, as their nephew was, of a vague click at first, and a week later, of a definite knock in the motor of his car. He did not mention it to them, but dreading the time when he would have to pay for repairs, he became more depressed than ever over the fact that his new car was failing them. To forget it, while the old folks drowsed during their afternoon siesta, he would stretch out face down in the grass, after leaping over an embankment or a fence, and immediately fall asleep himself.

Once, after a few minutes, he awoke, his senses unnerved and his mind confused by the terror of a dream he could not recall, to see the old people standing over him, waiting.

—You cried out in your sleep, Ferdinand, his aunt said, embarrassed.

Vaguely it came back—he had cried for some reason about them, and too terrified to look at their faces, he did not answer her. He continued to stare into the grass, wishing he could find the ease to confide his terror and so perhaps be rid of a spell. For he was possessed by the feeling that his dream instinctively had willed some vague terror to happen to them.

From that day on, though often on the verge of being driven frantic by their talk of the past, he listened to them, even forced himself to listen, repenting, as it were, in silence, that there were times when he wanted to shut them out.

One day he drove his car, sounding worse, over dirt roads and a detour, altogether fifty miles of a rough jaunt towards the ocean, which they had expressed a desire to see again. It was evening when they reached it. From the rock of a lighthouse, approached past clumps of bay grayed by blowing sands at the end of a point of land, they looked into the flood of waves. To the northeast the coast extended further into the sea—a fringe of trees whose species the eyes of the botanist could not probe because of their myopia. The three stood there unconcerned and alien, excluded by their desires from any curiosity as to the cottages of white painted clapboard impressively simple, old and alone, but part of the land behind them.

A full moon almost above the swell appeared to rock them and the flowing tons of water. After a short while they felt they were not people, but old costumes through which the wind flustered, supporting these strangely against the folds of the sea.

—It is red like the sun, said Ferdinand, his mind seeking

an image that he could not place anywhere but at the edge of an inland sea, perhaps more legendary than he remembered it these many years over three thousand miles away.

—This coast is different, but all of it reminds me of that evening we drove you back from Portofino with a fever when you were a little boy, his aunt remarked. You were able to talk quite fluently for your age, but all you said was:—fire—water.

—Rather elemental, he said. I could say the same thing now, he added with a laugh, mystifying them, as he thought to himself of his friend, the Englishman: of all people, throwing a coin over his shoulder towards a full moon for good luck when they were both somewhat drunk—and how his friend could pun.

—Nothing much grows here, he continued. I should think people who live on this barren coast might long for mountains that rise over the sea, like those where we come from.

—There's little need for humanity here, his uncle suggested.

—Yes, Ferdinand said, I am sure that a wine country bordering on the sea must be a legend to fishermen here. I believe it's quite usual to say that there are no peasants in America. I wonder what would happen to—his words ran out and stopped.

—To whom, his aunt asked him.

—Nothing. Let's go back to the car, he said.

—I wish you were happy, Ferdinand, his aunt said. I know it's foolish of me to keep on thinking of you as the small boy who once seemed to us very happy playing he was Columbus, because this name on a monument was a companion. Has our little nephew lost that bent of mind entirely?

Hurt by his silence which had estranged him since their arrival, she was forced to speak even at the risk that he might consider her maudlin.

—But I grew up, he smiled. He did not know what to say.

—You look ill, Ferdinand, she said. Perhaps we've been taking you out of your way, disturbing other plans. Maybe a change of landscape would do us all good.

He felt very sorry for them.

I'll drive wherever you say. Any landscape suits me, really it does.

She searched his face and decided for him. He suspected that they had discussed the matter before.—Let us go west then. We don't mind shortening the whole trip by a few weeks. After it ends, we may, all of us, want to get in touch with your brother and perhaps decide on another trip.

They were sitting in the car again, which he had not started though he had just pressed the switch lighting the dashboard. He did not answer her, determined he would never act on her last suggestion. They could not be happy with him. Why complicate matters with additional family. He was ready to start again, but with these two only.

—All set? he asked.

They nodded,—One thing, Ferdinand, his uncle asked, from now on please drive carefully. It would be foolish for us to end up in a hospital.

—You mustn't worry, he answered, I wouldn't have much courage for that myself.

He drove slowly over a dark road and stopped at the first garage in a sizable seacoast town where he put up the car for repairs during the night.

A month had passed since they first set out on their journey back into the byways envisioned by his uncle. But as if to stress that the world was rolling another way at the same time, the morning newspaper they read during breakfast told them that the enemy, who about a year ago had occupied their homeland, had broken another pact and turned on Russia. The enigma of what Russia would do was thus exploded. Ferdinand remembered his Russian friend had said to him that if their native land would be free again, Russia would not be on the side of their enemy.

But aunt and uncle refused to talk about it. If only they could go about their work in peace again while they lived. At their age they were justified, thought Ferdinand, considering that the compass seemed to offer no respite. For to the east of Russia the Japanese adventure in China continued, and since China was only one of the stakes of empire, adventure rolling like a ball might roll onto Russia; or offered less resistance down another chute of the world, roll into the Pacific, thus affecting the land through which Ferdinand and his relations were travelling. One might worry further about the ultimate attitude of The States towards the homeland which the old people had fled. For the present, refugees of their type were welcome, and perhaps that was the one fact of politics worth remembering to them.

The vague click in the motor of his automobile returned a few hours after he had paid to repair it. Annoyance after annoyance, and it would cost money and more money. He suspected piston trouble.

The summer wore on. Worried by the car, thirsty and made sleepy by the song of a bird in the afternoon heat of the prairies, he would be rived suddenly from dozing at the wheel—from a bad daydream as of being saved on a shore, his awareness still noisy with water; or eyes bloodshot, mirror in his mind the red eyes of a rabbit, suffering; or seem to be set down all at once in some burning city where, a stranger after twenty years of exile, on its streets he ran across aunt and uncle whose dimmed expressionless faces impelled him to drag after them with such heaviness he had to moan.

Fully awake then, he regretted that he never dreamed of his friends instead for whom in rare moments of his life he had felt true affection: the *rabbin* whose gentleness, unlike his own, could not hurt anybody; the Englishman whose thinking had approached the exhilaration of physical exercise; the Russian whose obstinacy in debate had amused him more than the insistence of his loves. He was anxious to hear from all three.

Aunt and uncle, scarcely realizing how he felt, took to the heat of midsummer better than they had to the cool spells during the eastern stretch of their journey. He impressed them as extremely fit and even happy in the mornings. But though each morning the light on thriving grain revived him, the summer brilliance by midday always succeeded in depressing him with a feeling of its absence. Before him the black hood of his car which no ray or color penetrated continued into the sunlight till every afternoon he literally saw black.

They crossed a table-land. In the evenings when the air cooled, the old couple were now writing their book. Hearing them discuss old classifications in the light of the little data they had gathered recently, he found himself drifting into the past with their voices in the whitish ring of lamplight where the moths thudded softly.

He was moved by a peculiar idea that if his uncle turned to him and insisted that he, Ferdinand, had lived before he was born, he could take the old man seriously, since belief of that kind was after all not too different from what students of the body believed who had isolated the persistence of the race in parts of its cells.

As he sat there, he even imagined these parts of cells separating till a new body was formed, coming to life again in the past. The strange reversal of sequence, assuming an air of fact, allowed him to relax and play with it for all it was worth, and as he looked up at the stars, he allowed the distance between them and him to lose most of its light years: so that the earth became younger and younger, making him feel that soon enough it would be lit up by the stars, quite close, as when they first began to shine.

At the western post office where he expected his mail, he did not hear from the Englishman or the Russian—who were, who knew where? But the *rabbin* had answered promptly as usual. He had been drafted since he was still young enough to come under the recent law, and wrote about it briefly: "The draft gives one a number and releases one into a virgin world. You realize, of course, that the army is no place where one may till one's bookish mind as it was. I suspect that like love or its absence it will teach me much in time. Then perhaps I will have something to say. But—

R.S.V.P."

He thought of the *rabbin*'s thin physique, reminding him of a slim statue of an Etruscan warrior in a museum back east and like the material of the statue serving, while it could be preserved, as but the stopping place of its sensitiveness, and asked himself: now what can the *rabbin* do in the army? But that image of the Etruscan warrior must have fought, too. It was a question that the *rabbin* had ceased to consider, Ferdinand thought as he glanced through the brief note a second time. Good old *rabbin,* he mused, he writes of his uncertain future hurriedly but modestly, to his friend in the past, as if I were still alive. He could not have thought of a more polite close than—Reply if you please. He would write to the *rabbin* in time. Why hurry to say he was becoming nothing to his friend who might be in active service soon and in danger of death?

They were driving southwest, through the region of mountains, arid and irrigated desert that along with the mesas, buttes, canyons, gorges, mountain ranges, lava flows, ice caves, and painted desert to the north, had been admitted to the union as the forty-eighth state less than thirty years ago. Its constitution, Ferdinand and his relations read in their guide, then provided for the recall of judges: whether with the aim of protecting people against unfair decisions or of abetting a minority's contempt of the law, Ferdinand could not guess. But as they travelled he came across evidence as to why laws were necessary among scenic wonders. Shales were a source of oil. Rocks yielded stones for jewels. The sides of mountains were mined intensively in some areas. The structures over oil wells and the entrances to the shafts of mines suggested triumphal columns ranging along avenues of empires of other times. Precious water, the sale of which conferred rights, flowed in ditches through extensive ranches thriving with the green of temperate zones, despite the hot dry air, in a desert setting of sand and cacti.

Beside the novelties which seemed but to have studded

the natural landscape, there existed the ruins of ancient building in the rock cliff and of irrigation canals in the valleys—the past work of extinct tribes of Indians, perhaps related to the high culture of the Mayas, Aztecs and Toltecs of Mexico further south, and glowingly recommended to tourists in the bulletins of chambers of commerce. The present tribes, some of them close descendants of the extinct, confined to modern settlements or reservations, fared none too well, though their former Indian character persisted in a seclusion of legend, handiwork, dances and ceremonials. In August or September, every year or every other year, certain tribes revived old rites that travellers like Ferdinand and his aunt and uncle, sympathetic to passing races, came far to study. The rest of the year the Indians subsisted on their ingenuity, making clay pots and baskets, hammering out metal ornaments, weaving blankets, mostly for the tourist trade, and attempting to grow a few crops—the yield not always enough to sustain them—, or just abiding by the restrictions of the reservation. Some, Ferdinand noticed as he travelled, hired out on farms—perhaps to keep from turning into rock. The red and yellowish rock of the landscape, often recalling human shapes, impelled this fancy. At that it was a twist in a white man's way of seeing the Indian in the colors of maize, potato, sweet potato and tobacco that identified his genius in the lay mind. Whether or not the natives of the region would become finally as inert as red or yellowish rock because the crops they had given to the world were hard to come by in a desert, the low humidity and the brilliance of the air insisted on fixing them in these colors in Ferdinand's mind. Bold colors of a pre-Columbian time contrasted, as he drove on, with the lustrous deep blue of the sky everywhere, by day or night, whether the sun shone or other suns flashed in the dark as stars.

The three continued in the car without much sense of time till one morning as they neared a prosperous ranch, Ferdinand saw a crude, dome-shaped dwelling on its outlying acres. He assumed that some Indians who worked on the ranch lived in the framework of saplings thatched with grass and leaves of shrubs, as others lived in adobes nearby. He did not point out the structure to his aunt and uncle who were trying intently to make out a spiny, unfamiliar plant at a distance. All at once he was aware of a young girl, of about fifteen, standing in the door of the dwelling. Her eyes looked elsewhere, yet her face was turned fully towards him, its clear reddish brown skin set off by a braid of black hair falling down in front of each shoulder. She seemed to have come into the surrounding air with no other intention than to appear benign, like the sun, against the blue of the sky.

Her face strikingly resembled the smooth, brown tones of an archaic earthenware or of primitive carving in wood that might give the same effect. A white linen waist and a peasant skirt woven of double cloth did not hide her arms and legs as deeply vivid as her face. Her bare feet, not small and not large, were evidently familiar with the ground. It was easy enough looking at her to feel the reason for conjectures about migrations of long ago, starting perhaps from the north of Asia separated from the Western continents by a narrow strait, or from hot islands across the sea, vaguely in coracles; but however it was, narrowing down to this moment and place. Devoted to he did not know what, the face might yet be looking at him through the windshield of his car as he moved up the road. She turned sideways to go indoors. He saw her profile and was aware of her entire body. His arteries beat faster to the thought that, young as she was, the fullest efforts of her race had begun to decay long before his own dying people started to live. But he could not sense any process of decay as fatal to her forbears as to his own in his own life. His uncle might say, had he seen her—the old couple had not—that she existed like the hidden petal of the Creeping Charlie. Though, with respect to her, the sky, whose blue resembled the petals that are seen and glared over the empty road in the sun, might be hidden instead of her.

He drove on, seeing little, conscious only after a while that he had trespassed on a private road. His aunt and uncle, in a reverie of their own, were remarking on the skill with which the desert had been made to bloom with fruits and flowers, vegetables and grain, by means of an orderly network of artificial runnels. The road branched into a driveway at the foot of a knoll, at the top of which a house, whose front was a substantial portico, adjoined a trellis forming a sheltered walk the length of its side wall. Large purple grapes, almost black, covered the latticework with a kind of hothouse opulence.

—How lovely, Ferdinand's aunt and uncle said in almost one breath.

The scene reminded them of their house on the Riviera that they had shuttered over twenty-five years ago.

A man who came up to the entrance of the walk leaned slightly forward, each hand holding on to a side of the trellis structure, and looked down at them. For an instant Ferdinand could have sworn to his aunt and uncle that the man was their former gardener. Very likely they, who dwelt even more in the past than he, had the same thought. To say it would but tug their desires for what had gone out of their lives. The old routes they had sought, they must know, were no older than their memories. Overlooking the Atlantic, he had stopped himself from speaking to his aunt and uncle about the gardener, and he stopped himself now.

He stalled the car, trying to turn around in the small space and drive off. Too old to endure exile or to expect a haven such as the place they were leaving might have offered in other days, their looks of regret probed their happiness that was past—a house, a vineyard, and a gardener who made plants of a season intimate; as his own regret reverted to all these, as well as a sudden swirl of sea from which he was saved, and a little girl about whom passion had not dispelled the thought of first love.

Like the dying said to see images of their earliest life—or all their past through a child's eyes—the three were stalled as if they still had a moment in the present.

The man who reminded Ferdinand of the gardener might

have spoken in any one of several languages and been understood. But as though he guessed something of the memories he had stirred, he addressed them in their own language.—Yes? he asked, as he approached the car, can I help?

They picked up to their own speech which had lost meaning spoken for three months only among themselves. Even Ferdinand could not be so rude as to drive off without answering.

—They were admiring his estate, he answered.

—Yes. A beautiful estate. But I am only the caretaker, the man said, not that I wish to be more.

He spoke their language with a familiar accent.

—You are an Italian, Ferdinand's uncle said, answering his own question.

—Yes, the other said.—I did not relish the idea of my country fighting yours, so I came here. Victory to the leader of our state is a matter of how well people can draw in their belts.

He said the last, sticking out his jaw and affecting a martial pose that made him look comically pigeon-chested. The glare of the sun clashed with the white of the desert in the distance, and Ferdinand wondered what other choice people had—unless they could find some plot of earth to work, like this caretaker, undisturbed.

The man did not mind talking about himself. As no doubt they guessed, he had fled. Stayed in hiding a year in Portugal. By a miracle he met the owner of this estate there who needed a practical agronomist. And this is what I've done since, he said, indicating the grounds.

He had mentioned the name of his employer, whom Ferdinand had met once. The official and his family were away on a special mission in the East, but were expected home soon. Chances of avoiding war in the Pacific were none too certain, the caretaker gathered. Ferdinand's thought drifted back to the embassy. He wondered if the youngster who had replaced him there had made good, if anyone still could make good in a bankrupt economy.

All his family, father, uncles, distant cousins on both sides had been either farmers or gardeners, he heard the man say to his uncle.

—Did he know? his aunt and uncle mentioned their former gardener by name.

—Yes, a very distant relation. But he knew his son-in-law well. His wife, a very pretty girl, had a baby.

—What happened to them?

He did not know. But most of the men came home from Greece, after fighting the winter campaign without shoes, with amputated feet. Only infants in cribs and the very old had not been put into uniforms. And yet all that his people had done was to become unwilling appeasers of the common enemy who had forced the war on them.

Ferdinand listened from time to time as he twisted a blade of grass. The three talking seemed to blend their separate voices in the sun. He saw one European nation after another sink into a crater where no agronomist could exercise his genius, for ever so many years to come, with the same facilities as in this desert.

It was too hot to drive, so they were having lunch with the caretaker. He was saying to Ferdinand's aunt,—Most of the time it does not seem to matter what happens to anyone. I suppose one needs food and drink and grows it.

They were drinking wine.

Because there seemed no point in listening consecutively, the talk was not always easy to follow.

—Certainly I am lonely sometimes, the caretaker said.—Without my family I feel orphaned. Like the Indians about the place, I work here and may die here. One of them, a young girl, tells me some of their stories. Nina says—

—Is that her name? Ferdinand asked, tasting his tenth glass. His aunt and uncle did not seem to hear him.

—Yes, the man went on, Nina says that all tribes came from the top of a mountain not far from here. The top is a square like a map—those are their words—and there each tribe received what it would require in the place where it was to live. But today some of them sing a song, "I have no money to go to the ranch." I daresay the red evening—the sunset on the mountains—was also given to them in that square. Nina tells me that Elder Brother, the hero who gave it to them, was killed. And he was dead a long time. Children played with his bones and made bridges of his ribs, till one day they ran home to tell their parents Elder Brother was sitting where he used to, fixing a clay drinking flask.

The thought of his older brother passed through Ferdinand's mind. It was cool in the lodge. They were out of the sun.

The caretaker was telling another story:

—Two brothers and their grandmother travelled in the throng with Elder Brother. Rather, the three always lagged behind. Grandmother was so old she could not keep up with the rest. Every evening the two brothers built a fire and left their grandmother there, and ran to catch up with the others to find out what everybody must do the next morning. Then they went back to their grandmother. They did this for a long time till they grew sick of it. The older brother said—I guess we had better kill our grandmother and stay with the rest for good, so we will know what is going on all the time. There might be a good fight down that way, and we'll miss it.

—The younger brother said, Alright, but let us first ask grandmother and hear what she says.

—They begged her, grandmother, you know how hard it is for us to keep up with the others. If we kill you, it would be easier for all of us. What do you think?

—Because I have lived long and have seen many things, grandsons, I know it would. And I would like you to be over there with the rest and see all that goes on. She sang a song and wept, I have seen many things in this world, and I have been in this world a long time.

Ferdinand was curious why his mind kept weighing whether the story were in good taste. The faces of his aunt and uncle were wrinkled and sad.

—No, thank you, each of the three said to the caretaker in turn and shook his hand. Ferdinand made out each speaking face distinctly. Aunt and uncle were grateful. He, too. But they had overstayed as it was. Good-bye came more glibly to his lips than it ever had.

He was thinking of the prestige of some one called Elder Brother in the stories he had heard and deliberating vaguely on associations connected with the first born among civilized people. The caretaker was saying—Fog settles in the mountain paths as soon as night falls. There are no places to stop at till the other side—and waved good-bye in the distance.

There was more point to driving a car after drinking. He insisted the risk made him see better. The desert sand on the left shoulder of the concrete road piled up in ridges. Graying hair, like his own it seemed, thinning out. Matted sage that no comb need part like hair disappeared from the view before him. A rickety planking replaced the concrete, and the car jogged and sagged across the crevices of the planks. Together they saw pronged cacti higher than a white brick wall, the last of a gas station, left standing with empty cans that must have been unprofitable to ship when full; a mesa, a congealed fall of color, too remote to take up more than a flash of attention; and nearby, a gorge, once a torrent, become a dry run. In the shadows of mountains making the daylight grow dark, the road now cut through rock and climbed around it in terraces. He felt unsafe gauging how many feet down their steep faces measured while he tried to look ahead at the same time. They drove as if over a prolonged wave, barely the width of two cars, its low broken curbing distracting to the eye.

—The caretaker was right, he said. I should have had more wine before trying these mountains.

—Who? his uncle asked.

—Père Noé, qui plantastes la vigne (Father Noah, who planted the vine) and since he had spoken listlessly, he persisted—that would be my testament, as well as Villon's. Yours, too. What hogs can forbid it or lay waste to our people?

Why weren't they talking?

—The evil piston rod knocked again.

Ample room to make the next, right turn, downhill, around two rocks that met at a right angle. Were they out of their minds saying he had swung out left and the curbing held him to the road? Or had they not said anything?

He was out of their old world again and in the New, no better.

—This is the burial space mentioned in the travel guide, he was saying to himself. The name Antigone passed through his mind. On all fours, growing used to the darkness, he carried their bodies one on each shoulder into the low cave, its floor a pile of broken rocks and its roof of heavy timbers thrust into the hillside.

—I am coming back, aunt, uncle, he sobbed to himself and looked into their eyes, the eyes of needles between eyelids. He crawled out, brushing against a decaying saddle that once belonged to some Indian. He had been fortunate not to see his mother's eyes in death. Fortune did not repeat itself.

They must not lie here more than one night. His word would not be believed. He pleaded his defense beforehand; all the time his eyes had been fixed on the road. But all the time. Why would he wreck his new car to be rid of them? They were weak enough to handle otherwise.

He hurried faster than he thought his heart could stand to retrace the tracks of the car through the desert on foot—positive that the caretaker was not at the ranch. He had not a second to spare, and it was too dark to look into a mirror to see if his face bled.

Out of breath, he stood at last at the caretaker's door. As he had expected, the door was unlocked, but the room in which he had spent the early afternoon with aunt and uncle was empty. Running out through the side door that led through the trellis, he seemed to see each grape on the vine he could not see in the dark.

There was still a chance that he might find the caretaker

before sunrise. He stumbled down the driveway where the car had been stalled that morning at the foot of the knoll, and scrambling to his feet again ran down the road that led to the edge of the ranch.

For once his mind was made up. As he ran he thought, all his loves, all his friends, had always sought him first. He had isolated himself from the world till he was afraid to hear his own voice speak in company; afraid to discuss the errors of his fellow nationals at the embassy and at home before more than one person; afraid to tell the sick they were sick, and the dying that he feared their death more than fear. But now he was making up for it. He would come to her whose people had been depredated, like his own, and speak to her, for no other reason than that he had seen her come out in the sun that morning. This was the worry that all his life he had hoped would fall off from him, the fear that everyone would say he was maundering if he as much as declared his daydream.

Silver patches of desert reflected upward, and caught his eye, at the domed hut of saplings where he had first seen the girl.

—Let me in.

Word for word, he had echoed—as if it were not he who spoke—a bawdy but admirable ballad that the Englishman once sang for him. He was not dressed in sailor's togs, but at least in corduroy, not too civilized.

There was no answer.

—Nina, I must find Pietro. Where your tribe, the Indians, are buried—his memory failed him, but he was quite sure he had their names right.

He could not recall turning the knob.

The floor he looked down at was a dimly lit square for eating and a mat for sleeping. She stood between these.

—It is her name, she said gently, not mine.

And he knew that what he had forgotten had stopped to deprive them both of their love.

—My own thought, he said to her, his cheek to her face as

he had seen it that morning.

She did not speak after that. Her silence retained the thought that his love had created it and that he could never stray from it further than from his thought.

They were together now in the time when the Aztec calendar was correct and the Old World calendar of that period in error. No hands of a clock crossed the figures of hours. There was less difference between them than between the Americans and her. She had planted a sprig of Creeping Charlie—her eyes like stars moving—and was oblivious as to whether it was called Wandering Jew or a weed.

But as it might happen to one who lived to himself, one afternoon he saw his three friends in soldiers' uniforms, their old characters come out of the guise. From their looks, they did not chide him for not keeping in touch with them. Of course he had not told them of her.

The Russian told him what the Chinese were doing. The Englishman had not the time to talk abstractly. The *rabbin* walked with them and smiled. Ferdinand did not always catch the meaning of the *rabbin*'s smile.

They had sauntered as far as a little village cinema and stood looking at two billboards on either side of its entrance: one advertised an old Chaplin comedy: the other, a Walt Disney in which a baby elephant was the principal character.

—Art's long, the Englishman mumbled, and life is too short to miss these. Let's go in.

They lowered four creaking wooden seats, near a side aisle, and sat down. The screen flickered and lit up, blank. During the minute they had to wait until the broken film was fixed on the projector in the operator's box, the *rabbin* asked Ferdinand about his brother. Constrained, he wondered when he had ever mentioned his brother to the *rabbin*.

—I will tell you later, he said.

The film was running again: something not advertised on the billboard and which they had not come in to see—highly original and yet disjunct. It did not seem possible they were showing it in a suburb:—something that one remembered of one's own lifetime, the kind of thing which, if it were a novel, would have been discussed in salons or at drinking parties in the nineteen twenties; those doing the talking never coming to any conclusion as to its value—a verbal and conceptual fineness too kaleidoscopic and yet of its time. The social life that judged it too diversified in itself to comprehend the whole thing from the shades of a difference, Ferdinand remembered. The roll of film, streaky, probably old, seemed washed by a thin, white rain. He had the feeling that the rain must stop soon, as appropriate titles tied into the sequence of broken narrative: something about Columbus, a millionaire, a small boy's toy automobile upset in the sea, the hull of a ship, and a close-up of its name: La Niña. The title translated: the girl. And continued: Columbus on his first return voyage entering the harbor of Palos. Suddenly the little theatre went dark.

—The film is always breaking, he said to the others. They did not answer and he could not see them. His heart pounded, causing him to recall that the piston rod of his car had leaped through its hood and breaking the plate glass had killed him.

Someone said, it's a pity he's going to sleep through the Chaplin.

He woke up. His first thought was of his relations. The whole dream must have passed in less than a minute. For aunt and uncle, waiting for him on the running board, evidently seemed to think that he had lowered his head over the wheel only for a moment, to recover from the shock of hitting the curbing. At least they were not going to accuse him of carelessness. He stepped out of the car, half dazed, and looked over the damage. Only a dented fender. Overhead a bird sang in the late afternoon, and as he searched for it, he wished he knew its name.

The road led down to the other side of the mountain and still another stretch of desert. A few insects leaping to die against the impact of his windshield did not obscure the view. It held in his mind the bronzed image of a girl whose race had been hurt like his own. But part of the time he drove on, thinking of another image: a street from which he could see the steps going up to the columns of the porch of the Capitol—not much more than a hundred years old.

He might please his aunt and uncle and speak again to his brother from whom he had become estranged. In that case, he could never get himself to tell this story or as much of it as the *rabbin,* who had lived in his time, could guess.

Thanks to the Dictionary

Preface

And what will the writers do then, poor things.

"A". Quoting the dictionary. Remembering my sawhorses, my little a.'s abbreviated for afternoon, perhaps for years, this afternoon. Another acre, one, any, some, each, aback, as aloof, till before a vowel will stand accepted, "An", active, tho not as a vulture. Perhaps next Ab, when the fast will not commemorate a Temple in ruins, Aaron's rod, the serpent to blossom, will grow, goldenrod which flowers on long stems in that vacation a part of July and of August. David, then, on his page, not like a slab forming the top of a capital, but not unlike an abacus, a reckoning table telling its sums will embrace all the words of this novel. For, David, anticipated, appears when the groundhogs are not in Abad. Abad is any cultivated city. But David who resists all its agents is free from iridescence, and without accidentals. If there is iridescence, it will be at his toes. His name, these words till now, are almost his story.

Not otherwise provided for, the son of Jesse stands by the water-raising wheel, the one bucket on its rim. On the ground, the prickly-pear is still, as before he stood he sat still. Type of the rule, there is neither blame nor praise for a boy's work.

North by west, i.e. one point or 11°15' west of north, he sees the black crow fly, the gray sparrow hop. He knows the normal color of the crow is black, the normal color of the sparrow is gray. He knows, according to nature, that one is as natural as the other. Steady and constant himself, the birds' to him, fly, circle and fly and are not fitful nor changeable. If there were a deformity in them he could pick it, but that again would be as expected as their symmetry. As he turns the water-wheel, he knows the birds in an assemblage of their qualities.

Follows a perpendicular of sight to a curved surface and that is a normal. But shifts slightly and becomes the line of his thought. Northward is a land. To the south is land. To the east is sun, which climbs to set. To the west is sea. He thinks his life. His life is not yet the present. His future is monstrous. In a heat he brings to himself seven wives and the eighth is childless."—David! your muscles, cold, the pole-star, your wives oxen, your wives are stiff, your person, it turns, loves, turns, as the sakkiyeks making even the beasts slaves! You will die unable to warm yourself." He sees a noose, the knot of which runs. Thirsty, he subjugates peoples. But he stands still, the prickly-pear seems to sit. The grief for a body, hung, repaid to his compact boy's body before he has been responsible for its birth makes him turn the wheel so that buckets multiply, and the winds in the twilight shifting around him, become common to his eyes—

Item:

Joseph Deniker 1852—French anthropologist, not therefore a member of the people he "so-called" nordic

—in a series of organic isomers designating a compound in which the chain is continuous and not branched,—his eyes, the winds in his eyes, the winds and his eyes become an ultimate substance—identical as their composition.

✲

The spring after the winter everybody in Bethlehem had the flu, David took a horse and cart laden with two sacks of the ground and bolted substance of wheat, three hot dishes of newly baked potato scones, four bottles of vermouth, one for each of his three brothers, and three pasteboard gills of blanc-mange for which he had no taste himself, and started on a long walk which would take him to his brothers in the army.

The lanes all led past the stream. The country of the trees swung and waved around him, in the early March, sunned still without embellishment, but in brilliant and dashing style, thriving and prosperous,—as an author, David ventured,—as at one's best. Musically speaking, the air flowed, as its compression sometimes, from an organ-pipe, flute or diapason. Domestically, it was one consistent square of chimney which had rid itself of all the gases of combustion. He walked.

The dense head-like clusters of the sessile florets lined up a passage for display. The stream was one issue, the flow-moss rising and falling with the water, and not forming a bog: imperfectly fluid, and a deformation of a solid body, but a gliding of interglobular movement such as might be rendered with an easy, gentle movement of speech—the brightest, finest, choicest of a period. So that the glaze abounding over the breadth and length of the stream, coated colorless, was nothing but a little wind, slack as the tiniest sheet, cased off, as one can almost imagine, like so many imaginary small ropes. The horse, trotted.

The dust the horse revoked from anywhere and everywhere for David's eyeballs, met them—a very light powder of sublimation. The mosses, their reproductive organs with their enveloping and associated leaves imagined themselves brown in the complimentary pupils of David's eyes. These, presently, had it that the little wind had veered, more accurately aboutfaced, and steadily held the new direction. One of the two wheels of David's cart flumped.

He stopped, got down in the mud:—as regards the spider, he said examining it,—and as regards the wooden rim and mental states, he who hesitates sticks; as regards the—as regards the tire, he who vacillates decides now one way and now another; as regards the spokes, he who wavers does not hold by a decision; as regards the hub, one shifts between contrasted decisions or actions; as regards the axle-nut, he may waver between decision and indecision, or between action and inaction.—Feelings, in general, fluctuate or vary.—Compare SHAKE. Let me see, what *is* that very significant stock ornament of catechism? *flow:* that which flows, a continuous stream or current, incoming tide, the quantity of water which passes thru an orifice or by a given point in a given time, a copious outpouring, also gentle movement as of speech.

—There now! that one's fixed—how's the other—. Said David:—Well!—as the wheel keeping the same volume rolled round again—I seem to have been flowing ever since I was a kid. It was that way he met the Philistine.

✲

Before, back to, the distyle, David differentiates and abstracts. Alienating him is the deformity he marks visibly as different. There is a disturbance, a change from a condition of order, as of a compound containing sulphur in its highest state of oxidation. Imminent, the distinguished is not distracted. The strained meaning before David interprets falsely, distrusts and suspects. He might be a distome, one of a genus of parasitic worms called flukes, from their short flattened triangular shape. He might be among a number, but only the distinguished back to the portico in antes will regard his ultimate distribution. The scene might be the District of Columbia.

✲

La; look; O; truly;—the expression of each face bore the effect of the sixth tone of the diatonic scale! The campers in the defensive enclosure formed by wagons were definitely there against any kin generated from Laban, father of Leah and Rachel, wives of Jacob. Historically yet incapable of being led by the Roman military standard adopted by Constantine, bearing the cross and monogram of Christ, their labarum or otherwise affixed an inscription indicating strong character and ownership. They did not know, but where some of them had gathered under a wall-opening to discuss *Le Voyage de M. Perrichon* a dipterous insect projecting its proboscis over the dripstone spelled—*tottering!*. Of some the labia cerebri had been impinged upon by labia majora, and to their always nasal regret still not by labia minora. So that they glided from place to place, footrest to footrest, as electric currents over diseased areas, themselves not prone to undergo essential change of their unstable atomic structures. Structureless, some of them slept, laudanum up their noses. In their incoherent series of apparitions, military departments stacked with cartridges, torpedos and everything every arsenal has, sought for analyses and explosives heard of by the independent labor interests of parliaments. With their refusal not to hear it was no queslion of parturition or rolling, or pitching of a heavy sea, or exertion, or effort, or stress or difficulty. A huge face with a labret stuck thru the left side of the upper and lower lips, stood sentinel. The sleepers continued seeing asleep, startled repeatedly by thoughts of rebellion.

It was among these that David, disguised, betokening a hidden meaning, and emblematically seeking his man, David illuminating darkly the night's fires he had wandered into, spoke affectionately:—My three unequal and dissimilar axes with oblique intersections, I say this of you my crystal forms, your initial letter, in Egyptian a lioness, in Phenician called *lamed* means rightly an oxgoad. My time comes when it will be *lagu,* a lake! In English the sound of this letter will be one of the most uniform and changeless of the sounds in the language, especially prolonged so as to continue a syllable! It is not in my name nor will it be pronounced in *folk.* But you will hear it in *holm,* my labradorite, my feldspar, L, 50, L̄ 50,000 upon 50 thousands, when one will write in a city, attributively, as L roads, in the time of sounds and the—then—lighted passing of symbols. And, by the way, let's make it liquid.

✲

Clove and clover are on his head. He steps forth, hastens forward, as out of a mass of visible vapor floating in the air at its various heights. The water will be returned to a channel after flooding this land. The three-leaved flowers are on the head of no clown. Clotho! and he swings no club whose birth you preside at!

And the other with his stout stick who clumps to meet the youngling sprinting against clostrophobia! Fear of closed spaces the other has it whoever his trick clothier. See, he should be cloven-footed, but he clumps each foot never divided! Boor, clout of the clud . . .

Cloudburst and cloudlet!

He has clumped his last, the clodhopper. Darkened by the shadows of the great multitude he lies foolishly provided with clothes, a dimmed appearance. And Clotho! you thread your distaff from what cloudlet? the skein out of what clover? The youngling bends over. The cloudlet suns: a smile.

*

—So will you give me the doom-palm, David?

—I give gingerbread to the dormouse; I will give you the gingerbread-tree.

—Am I trim?

—Are my loves dunderheads?

—You're a doodle-sack; what's in the knapsack?

—Well, for poetic measure there are a door-nail, a door-sill, or, if you wish, a door-stane, and dead as a door-nail, a dorking!

—Donkey!

—Donna!

—Are you going back to the dormitory, David?

—Not unless you wish a travesty on chivalry.

—Who's my attendant?

—Not David!

—Who'll look to my dormer?

—David!

—I'll put that into my vanity box.

—Don't! I like you.

Thru the Eyes of Jonathan

My what a ritual! Out of the rivulet onto the road and into the roadster. For all your rix-dollars, I wouldn't describe it. Ritardando, ritornelle, if you rise to meaning—sure It! No, not music, nor rivage, or how could riverine into a roadster?! Riverhorse?! Nonsense! Riverhorse in a roadster, what rivals could rival it! Come, come, my good man, hitch up your risibilities! Rive for the secret, turn your teeth bridges into rip-saws! A chaparral cock in Westchester, no! nix, not that road-runner! A plain roach, I mean! What a ripuarian y'are, not the European fresh-water carp. Rivet you! A plain cockroach! That was the little, sure, It stirred up the road stir!

*

O he was not difficult to raise, our youngling; he was the dosser! No rich hanging for a ball or church, but not dorty! Dungbeetle well known by its droning flight, or wall-eyed pike-perch, he knew them, not afraid to walk where the trees were doaty. At two he was already thru with his doses. At three he was already informed about dosage—how he put the liqueurs into the sparkling wines, and improved their quality, and gave them distinctive character! At four, tho, he was ignorant of plug or spigot, for they always stood their chance. And if re-spectably he rode in the dos-a-dos with *maman*, his Dot was on the same seat with him. Should maman look, he could al-ways diversify with a dotted half-note, so that Dot would not even seem the dotterel. And sometimes he affected doting. But at five even affecting was unnecessary, for the fishermen his friends would lend him the dory, and he made good use of the flat-bottom. He was regular,—Dot was pleased with do-simetry. At six, he was tall; straight, dorsad; dorsiventral, he seemed to turn and his both sides go back, parallel. At seven, he spent the year for ten minutes a day, considering the vir-tues of his double-breasted, now buttoned right side, now left. At eight, his boats were double-banked. Were so, for four years. At twelve, he found it only in his heart the pledget for cleaning a wound. Soft, and he read Feodor M. Dostoyefsky and left him in a doss, after the reading.

*

Daedal: cunningly formed or working, ingenious; variegated, rich, The daimon does not clog with mire but grows over the daffodil. The bank does not wall the watercourse despite the damage. Happening as the daimon—dalliance or dawk: the dahoon bearing red drupes in the southern United States; transport by relays of men or horses. Or the dahlia; and the smudge on the early daguerrotype. Dagon: half man and half fish, the god of the Philistines, trailed with the land mud and wet, his tusks thru the water, and bearing between them a flower. The dairy produces milk; Damascus once produced steel with peculiar markings as well as silks with patterns of flowers; the inhabitants of the rocks fall over the dalles.

✲

The reamer reanimates reality; the rearrangements of the reaper are a reanimation. What is reason but a cutting edge, the rearmost have no realty in. Réaumur, Réaumur, the fineness of your thermometric scale, rearguing freezing and boiling point, what can it mean to the mantis its legs, arms, folded in prayer. The rebellion against reason's reassurance is another rebec other than the tingling of the prayer of those who rebaptize, if you would only listen to me, my little Rebecca. Your Isaac, my little Rebecca, was reanimated if not by a reamer, at least by a cutting tool.

✲

A visiter making a visit goes where it is visitable. Where *it* is visitable. IT makes visitation socially acceptable. The visiter lifts his vizor. He wears it naturally to protect his eyes. Moreover, when the visiter lifts his vizor, it is visual. And like a vista. IT has become visitatorial.

"Instead of a vitamin put that into your vitellus!" as the visiter further said during the visit: "if you would only realize your vitals are parts essential to the life, health and soundness of anything such as heart, lungs and brain!", lowering his visor, while IT pondered: "flyforce, my vitellus is not invalidated".

⚙

Stereopticon: the screen, notwithstanding the intense light, given over to planimetry. The figures, the eyes see, the mind knows as not solid. No stereogram can relieve the moving planes' successive flatness the intense light reveals. And yet these move, not fixed in a lasting form: the vessel stern foremost, blunderingly; the sea upon itself mixing as with vast tracts of steppe simultaneously seen as thru a stereoscope. So that as we approach as at the stern ourselves, we see the lover stertorous climbing the portable set of steps, the love thru the rungs, under the hinged back frame of the ladder, her face, a stercorary, his sterculiaceous, beginning the stern-chase as she veers sterile.

⚙

The eland's ejection. But the eland is practically exterminated. What then of Elaine whom unrequited love makes elaborate? Her story elapses. Here where there is no elation for the elect, no elasticity among elders, no elbowroom among the unripe elderberry, only the snap of the tapering jumping beetle—the reference is to the seniority of these elders—What maid, what lily maid, will permit hermit herself be taught the unity of being, the unreality of motion and change. Or as well say to the Elamite—his ancient kingdom in the mountainous country east of Babylonia—"And Zeno the Eleatic—look for his election in El Dorado!"

⚙

Mind, that abstract, collective term for all forms of conscious intelligence, or for the subject of all conscious states, it walked along with David. What to do with the minim? To measure it roughly, the downstroke one drop? To mind, to occupy oneself, to regard as of importance; to be concerned for the signs of the times: I do not *mind* the noise; one Minié ball its plug driven by the explosion of the charge to expand the lead. But to have a mind to work. The instinct of animals is now held by many to be of the same nature as the intellect of man, yet the apparent difference is very great. Certainly not in *opposition* to matter—or the spirit or intelligence pervading the universe. What faculty of relations and comparisons can that be? To mine, not like mineral jelly for the lubrication of everybody. Not to minify, to undermine. Not mine, not mind-reading, not that disease independent of the ordinary channels of the senses. Not belonging to me that possessive of I, that flying of higher cognitions. The pie is made of mince-meat. It has mingled but is chopped. But propensity is experience independent of and dependent upon its instruction.

✲

The boon companions feast, and the feast lasts—no argument or evidence addressed to the intellect of flukes. Parallel to the affections and the will, rolled one part on another or inward from one side, wind the coupled, coupled, twining herbs with their convoys of large showy trumpet flowers, accompanying their property as of ships storing food at sea; the baggage train on land. The story continues thru 36 genera.

The convulsive spasms, the Jansenists ascribed to supernatural influence emanating from the tomb of François de Paris, have thrown their last at St. Médard. With cony at table, the combination of nervous impulses in motor centers insuring the cooperation of appropriate muscles in reaction, David, to this his, your, feast, has invited his boon companions to celebrate the songs of degrees.

—Eat now, we will play conquian later. Have this small and sweet cake. All the food has been prepared here, subject to the action of heat. We were bothered with much coom before to-night, but now there is sawdust only so that after dinner you do not slip in the rain. Who remembers the cooee of the aborigines to spite the coo of the dove? This is my friend, Jonathan, helping me celebrate to-night, not a coolie tho he serves us.

—After the chilling and slighting of the unions of apprentices and small capitalists, after the advantageous manufacturing, buying and selling of goods, after the joint action of profit-sharings, after the false modes of falsely mutual benefit, who would have thought of the possibility of a convocation without summons, a dinner for which no troops have been mustered, a friendly court without jurymen, a synod without preferment.

—Drink, my friends, would you believe it, we are a member of a system of lines or angles by means of which position is determined? And would you believe, it, position is only determined . . . And you, mister cooper, whose job it is to make casks and barrels,—it was *only to-night,* rabbits were freed from their coops, their still timid eyes will appreciate cool colors—so bring in only your barrels and casks of blue, green and violet.

David and Michal

The twelve peers of France, celebrated in the Charlemagne romances, dove. When love is extinguished, the wedge-shaped tenons and spaces are put out, in the cote of the cushat, she broods over a dowcet in her bed. So historic characters, for too much love, become spiritless in their personal lives.

When the strong unbleached linen cloth still serves his youth for a shirt, such as David do not want the property a wife brings to her husband in marriage.—Gentle, innocent, loving Michal, if you should become in bad taste, know that the writer of five books of psalms and as many doxologies will not declare them a reward for a wife. How many deans of diplomatic corps in our years to come will down a filament of the blade of a feather, down, or a fiber of down. Overthrown, old, I shall not even go in the downpour, and, never wanting to grow old, over the turf-covered undulating tracts of upland I will not take you to give you up—"The downpour is for the downtrodden".—All the same, the black guillemot visits the southerly coasts in winter, the pipe which receives the outpourings from the eaves of the roof is a leader. The dovekie about 7½ inches long is black above and white below. I have not been equivocal. I have been plain. I have been outspoken

✲

—Alright, because I am not a fish and you want all of its firmament! The government will have its own fiscals, but I shall stack so many wooden vessels for lard out of that monster. Solidity will be another kind of compact. That will be the break, the voice separating into so many layers, because you want the upper part. Because I shall always be nine and nine, and no other multiple, preceding all others that way in the order of numbering, always at first blush, without blush. You can have it that way. Because I don't want a firm, a union of two or more persons for the purpose of conducting business. You can cut an arm of the sea with a firmer maybe, That's how you'd measure me? Well, there'll be no pisciculture. There'll be at least not that industrial art. No fish-slices, no fish-trowels, because shape or action is not always a fish-tail, and there are so many Ham-fishes already among fish-crows.

✲

A division of long-legged birds and waders on the Grain

Coast—in the watching grain is the innate quality of a face, Michal's. The features of the young men evidently dabblers in gramarye. Like their leader, however, they are not self-advanced thru political or official connection. They have never graduated, nor are they concerned with graduation. He is David, such and such an one, interested in a pictograph scratched on a boulder; or on a wall; or in an escarpment;—running on legs or adapted for walking—and in his mind more than mechanically played, a postponed collection of graded exercises. He is impatient with speech or writing considered with regard to its correctness. On the other hand, there are paint or stain, in imitation of their grain to be applied to wood or marble. There are scions to graft. They are, nevertheless, not ineradicable, if they prove unpleasant. Consider the gram-molecular weight of 15.432 of vital air, and wear gamashes.

*

"I will be more vile"—you are not here, Michal, but I shouldn't have made so definite a statement. It will enure. My anger truckles like an incontinence of urine. What a machine! a reaction motor consisting of a hollow sphere upon trunnions above the boiler connected with it. At right angles to its trunnions the sphere has radial pipes with ends at right angles to them and to the trunnions. Escape of steam from the radial pipes rotates the sphere oppositely to the current. Be your own minister, hollowness, to yourself: a detailed succession of things in succession. My *superiority* to which she has no right or claim has envenomed her? Envy? Her body is little, its seeming makes want of possessions impossible. I have seen it so, small, bearing a kind of love to me, maintaining itself, self-contained for its own right or claim. Jealousy? When her eyes looked at me? of intrusion upon that which is its own? Suspicion? Of a knowledge of wrong, of my previous conduct, or even without reason? Doubt? The last maybe rules over the three former. In that case, the one eye which they hand from one to the other. But if this myth exists, it merely guards, she has not assumed actual possession of my lands or emotions by entering upon them . . . Neither does *this* thought encompass my head with a wreath . . .

What, then, is the index of the relative amount of unavailable energy in a rude implement of bone—hollowness? It would seem for an incalculable period of time, at least, that the emotions will not be that stringed instrument that gives forth musical sounds when exposed to a current of air. What then shall my life, as of nebulous matter rising and expanding as from the nucleus of a comet, on the side towards the sun, say to the sun every repeated morning? Maybe that unorganized compound of vegetable or animal origin that causes chemical transformation in the brain will entwine a word: see *eon* and present itself with the image of an age; look into the face of age and calculate an infinity. And eons, externalized, give shape to one's circumstances collectively: if not a small hallway, an entrance for coming and going, the total development of a particular vegetation throughout a period of dominance, of a distinct number of plants over an area, as of ferns, conifers, or flowering plants; and that eosere be David, and Michal, and sun, and the end of the month. And live in those "historical processes" when "twenty years are but as one day—and" when "may come days which are the" concentration "of twenty years"—and the apprehension envisages several milleniums before and ahead: "the free development of each the condition for the free development of all."

*

She stood among the very numerous. If her companions saw him too, they could not, when they pushed her elbow gently. At the field's end, the dry, small bed of a stream rose miraculously, vertically, upon itself, a nun-bird, black plumage, white about the head. She was then one who had never borne.

Where he stood, in the field's center, the use of existence never damaged. The power of sensation in its free state (she breathed, coral, seaweed, breathed), had become the curls of his hair. History was inoperative. Already at that time they could see South Carolina refuse obedience to the laws of the United States. They could see 1832. They could sing Canticles. Or, they could dispense with "Lord, now lettest thou"—

Or her mind's eye became her, became an eye. A microscope: the red-blood corpuscles stacked up like coins. Their columns? He was nude. The Numidian-crane, the demoiselle, the two censuses of Israel, had blended. She did not receive him, but she had become numberless.

David and Bath-sheba

A proposal of David to Bath-sheba—I have found you, even if one would say without an arm, yet like Venus. See the milt in the water, and, believe me, I am not of threatening or menacing character. I do not mince speech, so on the balcony of this minaret allow me to ask you to forget your General-husband—did you say Miltiades was his name?—it will be better for a million, for a thousand thousand of the ordinary units of account, for the shortening of the history of one civilization. I don't want to diminish the strength or force of anything, so if I say the mina is often tamed and taught to speak, and has the amusing and mischievous manners of the magpie, but that you may not succeed, I hope you will not consider me threatening destruction. The majestic style is often for milliners—they create forms mimicking another found in a different country, and only distantly related. Let me put it this way—I see an imitative resemblance in you as animal, and in your short steps the beauty of some—I don't know what—inanimate object. We're of one country. We're of no country. We're not wearing hats today, and that's why I assume we both hate P. Nik Yuk the historian, I should say statesman, writing on

Russia and its crisis.

✲

—You were not afraid of consequences?

—I assumed Uriah Miltiades was not negligent. I had heard of the Ulotrichi before that, they were said to be happy, I could also imagine the comforted of Jehovah recounting the building of Jerusalem, wooly-haired, but golden. I was David, propensity. Also, void.

—A wife may suffer from her husband constant neglect, while the negligence which causes a train accident may be that of a moment, and on the part of one ordinarily careful and attentive; in such cases the law provides punishment for criminal negligence.

—The negligence which friendship loves?

—Is not found!

—I found you. In the loose gown you wore indoors. It was not careless nor unceremonious either.

—Intensive terminal!

—The negative—I shall not say acid—of your speech, Bath-sheba, is your present love a kind of electricity assumed by sealing wax rubbed with flannel, a positive, I'll grant in your case, taken arbitrarily to correspond with previous assumption—love's beginnings—denoted by a minus-sign. You know it, your feelings are resinous. As you speak to me, you would have it we are now a negative picture having the lights and shades reversed. But in love, its portrait, only a quality, negatively intensifies the negative, as people of a certain speech, "I didn't see nobody", and the nobody—a Body—shines.

✲

An aside of Bath-sheba sitting on the ashlar of his roof—

His, the attribute of the subject, Lent goes, and I am still

Astarte, female of forbidden divinity to all our known friends, David's, on the squared stone of his mason-work. Thru all this season of penitence I have been able to look with a side glance. It is really that not on a vessel nor at sea, I am his largest continent of the world. Fault to him means nothing, nor to me. Now he sits actually in that oblique position, far enough to be facing me, near enough for me to make inquiry of his eyes, as of the stone. He is pleased that I have not spoken, more pleased that an aside has been my figure. He need not hurry to answer them while his thoughts are of—anything?—plaster-studs running from the floor of a garret to the rafters. His ability to occupy himself this way as he looks at me is his only humility. I am in love with what he knows he does not have to ask.

The propriety of a bath one takes, so as not to be overheard apparently, by the polite forms of slight request, has come to feel what he may fairly claim and reasonably expect. I have heard of Askja occasionally not dormant. I do not know where it is. His son should know of it. If he would—be wise with something of me. But it is the sleep of one like me who, taken, goes up aslope, that I almost wish for David that his son may never meet. May his, our son, be the light waking ash, tough, elastic wood, our ornament, lovable and with gifts to love. But to his father, to me, only, let be known the perished impropriety, the unplanned, which need no consolation.

I love my husband, but if he goes,—how should he go, I know he has happened—, it must be that certain performances will happen without commerce, like over my being here the powdery residue of substance that has not been burnt.

I will wait for what has happened, which seems never to have happened, for what will happen. I will tell David and I will know all,—as to, or towards the sea, his sight now happens, almost out of sight from my being here,—our love again.

✲

—Design!

—Who wants a design?

—We want a design! Desmoulins!

—Wants a design? Where's Desmoulins?

—Where's Hernandez De Soto!

—Does the Mississippi want a design?

—The bishop designate wants a design!

—Is he consecrated?

—Even the desperado wants a design!

—O! It is argued that the marks of design in nature prove it the work of a great Designer!

—Aim, cause, end, idea, model, project, purpose, reason, the families of minute, bright-green, unicellular, mainly solitary, fresh-water algae, the individual usually divided into symmetrical halves or semi-cells connected by an isthmus, want a design! The desk wants a design!

—Dispatch it!

—A derivative verb expressing desire wants a design!

—What a desiderative!

—Intention is simply the more familiar form of the legal and philosophical intent!

—And it wants a design! Give it a hankering!

—A glass vessel, tightly covered, containing substances, drying, with an arrangement for absorbing moisture and Des Moines want a design!

—Give them the Des Moines idea!

Intent and *purpose* overlap all particulars and fasten on the *end itself.* But David is distinguishable, and, even beyond this end. Desire has a wide range, from the highest objects to the lowest; desire is for an object near at hand, or near in thought and viewed as attainable; a wish may be for what is remote or uncertain; or even for what is recognized as impossible.

—Hey! this novel wants a design!
—Okay!—says David—you find it!

Degrees

Thanks to the dictionary, this book will be prefaced. As against any dictator, there is that book containing the words of a language, modes of expression, diction. As a gardener dibbles earth, as a duck dibs water for bait, chance or mischance, the page by the hand opening that book will be cast, and the print lie like cubes of bone or ivory marked on every side, with, from one to six spots. (More!) As against any dictator, dicast or reader, that modern juryman with functions of a judge, the words, single pulse-beats to each systole of the heart will command for two heads—like diazins their own cyclic class of compounds, their rings, that hold up, composed of their own atoms: Dicentra; low, delicate perennial herbs, racemes of nodding rose-colored or yellow heart-shaped flowers, the bleeding heart is well-known; doubly refracting crystals exhibiting different colors when viewed in different directions; solutions variously colored by different degrees of concentration; dicasts unaffected by blue-green- or redblindness; Dick, bunting; dicky, bib or a small bird; dicotyledons; dibasic, no dickering, on page 327, Dickson City a borough in East Pennsylvania; on page 303, the hand has turned back, there is David.

✲

Dates! dates! dates! the oblong, sweet, fleshy fruit! you headmen of barrios, in the time of some event, in a point of time—the dauphin in abeyance, removable as opposed to perpetual! Who paints coarsely or cheaply—a dauber, a dabbler. Trickery, a sticky occupation. But this may not be disposed of at will: a female child, a cell divided from the mother cell, psalms, a conceded fact, number, quantity, point. Knowledge is but Sorrow's spy. The lark takes this window for the east:

He was ruddy, cunning in playing. Jesse took an ass laden with bread, a bottle of wine, a kid, and sent them by David his son. David came to Saul. He became his David took a harp and played. Saul was well. The Philistines stood on a mountain on the one side, and Israel on a mountain on the other side: and there was a valley between them. Out went a champion, named Goliath, and said I defy the armies of Israel, choose a man for you and let him come down to me. David rose up early in the morning, and left the sheep with the keeper. He came to the trench as the host was going to the fight, the battle in array. David left his carriage in the hand of the keeper, ran into the army and saluted. As he talked, up came the champion. The same words, David heard them. And David,—Who is this Philistine? Eliab, anger. And David,—Is there not a cause? Said to Saul,—Let no heart fail.

Saul armed David. David said to Saul I cannot go. Put them off him. And he took his staff, chose five smooth stones out of the brook, put them in a scrip, and his sling in his hand. And the Philistine came on,—Come to me. And David ran, put his hand in his bag, took a stone, slang it, and smote the Philistine in his forehead. The stone sunk into his forehead, he fell upon his face to the earth. Saul said,—*Whose* son? And David,—The son of Jesse. And Saul took him that day, and would let him go no more. The soul of Jonathan knit with the soul of David, Jonathan loved him as his own soul. David accepted in the sight of all the people, eyed from that day. David played as at other times, a javelin in Saul's hand. And Saul cast the javelin. David avoided twice. Michal, Saul's daughter, loved David: and they told Saul and the thing pleased him, and Saul said I will give him her, she may be a snare to him. Saul gave him Michal to wife, knew Michal, Saul's daughter, loved him, was yet the more afraid of David. David behaved wisely, his name much set by. Saul to Jonathan, his son, and all his servants,—Kill David. Jonathan told David,—

Hide,—I will commune with my father. Jonathan brought David to Saul and—as in times past.   And war again: David fought the Philistines and they fled.   Saul sat in his house with his javelin in his hand, and David played with *his* hand. Saul sought to smite David to the wall with the javelin; he slipped away.   Saul sent messengers to David's house to watch and slay him in the morning. Michal let David down thru a window: he fled and escaped. And when Saul sent messengers to take David, she said,—He is sick. Saul sent messengers again,—Bring him up in the bed. And when the messengers were come in, there was an image in the bed, with a pillow of goats' hair for his bolster. Saul said,—Michal,—deceived me so,—sent away my enemy.

And he went, stripped off his clothes, lay down naked all that day and all night—Saul also among the prophets?

David fled from   , and came and said to Jonathan,—What have I done? Jonathan,—My father will do nothing. He loved him: as he loved his own soul.   The king upon his seat as at other times, David's place empty. Then Saul's anger was against Jonathan,—Son of woman!—chosen the son of Jesse! Jonathan answered, and Saul cast a javelin.   Jonathan knew his father was determined to slay David. Jonathan arose from the table in fierce anger, grieved for David, because his father had done him shame.   And Jonathan cried,—Make speed. And Jonathan's lad gathered up the arrows. And as soon as the lad was gone, David arose out of a place toward the south, and they kissed, and wept, and Jonathan said to David,—Go, and he departed, and Jonathan went into the city.

David came to the priest.—There is no bread but there is bread if the young men have kept themselves at least from women. David answered,—Women have been kept from us about these three days, and said,—I have brought neither sword nor weapons, the business required haste.—The sword of Goliath is here wrapped in a cloth, take it. David,—There is none like it. Fled that day for fear of Saul, and feigned himself mad and scrabbled on the doors of the gate, and let his spittle fall down upon his beard. And escaped to the Cave , and his father's house heard it. Went down, everyone in distress, and in debt; everyone discontented gathered there. He became a captain over about 400 men. David in the wilderness in strongholds, and Saul come out to seek his life. Jonathan to David, made a covenant in the wood, Jonathan to his house. A messenger came to Saul,—Come, for the Philistines have invaded the land. Saul returned from pursuing David, and David in Engedi. Saul returned from following the Philistines, took 3000 chosen men and went to seek David, his men upon the rocks of the wild goats. Came to a cave, and went in to cover his feet: and David and his men remained in the sides of the cave. Then David cut off Saul's robe privily. Saul out of the cave, on his way. David also, crying after,—David seeks your hurt? Whom do you pursue? And Saul,—My son David? Wept. Went home. But David and his men to the wilderness. A man, possessions in Carmel, Nabal; and the name of his wife Abigail: and she was a woman of good understanding, and beautiful: but the man was evil. And Nabal,—Who is David? Shall I take my bread, my water and flesh killed for my shearers and give it to his men? David,—I kept all this fellow had in the wilderness, and nothing was missing,—if I leave him by morning any that pisseth against the wall! But one of the young men told Abigail. Then Abigail took two hundred loaves, and two bottles of wine, and five sheep ready dressed, and, and, and, and saw David. And in the morning when the wine was gone out of Nabal, his wife told him. About ten days after, he died. Abigail after David, and became his wife. David also took , and they were both of them his wives. But Saul had given Michal his daughter, David's wife to Phalti. Saul down to seek David in the wilderness. David—spies—and came to the place where Saul had pitched. David,—Who will go down with me to Saul. So David and Abishai, by night, and Saul lay sleeping in the trench, his spear stuck in the ground, Abner and the people lay around him. So David took the spear and the water from Saul's bolster. David to the other side, on the top of a hill, to the people and to Abner,—*See where the spear is and the water that was at his bolster!* And Saul,—My son David? And David,—*My* voice; What *have* I done? So David on his way, and Saul to *his* place. David to , and he sought no more again for him. In the country of the Philistines a full year and four months. The Philistines against Israel, and Saul dead, and his three sons, and his armour bearer, and all his men that same day together. And David—lamentation,—Saul and Jonathan lovely in their lives, in their death were not divided; my brother Jonathan, your love to me was passing the love of women. The weapons perished. David over the house of Judah. Ish-bosheth, Saul's son, over Israel. Long war between the house of Saul and the house of David, Abner strong for the house of Saul. And Saul had a concubine. And Ish-bosheth to Abner,—Why *my father's* concubine? Then Abner,—Am I a dog's head, that you charge me today, with a fault concerning this woman? And Abner to David on his behalf,—*Whose is* the land? Make league with me to bring about all Israel. And,—Well, I will, but one thing, first bring Michal, Saul's daughter. And her husband went with her weeping behind to Abner to him,—Go, return. And he returned.

Joab come out from David, Abner returned, took him aside the gate to speak with him quietly, smote there under the fifth rib for the blood of his brother. And David,—I and my kingdom are guiltless from the blood of Abner. And David to Joab,— Mourn Abner. And the sons of , and Ish-bosheth on a bed at noon, and they smote him under the fifth rib and beheaded him. And David commanded his young men and they hanged them over the pool in , the head of Ish-bosheth buried in the sepulchre of Abner. So, David over Israel. Took Zion, the City of David. Took more concubines and wives out of Jerusalem and there were yet sons and daughters born to David. David returned to his household—and Michal,—How glorious who uncovered himself today in

the eyes of the handmaids of his servants, as one of the vain fellows. And David,—I will be more vile, and of the maidservants spoken of be had in honor. Michal of Saul had no child to the day of her death. David put garrisons in Syria of Damascus.   And in an evening-tide David arose from off his bed, and walked upon the roof of the king's house, saw a woman washing herself, very beautiful. And one said, Is not this Bath-sheba, the daughter of   , the wife of Uriah the Hittite? And David sent messengers, and took her, and lay with her. And she returned to her house, conceived and told David. Uriah, come to David, demanded, how Joab did, and how the people, and how the war prospered.   And David wrote a letter to Joab sent by the hand of Uriah, and wrote in the letter, *Set Uriah in the forefront of the hottest battle.* And a messenger to David,—The men prevailed against us, and Uriah the Hittite is dead also. Then David,—Say to Joab, the sword devours one as well as another.—Encourage him. And when the wife of Uriah heard her husband was dead, she mourned. And mourning past, David sent and fetched her to his house, and she became his wife and bare him a son.   The child of Uriah's wife, very sick, and David all night upon the earth. The child dead.—"He shall not return to me". And David comforted Bath-sheba.   A son, his name Solomon.   Absalom the son of David had a fair sister, whose name was Tamar; and Amnon the son of David loved her. Being stronger, forced her, lay with her, then hated her exceedingly. Tamar crying. And Absalom her brother. "Peace, sister, he *is* thy brother.
   Amnon dead; Absalom fled. And the soul of David longed to go forth unto Absalom—comforted concerning Amnon, seeing he was dead. Said to Joab,—Let him turn to his own house, and let him not see my face. So Absalom returned to his own house. In all Israel none so much praised as Absalom for his beauty.   Two years, and saw not the king's face. Said to Joab,—Let me see the king's face, and let him kill me. Came to the king and the king kissed Absalom.
   Spies.   And with Absalom went 200 men out of

Jerusalem. And they went in their simplicity. And the conspiracy strong, the people with Absalom. And David,—Let us flee we shall not else escape Absalom.   Battle scattered over the face of all the country. *And the wood devoured more people,*
   Absalom upon a mule, Absalom under the thick boughs of the oak, his head caught, taken up between the heaven and earth. O my son Absalom, my son, my son Absalom! O Absalom, my son, my son.

Famine in the days of David, and the king took five sons of Michal the daughter of Saul and delivered them into the hands of the Gibeonites, and they hanged them in the days of harvest, in the first days, in the beginning of barley harvest.
The last words of David,—As the light of the morning when the sun riseth, even a morning without clouds, as the tender grass springing out of the earth by clear shining after rain.   David old, covered with clothes, but he gat no heat.   A young virgin, that my lord may get heat.   Throughout the coasts, and found Abishag, very fair. Cherished the king, but the king knew her not.   All the sons of David, besides the sons of the concubines, and Tamar their sister.

And he built the city round about, even from Millo round about; and Joab repaired the rest of the city. And the Philistines again spread themselves abroad in the valley.   And David made his houses in the City of David.   Singers with instruments of musick, psalteries and harps and cymbals.
Chenaniah instructed about the song, because he was skillful.   Cedar trees in abundance.   Instruments which I made, said David.   The small as the great, the teacher as the scholar,   Solomon yet young, the work great.

Knowledge is but sorrow's spy.   Wake all the dead! What ho! What ho! How soundly they sleep on the decks of the world in storms of love. You, that are more than our discreeter fear, Leaves scarce reach green, As if the silver planet, In this small lanthorn, would contract her light, and to implore your light, he sings.

✲

There was a horse, its face bauson, and they used its back as a batule. There was a flower of the convolvulaceae, and it seemed to account to the horse's back become a circus-man's springboard and to its face marked with white, the incitement of a vaulting-plank, when it touched them. And the flower was for, and of all of them: one sepal of the calyx, Michal; one sepal of the calyx, Bath-sheba; one sepal of the calyx, Absalom; one sepal of the calyx, Jonathan; one sepal of the calyx, David. They were together gamosepalous. And David said,—When it is this way, the corolla above us, gamopetalous, is indistinguishable, and I am perianth, as if Saul were locked in me against them. Wherefore should I go to battle?

And Michal brought an old, run-over shoe, and Bath-sheba brought a baudekin, and Absalom a battering ram, saying—kill me if I use it against you; and Jonathan two companies, saying—Draw them up now, I will die in one of these battles, make it a heavy blow. And it seemed to David that they were all saying,—This one time, this time, because we are all dashed together. And David,—Action is so brief and partial, wrap me in the baudekin, Bath-sheba, it is so meaningless, despite my love for you, that I will go in it to battle. And David,—Jonathan, what is that thrumming? and Jonathan—It is the noise of siege-guns. And David—I should have known, it is empty like the harp I played when Saul was against me. You are all here, sending me, maybe you expect a report of the original meaning. It was that one morning springing shining out of the earth after rain, and that morning, too, I was going to battle.

And David seemed to hear the driving of guns from cover within reach of Michal, Bath-sheba, Absalom and Jonathan, all previously posted. And they were beginning to stand apart one calyx, but four leaves, missing a fifth.

Swift. Somehow he had never been there, or together. Then he sighed, saw a batule, then a run-over shoe by the head of a battering ram, and then a baudekin dragged by two retreating companies, and four names: and one of the names was Michal; and one of the names was Bath-sheba; and one of the names was Jonathan; and one of the names was Absalom. And as David mounted very near to the eye of the horse, he saw its face, bauson.

✲

Turn, turn, the leaf. Who was the mother of Absalom that David loved him so? Volti—Solomon was only favored! Swoop toward the earth from a height at an angle much greater than that of gliding, speak of David as volant over obsidian so that in its cracks at least may be seen a few individualized crystals. The heated matter of Michal, the dormant of Bath-sheba. Fold, turn the papyrus. $V={}^{m}/_{D}$. The amount of space includes the bounding surfaces of the solid—in music, the fulness of quantity, of tone—always the volume equals mass divided by density!

Apply then the difference of potential to this book—this conductor—whose resistance is one ohm, to produce a current of one ampere. Or complicate the experiment—a number of disks of two metals—the wives of David, the lives of David—one more oxidizable than the other and having between them this paper moistened with acids: who was, the winning of all the tricks in the deal, the entire range, does not tell, who was the mother of Absalom that David loved him so?

Direct, if you can, towards the chosen end, all the characters moving by their volition: if the tumbler falls, raise him up, while it is for him as if horse moves partially sideways round a circular tread. David speaks, Michal receives the thrust, he is cherished by Bath-sheba, his baby dies of Volhynian fever, David weeps.

Speak Volapük—what does the tongue matter! Any of its turns is volta, time, duration, value of tone, measurement by comparison of volumes.

David! David! hears . . . the note, the note above it, and the semitone below it. Absalom—who was his mother that David loved him so?—Absalom, the voix celeste?

The Baron Speaks

TO WHOM IT MAY CONCERN

The novella by Louis Zukofsky, entitled *Little,* that you presumably have (just) read, purports to describe the life of one Baron Snorck von Chulnt. This is, of course, a libelous lie, as we do so attest.

What the book actually is is not quite clear, but it would appear to be a chronicle of the activities of one Paul Zukofsky, yet another Jewish violinist (good God—will we never see the end of them?) of (we are told) not inconsiderable merit, although that is hardly a sufficient excuse to usurp our family title and pedigree. *Why* this particular personage was chosen as the protagonist of a novella shall probably remain forever shrouded, although the fact that he happened to be the son of the author (nepotism again!) probably didn't hurt.

Our attitude to this offense against all common decency is somewhat ambiguous. We have been asked why we have not considered legal recourse. We have actually done so, but our investigations have revealed that the Zukofskys are a notoriously difficult lot (we are of course aware that parents Zukofsky are currently deceased, but given the hushed tones in which they are still spoken of, *are* seems more appropriate than *were* as regards difficulties). Indeed, violinist/now conductor Zukofsky actually numbers among his friends members of the legal profession, and recently, a music critic of some Western newspaper has privately described him as being insane. Furthermore, the idea of dragging our name through

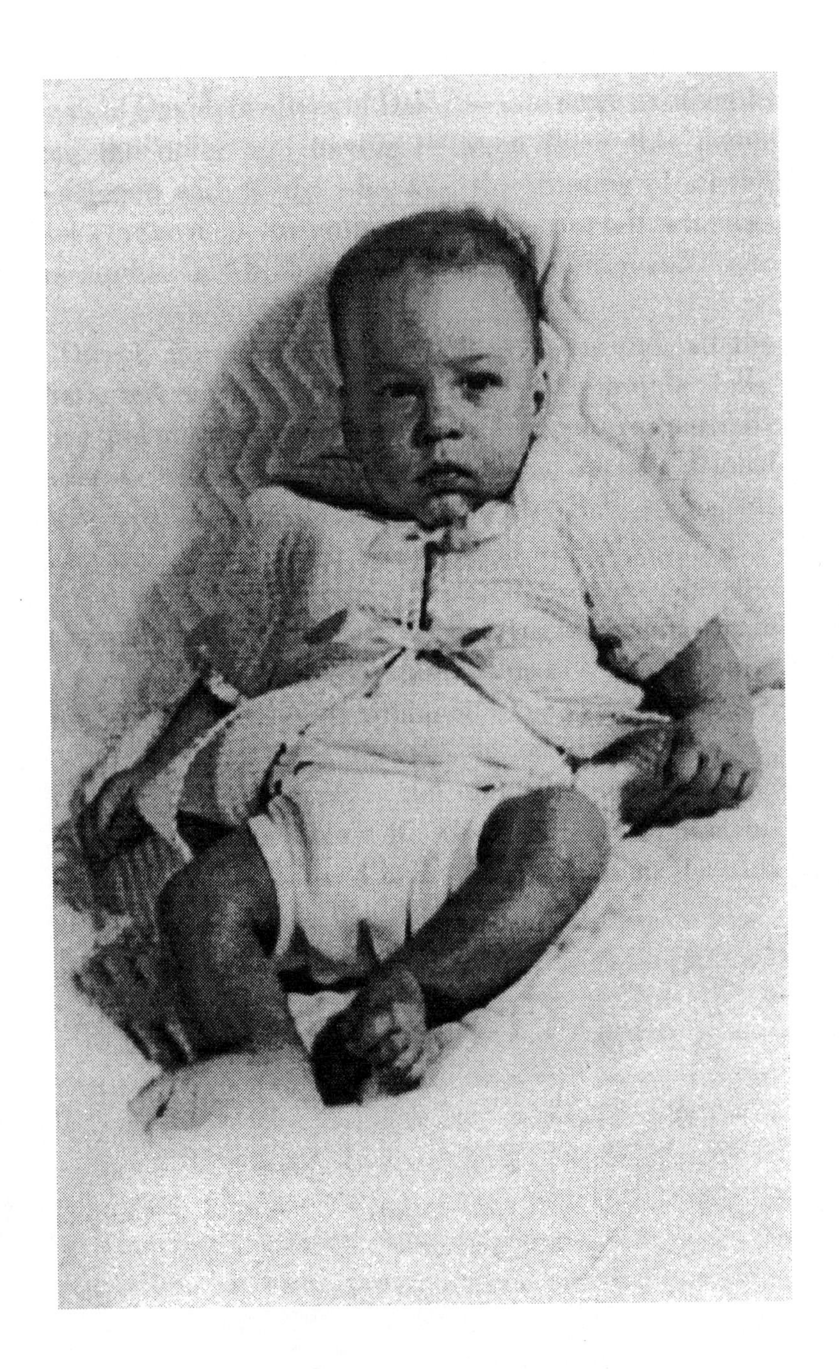

Paul Zukofsky, February 26, 1944

the courts is of course anathema, and as the outcome is at best Whistleresque there is no point in such proceedings.

Our greatest complaint has to do with the fact that there are those—mistresses and other such acquaintances—who, presuming upon their supposed intimacy, choose in moments of endearment to address us as "Snorckie," or sometimes as "Little." This we abhor. The correct form is of course

"Baron."

It says much for the courtesy and breeding of Mr. Steven Moore of the Dalkey Archive Press that we were offered this opportunity to disclaim our connection with the base(less) fabrications of the foregoing. In-grate-itude for this we have agreed to release the confidential files our agents have prepared for us on this (piece of) work, thereby lifting, without revealing "*All,*" the codpiece of obfuscation which is this goulash.

As, at the time of this writing, violinist/now conductor Zukofsky was in Iceland, pillaging and generally being riotous with his good friend and cohort Egil Skallagrimsson, our agents were unable to corroborate their findings. Therefore, none of what follows may be construed to be confirmed fact.

Report of our Agents, and miscellaneous Comments

p. 1, ¶ 1: The proof that this work is not about us lies in this first paragraph where our ability to "speak" or use words is impugned. Obviously the author is referring to someone else entirely.

p. 4, last two lines: Obviously the Western newspaper critic is correct. Anyone who thinks being a poet or musician constitutes a profession, let alone a good one, is patently insane.

p. 5: This is probably a description of the Mannes School in New York City. Legend has it that pp. 6-7 usw is not exactly inaccurate, especially the scowl; ditto p. 12, ¶ 2, except it was supposed to be a painter.

p. 16: There was indeed a teacher of this type.

p. 19: Count Murda-Wonda, alias Al Wand. This is a somewhat different view of the person who was so beautifully eulogized by Louis Zukofsky in his poem "Atque in Perpetuum A.W."

This is also the person whose brother, a sidekick of a famous Jewish mobster, was machine-gunned (murdered) in a telephone booth.

p. 21: The initial four lines of German poetry are actually by Tearilee. To libel, nepotism, and fabrication, we may now add plagiarism and improper citation.

p. 28:	Doctor Prunejuice = Gluillens. The name was Givens, and he consumed vast quantities of prune juice.
p. 32:	Sider & Sweetsider = Lyme & Old Lyme, Conn.
p. 33:	James Madison = Helen Taggart, a lovely lady who became a close family friend of the notoriously difficult Zukofskys.
p. 40, ¶ 2:	Edward Dahlberg, upon a visit similar to that of the Esfelts, having been fed a similar canned ham, accused Louis and Celia Zukofsky of trying to poison him, and thereafter refused to associate with them.
p. 41:	"Pia Mia": Only too true.
p. 44, ¶ 2:	It is encouraging to note that long before semiotics became fashionable, the Zukofskys were already pondering anti-semiotics.
p. 55:	"The old director" = David Mannes of the Mannes School.
P. 55. ¶ 3:	"Signore Agire Onesto Proba": There was indeed a teacher of this type.
p. 57:	"Mr Athens Olympus" = Roman Totenberg, the violinist.
p. 57:	"Rutar Neitsnebur" = Artur Rubenstein, the pianist.
p. 58:	"Ztephiah" = Jascha Heifetz, the violinist.

p. 61: "Warlock Endor" = Arthur Judson, the doyen of CAMI.

p. 62: "Imam Betur" = Ivan Galamian. "Betur" because better was (quite properly) the highest word of praise that he knew. Violinist/now conductor Zukofsky dedicated his recordings of the twenty-four Paganini Caprices to Galamian, "with great respect and affection." Galamian said of v/nc Zukofsky that "he has one of the finest intonations I have ever known . . . he has a very good head which does more than hold the fiddle" (Richard Kostelanetz, chapter on Paul Zukofsky, *Innovative Musicians,* New York: Limelight Editions, 1989).

p. 63: "Great Hall" = Carnegie Hall.

p. 64: "Sib and Gesib" = Mischka and Beebee, the Galamians' boxers.

p. 66: "What Bach? Any Bach." Actually happened a number of years later, to a long-tressed older heartthrob of v/nc Zukofsky.

p. 71: "Dr Vasily Presha" = Valentin Blumberg, from his habit (described on p. 73) of squatting whilst trying to teach about bow pressure. A very gifted teacher of basic technique.

p. 75: "My Institute" = Polytechnic Institute of Brooklyn, at which Louis Zukofsky taught. It was famous at the time for its research on polymers, not shellac. "Dr. Cubinis," a rather fey gentleman who bathed frequently, was actually a head of the English Dept.

p. 82: "Dlopoel Reua" = Leopold Auer, the teacher of (among others) Jascha Heifetz.

p. 84: "summer school at Garden" = Meadowmount School, Westport, N.Y.

p. 84: "Pamphilia" = Elizabethtown, N.Y.

p. 86: A photograph of the snapshot species has been recovered, showing a voluptuous Unzung wearing the briefest of bikinis (at a time when that would have been spelt with capital letters), with Unzung's arm enveloping a painfully callow and embarrassed youth who, at the time, was still (unfortunately) unable to partake in the treasures thrust before him. How sad that youth is wasted on the young. Even we, injured party though we are, cannot but help feel compassion for this usurper who never got to sing Unzung.

p. 86: "without vibrato": Obviously this characteristic of v/nc Zukofsky is of long standing.

p. 90: Mrs. Rilty "is this a fingering for a boy or girl": Mrs. Rilty, desiring to borrow v/nc Zukofsky's music with intent to purloin his fingerings, once actually asked this question of Celia Zukofsky.

p. 91: "Serp" = Louis Persinger, the teacher of Yehudi Menuhin, = "Nihunem." "Eichel Practice" = Michael Rabin, from his habit of constantly saying "I have to practice" (and never appearing to do so).

p. 93:	"Hemdlach sisters" = the Camps, so named because their money had been made in undergarments.
p. 94:	"Caasi Nrets" = Isaac Stern. "Guy Esor Octa Leber" = Leonard Rose, the cellist. He ate large quantities of chopped chicken liver (gehackte leber).
pp. 101-2:	"Onangni's" = Pugnani's. "Ztirf Relsierk" = Fritz Kriesler. "Oniz Narf" = Zino Francescatti, the violinist.
p. 108:	"Roger" Yksrogi" = Gregor Piatagorsky, the cellist.
p. 112:	Three spindle-back hickory chairs. These are currently (1989) on display in the Zukofsky memorial museum, located in Piss-cat—away!, N. J.
p. 115:	"Cochon *Concerto*" probably = Conus concerto.
p. 119:	"don't dare write for me—and if ever in fiction, to spare me, condense," Obviously, neither of these requests were honored.
p. 121:	"R. Z. Draykup" = Ezra Pound, from his habit of "draying" on one's kopf. The madhouse was St. Elizabeths in Washington, D.C. According to Barry Ahearn in *Pound/Zukofsky: Selected Letters of Ezra Pound and Louis Zukofsky* (a primer in economics), the visit took place on July 11, 1954.

p. 127: *The Mabinogion and "Manawyddan the Son of Llyr,* third of the four-branch tale of the Mabinogi." A combination of Sir Walter Scott "Waverly" novels and J. F. Cooper "Leatherstocking" tales. The author is obviously envious.

p. 131: "or could it be *we* are a bit envious." Our conjecture is confirmed.

p. 134: "Mihcaoj" = Joseph Joachim, the violinist for whom Brahms wrote his violin concerto. The statement about the prodigy growing up is a corruption of what happens to a "wunderkind," i.e., all too soon the "wunder" disappears, and the "kind" remains. This statement is most frequently attributed to the pianist Leopold Godowsky.

p. 141: "Phaethon Weaver" = Anton Webern. "I. Gloss Dazzling" = Igor Stravinsky.

pp. 146-47: Letter of R. Z. Draykup: See *Pound/Zukofsky*, pp. 214-15.

pp. 150 ff.: This recital in Carnegie Hall took place November 30, 1956.

pp. 160-61: This reaction of Betur's was to a graphic score of John Cage.

p. 161: "Upper School" = the Juilliard School of Music.

p. 162: N.B. from Little: "In defense of Unzung, it was not she in the Greek class, and the confusion was over Oedipus."

p. 165 N. B. from v/nc Zukofsky, re Tourte bow: "No such bow was ever purchased by or for me." For further views on the subject see Zukofsky on Strads in *Arts & Antiques*, January 1989, and Ross & Zondervan on "Capital Gains and the Rate of Return on a Stradivarius," in *Economic Inquiry* 27 (July 1989): 529-40.

pp. 164-67: For another view of this trip see Louis Zukofsky, *Barely and Widely*, #7, "Stratford-on-Avon," & #12, "Four Other Countries."

p. 168: This second concert at Carnegie Hall took place February 6, 1959.

P. Z.
11/17/89

DALKEY ARCHIVE PAPERBACKS

STEPHENS, MICHAEL. *Season at Coole*	7.95
WOOLF, DOUGLAS. *Wall to Wall*	7.95
YOUNG, MARGUERITE. *Miss MacIntosh, My Darling*	2-vol. set, 30.00
ZUKOFSKY, LOUIS. *Collected Fiction*	13.50
ZWIREN, SCOTT. *God Head*	10.95

FICTION: BRITISH

BROOKE-ROSE, CHRISTINE. *Amalgamemnon*	9.95
CHARTERIS, HUGO. *The Tide Is Right*	9.95
FIRBANK, RONALD. *Complete Short Stories*	9.95
GALLOWAY, JANICE. *Foreign Parts*	12.95
GALLOWAY, JANICE. *The Trick Is to Keep Breathing*	11.95
HUXLEY, ALDOUS. *Antic Hay*	12.50
HUXLEY, ALDOUS. *Point Counter Point*	13.95
MOORE, OLIVE. *Spleen*	10.95
MOSLEY, NICHOLAS. *Accident*	9.95
MOSLEY, NICHOLAS. *Assassins*	12.95
MOSLEY, NICHOLAS. *Children of Darkness and Light*	13.95
MOSLEY, NICHOLAS. *Impossible Object*	9.95
MOSLEY, NICHOLAS. *Judith*	10.95
MOSLEY, NICHOLAS. *Natalie Natalia*	12.95

FICTION: FRENCH

BUTOR, MICHEL. *Portrait of the Artist as a Young Ape*	10.95
CÉLINE, LOUIS-FERDINAND. *Castle to Castle*	13.95
CÉLINE, LOUIS-FERDINAND. *North*	13.95
CREVEL, RENÉ. *Putting My Foot in It*	9.95
ERNAUX, ANNIE. *Cleaned Out*	10.95
GRAINVILLE, PATRICK. *The Cave of Heaven*	10.95
NAVARRE, YVES. *Our Share of Time*	9.95
QUENEAU, RAYMOND. *The Last Days*	11.95
QUENEAU, RAYMOND. *Pierrot Mon Ami*	9.95
ROUBAUD, JACQUES. *The Great Fire of London*	12.95
ROUBAUD, JACQUES. *The Princess Hoppy*	9.95
SIMON, CLAUDE. *The Invitation*	9.95

FICTION: GERMAN

SCHMIDT, ARNO. *Collected Stories*	13.50
SCHMIDT, ARNO. *Nobodaddy's Children*	13.95